# A FRAGMENT
## OF GLASS

# F. L. GREEN

★

# A Fragment
# of Glass

London
MICHAEL  JOSEPH  LTD

*First published by*
MICHAEL JOSEPH LTD.
*26 Bloomsbury Street*
*London, W.C.1*
1947

*Set and printed in Great Britain by Tonbridge Printers Ltd.,*
*Peach Hall Works, Tonbridge, in Times nine on eleven point,*
*and bound by James Burn.*

# Contents

*

*For*
BARBARA and PENELOPE

*Part One*

# THE TOPIC

★

# ONE

*

He was the last of the short-listed applicants to arrive shortly after three of that April afternoon at the premises of the 'Daily Summariser.' Coming in, Bessing glanced slowly at the five applicants who were already seated in the ante-room. As he crossed to the vacant chair in the little row against the wall the mumble of their conversation subsided, and all five of them returned his glance with a stare of nervous criticism that hovered upon him to assess his character, talents, experience, and his chances. He knew it and felt all the more perturbed by his venture into the society which their presence expressed so forcibly to him.

In that shabby little room whose distempered walls were a drab green and whose only adornment was a calendar, the five artists sat like five men condemned by their destiny to meet there in a humiliating rivalry which was conveyed by their presence, and which none of them could prevent from giving an uneasy quality to the air of the room. Looking again at them, Bessing felt the impact of their five distinct personalities upon his sensibilities. There, like a figure of farce, was the inevitable eccentric, elderly and heavy, with his features dragged by the passage of all hope. There, too, was the booser, over-confident, sitting between the obvious, precise man and a snob. A youngster fresh from a school of art completed the number. All of them possessed an identical characteristic which glimmered in their features and took shape in their attitudes. It was hope.

Bessing felt completely foreign to their common attributes and to the kind of world which they created. His spirit was without ambition. He was there, it was true, because an urgent material crisis had compelled him to seek a salaried appointment; but he had never expected that his letter of application to the editor would result in a summons to attend for an interview. Like all the other letters which he had written to various employers, his letter was only an expression of his desire—addressed to an indifferent world and not to an individual—for an opportunity to earn money, and some attention to himself out of an illimitable source of generous attention at present accorded to millions of persons who could easily have done without it.

Thus far in his career as an artist, he had acquired only a slight experience. He had been an earnest student in London and Paris. During the war, he had worked as an artist in an aircraft factory where, for scores of workers, he had explained blueprints by making drawings of various objects in three dimensions instead of in one. After the war, he had returned home to pursue his own work and his own vague ambitions with a talent which was timidly individualistic and which was expressed with no particular emphasis and only a modest vision. He was one of thousands; and his temperament in its limpid ease, and his character in its passivity could not render his work with force or distinction or take him ahead of his contemporaries.

Nevertheless, he sold a few pictures to discerning dealers as well as to private patrons, so that there were always a few pounds between his security and the severe face of poverty. Also, there was the family house in Half Moon Street in which he lived with his sister, Lenora, and his brother, Quentin. And there was Lenora's salary as a typist. Once, there had been her savings, as well as his, all of which had dwindled during the three years in which Quentin had been ill, until the last five pounds had vanished and a chilly necessity had compelled him to apply, amongst other vacancies, for this appointment as strip-cartoonist on the 'Daily Summariser' staff.

Strip-cartoonist! He imagined that he knew what the job would demand from him. Day after day, an idea, a bit of funny stuff, a joke or a pun, or an adventure of some sort for a character who would grin at readers from the bottom of a page, with appropriate drawings in line which must be submitted two or three days before publication. Apart from that, he had not considered either the responsibilities of the job or the opportunities which it might afford him. He had no real desire for the appointment, nor any hope of success in it. It represented an income and a release from financial difficulty.

The summons to present himself to the Editor had not pleased him or encouraged him. At once, he forgot the liberal income, and his own poverty, and he anticipated only the daily compulsion, the effort, the noisy scene into which he must project himself if he were selected, and the loss of a very precious sense of personal freedom.

'This Editor,' he remarked to Quentin, handing him the letter, 'wants to see my drawings. I haven't any that would do.'

'Then make some,' Quentin retorted from the long chair on which he was lying.

Of the trinity, Quentin was the intellect, the subtle mind, the daring, positive thinker. Thirty-one, with a brilliant academic reputation behind him, phthisis had prevented him from taking an appointment and had chained his tall body to chair, bed, settee. But it had not destroyed him.

To know him was to appreciate at once the robust, fascinating world into which he had travelled during years of enforced physical idleness. And it seemed to John that Quentin's sudden enthusiasm for this possible appointment on the 'Daily Summariser' was not only the one pleasing factor in the affair but indicated his intention to assist with the daily cartoon.

'Make some drawings,' Quentin repeated. 'Create a character!'

He sat up, and with a zest which was infectious he went on:

'Get some paper, and pencils! I'll pose for you.'

John smiled lugubriously. 'D'you think you are comic?'

The gaunt face was upturned to him.

'Need your creature be comic?' Quentin said. 'Aren't there enough funny little caricatures, and supermen, and voluptuous girls? Create the Average Man. I'll pose for you.'

He laughed softly and continued seriously: 'Let's make him a thinker, as well as an adventurer. He can be picaresque, too.'

From the first, his enthusiasm brought it all into being and swept John into it, until the Man was drawn in Quentin's likeness and endowed with ideas that were Quentin's. John was merely the illustrator of the creature.

'Now,' Quentin continued, eagerly and earnestly, when seven drawings were made. 'Now give him a name. Christen him. The Adventures of . . .'

'Adventures?'

'Certainly!' Quentin exclaimed. 'He's a forthright fellow, with a venturesome spirit. Think of him! Just recently, he has saved a Civilization from a decline into a hideous era. Now he believes in the Individual. . . .'

'Wait a bit!' John said, standing before his brother. 'Who is he? What is he? What have you in mind?'

Quentin said quietly: 'Oh, he's Man, in this generation, journeying through the contemporary scene and . . .'

'You want him to convey your ideas!' John declared.

'It's such a good chance to say something about the world of to-day. Other centuries had their Don Quixote, or Mr. Pickwick, or Prince Myshkin, to examine and comment on what was current. So far, we have had nobody to poke a bit of fun or make a laugh, or draw serious comment.'

'Suppose the Editor wants a caricature?' John said.

Quentin laughed. 'He can't have it. He must have our Man! Tell him so. Tell him you have something original. Make him listen to you.'

'Well, a name . . .'

'Call him PEEPER,' Quentin said, pensively.

It went down in bold lettering. It was a name which had relation to all that Quentin intended for him; but John doubted whether any editor would accept either the name or the tall, gaunt figure which smiled and strode amiably through the drawings. He was not convinced about the idea. Indeterminate himself, he flinched from what was positive. Thus he sat in the cheerless ante-room, with his small portfolio of drawings that contained the germ of an idea which he knew was far too subtle for him to express. PEEPER belonged to Quentin.

Bessing at that time was twenty-nine. His fair, tall presence in its attitude of easy grace suggested his limpid character and his general detachment. He had the candour of expression which invites conversation, principally because in that countenance there was something which was so far untouched by the conditions which vex and possess the minds of most people. He was a free man.

'Mister John Bessing, please!'

All six applicants stirred under the glance which the clerk at the door threw at them. Bessing came from his reverie and stared back at the clerk, and then turned to the others, as though he could not believe that he was to precede them. He rose slowly and unwillingly.

To hear his name spoken aloud, and to realize that he must present himself to the Editor aroused a sudden revulsion in him. The momentum of enthusiasm which Quentin had encouraged and which had brought him thus far, ended. It was the clerk who now took charge of him.

'This way, please, Mr. Bessing!'

He followed the clerk dejectedly along a short corridor in which the sounds of telephones, voices in rapid conversation, voices dictating, voices reading proof copy, bells clanging, machines thudding and typewriters crackling rattled in his ears. He felt that he was being conducted to some kind of doom which was the direct consequence of his impetuosity. The smooth young clerk kept glancing back at him to beckon him forward, until the two of them stopped at a glass door upon which the clerk tapped and which he opened wide and once more spoke Bessing's name in loud, precise tones.

In that large room, a burly, morose man of about fifty was seated at a desk. He glanced up aggressively from his papers and saw Bessing, whereupon something akin to motion beginning in a large unit of machinery began in his swarthy square face. The door closed behind Bessing.

Bessing remembered that moment ever afterwards, for as he approached the desk and saw in the hirsute hands of the Editor his letter of application, he felt that in that application all the momentous, extraordinary events that ensued had their source. And at once he wanted to remark that he was temperamentally unsuited for the appointment. He felt that he ought to disclose that he had had only a slender experience of life and that at the age of eighteen he had gone straight from grammar school to a school of art from which, three years later, he had been sent to Paris where he had remained for two years, after which he had returned home, where his parents had given him a studio. And that he had lived at home until the war, when he had been sent to work as an artist in an aircraft factory. And that his parents had been killed during an air raid. And that he lived at home with a brother and sister. . . .

But the Editor was smiling. He pointed with a gold pencil to an armchair and invited Bessing to sit down. He made some comment on the letter. No sooner was Bessing seated than that redoubtable personality—thick, solid, dominant—aimed questions at him and took him through the first part of the interview at such speed that Bessing felt as though he had been carried far out of himself and his environment to some kind of island inhabited at that moment solely by the Editor.

It was bewildering. It was the direct result of an act of bravado committed by Bessing when he had made application for the appointment and now slowly mounting against him in all its unpleasant consequences.

Suddenly, the questions ended and a pause ensued during which Bessing heard the stertorous breathing of the Editor whose hand shot out.

'Show me your drawings, please!'

Bessing unfastened his portfolio and removed his drawings and passed them to the hand which all the time remained outstretched, and which gave one almost imperceptible flicker of impatience, and then grasped the sheets as though they were trivial things with which he was not much concerned.

13

The questions began again, coming quickly and affording the applicant no pause in which to assemble his thoughts or pass any remark. Had he much experience of line work? Cartoons? Was he happy in that medium? Had he ideas for it? Had he studied the work of other cartoonists? What were his interests?

Mr. Julius Belfwig examined all the drawings very closely without once taking his eyes from them or pausing between one question and another. He did not appear to afford much attention to what Bessing said, but swept on, as though he spoke merely from an edge of thought, his mind being given to the work of this young man whose character in its curious negativeness seemed to him to be exactly the sort which he had hoped to find and which had the pliancy that would allow it to be moulded to his own forthright purposes.

The questions ceased abruptly again. Belfwig pushed all the drawings a little distance from him. At the same time, he sat back, folded his hands, and turned to Bessing.

'I like your drawings, Mr. Bessing,' he said. 'I like them very much indeed!'

His smile began. His dark gaze was fastened upon Bessing who had the distinct impression that the Editor expected him to note the fact that the drawings had been praised. An acknowledgment was awaited. Bessing smiled slightly. That was all.

At once, Belfwig's smile dropped like a heavy curtain excluding sunlight. He looked faintly annoyed as he inclined his body backwards and stared at the ceiling. His hands were joined on the desk. He might have been praying. Impressive as he was, in that magnificent room in the lofty, busy building, he failed to awe Bessing.

'Our circulation is well above the three million mark per day,' he recited. 'That is an achievement resulting from a progressive policy in every direction into which this newspaper extends. Our purpose is to afford our readers a daily presentation of news conveyed by an expert staff in such a manner as will instruct, guide and inform. We are democratic. We are without class. Our staff has an original, frank approach to the many problems of contemporary life, as well as to this newspaper's heavy responsibilities. We go forward with our millions of readers into a New Era, harnessed to no political party but determined to uphold the national dignity and honour. That, I believe, is an outline of our policy.' He continued after a pause during which he glanced at his fingers and flicked away a grain of dust from them.

Bessing was not listening. He was absorbed in his study of that square head with its mane of steel-grey hair flowing over the nape of the neck. And he was still lost in thought when Belfwig turned to him and shot another question.

'What was your exact intention with this . . . this PEEPER?'

Bessing struggled from his reverie and tried to find words. He hesitated to utter them, for they were not his but Quentin's.

'I notice,' Belfwig went on, glancing at the drawings, 'that you have contrived this personality and given his daily appearances some continuity. Did you intend to create a story round him?'

Bessing spoke. He heard himself repeat what Quentin had said of PEEPER. It all came readily to his lips, while Belfwig sat with his gaze upon his large, hairy hands and his head down as though he were very much bored. Suddenly, Bessing was silent.

Belfwig flung his whole body round and faced him.

'I think it's highly original!' he exclaimed. 'I like it. I like it very much!'

He smiled. He paused.

'I have never liked any feature so much!' he added.

Bessing was silent. Again, he heard his drawings praised and PEEPER extolled. Belfwig had ideas and he got up and walked about his room while he expressed them. PEEPER could do this. He could do that. Soon, the newspaper was conducting a Drama revival. PEEPER could assist.

Finally, after having woven so many irrelevant ideas into PEEPER, Belfwig drew breath, paused, and offered Bessing a contract.

'Think about it . . . for an hour or two . . . Mr. Bessing, and then give me your answer.'

He turned his back on Bessing and touched a switch on his desk. A secretary entered. Belfwig said:

'Tell the others not to wait, please. And thank them for their attendance.'

Bessing exclaimed suddenly: 'But just a moment . . . I . . .'

Belfwig smiled and dismissed the secretary with a sharp little gesture of his hand and turned to Bessing.

'I think you'll enjoy this appointment, Bessing!'

His smile appeared on his heavy, square face, like a chink of sunlight struggling into a roomful of massive furniture.

'You'll be happy here with us,' he said; and after a pause, he added: 'What do you think?'

Bessing was thinking of the six hundred pounds per annum which was his salary in the appointment. And of his duties. But principally of the curious fact that he had been selected, and that he was now committed to PEEPER because Quentin had created that character for him, and because Quentin had plans for PEEPER. It startled him.

Belfwig spoke again, rubbing his palms slowly together and fastening on Bessing his heavy, dark gaze.

'I want you to feel that I am here to help you. Never hesitate to ask my advice. And never forget that once we have agreed on a course I shall back you to the end in it.'

He offered his hand.

'Thanks,' Bessing said.

'You'll be here to-morrow, with some more of your work,' Belfwig said, retaining Bessing's hand, 'but before that you'll 'phone me? Have I your number?'

'I'm not a telephone subscriber,' Bessing said.

'I'll arrange for a 'phone to be installed at your home. I have your address.'

The handshake ended and they parted.

# TWO

Bessing came out into the first seething wave of the rush hour. He was thirsty and wanted a cup of tea. The snack bars were crowded. The little cafés were full. The 'buses, when he turned to wait at the stage, were crowded. He walked, feeling nervous and thirsty and no longer free. That delicate sense of personal freedom was gone, sold for six hundred pounds. In its place there was a weight of responsibility which he found oppressive and which seemed to him to be represented by the throng everywhere about him, and the rattle and thunder of the traffic. During the war, he had accepted the idea of work. It was essential that all should work. But this job . . . this was so completely new to him that it agitated his character which, in its foundation, had an obstinate indolence. Or was he oppressed because his sensitive spirit was unequipped for contact with reality. What did he fear? What had he to lose? His contract stipulated that a month's notice from either party could terminate the agreement. Therefore, the door was always open for him to march out to his precarious, personal freedom.

He trudged the whole way home and felt happier when, entering Piccadilly, he was on more familiar ground. He found something of himself in that locality. Echoes of days and nights, the beginning and end of happy excursions, the dinners with Lenora and Quentin, and the return home with them, as well as years of life with them, seemed to meet him in the hot gust of air from the Green Park Station, and from the Park itself with its first green mist of foliage on the black boughs. The exquisite enchantment of his life with Lenora and Quentin in that trinity recurred again to him and composed his thoughts. As before, life could continue from that heart. Nothing was lost, nothing had been sold or given away. And with six hundred a year . . .

But the Thing to which he had given himself! It was likely that it would consume the whole of his talents. He could be witty. He could make one apt pun per day, were it required of him! But to keep PEEPER going, and to give him purpose and direction and to make him trenchant and interesting . . . that would be a task of some magnitude which would demand qualities from him. And although Quentin was beside him to direct him, and despite all the opportunities which the job would afford him, he could not rise to it with enthusiasm.

Already, PEEPER was alive, a personality who dominated his life. He could not ignore him.

It was not often that Belfwig became enthusiastic. A lifetime of extensive experience had acquainted him with so many crises, sensations, features in a range of ideas that expressed the entire chord from the sublime to the ridiculous that his response was cautious now. Yet no sooner had Bessing gone than he grabbed the telephone and made a call to the Chairman of the newspaper's Board.

He spoke to Lord Ecks who, at that time, was at his club. Could Ecks come round? Or perhaps Ecks would prefer him to come to his club? The gruff, terse voice asked Belfwig if the matter was urgent.

'I think you'll find that it's more than that,' Belfwig said.

'Serious?' the voice said.

Belfwig replied that it was imperative that the two of them should discuss the matter immediately, whereupon Ecks with characteristic caution, stalled, prevaricated, and exhibited his complete lack of courage while Belfwig laughed.

'It will charm you!' Belfwig said.

Ecks coughed. He promised to be over within fifteen minutes.

Belfwig replaced the receiver, called for his secretary and dictated what he called a 'Cartoon Campaign.' And he was still walking to and fro in the room and dictating when Ecks arrived.

In appearance, this press lord was grubby and slipshod, with his greying hair seldom brushed, his collar always crumpled by his energetic movements, and a quantity of his native soil under his fingernails. He looked much younger than his sixty-two years, probably because of his abundant mental and physical energy. A stranger might have placed him in the late forties and speculated without success on the trade, profession, or occupation pursued by this restless, unkempt person in shaggy tweeds and heavy boots whose wealth and influence extended into so many roots in the national life.

Belfwig liked him as a man but found him an exasperating employer, despising him for his politics which were evasive and fluctuating, like those of most puritans. For Ecks was a notorious puritan; and it was only by extreme opposition to his ideas that Belfwig prevented him from hurling the 'Daily Summariser,' together with its attendant advertising and publicity organizations, and its vast resources of influence, into the ridiculous 'Causes,' 'Reforms,' 'Campaigns' and 'Crusades' which, from day to day, excited his imagination.

Nevertheless, on this occasion, it was through the medium of his weakness for a noisy shout across the national life that Belfwig induced Ecks to sit down and hear what he had to say. Within five minutes, he had told him. A new, original cartoon. He showed him the drawings of PEEPER.

'With a personality like that, we could grasp the public imagination and direct it, mould it. . . .'

'A crusade against obscenity in the music-halls!'

'Possibly. Later on. But at the moment, something . . .'

'Would prefer action against obscenity on our stage . . .'

'Why not?' Belfwig agreed. 'But initially . . .'

'Quite!' Ecks said. 'You mean, the feature must be established?'

'Rapidly. A campaign of publicity.'

Ecks demurred. He wanted time in which to ponder it.

'Publicity for what purpose? Must have an object in view. Can't spend thousands and thousands on nothing. Can't gear up our subsidiary companies and pelt off to nowhere!'

Belfwig explained. PEEPER must be the subject of the campaign. If the publicity organizations could act for boot polish and toothpaste, they could do the same for a personality with which the newspaper

18

could achieve an access of power and influence hitherto scarcely dreamed of by the Board.

Ecks stared sullenly at him. He said quietly:

'What will you do with him?'

'With a creation like this, there's hardly anything which we could not do,' Belfwig said.

Ecks grinned. Then very slowly, his grin extended across his face. He got up. He walked about the room. He chuckled.

'Biggest Cause in the history of journalism! An uprising against all that's . . . all that's evil in our national life! Finest thing we've ever attempted, Belfwig!'

He dreamed aloud while Belfwig listened and made his own plans and notes. Then Belfwig interrupted him.

'I propose that we leave PEEPER in the hands of the artist, for the time being.'

Ecks disagreed. 'Too great a responsibility for . . . a fellow like that! Must direct him. Must decide policy ourselves.'

He strode about the room and stood at the big windows.

'Some aspect of modern life,' he suggested. 'Something we can uproot and destroy, for the betterment of the lives of the people. Something which touches them all. Some kind of burden, or racket, or . . .'

He had come to the end of his flight of fancy. He made a gesture and sat down. Belfwig was waiting for him with plans for the advertising campaign.

They began next morning, like an intricate, immense piece of machinery commencing to revolve and hum. First, the department of the Advertising Director. And his branches in the provinces. And their subsidiary departments and their hundreds of agents. Publicity was composed and distributed. Space was purchased for thousands of pounds: on hoardings; on public vehicles; everywhere to which the eye might travel. Even on roadways far out in the country and controlled by pompous little Urban Councils who gaped at the offer of hundreds of pounds for the mere right to paint across arterial roadways the single name, PEEPER. The name went out like a shout which cost a fortune to utter. And behind it were the scouts and analysers, studying the response from the public. All was going well. The public was mystified, intrigued. WHO IS PEEPER?

Only a dozen people knew. But millions were asking.

# THREE

★

It was a quarter to five when Bessing entered Half Moon Street and ascended the four steps of Bessing House and opened the door. He had been born in this faded house that was now so much in need of repair after the deprivations of warfare. Here, his life had commenced. To this house he had returned after journeys to find an especial flavour of his life awaiting him. He felt whole in it because it seemed to him to retain all the fragile ideas which, at one time or another, had informed his art. And although his lackadaisical temperament might resign one after another all those delicate fancies, the house itself seemed to preserve them for him, so that they were never quite lost but remained to spring again and with freshness into his imagination, perhaps from Lenora's presence or from some remark passed by Quentin.

His brother and sister were of a more definite character than himself. He knew that. It was all the more disturbing to realize that for the first time in his life he had assumed some responsibility and committed himself to a task which was more suited to Quentin's assured character or to Lenora's eager spirit than to his own impractical nature that met life with an indifferent glance. That, indeed, was a fact which he could not escape.

It overtook him. It flew ahead of him and turned to confront his speeding thoughts that sought a release from it in flights of fancy. It was awaiting him when he went upstairs to the big room, overlooking the street, which was his studio and the family lounge. It met him in Quentin's glance of interrogation. He handed the contract to his brother and sat down.

'I can't sign it,' he said.

'Why not?' Quentin returned. 'You applied for the job. We've gone over all this already. You have the job now. . . .'

John saw that Quentin had prepared a meal during his absence. The table was set attractively, and Quentin was saying: 'You have forgotten that PEEPER will justify my existence!'

Glancing at John, he saw that he had sat down and was swinging his feet on their heels.

'I don't like it,' John said. 'I wish we hadn't created him. I'd much

rather have made an amusing little caricature, instead of this . . .
this . . .'

'Awful!' Quentin said, grimacing. 'A hideous little monster! That's
what they are. Trolls! Monsters! No point to them. . . .'

'But at least he wouldn't tyrannize us!' John said.

Quentin laughed. 'PEEPER isn't a tyrant! He's ours, and we can do
what we like with him. We can decide what he is to do, think, say, and
where he is to go. . . .'

'Belfwig has decided . . .'

'Is he the Editor?'

'He liked him so much that he's working out an itinerary for him. . . .'

'Listen!' Quentin said, sharply. 'What's the matter with you? Aren't
you pleased? Don't you appreciate that this is an opportunity which
doesn't happen, except once in a century?'

John got up. 'But this Thing . . . this PEEPER . . . he's alive already.
He's larger than us. Every day, we'll have to do something with him.
Which means that he'll stand here, in this studio, in this house, waiting
. . . all the time.'

Quentin regarded him gravely.

'Why are you afraid?' he said.

'Because he'll become so real,' John said. 'He'll determine our lives.
He'll be here . . . like a presence, at table with us, waiting for us to
project him on another adventure . . . every day . . .'

'That,' said Quentin, 'will be the fun of it!'

'Fun!' John shouted. 'Fun, you call it. When all the time we'll have
to obey him! He'll become an idea which will drag us with him. We'll
be nothing but his hapless narrators!'

Quentin came across to him and laughed.

'At last,' he declared, 'you've understood the idea. Of course PEEPER
is to be real! But he'll be fascinating and amusing. Listen; let me
explain.'

They sat down, and Quentin went on:

'What sort of Image have the Scientists made of man? They have
imposed on all of us an idea of Man as an inexorable creature who can
kill at incredible distances, travel at fantastic speeds, explore the outer
regions of Space, see through fog to incredible distances, hear things
at a great range, speak across great distances. And exterminate his own
kind in tens of thousands within the flash of a bomb. That Image of
himself in the minds of men doesn't remain static. It increases, day by
day, in power.

'And what Image have your politicians and statesmen created of Man? They have made a stupid, savage thing of him, only capable of being moved in masses, or influenced in masses about national boundaries and other silly matters, and blindly obedient because real freedom has been stolen from him and because he is deluded by them into supposing that the most hideous barbarities are his Duty.

'Next. What sort of Image have the lords of Commerce and Industry made of man? A machine of fantastic efficiency. The helpless slave of economic terms which can be applied to any device after a crisis, in order to explain away a deliberate crime. Hapless Man, chained to price levels, exchange rates, interest rates!

'And your Theologians? How many gods must Man obey? How many heavens and how many hells await him? How many opposing moralities threaten his individuality?

'And the Artists in all their subtleties? What is their Image? They, at least, never insist it on Man. Once in every two or three centuries, the truth is told. Don Quixote journeys through a proud civilization and discovers its rags. Gulliver discloses the abject creature. Prince Myshkin, coming from his mental hospital, discovers a lunatic world. Mr. Pickwick sets forth. But now it is PEEPER's turn!'

Moment by moment, the idea took shape in his words while John sat listening to him. PEEPER assumed dimensions, like a being coming to life in the mind. He was to be the Image of the Average Man, and as such he was to examine the contemporary scene and its ideas that composed the modern civilization. Politics, Science, Art, all were to be within his mission; and he was to make sport of their solemn errors and their faults, and acknowledge their virtues. His journey would be a considerable one; but such would be his appeal that the least of men would relish his amiable character and find him lovable and fascinating.

The prime fact which emerged from Quentin's words was that PEEPER was a creation of size and importance, invested with a penetrative mind and a bold vision, clothed with Quentin's character and drawn in his likeness.

John's function was nothing more than that of an illustrator.

# FOUR

*

It occurred at once to Lenora when, arriving home twenty minutes after John's return, she was told the news. A feeling of apprehension took hold of her and robbed her of any pleasure which she might have experienced at John's success.

There had been meals in the past during which many material problems and anxieties had kept the three of them in a silence which, once broken, had released them. The harsh conditions which had confronted them during difficult periods in the past seemed now to be trivial compared to the curious responsibility that Quentin had set upon John and himself. Obviously, it was Quentin's idea, his fancy, his release from frustration. As such, she dared not condemn it, although she could say nothing for it. Nor, when she envisaged PEEPER's development and his progress in the weeks ahead, could she feel anything but foreboding.

Of what? The betrayal of the delicate, exciting spirit which Quentin created for himself and all of them, and which was the greatest achievement of his mind? Of the fact that John's part in PEEPER was almost fraudulent? Or of the sudden good fortune which had visited their lives, and its consequences?

But she concealed her fears and pretended pleasure at the news, and was relieved when Quentin, opposite her, drew so many amusing fancies regarding PEEPER's future, for while he spoke she could relapse into silence and attempt to grapple with her peculiar problems. Yet, as the meal progressed, and she heard all that was to be done with PEEPER, there was no longer a small loophole through which she might escape from him.

PEEPER, while solving so many immediate difficulties for them, only presented fresh ones. The old, in comparison, were insignificant, for they were personal to the household and might, in time, slip out of their lives. But the new were of another kind. They would come from outside, in the great gusts of publicity which would blow into the household. She foresaw, as well, so much controversy and sensation, for Quentin was not content for PEEPER to be a caricature. PEEPER was to represent something much more actual than a figure of farce. And through PEEPER, the whole fabric of some especial atmosphere which, at present, sprang to life from Quentin's character and personality and gave an essential quality to the household, would be expressed for the whole world, if it wished, to savour.

She deplored it. She had only to listen to Quentin to be convinced that PEEPER would become a force in contemporary life; and in much the same way as Quentin himself had destroyed in the household so many outworn ideas, traditions, conventions, and rendered others in their place, so would PEEPER influence the minds of people. She knew and understood Quentin so well. His mind was a power that fascinated her. His philosophy created in the house a mystical existence, so that it was enchanting on that little island which the three of them made, in this precious seclusion, to resign ideas and exist upon others. But it was another matter to realize that PEEPER's mission was to offer those ideas to the world at large.

'He won't be popular,' she remarked to Quentin.

He laughed. 'Give him time! He isn't quite perfected yet.'

'You'll make him a prig,' she declared. 'He'll be hated and despised.'

'Why?'

'Because he's destructive,' she said.

There was silence over the table. Presently she saw Quentin lift his dark eyes and glance at her.

'So you don't like him?' he said.

She shook her head.

'I wanted him to be humorous,' she explained. 'I wanted him to make people laugh. If he could do that, think of the result! The world hasn't really laughed for . . . for how long? We ought to recover our sense of humour. We want to be able to enjoy life. That's what it's for, isn't it?'

Quentin almost groaned: 'Oh, the quips, those little puns, and the little tricks that bring sniggers and giggles . . .'

'Not those,' she said. 'Something much more subtle. Make him a great figure of comedy!'

'He'd become a buffoon.'

'Make a comedy,' she pleaded. 'You could, if you wished.'

He shook his head and grimaced. 'It would be nothing but a burlesque, or a parody. . . .'

'Let it,' she said. 'What harm would that be? Make us laugh. Destroy all this solemn pressure under which the world lives. Look at our hideous world: every scrap of news is puffed into a monstrous drama, or a nerve-racking crisis. Can't we laugh at something? Couldn't PEEPER make a comedy of it?'

'How?' John said.

Quentin turned to her. 'Tell us.'

'All the conferences,' she explained, 'all those delegates travelling thousands of miles to wrangle about the rights of millions of people who really care far more about their chances of having nice meals and enjoying life than about . . . what is it? . . . sovereign independent rights. All the huge staffs that accompany the delegates. All the reports and documents, and the telegrams, and the speeches, and the newspaper correspondents' awesome reports. That's the greatest comedy one could ever devise! It is. It's the most farcical drama ever conceived. Because all the time, Peace or Security is waiting in the hearts of all people! Nobody wants War and Insecurity, except the few men who cannot agree. The rest . . . the millions . . . want what all people really want: food, comfort, happiness. Those stupid conferences are composed of the actors in a farce, that's all! It is all a big game of bluff.'

'It is an enormous tragedy!' Quentin asserted.

But Lenora was laughing, and presently John joined her.

'No! It's comic!' she exclaimed. 'It's the best comedy yet. Those delegates represent nothing but their own cunning, or their own stupidity. The real people want only food, work, laughter, comfort, things like that.'

'It depends on how you look at it,' Quentin said.

'Well, look at it!'

John laughed again. 'She's right, Quentin! Conference after conference. The age of conference . . .'

Lenora said seriously: 'One thing I want to insist on, no matter what else you do. I want PEEPER to be our secret. I don't want our friends to know where he came from,'

She got up from the table and left them staring at each other like two people in a dilemma of mischief.

# FIVE

★

The spiritual life of this trinity sprang from Quentin, but its material well-being was safely contrived by Lenora who, in appearance, resembled Quentin, but who was completely unlike him in character and temperament.

She was practical, positive, and an egoist. She had resources of nervous energy that could rise to a considerable pitch of effort when Quentin was ill or when financial matters fretted John and drove Quentin into moodiness. She could apply to Quentin's outbursts of anger a tranquillity and patience which melted them as effectively as warm sunlight thaws ice. Over the household, she insisted reason until it was law. It had to be, with one man who was an invalid and another whose character was too abstract to continue without some kind of discipline from her. And she managed all this with a deft, practical ability and a force of example which was a constant influence over the frailties, the crises of temperament, the alarms and everything else that had expression in their lives.

Of the three, she was the sole inheritor of that virtue from a practical-minded mother. In the same way, she was the heiress of the family property which consisted of the house in Half Moon Street. Frequently, during lean financial periods, she had been tempted to sell the house or convert it into flats. It would not have been difficult; and the resulting income would have doubled the family revenue. But only at a cost to an indefinable yet precious sense of space and freedom and individuality which had its source in her love for the house and the spirit which the three of them had created in its atmosphere. Consequently, she had done nothing except remove her furniture from two rooms on the ground floor which she let to a friendly, eccentric personality named Hector Twigge, at a rental of twenty-five shillings a week.

She might have made a better bargain. She could have let other rooms. The notion of doing so still occurred to her. But other matters had lately involved her, and her talents of patience had failed slightly under their pressure.

It might be said that with the house she had inherited her two brothers, both of whom were heavy responsibilities. Her friends—

Riddle, Kitty and Matthew—appreciated that. What none of them realized was the world which was composed in that household. Its wonder, its joys, its perils and its conflicts, its entire enfolding charm, were secret. She alone experienced them, was enthralled by them one day and oppressed by them on the next. Her life was on two planes, one of which presented the activity of the Capital to her and afforded her work and a salary, while the other . . . what could she say of it? Where were its roots? What was its direction? It fulfilled her so completely that she had never envisaged anything else for herself. Nevertheless, she was often fearful of it.

Dominated by Quentin, it often seemed to her to belong to the spiritual. Hours seemed to her to lengthen into strange, prolonged periods in which Quentin, John, and herself existed by their unity, their proximity to one another, their ideas. It was a state of such tranquillity in its heart that it often appeared to her to be in danger of detaching itself from the reality of life which beat vigorously about it, like the breeze that rattled the windows. That had an enchanting temper. But alone in her room, she wondered how long such conditions would last, and what was their ultimate purpose, and what was the nature of the journey which she was making with her brothers.

Once admitted, the questions assumed importance. They belonged to the atmosphere of the house in its peculiar individuality. Outside, there was the world: the pulsating, activity of the City. Here, there was a personal life that had come to represent everything of existence to her. She was completely identified with it. Yet, like everything of the outer world, it was subject to change. It might disintegrate. It would end if Quentin were to die. And then?

She was twenty-five. At a glance, the essential quality of her character was apparent. Slender, slightly above average height, she had long, graceful limbs and a slight figure. Although her dark features were composed calmly and her manner was invariably self-absorbed, behind all her moods there was an animation which expressed itself in her movements, her voice, her smile, so that it was impossible to suppose that she was anything but spirited and buoyant, happy, and supremely confident in character. Nevertheless, she was often subject to secret periods of devastating doubts and a sense of failure that came from the conflict which, paradoxically, had its root in this trinity.

It was paradoxical, perhaps, that there was this fundamental conflict between three people who were united, happy and apparently indispensable to one another. But it was true: the conflict was there, like an unyielding, inimical condition with which she constantly grappled while, at the same time, she appreciated that without it none of them would have belonged to actual life or would have understood themselves. But it was chiefly her problem. To maintain her supremacy. To possess an inexpressible authority over these two men, and never to lose it. To direct their lives because they were a part of hers, and because she loved Quentin and John.

To lose that advantage in moments when Quentin carried all of them into regions of mystical ideas, and to realize that it was not she who possessed them but they who possessed her was an anguish from which she struggled only after days of effort. She dared not lapse profoundly into Quentin's mysticism. Her materialism was the warrant for her existence in this house with her power over these two men. She was the apex of their trinity. She was fulfilled in it. To doubt that she was not at its apex, not dominant, but only the servant of it, and that her profound love was sterile, spiritual yet fruitless, was poignant and bitter to her, until she reaffirmed to herself that she was mistress of it all, the element of some pervasive power which afforded her a purpose.

Not long ago, Riddle . . . jolly, affectionate little Riddle who was an accountant in the City, and who certainly had nothing of jealousy in him, had lent her a book. Her amiable friend, Riddle, who could be absolved from all subterfuge or slyness, had lent her a biography of William and Dorothy Wordsworth. He had followed it with another which was the history of the Brontë family. Riddle, who enjoyed biography, had lightly given her these books to read. That was all. Wasn't that all? Or had he intended them to speak for his discreet tongue which wanted to tell her that she was foolish to ignore his love for her and render her life to her two brothers who might one day leave her with nothing but a prospect of spinsterhood.

With the advent of PEEPER, would not that happen? Would not PEEPER dissolve the spirit of the house and carry John into another, noisy world. And would not Quentin drift away from her into his ideas? She would lose her advantage and her influence over them; and of that enchanting life which the three of them had created for themselves only her memories would remain. That, surely, was what Riddle attempted to tell her.

His kiss . . . his swift kiss, and his sudden ardent proposal of marriage that seemed to her to come so incongruously from his unemotional nature, augmented so much which he had never expressed in words. It was like a retort to Quentin's fascinating theory of life in terms of

Time, Space and Prayer; and as such it was eloquent of all that was lacking in her life.

It was also an opportunity to resign the conflict and step forth. But to resign! To yield at this juncture when, after another effort, so much might be achieved!

The advent of PEEPER suddenly rendered the struggle more intense, for he was not only a threat but something which she might turn to her advantage. He represented the conflict, and it was around him that it would move.

She had enjoined secrecy upon Quentin and John. She too would preserve the secret. But she longed for someone in whom she might confide. Quentin and John made a pair, but for herself there was only old Twigge, downstairs. He understood the life of the household. Already, he was a part of it.

She went down to him.

## SIX

*

His door was open as she passed with a bucket of rubbish for the bin. She knew that as soon as he heard her coming down he would enter the passage and pretend to be surprised to encounter her. She could see him through the open doorway. He held a long poker in his hand. Turning at the sound of her step in the passage, he grinned and approached her.

'Come in,' he said.

She set down the bucket outside and entered the room. He pointed to the fireplace. It was heaped with fine ash on top of which he had added coal dust. A thin stem of smoke arose from the mass.

'Look at that!' he exclaimed. 'As faithful as the best of friends. Before I go to bed at night, I give it a taste of slack. And when I get up in the morning, I stir it and it warms up and smiles at me! Of all the things in the world, he gives me the least trouble and the greatest comfort.'

He chuckled softly and drew forward a small easy chair.

'Sit down,' he said.

When she was seated, he settled himself opposite her in an office chair which was his favourite. He crossed his thin legs and joined his hands.

He was sixty-four. He had occupied the rooms on the ground floor for two years. Where he had been before that, Lenora did not know. Somewhere east of this part of London, she supposed. Somewhere at the top of a draughty, damp building in a room whose windows overlooked the great sea of towers and roof-tops. And before that, north somewhere, in a basement. And previous to that, in another garret. At one time or another, he had comically related some of his adventures in a London which seemed to Lenora to lack any sort of charity or goodwill and to be as ruthlessly 'on the make' as any sour old miser in his ancient den could be. Twigge laughed over his adventures. His life had been like that of an imperishable speck of dust blown to and fro by the curious currents of life in the city. And instead of disintegrating, as did other particles, into smaller ones, the grain of dust had increased in size and strength. The forces of life had enhanced it, polished it until it shone and reflected vivid things. The peculiar harshness of life in the City had engendered in it a resource and optimism, and a complete, fascinating philosophy of life. He was identifiable with formidable yet kindly currents that moved below the harsher ones and carried him towards security, favourable opportunities, where his wit and shrewdness found expression and some kind of reward. And all the time, they moulded his distinctive character and personality into a glittering thing below whose rough surface there was generosity and gentleness and wisdom.

In appearance, Twigge was small and sharp. His feet and hands were very large and disproportionate to his thin body which was clothed always in a suit that was quite three sizes too big for him. He had a small head and a small face, round, on a thin neck. His hair was plentiful and white and untidy. His brown eyes were clear, like a child's. His nose was large but handsome, with its tip like something that seemed to sense the world. Below, his full lips suggested eloquence and a love of conversation. And the whole of that vivacious countenance was glowing with a single quality. Inquisitiveness. An insatiable interest in people, things, in facts, knowledge, words, sounds, events, and positively everything that could be gathered or experienced by the five senses and transmuted into comprehensive thought.

And his profession, occupation, trade? His means of livelihood? It had many ways and means. He wrote sermons for a confidential Bureau that supplied them on subscription terms to ministers of religion who lacked time or the ability to write their own. Similarly, through the same Bureau, he composed speeches at short notice which were supplied on demand to such persons as chairmen of public bodies, and mayors, presidents, secretaries. He posed privately for artists and sculptors, as well as for students of art at many academies. And at various occasions during the week, he took his pitch in the Park.

## HECTOR TWIGGE. THE HUMAN ENCYCLOPÆDIA

Apart from all that, he was accomplished. He could draw and paint in a delicate fashion. He wrote little verses that had a quaint originality. He played Chopin on his piano which he regularly tuned himself. He had read widely. And he had formulated his own ideas and his own philosophy.

Nevertheless, it still did not explain him. The stones of the city sheltered him and afforded him bread. But who was he? From whence was he? What did he hope for?

He was so much a part of the City's life—the speed, the pressure, the liveliness, the quick response, that there did not seem any necessity for a definite answer to the question. His presence inspired not only the question but supplied an answer as well. Lenora might just as well have asked herself what was the history of any cornerstone, any pillar in the City, any familiar little landmark. Twigge belonged to what was visible, tangible, perceptible.

'Something on your mind?' he said, interrupting her thoughts. He laughed softly and went on: 'Come on! Let's have it!'

His voice was hoarse and hollow. Coming from such a wispish body, it was startling and amusing. Lenora looked at the fire and smiled.

'You know, don't you, old Twigge?'

He nodded as he smiled back at her. 'Plenty!' he said. 'General and particular. Concrete and abstract. Rhyme and reason. The good, the true, and the beautiful. It all amounts to one thing.'

Leaning forward, he took the poker in his big hand and gently stirred the heap of warm dust in the fire until a small flame rose.

'Listen,' he said. 'D'you worry yourself with what happens to you when you dream at nights?'

She shook her head without looking at him.

'Then why fret about what happens to you when you're awake?' he said.

'Because,' she began, 'what happens when the mind is conscious . . .'

She stopped because his nutty face had become creased in a grin.

'Go on!' he exclaimed, softly and sardonically. 'Go on! When the mind is conscious it is sensitive to the actual. It is the recording instrument of the five senses that inform it and help it to co-ordinate thought, etcetera, etcetera, etcetera! Don't you believe it! That's an old, old story. But that's beside the point. Conscious or unconscious, there's only one mind. Agreed?'

He cocked his head on one side and, with his hands outspread, awaited her reply.

'Well, yes. But . . .'

'Agreed, or not?' he insisted.

'Yes.'

His hands dropped to his thin thighs. His head remained in its attitude.

'If there's only one mind—one phenomenon of the human brain—to experience existence, wouldn't you concede that what happens to it at any time of the day or night is important? Asleep or awake. Conscious or unconscious.'

Lenora said: 'But when it is awake it acts consciously. It's under control. It is reasonable. It thinks sensibly.'

His head returned to its normal angle.

'Does it?' he said. 'Does it?'

'That's its function: thought.'

Old Twigge was slowly shaking his head.

'Why!' he exclaimed, 'if the human mind is under control and is capable of thought, then there's no excuse for all the wars and tragedies and mistakes, or for the wranglings and spite, or for everything else which is bad!'

He pursed his lips. The white hair on his head shook like grass in a wind.

'No, no!' he said. 'We can't agree on that. Sorry. No!'

'Then what?' Lenora said.

Again he stirred the mound of hot ash and dust with the poker. The glowing heart of the fire appeared.

'It's all a dream,' he said, looking at the fire and speaking softly. 'Everything. An involved dream. And just what you like to make of it, providing you play the game fairly by the rules. That's what life is. But there's much more to it than five very, very inadequate senses and one small brain can make of it. And the more you consider it, the more you appreciate it. And the more you do so, the simpler all the problems become.'

He glanced at her. 'So you see, whatever you've got that's worrying you isn't worth fretting about. Is it?'

Lenora rose. 'Isn't anything important?'

His keen, lively face turned to her. 'Precious little!'

'What are we to think of it all?' she said. 'Of all that happens? Of the whole of it, and the past, the present and the future?'

'What we know of it isn't the whole of it,' he said, as though he were imparting a secret. 'It's only a fragment of the rest, which is so large that the mind cannot comprehend the whole of it.'

'Twigge!' Lenora said, earnestly. 'Tell me this: what are we to think of it? Is it tragic? Or is it comedy?'

He spread his hands. 'It's just how you want it!' he exclaimed. 'A tragedy or a comedy . . . what you will.'

She looked down at his upturned face which was lifted in an expression of happiness.

'Is it?' she said, pensively.

'It's a comedy,' he said. 'A grand comedy . . .'

'Then why don't we laugh? Twigge! If only we could laugh! If we weren't all so solemn!'

He rubbed his hands briskly together; and chuckling softly and rising from his chair to stand with his back to the fire, he said repeatedly: 'Now you're talking! Ah! Now you're talking!'

She smiled at him and went out. In the yard where she emptied the bucket of rubbish into the bin, she heard his laughter sounding softly and gaily on the air. And although she had related nothing of the subject of her anxiety, over it all he had cast his curious philosophy and melted it, as well as having revealed to her an interesting conception of the world which had a warmth and humour that were refreshing to her.

# SEVEN

★

A week later, when PEEPER first appeared before the public on that Friday morning, she had to admit to herself that he gave her little cause for anxiety. During that week, she had seen on hoardings, on 'buses, on the Underground, as well as on the backs of 'bus tickets, the name in bold type. PEEPER. WHO IS PEEPER? It was everywhere. It met the eye in moments when one hurried to and from work or leisure, and it captured one's mind for an instant. It was up and down the country on all the hoardings rented by the 'Daily Summariser,' and the newspaper itself had excited the public interest by pretending complete ignorance of PEEPER and by commenting upon the extraordinary attention aroused everywhere by the advertisements which had percolated so deeply into the national life that it was impossible for anybody to escape them.

The campaign of publicity had succeeded, for the original question had been followed by an answer. PEEPER IS COMING NEXT FRIDAY. And on this morning's 'Daily Summariser' the entire front page announced him

A world hurrying to work and absorbed with immediate matter gave him nothing but a cursory glance. There he was, nothing more than a figure in a new strip-cartoon. It was later that he swung into public attention. At eleven, at the lunch hour, and throughout the afternoon, he was there for the millions to discover at last. And by that time, the Continent which had been intrigued as to his character and purpose and identity was satisfied with him. The secret was out in America where the identity of the individual whose name had mystified all the British Isles for the past week had excited a considerable volume of comment. Cables related news of him and some headline in the afternoon newspapers falsely attributed a sensation to him.

## ADVENT OF PEEPER HITS BRITAIN

From America, the wires agitated for news of PEEPER. London replied. And the fact that America craved for facts had repercussion in the City. By the late afternoon and early evening, heavy ripples of the volume of interest in America demanded facts. Who was PEEPER What was he doing? What was his speciality?

The three million four hundred thousand readers of the 'Daily Summariser' had seen only a rather personable figure, yet about him there was a potentiality which promised . . . what? The newspaper itself promised much from him. ' . . . an extraordinary personality destined to adventure into the national life and create controversy.' America headlined the news; and back came more ripples, drenching the Press.

It gathered weight as the day passed. Then Lenora heard it all more clearly. PEEPER, the caption said. THE ADVENTURES OF PEEPER. By Jayby. And there in the cartoon, she saw Quentin. He looked amusing, candid, thin and dark and brisk. Carrying a small suitcase, he strode past a group of world-famous statesmen who stood beneath a wall on which the initials of an International Organization were printed.

I'LL DROP IN SOME DAY, he said, passing by.

AND SEE FOR MYSELF WHAT GOES ON.

With an interesting glance backwards at the group, he walked on. With their heads together, the great statesmen took no notice of him, for he was merely a passing individual. In the last frame of the strip, he was shown stepping quickly from the cartoon and walking off the page.

It was no more than an announcement, yet it had effect principally because from other Continents had come the wave of excitement about him. The campaign of publicity had succeeded in establishing him. And a populace which had been at work all day and was now returned to leisure in which it could review the events of the day had time in which to discuss the feature. Its opinion was that PEEPER was worth watching.

On the following morning, PEEPER appeared again. Below a large placard which stated: CRISIS AT CONFERENCE. RUSSIA OBJECTS. FRANCE ANGRY. AMERICA IMPATIENT, PEEPER was shown walking in the Red Square at Moscow amidst people who certainly did not seem to express objection. In the next frame of the cartoon, he appeared amongst the throng on a Parisian boulevard where, seated outside a café, he was watching the cheerful, animated scene which certainly did not depict an angry France. In the third frame, he was visible at a baseball match where the cheering multitude was obviously intent only upon the game.

NONSENSE! PEEPER said. THE PEOPLE ARE AT PEACE.

That was on Saturday morning. On the following Monday morning, seven thousand, eight hundred and thirty-four letters reached the Daily Summariser' and were passed to an expert staff to be analysed. Belfwig impatiently awaited the report.

Adverse, pro, contra, constructive, abusive, anonymous, facetious a few examples from each heading were passed to Belfwig. He read them and was satisfied. He placed much importance on the adverse ones and was pleased by the measure of anger and disappointment expressed in them. His plan for PEEPER was to arouse exasperation first of all; and he was prepared to excite that feeling two or three times and then swing neatly over to something which would satisfy his most critical readers and, at the same time, gratify the minds of other readers who expected PEEPER to be maintained on a serious level PEEPER was to be for all minds and not for the minority or the majority If, at first, there was exasperation and derision, Belfwig wished to measure it. Praise would come later. And still later would come controversy, which he desired so that PEEPER might rise into reality from its hot breath and become a figure of fact in the lives of . . . how many? Millions, he hoped. In England, in the British Isles and Europe as well as in all the other continents. He wanted PEEPER to become famous everywhere. And more than famous. Something . . . something new in the history of the planet.

That morning, PEEPER made his third appearance, and was shown standing outside the House of Commons watching the Chancellor of the Exchequer arriving at the House.

IN THE BAG.

It was not especially pointed, although it was apt, for this was Budget Day. It caught and held the public attention for an instant longer than before. It quite likely caused a few wry smiles, for there was nothing which the Chancellor represented so much as the staggering load of taxation which the people bore and which impeded their progress. Apart from that, it merely promised further comment. There was no doubt of that, for by midday thousands of letters addressed to PEEPER had been delivered at the newspaper's office.

Belfwig made only a brief reference to them when he and Bessing met that afternoon. He spoke, instead, of PEEPER's previous appearances, saying that the feature had made its roots and excited interest and comment and, he hoped, given promise of better things to come When he mentioned the enormous volume of letters, he advised Bessing not to take them seriously but to regard them as flashes from the public mind. In his opinion, the best and only course was to pursue a consistent attitude, clear and emphatic. With a slight smile which was intended to flatter Bessing, he went on to remark that while he, of course, could not create PEEPER's adventures or even decide the detail of his character, he could speak as the Editor of this journal and remark that consistency and emphasis were qualities which men and women not only admired in the end but which influenced them all the time.

After that, he gave his enthusiastic approval of the following day's cartoon and handed Bessing a parcel containing a selection of the letters from readers.

An hour later, Bessing reached home and untied the parcel and read the letters. A feeling of horror and despair grew in him, and his hands trembled as he held the sheets of blue, pink, white, yellow and green paper, some of which were heavily scented. Fantastic styles of hand-writing seemed to him to express far more than the words themselves. This, he thought, with revulsion, this is a vision of hell! These obsceni-ties, these ravings and the incoherent ideas, and the scent from the pages, and the vanity of the expensive paper and envelopes with their deckle-edges and their embossed addresses and their seals . . . all this was madness! And all had been addressed neatly, sealed, stamped and posted, and delivered by postmen. His Majesty's Mails!

It presented to him a kind of lurking, tenebrous world that was very terrible in its manifestation of the narrow, secret paths in the human mind. Who were these correspondents? What was their occupation? From what environment did they come? Amidst the great morning and evening throngs did they mingle? Did they work all day at office, at desk, at counter, and appear normal, efficient, cheerful? Did they com-pose the great scene, the comedy or tragedy, or were they separate, apart, in their madness?

Quentin had come beside him and taken a few of the letters. They dropped quickly, one after another, from his hands as he read them. Suddenly, he laughed explosively. Was there one that was amusing in the sad bunch?

Turning, John saw Quentin holding at arm's length a letter written in a small, dainty hand upon heavy deckle-edged paper in a mono-grammed envelope. Reading it, he was as startled as he had been by the others, for here again was the revelation of a baleful, personal world. Quentin's laughter shed a kind of light upon it and brought it forth and somehow rendered it in a new way.

The letter was like a climax to PEEPER's three appearances. Frankly, tenderly, and sincerely, the writer offered herself to PEEPER in marriage. She described herself, physically and mentally, gave her age as thirty-five, and having concluded by remarking that she had a private income of a hundred and fifty pounds per annum, requested the favour of a reply by return of post.

Their laughter ended. The letter was on the table which stood between them.

'She is the first to believe in Peeper,' Quentin said.

Lenora entered the room. Quentin handed the letter to her. Reading it, turning it over and examining the fine paper and seeing the envelope with its monogram, and reading aloud the woman's name and address, she suddenly looked at Quentin and John.

'Is she . . . is she serious?' she exclaimed.

'Look at these!' John said, pointing to the mass of letters littering the floor.

Lenora was laughing softly and without restraint.


# EIGHT

★

Whatever the three of them had to say about the letters was interrupted by the arrival of a messenger from the 'Daily Summariser.' Would Mr. John Bessing come at once to the office, where Mr. Belfwig wished to see him regarding an urgent matter?

John was not yet accustomed to such requests. Moreover, the life of this national newspaper with its popularity and importance, its vast organization in Departments and Syndicates, as well as its extension into subsidiary companies that existed solely to direct such matters as advertising, distribution, finance, presented him with an idea of something so large that his sensitive imagination flinched from it. On two occasions within as many days, Belfwig had offered him a studio in Summariser House, as well as the services of a clerk and secretary. I was an invitation amounting to an order, tactfully conveyed, that Bessing should identify himself with the intricate, massive life of this Press and become one of the thousands of members of its staff. But there was something else as well: Belfwig was attempting to gain influence over this new member of the staff.

On the present occasion, Lord Ecks was impatiently awaiting with Belfwig the arrival of their staff artist for whom they had sent a messenger. An hour previously, Ecks had appeared unexpectedly flushed with nervous energy generated in his impulsive temperament by his plans for yet another 'Cause.' Belfwig, as ever, was accessible; but it was almost a rebuff to Ecks to discover that the creator of PEEPER was not in the building and had not yet attached himself physically to the immense team which the Board controlled. It was left to Belfwig to explain cleverly that in regard to this young genius the process of adaptation to the organization was something which he was loth to hasten.

'I don't want to break down his background which, after all, has produced PEEPER,' he said. 'A genius is entitled to special consideration.'

Ecks glowered at the mention of genius.

'What's he like?' he said. 'What's his outlook?'

Belfwig was amused. 'Sluggish,' he replied. 'And obstinate.'

Ecks was not only amazed but horrified.

'Won't do!' he declared. 'Can't have that! Can't possibly tolerate it!'

Belfwig lapsed into gravity.

'I'm afraid we shall have to,' he said. 'We must remember that a mind which has presented us with this opportunity . . .'

Ecks exploded. 'God bless my soul, what's all this?' Then he shouted. 'Genius!' he snorted. 'We've done without him ever since we bought this newspaper! Genius is not indispensable. I can create it.' He strode about the room. 'He'll listen to me, Belfwig, genius or not! I want this call for Reform to be heard!'

He pointed to the mass of notes on the desk. Belfwig smiled, shrugged his shoulders.

'You can try him,' he said. 'But be gentle.'

When Bessing appeared, Ecks behaved as though he were in the presence of nobility. He was courtly and gracious. He was the personality famous amongst political hostesses who longed for the power of his Press on their platforms. Bluff, tactful, charming, he put Bessing into a frame of mind which was the prelude to his next move.

'I was keenly interested, Bessing. From the outset. Particularly with your idea of projecting PEEPER upon a journey through contemporary life. That appealed to me.'

'I'm very pleased, Lord Ecks,' Bessing said.

Ecks lit a cigar. 'I want you to do something for me, Bessing,' he went on. He walked to the end of the room and turned. Then he spoke from that distance, at the same time returning slowly to Bessing.

'This Press has decided to attack what it feels to be an absurdity in our national life. We have organized a thorough campaign which we propose to direct against the system whereby Income Tax is levied.'

39

By that time, he was standing before Bessing.

'I want you to help us, Jayby,' he said.

Belfwig nodded encouragingly behind Bessing.

'How?' Bessing stammered, looking up at the vigorous face which suddenly beamed at him, laughed, and exclaimed:

'I am the last person to attempt to tell you! Your genius alone can do that.'

But Bessing had no sooner assented to the request to enlist PEEPER'S assistance in the Cause than Ecks presented his plans. There they were, on paper, masses of paper, gigantic conceptions that would transform themselves into printed words upon the pages of the City editions, the dozens of provincial editions, and the special continental editions. The 'Weekly' which the newspaper published would carry them. So would the overseas editions which, daily, were bundled off to the world's capitals. And a surprisingly noisy, energetic Ecks explained them.

'Not political,' he exclaimed. 'Nothing of party politics in it. A pure call for Reform. Nothing more. I sent for you because it is my opinion that here is the perfect Cause for your PEEPER. Now!'

Bessing listened not so much to the involved, extensive plans as to the voice and personality and temperament of Lord Ecks who, presently, rang for Belfwig's secretary and sent her out to find someone who would purchase immediately some Watman paper, and charcoal, and some kneaded rubber. And when that was done, Ecks and Belfwig led him to other Departments in that big building. He met Feature Editors, Leader writers, Advertisement executives; but all the time he was secretly listening to headlines and seeing in imagination the bold type proclaiming a Cause.

Under Ecks' shrewd influence, he drew another cartoon to replace to-morrow's which was now put aside. And when that was done, Ecks coaxed him to draw yet another. The telephone rang incessantly, and Ecks bawled into it, laughed, became angry, and then gentle and courteous. Dazed, yet conscious of the increasing momentum of the plans for the Cause, and aware as well of the fact that it was in PEEPER that the whole impudent stunt would be concentrated, Bessing finished his drawings and fixed them.

Ecks examined them with Belfwig. He tossed them aside.

'I am satisfied,' he said, in his brusque fashion, as he scrambled into his coat and clapped on his hat. He held out a hand to Bessing.

'Come and dine with us, my boy. Glad to see you, always.'

He strode to the door. 'Back in a couple of hours!' he bawled, going out.

Bessing turned to Belfwig who sat back and grinned.

'You've impressed him, Bessing,' Belfwig said. 'Unless I am very much mistaken, you will find that PEEPER is going to create a sensation!'

'That wasn't my intention at all!' Bessing retorted. 'I didn't intend to create sensations. I envisaged . . .'

Belfwig listened to him for several minutes, then he quietly interrupted the angry flood of words.

'What does it matter? Lord Ecks has vision . . .'

'Wind!' Bessing shouted.

Belfwig laughed. 'Never mind! Just go on with PEEPER as you have done so far, Bessing. Don't worry. Leave the rest to me, and Lord Ecks.'

Bessing went home. He felt as though something in him were caught up in a sound, a force, a mighty machine which was capable of hurling ideas at the minds of millions of people when they opened their newspapers in the morning. He was no longer an individual, detached, with a personal freedom which enabled him to create his own artistic fancies. Instead, he was harnessed to an organization which was committed to a Cause. He knew what happened to such stunts: the Causes; the Calls; the Crusades. They made a slight dent on the public mind which, after two or three days, recovered its original shape. Yet, in this instance, he had forebodings which, when he reached home, he explained to Quentin. He expected from Quentin a reproach, or at least a sympathetic reception of his anxiety. Instead, he was greeted with boisterous laughter.

'Why not?' Quentin declared. 'It'll expire in three days! Those stunts never last longer. But after that . . . we'll have PEEPER for ourselves. And by that time, he'll be familiar to people. Ecks will have established him for us.'

It did not encourage John. He was afraid. In his characteristic way, his thoughts flew into the future and returned in terror to him. A sensation! And again he felt the harness of that immense organization confining him, driving him.

He sat down and took up once more the letters from the 'Daily Summariser' readers. Crude, obscene, fawning, with their fragmentary ideas and their meandering sentimentality, they were like the gibberings of deranged minds making sound across life. And that woman who offered herself in marriage to PEEPER, and who mentioned as advantageous her tiny income! Marriage to a figure in a cartoon! Was that the public mind? Was that the substance which the newspaper' enormous organizations intended to wring for a sensation?

'She wants to marry him!'

Then he was silent. If PEEPER were real enough to that woman to inspire such an offer, what else would happen when other minds accepted him as a reality?

## NINE

*

On the following morning, PEEPER appeared in his place at the foot of page three where readers of the 'Daily Summariser' expected to find him. Yesterday, the Chancellor of the Exchequer had presented his budget and delivered his long speech. An expectant nation, anxious for relief, had been offered instead some new and involved form of Relief which was similar to other Reliefs within the terms of the multitudinous Finance Acts. And the nation's hope was once again swallowed in the revolting vision of the lunatic tangle and incomprehensibility of the system of Income Tax. PEEPER had, of course, only been able to guess beforehand that some such form of Relief would be offered. He had taken a chance. With his hands extended in appeal towards the Parliament Buildings, he was saying:

'THE INCOME TAX SYSTEM. RELIEVE US OF THIS GIBBERISH! CLOSE IT DOWN! SIMPLIFY IT!'

Lenora saw it when the newspaper was delivered shortly before breakfast. It was apt. It was trenchant and timely. A patient nation had tolerated for years those idiotic phrases and the entangling jungle-growth of this enormous piece of official ritual that had spread beyond its original limits and become an assault upon commonsense. It belonged to some muddling process of an earlier age, and was nonsense upon nonsense. The highest and the lowest intelligence alike turned with exasperation and hot disgust from it as from the eccentricity and curious prejudices of any asylum inmate. Only its high priests and its millions of servants, and the many accountants who derived an income by disentangling their clients from its maddening clauses, sustained it.

But Lenora was worried. This forthright call for reform was a voice that had its source in her home. What answer would come and disturb her? What controversy would begin and sweep like a gale of voices pressing into the home? What was being commented in the trains and 'buses moving towards the City?

She left home that morning as though she were venturing into an ocean of sound that might presently heave its volume in derision or agreement at PEEPER. What would she have to say then? What must she do? How could she pretend ignorance of the source of that provocative creature?

The distance from home to the estate agency where she worked was short enough to cover in seven minutes. But her route was along Piccadilly which at that hour was full of the throngs from the Underground and the 'buses. She watched. She listened to snatches of laughter and chatter.

She need not have worried. The pace and mood of London going to work was not marked by references to PEEPER. The long stream of 'buses swept noisily from Hyde Park Corner, with the April sunlight flashing in reflection from them. Private cars and taxis pressed around them; and the thunder of this stream rattled against the high buildings to her left and broke into fragments which poured out across the spring freshness of the Green Park. Ahead, from the Circus, another stream pushed, nosing from between the two sheer walls of the chasm. On the pedestrian islands, little crowds gathered and then darted over. The queues at the stages appeared indifferent to anything except the approaching 'buses. And the voices which broke from sudden, curious moments when the traffic's commotion subsided slightly and the spring wind sped gently over the city's face, spoke only of what was personal.

Lenora halted at the corner of Old Bond Street. The 'buses sped dexterously round, drowning the voices. Behind her, a man laughed.

'He's right,' another said, loudly. 'The thing has gone mad. It's overloaded with . . .'

The rest was smothered in the crash of traffic and the pattering rattle of footsteps and chatter. The little crowd, waiting to cross, gathered itself and sped over. Lenora did not go with it but remained on the curb feeling cold and afraid, wondering how many others would add to that remark and make a chorus which would ascend vociferously and create controversy. And then what repercussions? And in the office . . .

She need not have anticipated it, for at the office there were only the usual sluggish efforts that gradually rose to full activity and set in motion the daily life of the building. There, over hats and handbags which remained on desks while letters were sorted and covers were removed from typewriters and filing cabinets opened, the conversation was similar to that of innumerable yesterdays. The subjects of talk were threaded into character and individuality and were of some rapidly comprehended event or personality: the arrival in England of a famous film star; chances of a glimpse of him to-day. A new film. A new novel by Peter Cheyney. A delay on the Edgware-Morden line. A quarrel with a 'bus conductress. Certainly not the Budget, or UNO (again in full session) or anything else that was of government here, there, or anywhere. For the film stars, the novelists, the personalities of the stage, were nearer to one in the actuality of daily life. One could see them, write to them. They were concerned with people. They existed by some contact with people. And life and all that it offered was nearer to one in the pages of a novel, or on the screen or stage, than it was in the august councils of statesmen or the meetings of Cabinets or the ponderous ritual of Parliaments, all of which was beyond a gulf which the statesmen, once they had gained power, would not cross.

Listening, Lenora heard nothing of PEEPER. Collis, her immediate chief, came in quickly and hung his hat on a peg and set his overcoat on a holder. He tossed his copy of the 'Daily Mail' on his desk and lit a cigarette. A bell rang. He looked up and frowned as he extinguished the cigarette.

'Is he in already?'

Lenora arranged her desk while he was away. Filing baskets, notebooks, pencils, quarto heading. Chester put his head into the room.

'Not here?'

He came in and stood at her desk.

'He's with Charlie,' she said.

'Charlie here already!'

He was carrying a folded copy of the 'Daily Summariser.' Her glance resting on it caught his attention. Always affable to her, always anxious to please her, he opened the newspaper.

'Seen PEEPER, to-day?'

He laughed as he looked down at her and showed her the strip from which Quentin beamed out at her like something intimate and personal to her which had escaped to the page.

'Oh, PEEPER!' she murmured.

And fortunately at that moment Collis returned noisily and flung down a bunch of letters and came across to laugh at PEEPER, and to say that Charlie was laughing. Chester strolled away. Collis dictated some letters. Then gradually she heard the laughter rising in little gusts from the other rooms. She met it, later, when she entered them. PEEPER! Oh, yes, I heard . . . they say . . . did you know? If you ask me . . . and this fellow was saying . . .

Into it all there came a telephone call for her from Riddle.

'Len, could you lunch with me?'

Could you, he was saying, at Verrey's, at twelve-thirty. I've reserved a table. She was silent. PEEPER was so much a topic that she feared to go far. Sandwiches and coffee in the Snackery round the corner, and then a quiet half hour to herself. That was what she had anticipated. Not the crowded restaurant, and the talk about PEEPER.

'Not to-day,' she said. 'I'm afraid . . .'

'I'll be round just before half-past,' he said. He laughed and rang off.

He arrived at a quarter past twelve and stood chatting with Collis while Lenora put on her hat and coat.

'Question in the House, this morning,' Riddle said. 'At Question Time. Opposition back bencher asked the P.M. if the Government would scrap the existing methods of levying Income Tax. Wanted a Select Committee to examine the whole thing. Said it was outdated. Decrepit, he called it. Said it was a Bogy in the nation's life.'

They laughed uproariously. Riddle continued: 'No wonder the Yankees want to know about PEEPER! But in Parliament . . . Old Colport asked if the Government would consider Socializing the System! Opposition laughed like mad, and cheered. Government supporters shouted back that it was a Tory system. Then the lid was off for five minutes.'

The telephone rang, and while Collis was speaking Riddle left with Lenora. At the 'bus stop in Bond Street, he turned to her with a mildly aggrieved air.

'You never told me, Len!'

His round, plump face confronted her, and he waited for an answer which she could not give him. Inside the 'bus, he went on:

'About PEEPER.' And glancing at her he smiled again.

She was silent, staring ahead of her.

'As soon as I saw him,' he said, quietly, leaning towards her, 'I recognized Quentin.'

She gave him a quick glance, more to check any further remark.

'There's no mistaking the family likeness,' he said.

She had nothing to say to him. Her silence made some sort of response which enjoined silence on him. It was not until they alighted at Oxford Circus and he steered her across to Regent Street that she spoke.

'It's a secret,' she said.

'And a pretty good one!'

'I want it to remain one,' she said.

He laughed. 'It'll . . . I should think it will bring John a fortune!'

And he went on in his flat, matter-of-fact way. A real fortune. The idea was not new, of course. There had been PEEPERS . . . but they were caricatures. PEEPER . . . this one . . . was original. Unique. He had come at the right moment. People were tired of caricatures. They wanted something nearer to themselves. . . .

He stopped suddenly, for a glance at her showed that she was not listening to him. In the crowded restaurant, the kind of conversation which he desired with her was impossible. Silence was enforced on him by the brisk activity and noise about them, as well as by her mood which appeared to him to be held by anxiety and anger. Something he had said? Some tactless remark? He tried to entice her from it into his own cheerful mood and his genial spirit.

For the first time in their friendship, he failed. She defeated him with her silence and absorption. He ordered the lunch and then sat back hating the cheerful sounds around him and the hollow roar of the traffic up in the street. He lost his buoyancy, and his appetite. The whole of his life suddenly seemed dull, heavy and lacking in attraction to him.

Lenora looked quickly at him. Then she laughed. His round, smooth face with its complacent, patient expression was the countenance of the sane world, comforting and purposeful and discreet. But the faint shadow of unhappiness upon it was too eloquent of his thoughts for her to ignore it.

'I'm sorry,' she said, leaning slightly towards him.

He grimaced. 'Why are you worried?' he said.

'Oh, PEEPER . . .' she told him; and she continued: 'He's every-where!'

He listened while she explained. Hadn't he heard? The people in the 'bus? And around them at the tables? All the talk! And Charlie buying back numbers. And the prices for back numbers on the Exchanges. And what he himself had told her about John making a fortune. And the news about the question in Parliament.

Riddle looked up from his soup. 'No harm in that!'

'But it's not what I wanted PEEPER to be,' she said.

She told him: she had wanted PEEPER to be light, gay, so amusing that he would create laughter. She had wanted a comedy, not this . . . this priggishness.

'And he is a prig!' she declared. 'A sardonic reformer! And that's only the beginning. . . .'

'But he's harmless!' he exclaimed, in the face of her pallor and distress. 'If he can clear away all the old rubbish piled on us which we carry forward year after year, prig or not, he'll be a useful man! In any case, he's made us all laugh to-day!'

Her silence came again. He did not know that it was not so much what PEEPER would do in the world but the effect of it in her home that mattered. And her loss of advantage and influence over her brothers. And the gradual loss of that enchanting atmosphere in their lives.

Riddle said: 'You're too serious, Len!'

He tried to extend his buoyant mood over hers. All the time he was struggling as well with his own large convictions of doubt and anxiety and suspicion.

'You don't enjoy life, Len!' he said. 'You stick at home. You . . . you don't give yourself a chance!'

It was his only theme. Throughout the meal, he went on. She did not dare to interrupt the theme. It beat against her like soft rain and was strangely refreshing to her. She knew what he was trying to say, and she was attentive because she wished to discover if he really understood her life. But he was always the same: constant, unvarying, he merely repeated in so many words that single theme. He understood nothing of her. It was satisfying to realize it, and yet disappointing. And she could not help being amused by him.

Looking at his clear, round face, she knew that he was good. He had virtues and qualities. He was respected in his profession where, one day, he would be a partner in the firm which employed him. His solid, unemotional nature would continue in that vein all his life. He would never be anything but sensible, reasonable, kindly, so that upon his character one could establish an empire perhaps, and at the least find a remarkable constancy and faith. All that was good. But his fault was that he was so predictable. To-day, to-morrow, a year hence, a lifetime ahead, he would still be the same. And he failed in her sight because of that unchanging character of his. He loved her and wanted to marry her. He had just now lightly decried her life at home; but he did not know that compared to her brothers he was dull and unattractive. The very things which, had she disclosed them to him, would have brought his immediate criticism, were the factors that enchanted her and conflicted with his massive virtues.

Quentin's character with its curious moods, and his intellect which conceived such sharply-defined ideas, as well as those exquisite moments when he expounded some abstruse theory, compensated her for the heavy responsibilities which his illness put upon her. In the same way, John's procrastination and indolence, as well as his habit of living more by his vague ideas, his sensibilities and impulsive whims than by habit or convention, presented him to her with a freshness which never dulled. And both of them belonged to her. She was somebody to whom they turned with implicit faith. They were hers, even to support. They might vex her. They might be inconstant. But in some degree that was what bound her to them. That, and her authority over them, and her place in the trinity.

Could marriage offer her more? Could Riddle make her life as exciting as this journey which she made with her brothers? Would each day appear new, different, varied, with all manner of horizons constantly appearing? She knew what he offered her. It was love, comfort, security, children; and she did not scorn them. What he could not render her was the sense of fulfilment which, merely by their proximity to her, her brothers granted her. Even her responsibilities and anxieties were unlike those of the life which Riddle persistently presented, for they had their flavour of another world. Even this present anxiety was unlike anything which Riddle's orderly life would have raised in hers. It was so large and pervasive in her life that it evoked all her resources of courage and strength, and demanded a constant effort of every nerve. It brought her alive. And the result was that she felt the conflict as something which, to lose, would end in complete defeat but which to win would offer a prospect of immeasurable triumph. It was worth all effort. And compared to it, what Riddle offered her was trivial and commonplace.

Suddenly, as though he had realized it all, he leaned forward.

'Well, leave it all!' he said, roundly. 'Stop worrying about PEEPER! If you can't stand him, think no more about him! That's the sensible thing to do. Not this . . . this moping!'

He was angry. His good-humoured face was deeply flushed. His right hand was clenched and he struck the table lightly with it to emphasize his words.

She understood him so well, whereas he had only the thinnest

48

realization of her life. She could not enlighten him. With a kind of pity which must have betrayed itself to him, she rested a hand on his arm.

He moved back from it. 'No!' he said, emphatically. 'Don't do that! Just think about yourself and do the proper thing! If we're friends, you should listen to me.'

He leaned forward. 'Give it all up . . . leave it! It worries you. Very well, come away. We'll be married.'

She was silent. Her grave face with its secrets was the whole of a delicate fabric which his gaze assaulted as he sat there and awaited her answer. His patience and tact and caution were all gone, and he was far out, beyond them, staring at her with his angry eyes, his heavy gaze ripping her senses in his quest for an answer. She could only retreat.

'Let's go now,' she murmured.

'Not yet! I want to know . . . I have a right to know how long . . . just how long you are going to let Quentin and John spoil your life!'

She rose more in fright than by intention. The waiter came across at once, and there was nothing Riddle could do except rise and settle the bill and follow Lenora up the stairs into Regent Street.

He took her arm firmly in his hand.

'Running away from it!' he exclaimed. 'Trying to . . .'

He was silent. His fury prevented him from speaking. He and Lenora walked through Hanover Square into Brook Street.

'For years . . .' he went on, heavily and sullenly, 'you've practically supported your brothers for years! You know you aren't happy, don't you?'

He regarded her angrily. 'Don't you?' he said.

She released herself from his grip. 'It's my choice,' she said. 'They don't compel me.'

'But you aren't in the least happy about it,' he went on. 'You know that.'

She did not answer him. Whatever he had said was related to so small a factor of her life that she felt no anger and no real necessity to reply to his arguments. She pitied him because despite his pursuit of her into this personal matter he still could not appreciate the richness and variety of her life at home, or realize that even in her conflict with her brothers there was something which fulfilled her spirit.

Behind the window of a small shop several prize kittens were on show, romping in and out of a lined basket. She stopped to join the little crowd which stood there. Above the basket a large mirror was fastened. She saw Riddle's reflection in it.

His face was taut and creased and florid, like that of a man driven out of himself and thrust into some desperate extremity. She slipped her arm through his and drew him away. His rage was the heavy, unfamiliar fury of the complacent spirit unaccustomed to emotion. It had overwhelmed him. He could not speak.

He knew that he had trespassed on Lenora's personal life and been rebuffed by her silence. Yesterday, he might have apologized for his fault. To-day, he felt that she owed him an explanation of some sort. He believed that she held secret some fact which she dared not disclose. What it was, he felt that he could accurately surmise.

He had no particular experience of women to guide him in this, but he had an active commonsense which sought what was obvious. In this instance, he supposed that Lenora's secret was nothing more than something trivial yet important, and so trivial that she dared not confess it, and so important to her that she dared not renounce it. Something like that. Some obstinate fancy, some sharp little disagreement with John and Quentin which angered her but which she wished to continue until she had resolved it all.

Her hold on his arm as the two of them continued their walk was better than words, he thought. He supposed that she loved him but that before she would consent to marry him she must decide about her brothers. An ember of rancour against her compelled him to keep silent. He waited for her to speak. He hoped that she would confide in him. But they reached her office without either of them having said a word more. Still he waited, standing squarely before her and watching her.

Her glance came up and rested on him. Her clear, fine eyes and the vivacity of that face!

'Riddle dear . . . I'm sorry . . . I spoiled your lunch.'

'Tell me what you are hiding from me,' he said, flatly.

He waited an instant for her answer and then went on:

'I know what it is . . .'

He paused because the expression of her face seemed to part and prepare to reveal what was in her thoughts. She did not speak.

'It's something you want to decide with Quentin and John!' he declared. 'You stay in the house with them just to decide it all. You want your way with PEEPER. I know you, Len. You love things that have an element of conflict . . . something you can oppose and conquer! That's all!'

She heard it all with a curious, enchanting sense of relief. He had found her at last. His slow, inept sense of perception had glimpsed her. She waited for him to continue. She would have listened to him. She wanted him to discover everything which she herself could never express in words. That would have enhanced him in her sight.

But he waited for her to confirm his surmise. She said nothing. He gave her time. Finally, he shrugged his shoulders. She knew then that he had given up.

She smiled at him and said good-bye and appeared to linger there as though she did not wish to leave him. He made the usual remark that he would 'phone, would drop round, and raised his hat as she turned and entered the building.

He realized that neither anger nor cajolery could inspire her to confide in him or to accept his offer of marriage. Something more was required. He was puzzled and annoyed. Something which his character and temperament lacked and which prevented him from appreciating certain problems in her life?

Only Lenora could have told him.

She had features whose delicacy he could remember so well when he was not with her. Yet, whenever he was in her company, he realized how inadequate were his senses to gather the innumerable fleeting reflections of mood, character and sensibility that had their moments in those features, and which were far too subtle and transient for him to trace to sources in her thoughts. So much of her was beyond him to fathom; and the little of her which he saw and loved seemed to him to be offered by some grace of her spirit which was inclined to grant him that much. And he appreciated that his friendship with her was only upon some quick surface of her life below which there was a wealth of spirit which her silence concealed from him.

He feared to penetrate that silence which so often dropped between them. He waited. From experience, he knew how to evoke her gaiety, her laughter and smiles, her happiness. That much was sufficient for the moment. But what of the hours, the days and nights when the two of them were apart?

They were like impenetrable walls rising before him and concealing her from him. He had offered her his proposal of marriage which she had met with silence and a smile.

It was not an answer. He wanted something more than her silence, her smile, the surface of friendship. He had supposed that he had patience.

It was exhausted. And his hope, too, was at an end.

That was the impression he had left upon Lenora when he had parted from her. And suddenly, the idea that he was no longer in her life was disturbing to her.

To-night, to-morrow, soon, she would write to him or 'phone to him. He was indispensable to her. She could not understand why, but it was true. Her life without him had an alarming prospect which she could not face.

# TEN

★

Belfwig had been correct in his forecast of events. By noon of that day, his predictions were confirmed. The telephone calls were incessant. Telegrams in hundreds were pouring in. Letters in thousands were delivered, and more were on their way, while a city which was usually preoccupied with its own involved concerns paused, grinned, looked again at PEEPER's amusing figure and was suddenly conscious of the fact that for years the entire nation had meekly tolerated a system of taxation which, like a beggar's suit, had accumulated upon itself hundreds of stitches, patches, amendments, additions, rules, until the whole thing was a ludicrous scarecrow held together by red tape and glue and jerked into hideous life by armies of devotees. Millions of sane men and women knew that this thing was comparable to the chaos of a lunatic's dream, yet not until PEEPER said so on this April morning did the whole undignified, humiliating nonsense stand forth for what it was. A load of cumbersome gibberish which urgently required to be consigned into the pit of things past.

By two o'clock, it had become a topic that ousted all others. It blew about the City all the forenoon and afternoon. Some early editions of evening newspapers reported PEEPER's remarks on front pages, commenting on the general effect in the City. Some curious features of the affair were noted: final quotations on the London Stock Exchange had shown a steep rise in gilt-edged securities and a sharp decline in Industrials. The principal of an Income Tax Bureau in the East End had disappeared. An elderly eccentric carrying a placard on a pole had been forcibly ejected from Somerset House.

Yesterday, and to-day, the 'Daily Summariser' had travelled in trains with travellers who had heard nothing of PEEPER'S success. Together with crumpled numbers of other morning and evening newspapers, and the usual weeklies and illustrated magazines, monthly home magazines and some shoddy, it became part of the débris which littered local trains. Throughout the day and night it was carried by other travellers far away in the long-distance expresses and left in the compartments at the end of the journeys. Carriage cleaners, porters, attendants and ticket collectors gathered it, folded it and kept it for leisure hours. And in those distant places: Scotland, the Midlands, the East, Wales, Devon and Cornwall, PEEPER smiled, made his statement and evoked laughter. His appearance so far from the Capital and out there amidst the affairs of so many cities, towns, villages, might have submerged him had it not been for the long wave of interest which travelled out with him and awaited him in those places. That wave travelled with the speed of sound and made ripples across provincial affairs. Questions arose. PEEPER was there in person, in the hands of the porters, cleaners, attendants, and other railway employees, as well as in the hands of a few travellers.

He lingered in 'buses and trams, waiting-rooms, taxis. He blew about in gutters. He was rescued from salvage bins and pocketed by sharp salvage men. Many a steaming package of fried fish and chip potatoes smeared his face. He wrapped meat and repaired boots and shoes and was taken home to be read by the old men and women of the family who spent entire days mooning over any old scrap of newsprint. His destinations were remote and odd. Yet his advent therein coincided with faint echoes of news from the Capital concerning him, and with extraordinary advertisements displayed in big and little shops, pubs, halls, asking for back numbers of the 'Daily Summariser.' Questions were asked. What had happened in London? What strange news was stirring the life of the Capital? Hadn't there been a question or two in Parliament . . . something about Income Tax? And hadn't old Colport said something, and wasn't it on the wireless one night?

Know-alls in clubs, pubs, hairdressers' saloons, flourished their talents for sensational knowledge by relating the true story of PEEPER. Rumours began and gathered size, and expired like big and little waves that were followed immediately by others of larger and more fantastic proportions, until slowly and ponderously, the topic which PEEPER had created sank its roots into that mysterious substance, the public mind.

For this, Belfwig had hoped, had calculated and was prepared.

Always an adroit opportunist, with daring and purpose, he took this chance with a zest which rode deliberately through minor laws. The Provinces demanded a larger quota. He gave it to them in thousands.

He cleared whole columns of political titbits and crammed them instead with news of PEEPER, antagonizing at least three of his sub-editors. He laughed at their discomfiture and smoothed them glibly down. He gave his instructions to the staff. He wanted space for every large and small item of news concerning PEEPER in the City and throughout the land. He had his finger on the heart of the City, as well as on every flutter of the national pulse elsewhere. He himself edited scores of reports and shot them down to the old foreman printer. And paper? He stole it from the press's other publications, recklessly, and had it dumped at the printers like so much gold. Aghast, those old craftsmen stared at one another and shook their heads. PEEPER! What an edition!

He had an interview lasting an hour with Bessing and again congratulated him, and once more felt exasperated by Bessing's limpid, sluggish character which did not rise to his zest and which remained curiously impassive in the face of the sensation which PEEPER had created. And it was a sensation. Belfwig had to din it into him and show him the telegrams and cables before Bessing could be drawn into remarking something about the drawings which were to follow to-day's.

Walking home, Bessing heard the Topic everywhere about him. It was not clamorous; but it glanced out of every conversation which he overheard. He recalled what Belfwig had told him. The demand for thousands more copies in the Provinces. The questions in Parliament! All the hard little facts gathering and cohering! He stopped and looked about him at the face of London at dusk of an April day. And he felt that a weird force was released on the air. He walked on quickly, with the sensation beating on his ears from all around him.

By five of that afternoon, PEEPER had extended into higher and lower levels, like a flood. He had caught the entire public imagination. He was a word which sounded in the air and aroused curiosity to a pitch of excitement. He was in the great blocks of offices east, north, south and west, along the river, in the great squares and streets. His name travelled into the big shops. It had sped about all day in the Exchanges and Markets, and in the circles of shipping, insurance, banking. A million tongues told of him. He set out with great steamers on long voyages, and travelled off on long expresses, and sped about like a brisk mole under the earth in hundreds of trains of the Underground.

54

The waning sunlight released him, and out he went into the suburbs on the lips of thousands scrambling home at the rush hour. He was news. He had raised a laugh, but at the same time he had summoned a serious public mind to consider him.

Lenora knew it. Little exclamations about him slapped her ears and made her flinch as she walked home through a twilight which was like a promise of enchanting summer months ahead. This was always the happiest hour of her day. To turn the corner of Bond Street and see above the streaming throngs in Piccadilly the pastel hue of sunset or dusk always reminded her of the distant scenes in Dorset, Somerset, Devon and Cornwall below the sinking sun and the sea and forests and fields. To-day, that delicate fancy which had always hovered above the long line of traffic was spoiled by immediate things. There was no escape from them. They met her from all round, and grew from her own heart. PEEPER and his Adventures!

He had his source in her own home; and merely to consider that was terrifying. She made her resolve as she walked home. There was some sense in what Riddle had told her. End it! Leave it! Make up your mind! And that was what she intended to do, even if it cost her every particle of nervous energy as well as her present and future security. She had submitted in the past to so many of Quentin's ideas and had allowed him to insist upon herself and John the whole curious force of his mysticism. But she had done that because it harmed nobody. Now, however, the conflict must be brought to a decision.

She was prepared for it in every fibre of her being. The words were on her tongue. Her spirit was determined. This time there would be no arguments, no acceptance of Quentin's persuasive ideas. This time . . .

At the moment when she entered the house and went upstairs and heard John's shout, she knew that there would be no struggle.

'Len!'

He was leaning over the banisters and beckoning to her. He ran back into Quentin's room; and that was where she followed him and met his stumbling outburst and saw and knew all that had happened.

'I was out. Belfwig sent for me, and when I got back Quentin . . . I found him on the floor. Collapsed . . . a hæmorrhage. I managed to get him on the bed . . .'

Quentin, fully clothed, was lying across the bed. He was semi-conscious and mumbling and trying to rise. All around, was confusion: a basin of hot water, already discoloured, with a towel fallen into it and a sponge making a small pool on the dressing-table where John had dropped it; Quentin's clinical thermometer lying near the sponge; the bed quilt in a heap near an overturned chair; garments on the floor; some sticks and newspaper smouldering in the grate where the coal scuttle had upset.

'I sent Twigge for Nye,' John said.

She tried to settle Quentin on the bed. His lax body seemed to her to be heavy from a complete resignation to this relapse. Taking hold of him beneath the arms, she glanced over her shoulder at John who was tidying the room.

'Help me with him. Take his feet,' she said, peremptorily.

And when that was done, she loosened Quentin's garments. She was calm and practical and deliberate. She took charge and gave John instructions.

'Now fill all the hot water bottles . . . all of them . . . and bring them here.'

'What about the fire? Hadn't I better . . .'

'The hot water bottles first! Quickly!' she said.

She brought across the basin of warm water, the towel and the sponge, and wiped Quentin's face and neck and shoulders. She drew the curtains and tidied the room and wondered why John had not yet brought the hot water bottles. Running out, she found him looking for them.

'I can't find them. I've looked . . .'

'Hanging behind the door in the kitchen. I'll fill them. You go in and watch him.'

She filled a kettle and set it on the gas stove and took down the three bottles. Running into the bedroom with fresh sticks and paper, she saw that Quentin had moved. His legs dangled over the bed's edge. A thin trickle of vivid blood lay like a thread from the corner of his lips to the towel which she had set beneath his head. John was cleaning out the grate.

'Help me to undress him,' she said calmly.

When that was done, the water was boiling. She ran out and filled the bottles and brought them to the bed and arranged them around Quentin's body. A few minutes later, Nye arrived. By then, the fire was lit, the room tidied; a bowl of hot water with fresh towels and sponge stood beside the bed.

Nye made his examination swiftly. The temperature, the pulse and respiration, and then the lungs. Pedantic and pompous, he sat close to the bed, a little thin figure, strong and competent. As he applied his stethoscope, he looked like an actor repeating the triumphs of thousands of performances. Lenora thought of his extraordinary reputation as she stood behind him in the room which, for her, was bewildering with its firelight and paraphernalia.

Rest, Nye was saying in his suave voice, absolute rest for a long time, and nursing day and night, and, as soon as possible, sanatorium treatment. He rose and slipped off his stethoscope and said that he would return later in the evening. Meanwhile, he must warn them of the patient's critical condition. He felt confident that Quentin would survive the crisis but he could not yet say that the danger of pneumonia was past.

No sooner had he departed than Twigge appeared.

'Let me take over,' he said. 'I know what to do. I nursed my old mother for two years. Nothing I don't know about a sickroom. Off you go, you two! Get something to eat for yourselves. Take a rest. I'll call you if things go badly.'

Lenora was thinking: 'Sanatorium treatment.'

Her savings were gone. She doubted if there were more than two or three pounds in the house. Yet it did not seem to her to matter much. What was more important and gave her a sense of relief and satisfaction was the fact that for a long time ahead PEEPER would be hers to influence. The prospect was instantly brighter. There had been no conflict, no disagreement. Her victory was certain.

It gave her an access of hope and strength that would take her through this crisis. Looking at John and noticing his distress she could not help making a comparison.

'Just when PEEPER was going steadily!'

She smiled. 'Don't worry. We can keep PEEPER going!'



ELEVEN

★

Riddle was twenty-nine. He was the only son of elderly parents who had one other idol in their lives. It was the idea of Permanence.

For as long as Riddle could remember, his parents had resisted change in all its aspects, crushing its insidious currents, denying it when it confronted them in large facts, stupidly and yet courageously refusing its manifestations in their very beings. Long ago, whatever love they had had for each other had expired, yet they still held themselves in all the conventions of marriage, although both of them had become so extremely eccentric and stubbornly individualistic that they were a constant irritation to each other. At no real point did their lives meet in harmony, nevertheless they maintained the ritual of two people in the closest accord and love. It all had an element of extreme comedy. Only the result was tragic, for there was neither peace nor love, but merely an incessant friction.

Riddle's father was a retired railway official of the senior grade who, for half a century, had been tucked away in an office where his meticulous habits had gradually increased and ultimately devoured all that was sensible and reasonable in his character. When he emerged at last into retirement at sixty, he was a bore and an egoist who extended his habits over the lives of everyone within reach of him. Old but vigorous, clumsy, tactless and self-opinionated, he was not at ease at home where, for so long, his wife's habits had found their full expression. His pawky sense of humour did not help him when he settled into retirement. Nor did his miser's mentality.

From his habits as a senior official of a railway company he developed into a miser who could not part with anything. Newspapers, tracts, journals, pamphlets, letters, as well as odds and ends such as little boxes, cartons, bits of pencils, pens, fasteners, string, wire, literally anything which seemed to him to have some value still attaching to it in a utilitarian way, were all hoarded. He never discarded anything. Whatever came into the house remained in it, until the ocean of rubbish rose gradually and obliterated his wife's expression of herself in the neat rooms, just as his hard, unyielding character and personality smothered hers, in spite of all her pleading, her ruses, her desperate attempts to defeat him, and her pitiable courage.

She was a sharp little woman, clever and resourceful, with her own ideas and ambitions and friends, all of which were opposed fundamentally to his. She was entrenched in them and could not share them with him. Yet both of them constantly pretended to share their lives with each other, although the result was failure. They were two utterly different persons. Why then were they together?

First of all there was Marriage. That was sacred and must be maintained. Next there was Home. It must be 'kept together.' Finally, there was their son.

Riddle too, in his own way, was a disciple of the idea of Permanence. He loved order because it expressed a continuity of daily life around certain things which were fixed and which he regarded as permanent. He wanted to love Home, but it had become a place of increasing disorder and clashes in which his parents' characters had degenerated. Yet he could not leave the place, although he was uncomfortable in it. Nor could he love it any longer. The only thing to do was to depart.

How? On what grounds? His parents had been generous to him. They thought so much of him. Their love for him and their faith in him was immeasurable. And he knew that were he to announce his intention of leaving them, they would be deeply hurt. Moreover, if he were to go they would be left with nothing but themselves. He knew what that meant. A final cloud would descend on them and smother them. Therefore, he must remain.

It was intolerable. He was obliged to listen to their disagreements and to see about him the gradual decay which shed a depressing atmosphere over his life. There was only one way by which he could escape without hurting his parents. Marriage. It would please them.

Thus, the vision of Lenora was a glimpse of salvation for him. He loved her sincerely and devotedly. But at the back of his mind there was a conviction that his love was doomed to failure and that he would be wise to acknowledge that much.

He realized that his love for her was nothing more than a criticism of her life which, in response, could not be anything else but in opposition to his. He understood that his presence amidst that trinity was sufficient to declare his criticism of all three of them, and that his devotion to Lenora conveyed nothing more than his intense desire to engender in her an appetite for life as he envisaged it.

He was right to offer her that chance. If his manner of presenting it to her had been feeble, he would amend it now. He had something positive to say to her at last.

After a difficult afternoon, he hurried home, changed and bathed and dined. By half-past eight, he had reached Bessing House. He touched the bell and waited. It did not ring. He pressed it again and realized that it had been disconnected. The door was not locked.

He went in, closed the door quietly behind him, and went upstairs. Half-way up, he stopped. John was coming down.

'Oh, it's you!' John said. 'I thought it was Nye.'

'Nye!'

John told him: 'Quentin collapsed this afternoon. Nye got here fairly quickly. He's coming again . . .'

'And Quentin?'

'Not too good. Nye's rather afraid of pneumonia.'

'I'm sorry,' Riddle said. 'Is there anything I can do?'

'Nothing, thanks. . . .'

Riddle stopped at the top of the stairs. 'I won't stay, John. You're probably all very busy. . . .'

'Don't be silly! Come on in! I'm with Quentin. Len is in the studio. Go in. I'll be there later.'

When Riddle entered the studio and greeted Lenora, he was instantly puzzled by her mood and behaviour. Her expressive features showed no sign of anxiety. Her eyes were vivid, and as she looked up at him they sparkled, while her delicate lips seemed about to smile. She looked as though she were enjoying an extraordinary stroke of good fortune.

'Sit down,' she said.

Looking intently at her, he said slowly: 'It's bad luck, Len.'

'We're waiting for Nye,' she said, looking pensively at the fire.

'John told me.'

'He said that if it weren't for possible pneumonia, he'd have sent Quentin for sanatorium treatment. Fortunately . . .'

Riddle frowned. 'Fortunately?'

She turned her head slowly and looked at him.

'Fortunately, he wants him to remain here until he's certain the danger has passed.'

'I don't understand you, Len,' Riddle said, heavily. 'You say fortunately . . .'

She suddenly laughed outright.

'If Nye had ordered him off to a sanatorium, I'd have had to tell him it was impossible!'

'Why?'

She laughed again. 'Because there isn't more than a couple of pounds in the house!'

He was aghast. She sat there laughing like a woman without a care. Her nonchalance appalled him. Her laughter ceased, and with a curious brusqueness which made him imagine that she had discovered his pity for her and was scorning it she said:

'Why did you come?'

'Not because Quentin was ill,' he said, candidly. 'As a matter of fact, I didn't know about him. It was for quite another reason.'

Her smile returned. She was silent, watching him with that faint expression of mockery on her lively features. Her hand slowly rested on his.

'What was it?' she said.

She was laughing again. Often, when they were together, she behaved like that. He never resented it, since she appeared so amused by him, so happy. And even on this occasion, he was not discomfited by it. Even to be laughed at proved to him that she was aware of him and had at least found something of his character to consider. But this time, her laughter had a faintly nervous quality that disturbed him.

He got up and stood close beside her with his arm along her shoulder. He looked down at her upturned face. He loved its delicate form and the features with their quick, almost brittle expressions. But this laughter that fluttered from her lips . . . it was so full of mockery which, as he stared down at it, misted and was transformed into something else that might have been pity or a taunt. He could not analyse it.

It was as though he were peering closely at an oil painting and discovering behind the separate strokes that composed the face the entire inner texture of the work, as well as its character which, from a distance, was so apparent but which in this proximity had quite a different quality. There it was, crude in all its nervousness and turmoil, and completely frank.

He had that glimpse of her real nature. Her laughter did not cease until he stooped down and kissed her on the lips. She drew away slightly, for an instant, and then was still and silent while he kissed her again. He tasted at that moment an individual essence of her life which he could not describe in words, but which, later, he could define because of its effect on his senses.

It left an impression of subtle warmth, consuming warmth and turmoil and the mystery of her temperament in its curious conflicts and resolves and decisions. It was the flavour of another world, beyond his own circumscribed, orderly existence, and disturbing to him in its revelation of her life. He was a stranger in that world of hers, and it was poignant to him that her nature should condemn her to it.

But as he sat down he was thinking of what she had told him. Not more than a couple of pounds in the house! His left hand was plunging into his jacket pocket.

She watched him and knew what he was about to do. It was fascinating to watch him. He was like a delicate piece of machinery which took motion in a certain way according to whatever words were spoken to it. He spread his cheque book on his knees and unscrewed his fountain pen and wrote.

He was one and indivisible and completely predictable. It was his virtue and his fault. He had only one self, like a constant weather, unchanging, unyielding; and he would never understand that no matter how immense were the problems that rose from her brothers' lives, they were her happiness, her preoccupation, because they were part of the diversity of mood, character, personality which composed her existence and engaged her whole spirit.

He got up and showed her the cheque. Her name was on it and his signature was at the foot. That was all. The rest was left for her to complete. His hand folded it into her own, and he turned without a word and went out.

When she heard his footsteps in the street below, she looked down at her hand which opened then and disclosed the crumpled cheque. John entered the room.

'Where's Riddle?'

She did not speak. Coming towards her, John saw the small slip of paper at which she was smiling.

'What is it, Len?'

He stood beside her and reached down and took the cheque from her open hand.

'Good lord! What does he think?'

He laughed softly. 'Does he . . . does he think we're poor?'

She looked up at him and nodded.

'Well, we are . . . we must be . . . by his standards,' she said, gravely.

He let the cheque flutter to the carpet. He chuckled again.

'Poor!' he exclaimed. 'Good lord!'

Suddenly, turning, he stopped laughing. He walked about the room, realizing that if it had not been for PEEPER poverty would have been real in the household. He came back to Lenora and stooped down to recover the cheque.

Lenora snatched it up and spread it on her knee and smoothed out its creases.

'No!' she exclaimed, seriously. 'Don't laugh! It's unfair to laugh . . .'

'You were, too!' he said.

She tried to conceal her smile. With her head averted, she said: 'I know. But it's unfair, all the same. Don't misjudge him. He's really good.'

John could not regard the gift as anything else but ludicrous and amusing.

'But to do that!'

She glanced up at him gravely. 'I love him for it!' she said.

'What are you going to do with it?' John said. 'Tear it up? Burn it? Or return it to him?'

'I shall keep it,' she said.

'So long as you don't use it . . .' he murmured.

Use it! That was unthinkable. Its significance to her was not in its utilitarian value. Instead, it was like a part of himself which Riddle had left in her hands; and as other women received and treasured love letters, she would keep this slip of paper which he had signed.

# TWELVE

★

Later that evening, Nye returned to make a further examination of the patient. By then, Quentin was delirious. It did not surprise Lenora and John when, after a few minutes at the bedside, he turned to them and said briefly:

'Pneumonia.'

He rose and slipped his stethoscope into its case and stood facing the fire with his hands outstretched to the flames.

'To-morrow,' he said, speaking above Quentin's incoherent mumbling, 'a nurse. I'll do my best to engage one for you.'

He gave careful instructions as to what must be done for the patient. Absolute rest, quietness, warmth, milk foods. John accompanied him downstairs.

'I'll call during the night, if I possibly can,' Nye said.

When John returned to the room, Lenora was seated at the bed-side.

'Go to bed, Len. I'll stay here with him. I'll call you if it's necessary,' he said, crossing the room.

'I want to stay,' she whispered.

He came towards her carrying two bulky notebooks. Without a word, she stretched out her hand and took one of them from him and turned the pages.

'What's this?' she said, glancing up at him.

'They're Twigge's,' he whispered, in a desultory manner.

'In shorthand,' she murmured.

Turning the leaves of the book, she saw it there. Not so much the neat shorthand outlines which filled the book, but something of their meaning. Something which was intense, comprehensive, and which immediately excited her curiosity until she recollected that the notebook belonged to old Twigge. She closed the book and handed it to John.

'Can you transcribe it, Len?'

She shook her head. 'I don't understand that system.'

He crossed the room and opened a cupboard.

'Look!'

Inside, there was a pile of similar notebooks. He took several of them and brought them over to her.

'Twenty, altogether. Twigge told me about them.'

Her curiosity was again excited, for those pages of trim little outlines seemed to her to have relevance to the light delirium which poured in a mumbling sound from Quentin's lips.

'Twigge's?' she asked, looking up at John.

'His, and Quentin's.'

'What is it about?'

'Notes which Twigge took from dictation . . .'

'Yes, but what's the subject?' she whispered.

He told her while she turned the pages.

'Something they have worked at for nearly two years. Ever since Twigge came here and the two of them began to discuss philosophy.'

'A thesis?'

'I suppose so. But didn't you know?'

She shook her head. 'Oh, I heard them, sometimes. Arguing and discussing . . .'

He drew up a little chair near her and went on in a whisper:

'It's the history of a soul . . . an eternal phenomenon . . . something like that. Twigge told me this evening. A kind of history, from the first experience of human life at the time of Plato . . . when this soul first knew life . . . and down to the present time. A history of Thought and its effect on one soul. Man, the eternal soul. . . .'

Lenora was still slowly turning the pages. Again, while her brother told her that the notes related to a subject which Quentin and Twigge had conceived, she saw in the close lines with their symbols of words something whose meaning seemed to come from the pages and assume relevance to the swift speech which pressed into incoherent utterance during Quentin's delirium. And from all the millions of words that were concealed on the pages and which composed this voluminous thesis, there seemed to her to come something like an invisible presence, complete and profound, that hovered about the patient.

'I heard the two of them, sometimes . . .' she whispered to John; and rising slowly from her chair she stood at the bedside, settling the pillows and the sheets about Quentin.

'You go,' she whispered to John. 'I'll stay with him. I want to.'

It was not the first occasion on which, with John's help, she had nursed Quentin through a long illness. She had, as Twigge said, 'the constitution of a statesman.' She required more than that now. There was more than a sick man to watch. There was PEEPER, in the crammed pages of that thesis.

Sitting there, Lenora sank into a torpor. Whenever the patient stirred, her glance went to him. She heard the thin trickle of words pouring from his lips. Once, John entered noiselessly, smiled at her, handed her a tray with tea and some sandwiches, and quietly made up the fire. She drank the tea but ate nothing. The hours passed, so swiftly that they were like mere minutes of time. And all the while, she was in a mysterious region which was not of complete consciousness but of a mid-state that was dominated by the prone figure of Quentin, as well as by that indefinable presence which had floated from the pages of the notebooks.

She did not hear Twigge come in. It was not until he was within a yard of her that she was aware of him as he stood watching her. She glanced up. Her mind was instantly clearer.

'All alone?' Twigge whispered, cheerfully.

She shook her head and pointed to the notebooks piled on the table near her.

Twigge grinned. 'Oh, those!' he whispered. 'There's the whole story.'

'PEEPER,' Lenora said; but Twigge only gave her a glance and a half smile and went on to say that he would take a spell while she went to bed.

She was too tired to say more than a terse good night and to thank him for coming.

# THIRTEEN

★

When, on the following morning, PEEPER appeared again, Lenora had no time to study him; but once more he was a topic which grew quickly from the City's life. Never, even during the great gusting crises of wars, international wranglings, had she heard so much comment, laughter and speculation about one personality. For he was a personality. The interest which he aroused, as well as the gathering momentum of his influence, created an altogether new kind of sensation and insisted it on the mind. He became more real hour by hour. Like other personalities whose only appearance to millions upon millions of men and women was through the medium of a photographic reproduction in the Press, PEEPER came alive. He was famous, was trenchant and amusing, serious but not dull, controversial yet not bitter. It did not matter at all that he was not in the flesh. A generation which imparted a fabulous existence to so many personalities of stage, screen, radio, politics, without seeing them in reality; and which, on the Continent, had advanced a crude neurotic to the position of a demigod, was quite willing to bring PEEPER alive. In the hearts of millions who believed without seeing, and who had faith and love, PEEPER was actual. Nobody spoke of Jayby who drew him. Nobody wrote to Jayby or sought him. PEEPER was the man, the Topic, the lovable personality whose tall, lean presence and agreeable smile met everyone on the page.

Again he had thrust all the force of ridicule at the Income Tax system; and once more the public responded, laughing with him but at the same time looking fairly and squarely at that absurd, patched indignity, with all its mumbo-jumbo, and wondering why it had tolerated it for so long. And it admired PEEPER for drawing attention in such an amusing way to this dead-weight of rubbish which a government that prided itself on its progressive vision had not swept aside with a single vigorous movement of its powerful hand and reorganized from top to bottom. PEEPER was not some fantastic little caricature of Man. There he was, tall and personable and like the rest of men. And he was a thinker who was by no means pedantic. A glance at him revealed that he was wise, clever, and amusing. The world was full of thinkers, and a solemn crowd they were, except for the few who knew and understood the people. The rest were wrapped up in Thought which scarcely touched the lives of earth's inhabitants and which certainly did nothing to disentangle the conflicting muddles into which a tired, hungry world had drifted.

It was refreshing and new to discover this PEEPER every morning. And it was amusing to see him again making his tilt at the ponderous, implacable Income Tax system. In to-day's issue of the 'Daily Summariser,' he stood before a huge wheel which was hung with thousands of little tabs and tickets. Lofty ladders were against the wheel, and swarms of sedulous officials and clerks were intent upon hanging more tabs and tickets on the spokes, while down below a phalanx of other officials and experts was formed and was attempting to urge the wheel a fraction of an inch on its fantastic revolution. The faces of the phalanx expressed strain and a kind of fussiness over trivial detail associated with all the paraphernalia of the System.

THE LOWLIEST CITY, said PEEPER, WOULD SCORN TO LEVY TAXES BY SUCH METHODS!

Lenora did not see it until eleven o'clock when old Harry, the porter, brought cups of tea. Collis was out at the firm's Holborn Branch. Chester, having just entered the room and seen that Lenora was alone, was standing beside her desk. He offered her a cigarette which he lit for her, and handed her a cup of tea from the tray.

He produced his copy of the 'Daily Summariser.'

'Like to see?'

She accepted it principally to conceal her distress from him. Looking down at the page, she smiled while he chatted. Occasionally, she sipped her tea. Chester walked about the room, laughed, told her what he thought of PEEPER. But she remained silent.

'Do you know why they're so keen on him in America, Len?' he said. 'Can't you guess why it is? It's because he says what the people think! He's vocal about something which is small to most of us but which millions of us know is daft! And he's . . . you know . . . you feel that he's on a new track . . . and that anything might happen because he represents what millions think.'

She looked up suddenly at him. 'What sort of thing?'

'Something new,' he said. 'You feel that he brings everybody together. Look at the millions who shout for him! Look at the way they ask for him, in America, in the rest of the world! You feel that . . . that all of us are sick and tired of not being out of the Munich crisis yet. People want somebody to bring them right out of the mess. To tell them, straight out, the whole truth. To carry them along and make changes. That's why I like PEEPER. You feel that he'll put his finger on things.'

Lenora's face with its pallor was upturned to him. At that moment, Collis entered. He crossed to his desk and dropped his brief-case on it and turned to them.

'Any tea?'

Chester offered him a cigarette. 'What news from our connections in the wilds of Holborn?'

Collis laughed as he removed his coat and gloves.

'PEEPER,' he said.

The porter entered with a cup of tea.

'Thank you, Harry!'

Harry's sharp little eyes found Chester's 'Daily Summariser' lying on Lenora's desk.

'You done with that, Miss Bessing?'

'It's . . .' She indicated Chester.

'I only wanted to 'ave a look at PEEPER, Mr. Chester. If you could spare it for five minutes.'

'I'll leave it with you in a tick,' Chester said.

'Thanks,' Harry said.

Collis stirred his tea. 'There's a PEEPER Club at Lloyd's,' he said.

Chester guffawed. 'You'd better tell Charlie that, right away! He likes to be in on things like that.'

'Members of Lloyd's only . . .'

'What's it for?' Chester said.

Collis sipped his tea and opened his brief-case.

'Jack, at Holborn was telling me . . .'

Lenora heard them while she typed. A club to support PEEPER's remarks about the system of Income Tax. Badges were already appearing. An exclusive Club. And another amidst Stock Exchange members and banking circles.

Collis had, as well, some startling rumours to pass on. First, that the 'Daily Summariser' had been cabled by an American Syndicate which offered half a million dollars for the right to publish PEEPER for the next six months. Second, that some public disturbance had occurred in the Midlands during a political meeting at which PEEPER had been mentioned. Third, that the Home Secretary was taking steps to ban PEEPER from the 'Daily Summariser.' Fourth, that the Institute of Chartered Accountants . . .

Collis was all the time running through his correspondence, while Chester listened, laughed, and at the same time glanced at Lenora. She rose abruptly, the empty cups giving her an excuse to get away from all that alarming chatter about PEEPER.

She was at the door when Chester called to her.

'Miss Bessing!'

He had nudged Collis who, glancing up, saw her standing there with her head turned towards them.

'Isn't she . . . just like . . .' Chester exclaimed. 'The image of PEEPER? About the face . . .'

She tried to smile as she opened the door and went out. Her right hand, holding two cups balanced one on top of the other, trembled. She lifted the top cup and saucer into her left hand and left the door ajar. And heard Collis:

'You ass, Chesty!'

'Why?' in a round, almost indignant tone.

And then Collis's murmur: 'Didn't you know? Jack told me. It's her brother. Jayby. An artist . . . the artist one . . .'

Whatever else Collis said was inaudible to her, for she went quickly to Harry's little room and gave him the cups. A few seconds after that, she tapped at Charlie's door.

She went in, closed the door, and then walked towards his big, cheerful, florid face which lifted as soon as she entered the room. It was there: the inquisitive little gleam, in the jovial face.

'Miss Bessing . . .' And a slightly new tone in the voice which was at once kindly and ingratiating.

'Mr. Charles . . .'

He smiled. He gave her his whole attention.

'What is it?'

'My brother has gone down with pneumonia . . .'

'Oh!'

She could see that he was genuinely surprised. He interrupted her. 'Not the . . . the artist?' And at that moment he appeared really perturbed.

'No,' she said. 'My elder brother. Quentin.'

He blinked, perhaps because he felt slightly discomfited by his sudden disclosure of his inquisitiveness. He nodded.

'I'm sorry . . . sorry to hear that.'

'Would you mind if I took a few days . . .'

'Certainly not, Miss Bessing. Most certainly not!'

There was a faint effusiveness in his manner as he rose and came to the door and opened it for her.

'Let Mr. Collis know, won't you? And come back to us when you can. I hope your brother makes a good recovery. Let me know . . . drop in, if you can, and tell me.'

In Collis's room, she cleared her desk. Chester had gone. Collis was watching her.

'Well, I'm sorry, Miss Bessing. Pop in, won't you?'

He spoke as though she would never return to her desk opposite his. In his colourless face there was a look of regret which increased while she took down her coat and put on her hat. Perhaps he was right in his surmise. Perhaps she would not return to the office. She was hurrying away from it as from a gathering cloud which, when she entered the noon scene, seemed to descend a little lower and threaten her.

She was grateful for the quietude of the house when she reached home. Here there was silence and nothing audible of the outer world which was astir with a new sensation.

Twigge met her. 'They sent for John,' he said. 'The Editor wanted to see him. I'm with Quentin.'

She preceded him into the room and crossed to the bed. Quentin saw her. His large, dark eyes beneath the sharp brows seemed tardy in their recognition of her. He smiled slowly.

She could not fail to see the likeness. That gaunt yet attractive face with its wry smile was PEEPER, alive and watching her. She laughed softly.

'You are so like him!' she exclaimed. 'Just like PEEPER!'

'How is he, Len?' he asked eagerly.

# FOURTEEN

★

'I'll tell you, later on,' she said. 'No talking now!'

He pleaded with her. 'Just a word! What's the news about him? What do they think of him?'

She sat down and told him. 'He's very popular. All over the City.'

His intent gaze detected immediately her anxiety which she had successfully kept from her tone.

'I knew he would be,' he said. 'But you still don't like him, do you?'

'I'm afraid of him,' she confessed.

'Why?'

'Because he'll become so significant, beyond us, too big for you or anybody to control. Like a Thing in the air.'

He was silent. He turned his head on the pillow and stared at the ceiling and seemed to Lenora to have gone into a reverie. She leaned over him and straightened the sheets.

Slowly, and in a voice which was scarcely more than a whisper, he said: 'No need to be afraid, Len. I wanted him to become like that: a great personality, but not more than life-size. I want him to be something of all people, everywhere. Someone easily understood. This . . .' and he turned and smiled slowly at her. 'This is only the beginning . . . this poking fun at Income Tax. That's only a trick to gain a bit of popularity. After this . . . a few more tilts at things, and then . . . then he'll really set out on his journey.'

'Don't talk now, Quentin,' she said. 'Rest, please!'

'I want you to like him and enjoy his appearances,' he said.

'I could do that, if only you'd make him . . . well, comic. I'm terribly afraid of him. Already, there's a stir. I don't like it. I feel that anything could come from it. You know what sort of mood we are all in, after the war years and the years of crisis before them: irritable, tense. That's why I wanted you to make PEEPER bring laughter. Instead, he'll . . .'

She broke off and said slowly and with conviction: 'He'll make disaster.'

'But an ultimate good,' Quentin said.

'After what?'

'You'll see,' he whispered. 'They'll love him . . .'

She checked him. 'No more talking, for the present. Rest now.'

'Leave him to Twigge, Len,' he pleaded. 'He knows what he must say and do.'

She smiled. 'You two, with your notebooks!'

'A great story,' he said. 'Twigge understands it all.'

'And John?'

'He and Twigge . . . Twigge will show him.'

Soon after that, he slept. She took the opportunity to tidy the room and to clean the other rooms. Twigge, when she sought him, was absent. She had much to ask him, but it could wait, although as the minutes passed and the silence of the house grew around her, disturbing presentiments moved from all the questions which awaited Twigge and which she could not yet put to him. She sat down.

It was absurd to imagine that PEEPER would follow the course which Quentin had decided for him. Already, in the odd and disturbing events of the past two or three days, there was every indication of an effect which Quentin had certainly not calculated. And in how many ways, and to what degree, would that effect continue? He had not anticipated it. She knew that he had no knowledge of events in the City and elsewhere. Lying there in bed, he did not appreciate what was happening. He dreamed of the direction in which PEEPER would go, but he was too late. PEEPER was already drawn into another course. And the enthusiasts would hold him to that course.

It was not feasible that old Twigge could devise with John the exact progression of PEEPER, for PEEPER was an Idea which, powerful and persuasive, had settled into thousands of minds. It was impossible to imagine John—that limpid character—withstanding the current which insisted the kind of direction PEEPER must now take. Thousands wanted PEEPER. In the air, there was a kind of murmur which demanded an answer that John must render. The authentic PEEPER belonged to Quentin's intellect, Quentin's mysticism, Quentin's courage and wit and character, as well as to his spirit. PEEPER was Quentin. They were one, in some indefinable way, and only Quentin could express him and guide him. But this Idea, this creation . . . what would become of it now that its creator was ill and unable to direct it? It had gone forth. Somewhere, it awaited his entire attention. It would refuse John and Twigge and herself. Already, it had roots and was alive.

Out of the City, and from the cities and towns and villages of the land, a sound was rising. All the newspapers reported it, and she understood its exact nature. It was no longer a Topic. It was an Idea. It was PEEPER in the minds of millions of people. And in the sound there was a monstrous threat of power which would go beyond all that had hitherto been delineated as the bounds of human behaviour. Within the past six years, the boundaries had been so often obliterated, and mankind had so violently pressed forward, and then retreated. Into what? Into peace and security? Hardly! As Chester had told her, all of them awaited something, wanted a call, a leader, somebody to beckon them forward.

She knew that PEEPER was there, and that already millions were shouting for him. As they shouted for other personalities of sudden popularity who seemed to offer them release from themselves. But

PEEPER was larger than the living man. He was an Idea. Nobody, as yet, was beside him in Quentin's place to direct him.

A voice broke through her thoughts. Halting suddenly, she heard it again and recognized it. She hurried in to Quentin and saw him. His eyes were open and he stared up at her without giving any sign of recognition. He was delirious again.

She could not distinguish the words which came in a flood of sound from his lips. Entangled and fragmentary, some of them like brittle things, others proud and violent yet still lost to her, they disclosed only the pressure and chaos of the delirium which ejected them. Wiping his hot forehead and cheeks and composing his arms, she imagined for an instant that his rambling words were a kind of response to the voices in the City with their wild rumours and their fantastic enthusiasms. Suddenly, and mercifully, he was silent. Within a little while, he was asleep.

Her momentary panic ended. She heard the house door close softly and John's step on the stairs. She ran out.

All that she had to say to him was quenched at once by the startling change in his whole manner.

# FIFTEEN

*

He was transformed. For years, he had never been anything but mild and lackadaisical, a man who could not worry and who accepted life with grace and contentment. His complacent humour had dignity and geniality. It was all so much a part of her own life into which it had merged itself, that for her to find him so changed gave her a sense of solitude.

She felt as though the whole foundation upon which her life rested were suddenly swept away and that she was alone. She was suspended in a void from which she smiled because she frantically supposed that to see him smile in response might create again all that she seemed to have lost.

He went into the studio and sat down. A kind of strength seemed to have come to him. His attitude was different. Even his pallid face expressed a kind of confidence. But she was still frightened, for he looked exactly like a man who had suffered an ordeal and emerged, whole and resurgent, from it. His unusual pallor related that much. But his silence terrified her with its evidence of so many things which she had anticipated and feared.

He got up and walked into Quentin's room. Following him, she saw him looking down at the patient. He turned to her.

'It's fantastic,' he said, in a whisper, running his hand over his fair hair. 'If he had published that thesis, all this wouldn't have happened. Joad or Huxley . . . somebody like that . . . would have reviewed it. Joad would have been witty and perhaps encouraging. I don't suppose it would have been widely read, except amongst students of philosophy. But in this way, through PEEPER, and merely by illustrating a few points . . . there's all this wild excitement!'

Lenora sat down. 'Tell me . . .' she whispered.

He grinned and again ran his hands over his head.

'People are fantastic,' he said, sitting down beside her. 'I mean just the ordinary people. People who work, who manage big and small concerns and who somehow keep the world running. Nice, decent people, working hard. People in the top ranks and all the good sorts in the other grades: porters, drivers, 'bus conductors. They are incredible. They are mad!'

He laughed softly and told her what she had already heard from Chester and Collis. Then he showed her cablegrams. She could not understand them immediately. He had to explain them to her. They were from New York, Hollywood, Chicago, as well as from Paris, Cape Town, Bombay and Calcutta. Syndicates and independent newspapers offered immense sums for the right to reproduce PEEPER. And Belfwig had accepted the offers, as he had every right to do under the agreement between the 'Daily Summariser' and Bessing, but had made an extremely generous offer to John who would receive a half share of the income. From Birmingham, Manchester, Newcastle, and other cities, there were telegrams offering high fees for permission to use the name of PEEPER on toys, chromium goods, cotton fabrics, and so on. From Hollywood came an offer to reproduce PEEPER in film cartoon. A firm in Luton offered a substantial sum for the sole right to call their new range of male headgear, 'PEEPER' hats. And Belfwig had said that from all over the country the telegrams were pouring in, asking for similar rights for ties, gloves, boots and shoes, brushes, shirts, jackets. A firm of motor car manufacturers in Coventry offered twenty thousand pounds for the exclusive right to call a new car the 'PEEPER'

Ten. Three Parisian magazines offered generous terms for a few PEEPER cartoons. From Cape Town came an offer to name three new hotels after PEEPER. A Parsee publisher offered to publish PEEPER's biography on payment to him of a thousand pounds down and another thousand upon publication. A popular comedian pleaded for the right to make a farce around PEEPER.

'Money . . .' John whispered, sighing. 'Belfwig has signed all the contracts, and cabled acceptance of every offer. Now he wants me to enter a new agreement with him. He offers twenty thousand a year, and a percentage of royalties or whatever it is. And that's only a beginning.'

'And I told Riddle . . . was it yesterday? . . . that we hadn't more than two pounds in the house!' Lenora said.

John took from his pocket a cheque which he handed to her.

'From Belfwig,' he whispered. 'An advance . . .'

She read it. Pay John Bessing. One thousand pounds. And looking quickly up at him she exclaimed:

'Shall you go on? With all this . . . all this idiocy?'

He shrugged his shoulders. 'Yes,' he said, firmly.

'It isn't PEEPER,' she told him. 'Not the real PEEPER.'

'I know that,' he said. 'I know Quentin wouldn't have approved it. But I can't resign now. I can't disappoint Quentin. We've got to go on with it . . . until he recovers and can take over.'

'You can't do it!' Lenora said. 'You know that. Not without Quentin.'

John laughed. 'Oh, yes we can! We're in Twigge's hands.'

He got up to go. Lenora followed him into the studio and confronted him.

'Resign, do you hear! Stop the whole thing!'

He shook his head and turned away. Sitting down, he stretched out his legs and yawned.

'As a matter of fact, Len,' he said. 'I don't care what happens to PEEPER. All I know is that I am going on with him. I'm determined not to give it up.'

'Listen to me, John,' she said, standing before him. 'You haven't considered what a responsibility he'll become. Have you? Speak the truth! Have you? You haven't looked ahead.'

He laughed. 'I can accept it all,' he said. 'I'm not the sort that worries. I'm what they call a pococourante, Len.'

'You don't realize what you are saying! You must have heard . . .

you've told me yourself . . . what's happening. You said just now . . . you yourself said about people . . . Well! Well, they are fantastic. And they'll take PEEPER out of your control. . . .'

'Not mine,' he said, shaking his head and rising and patting her shoulders. 'But Twigge's! He has all the notebooks and knows what to do. I merely do what I'm told and illustrate.'

'As if Twigge could stop them!' she retorted. 'Already, they have taken PEEPER from both of you. The PEEPER Clubs. And what those cables and telegrams said. Don't you realize what that means? It's madness! It's banging right up against the windows of this house, and soon . . . soon . . .'

He took hold of her and drew her to a chair and stood over her.

'Len! Len!'

'Give it all up, John!' she pleaded. 'Before it all goes quite mad!'

'Now listen,' he said, sitting on the arm of the chair and running his hand through her hair. 'I can't do that. PEEPER belongs to Quentin, and when Quentin recovers PEEPER has to be there to meet him. That's that.'

He got up. He had determination and she could not shake it, no matter how she applied her arguments or tried to cajole him. He laughed at her, showing her the cheque.

'We were too poor, Len. We were, really. I don't understand money, but you do. Take the cheque. I've endorsed it. Go and buy things. Get all the medicine Quentin wants. Order a car, so that when he's well, we can take him out for a jaunt. Go round to Charlie and tell him we want a country house. Get some things for yourself. You deserve them.'

She tore the cheque into tiny pieces and flung them at him.

'As if . . . as if I want things! Things!' she exclaimed.

He laughed softly. 'It doesn't matter, Len. Belfwig will write me another cheque to-morrow. And you ought to think of Quentin. He deserves some country air, and a bit of luxury. After all, he has earned it. PEEPER is his.'

She had never been so angry as at that moment.

'You needn't say any more,' she said.

He was silent, looking at her with his solemn, candid eyes and shaking his head while she said furiously:

'All that! As if that's the kind of PEEPER Quentin wanted. The name on toys, chromium counters, hats, shirts, cars! Is that the best way to . . .'

She stopped because his expression had changed. He frowned. Then he said quietly: 'It's not my fault. I can't stop it. You know as well as I do what's happened. You said so just now.'

And sitting down, he said softly and pensively:

'It's PEEPER. All over the place. Everywhere. And out of hand.'

For a long time, both were silent. Presently, she got up and went in to Quentin. He was still asleep. She sat down and lapsed into thought, hearing his heavy breathing, seeing him stir feverishly. Her hand moved over the sheets and rested on him.

She was thinking: money . . . the chance to extend their lives. But she had no desire to do that. PEEPER was clamouring against the house, like a gale, and she wished only to remain secure here, as before, and to defend a way of life which had fulfilled her. Money would not help, except to cover Nye's fees and pay a nurse, and provide special food, and, later, the proper sanatorium treatment.

For the next three weeks, she entrenched herself in the house. She was heavily occupied; for although nurses arrived, there was still much to do. She had time one afternoon, when the crisis had passed and Quentin was slowly recovering, to visit the office and speak to Charlie to whom she offered her resignation.

To break that link with a life which she had always enjoyed, and to lose the feeling of attachment to a solid world, cost her an effort. She liked Charlie for his stable, affable character; and Collis who was a Cockney; and Chester who admired her. With the rest of the staff, they constituted a little society which met every morning and sustained one small segment of affairs before departing, at the end of the afternoon, for their leisure. Looked at in that way, their employment seemed odd. Yet, underneath it, there was something which all of them tacitly admitted but which none of them had ever defined. It was an aspect of life's purpose: the activity, the focussing upon something which furthered other human affairs of one's energies, thoughts, one's loyalty and integrity.

To renounce it demanded an answer from her. To what was she going now? What was her purpose? Charlie suspected that she was destined for a life of leisure. Collis and Chester probably imagined the same sort of thing. They were wrong.

Weeks, months possibly, would elapse before Quentin was fully recovered. Nye said so. The nurses said so. But when he was able to be moved and could go down to the sanatorium, or was it to be the cottage, there was still work for her at home.

She knew why she had resigned her job at Charlie's. It was because she wished to take charge of John's affairs. There was a fortune to manage, contracts to examine, letters to answer. That was the face of it, and behind the face there was something much more important.

Twigge had firm hold of PEEPER. Whether all that was happening was what Quentin had intended, she did not know and could not discover. But she was still anxious to maintain her place in the trinity. She had to keep herself at the apex. And, after a week during which odd and terrifying things happened in PEEPER'S name, she began to formulate her own plans for him.

She was determined that he should become a figure of comedy throughout a world which, by its fabulous offers of contracts, had opened its heart to him.

At the first opportunity, she went down to talk to Twigge.

## SIXTEEN

★

Of the two rooms which he occupied, the one facing the street was his study. Behind it was his bedroom.

Lenora had never seen his bedroom. Nor had she ever seen him enter it or come out from it. His life at home seemed to her to be spent in his study. She could never associate Twigge with the natural function of sleep, for whenever she had left home at about nine in the morning, there he was in his study, fully dressed and already at work or preparing his breakfast. He appeared to have been up for some hours. When she returned at the end of the afternoon, he was still at work. Later, he went out. He came home very late, although at what hour she did not know, for he came and went almost noiselessly. His habits intrigued her, and not until she asked him in a jocular way if he ever slept were they explained by him.

At some time during the day, Twigge rested; and again, for a few hours during the night, he slept. In all, for about five hours. The fact presented him to her in a new light.

He appeared to be absorbed so much by actual living, which he enjoyed, that he had no desire for sleep. Life to him seemed altogether delightful and fascinating. She knew how he earned a livelihood: from selling sermons and speeches; from park oratory and his displays of factual knowledge; by posing for artists. But it did not explain him. She had the notion that despite the time which he gave to such things, they were incidental to something which was much larger and much more important and which really absorbed all that was in that odd little body and that gentle but formidable personality.

Going down to him, she found him seated writing at his desk. Either the desk was very high, or his chair was very low, for only his head and shoulders showed above the books and the sheets of paper, the curious inkstand, the files and the other objects which littered the desk. His elbows were outspread and his head was on one side, so that he looked exactly like a diligent schoolboy. He glanced up at her and came out of his preoccupation to rise quickly and gravely offer her a chair, a cigarette from a quaint old cedarwood box, and his whole attention.

He asked for news of Quentin while he took the chair opposite her and spread his big hands on his knees. She experienced at once the enchanting warmth of his personality. Looking intently at him, she studied his features, enjoying their tranquillity which suggested to her so much knowledge of life and so much faith and love. He sat there, sustaining her candid scrutiny, patient, happy, as though he were content with her mere presence.

'Twigge,' she said, slowly, 'that book which you and Quentin have written.'

'A treatise,' he said, softly.

'Tell me about it.'

His hands joined slowly, and he looked reflectively at the tiny thread of smoke which rose from his fire.

'Ever heard of a gargoyle? From the old French, gargouille, which means a throat,' he said.

'I know,' Lenora said. 'On cathedrals and big buildings. Jutting out. Queer faces, and in the shape of birds' heads.'

'That's it. To carry off rainwater. A method of draining. Now think of a gargoyle, high up on a cathedral tower, looking out over a big city and the world beyond, century after century. And suppose, for the sake of illustration, that the cathedral and the gargoyle have been there for thousands of years. Just for the sake of illustration, let's suppose that it was first of all a temple, and then a cathedral. Well, century after century. Same expression on the face, looking and looking, no matter what time o' the day or night, or the weather. Looking and listening. What does it see, and what does it hear?'

It was a fascinating question. Lenora pondered it and then said slowly:

'Oh, the changing scene: the advent of kings, emperors and governments, and their downfall. Wars, revolutions. The birth of new civilizations, and their decay. And then the death throes of them. And after that, the birth pangs of another civilization. And all the time, the individual lives of millions and millions of people. And new ideas and habits. . . .'

She stopped because Twigge was laughing and shaking his head.

'That's always there,' he said. 'That's the surface. What else?'

Lenora said: 'You mean the nature of it? Well, a comedy?'

'That's only a name for it,' he said. 'I'll tell you what he sees. The same old things, year in and year out. First of all, the stars and planets, the moon and the sun, and now and then a comet. He sees rain and ice, sleet, hail and snow. He feels the wind blow softly and strongly. There is thunder and lightning. The years are marked by the seasons. Always the same: spring, summer, autumn and winter. And Man. Just the same, year after year and century after century. The same nature; the same emotions and impulses. The immutable phenomenon!'

'Oh, but surely . . .' Lenora protested.

Twigge laughed. 'I tell you, the same now as ten or twenty thousand years ago. Savage and terrible, as ever. Worse, perhaps!'

'I can't believe . . .'

'Because,' Twigge said, 'because you're like the rest! You are deceived when you imagine that Man isn't a part of nature. He is. A part, mind you, not the whole of it. Not superior to nature. And savage still, although lots of people would be shocked if you told them that. But the fact is, we are worse than savage. We are merciless. We kill in hundreds of thousands. Don't try to delude yourself that that isn't savage, We've done it twice within twenty-five years. Why? Because that's the nature of Man. Cruel, stupid sometimes, stubborn. All our so-called Progress hasn't taken us into wisdom. Your philosophers have no more influence upon your statesmen than the babes have. There isn't sufficient wisdom in the world yet to end the disagreements which lead to slaughter. And your scientists are quite content to render their remarkable discoveries to the generals in order to increase the rate of slaughter. It's human, but it isn't progress. It's just the same old savagery and paganism, year after year; and that's what the gargoyle sees.'

'And is that what your treatise says?' Lenora asked.

'Do you know what your brother calls me?' Twigge said. And he went on: 'A gargoyle! We talked it over, and I said to him: "I've spent a lifetime looking at it and talking about it. And you've spent years pondering it. Let's put it all down in a book. We'll argue it out, and I'll write it down in shorthand." And that's what we did.'

He got up and stirred the fire.

'But that's not all,' he continued. 'We have a hero in our book! A great fellow. A soul. The soul of man. And we began with him some four thousand years ago and brought him through the ages and showed him the kingdoms and cities of the world, and introduced him to the wise men: the philosophers, the writers, the artists!'

Twigge made little flourishes with his right hand as he spoke. And his tone was gay and lifting. Lenora laughed.

'Go on! What happened?'

'He met them all, age after age. He discoursed with them. Then he met the kings and other rulers, and the cunning statesmen, and the great fools of history, and the pompous generals who thought that victory in bloody battles gave them a warrant for managing the affairs of whole nations. And so he came down through the centuries to the present time. He is walking the streets of this city at this very minute! He is looking at mankind in this present century. And his name is . . .'

'I know,' Lenora said, quietly.

'Peeper!' Twigge said, with another little flourish.

'That's what I've come to talk to you about, Twigge,' she said.

Twigge grimaced at her. 'I guessed as much!' he said, setting down the poker and dusting his hands. Then he sat down again.

'Well, I'm listening,' he said.

The April afternoon had gone to dusk, and a light rain was falling. The gutters were full and were beginning to gurgle as the water poured through them. An occasional gust of wind hurled rain against the windows. Twigge had not yet put on the light. Only the flames, and the small, red heart of the fire illumined the room which, with its ranks of books and the shelves that stretched along the walls, and the piles of notebooks, papers, and its tide of disorder, seemed to stretch extensively beyond that tiny area of light and gentle warmth. Looking at Twigge, Lenora imagined that his stature had curiously increased. His small, scrappy body in the large chair remained as usual, but his fine head with its white hair was uplifted and seemed to give him additional inches. For the first time, she was aware of him as a being whose diminutive body had no relation to the size of his character and the breadth and width of his lively mind, or the extent of his spirit.

'Go on,' he said. 'I'm all ears.'

'What are you going to do with PEEPER?' Lenora said.

'Who? Me?' Twigge exclaimed.

'Now that Quentin is unable to take care of him.'

Twigge folded his hands and stared at the fire. He swung his feet which did not quite reach to the floor; and in a voice which was almost a whisper, he said:

'It's all decided, my dear, in the Treatise.'

Lenora was leaning forward. 'But what is he going to do?' she said.

He looked sharply at her and unfolded his hands and made a little gesture with them.

'Nothing much to tell . . .'

'What is it, Twigge?'

She was adamant in her resolve to make him disclose it all. He shrugged his shoulders.

'Nothing much. He'll illustrate all the features of life that make us what we are at heart. He'll hold up a mirror . . . a fragment of glass . . . so that people can see themselves in it. And he'll take that fragment of glass with him across the whole world and whenever he thinks it'll do some good, he'll hold it up so that people can see themselves. . . .'

'What for?' Lenora said.

Twigge sniffed and was silent.

'A priggish thing to do, isn't it?' Lenora suggested. 'He'll get into trouble . . .'

'I wouldn't be surprised,' Twigge agreed.

'Isn't there enough trouble already, without . . .'

'Plenty, but not the sort that he might get into. The trouble he'll create might do some good. Might shake things up for the better.'

'Not long ago, Twigge, you told me that everything is as we choose to make it. Comedy or tragedy.'

Twigge sighed.

'What is it to be for PEEPER,' Lenora said, 'tragedy or comedy?'

Twigge was silent. He would not, or could not say. He stared at the fire while Lenora waited for his reply. All at once, he chuckled and then quickly burst into laughter. And turning to her, and leaning forward with his hands on his knees, he told her:

'He'll win the attention of the crowd, first of all. That's the first step. After that . . .'

He broke off and laughed heartily. 'After that . . .' he panted, '. . . a comedy! You said you wanted him to make everybody laugh, didn't you? Wasn't that what you said?'

She admitted it. 'Yes, but not . . .'

'Not what?'

'Not something . . . mischievous, Twigge.'

He got off his chair and stood before her with his thumbs under his waistcoat.

'You wait!' he whispered. 'We'll get him set fair and square in the public mind. Then we'll have some fun!'

'What do you mean by that?' she said.

'What you wanted,' he retorted, with a flourish of his hand. 'A good laugh . . .'

'Twigge, I don't like it! I want to know . . .'

He was rubbing his hands together and giggling.

'Just a puff would do! But what a sound!'

'At what?' she demanded. 'Tell me . . .'

He put up a hand to interrupt her impatient questions.

'At all the bad things, and the wrong things, and the big errors which stupid statesmen load on our backs. Remember Joshua and the walls of Jericho? Remember how the shout split the walls wide open? This time, it won't be a shout of anger, but one big peal of laughter! In other words . . .'

As she sat there listening to him, he thrust his head forward and whispered:

'Ridicule!'

It was not only a sound on his lips but a purpose which his keen eyes reflected and which his whole being relished. It frightened her. It was the Idea which gave PEEPER life and purpose and which threatened the whole world.

She shook her head. 'No . . .'

'Oh, but they'll laugh, right round the world!' Twigge was saying. 'They'll laugh at the big fellows who fall out with one another and then call up whole nations to fight wars for them. They'll shake their heads and say: "Go and fight it out in single combat, and leave us in peace to enjoy life! We have no enmity against our neighbours in other lands!" And they'll show up the hypocrites, and humbugs and liars in just the same way, with laughter!'

Looking up at him, she saw that his face had a serious expression; and again he seemed strangely increased in stature. He went on telling her what he intended for PEEPER, and what the response would be. She herself had nothing to say against that determination. She had pleaded for laughter, a comedy, a release from the irritability and solemnity, a return to kindliness. And he stood there and promised it all to her in a kind of reckless abundance which was more than she had bargained for. He was still talking when she rose and crossed the room and went out. She could hear him, chatting away to himself in there, while she stood with a thumping heart and a mind which was full of entangled fears.

She closed the door on all that he was saying and hurried upstairs. She was looking for John. In the studio, in his own room. She found him in the sickroom. Standing in the doorway, she beckoned him out and preceded him to the studio and there faced him.

'I've been speaking to Twigge,' she said, rapidly. 'I want to ask you . . . about PEEPER. Do you know what he and Quentin have decided, do you? Do you?'

He was startled by her vehemence.

'Yes, of course?'

'What they have planned for him?'

'Yes,' he said, tersely.

'Does Belfwig? And the proprietor of the newspaper?'

He laughed. 'Good lord, no! Of course not!'

'Why not?' she demanded.

'Well . . .'

'Because you daren't tell them?'

He sat down and grimaced. 'It's not that at all. PEEPER has achieved some popularity, and that satisfies them. It's all they expect him to do.'

'And that's what you and Quentin and Twigge wanted, wasn't it? To get him firmly established, and then . . .'

He glanced up at her expectantly and nervously.

'And then do what Quentin and Twigge proposed!' she went on.

'I never thought he'd become so popular, Len,' he said, slowly.

'Wouldn't it be honest to tell Belfwig . . . to explain what PEEPER is going to do?'

He made no answer.

'Are you going on with this thing?' she asked, angrily.

'I can't help myself,' he said. 'PEEPER takes us with him. Belfwig wants him to continue. And Quentin expects it.'

'But when something happens . . .'

He got up. 'You've let it frighten you! For heaven's sake stop this! It's nothing but a cartoon. Why let a thing like that worry you?'

'It's more than that,' she said, refusing his persuasion. 'It's much more . . .'

He turned away. 'Oh, well, what if it is? It's too late to stop now!'

'It isn't,' she was saying. 'No, it isn't . . .' And it seemed to him that her words came from everywhere in the room and stormed his senses, imploring, insisting.

'You're thoroughly frightened, aren't you?' he said, facing her.

'Yes!'

'Why? Why?'

She had so many fears, all of them large and formulated by her imagination and extended into a future which he had never troubled to anticipate.

'Listen to me, Len!' he said, interrupting her. 'Do you want me to resign and finish the whole thing? Do you? I will, if you insist. I'll go at once to Belfwig and resign. And I'll tear up the contracts. I've told you already: there's only one thing which has prevented me. Quentin. PEEPER is his creation, his Idea. I can't destroy PEEPER behind his back, now, when he's ill. And another thing: we needed money.'

She walked to the fireplace and said pensively: 'The money . . .'

'That, and his Idea,' John said. 'At the moment, they go together.'

'I wish we were back in our yesterdays . . . in our own world,' she said, quietly and pensively.

'Do you want to deny him this opportunity?' John said. 'Must he always be without a chance to work and achieve something? An invalid, supported by you? Do you want me to resign?'

She shook her head. 'No,' she returned.

He walked to the door and halted. 'When you say yes, I will,' he said. 'I'll give it up.'

# SEVENTEEN

★

The gargoyle projected from the sheer, grey face of the building which overlooked the extent of the City. Only a pale light which was like dawn or the afterglow of sunset hung above the City and was reflected by the River which coursed in a twisting, broad way between the dark masses of buildings. Tiny pinnacles and turrets arose from the scene, jutting up from the extensive haze that floated like a veil across the expanse of the City.

Voices, and the murmurous roar of traffic, rose into the air in an endless commotion of sound which was frequently dispelled by the soft thunder of the breeze or the pricking of rain. But neither wind nor rain disturbed the expression on the gargoyle's face that was thrust forward inquisitively. It was a human face: keen, humorous and fascinating in its form.

Quentin had been studying it for several minutes and noting its shape and substance and expression. To do this, he had been obliged to make an effort of will which deprived him of reserves of strength. Yet to fail to make that effort would result in a relapse into the tedious chaos which lapped his consciousness. Moreover, the gargoyle's face was a focus for his entire will which, once it had concentrated itself in that way, achieved a powerful link with life.

The gargoyle's face was faintly luminous in some remnant of day light that lingered in the heavens where a few stars and planets were already visible. Some light rain was falling from a bank of speeding clouds and spattering the gargoyle's head. The eyes continued to peer out on the scene, without blinking. And the expression remained as before: eager, inquisitive and benign and somehow amusing. Its tranquillity soothed Quentin, for in that countenance he could detect the reflection of thoughts that were composed and reasonable; and he felt that the gargoyle understood the nature of what was happening in the world below him and that he did not condemn it or extol it. A faint smile waited behind the lips, and words seemed to hover there as well. Quentin waited for him to speak.

After centuries of observation and silence what would the gargoyle remark? It was surely time he commented upon the activity which year after year, he had seen below him. How lively that scene had been! How colourful, and how teeming, and at the same time how terrible! Over the course of the centuries, so many wars, so many disagreements and tragedies, and so many errors and evils! And always the sedate voices remarking that Man was the especial regard of the Almighty! And the clamour unabating, and wars still occurring. What was the purpose of all that activity which, century after century, continued without pause despite the catastrophies which struck it?

Quentin waited eagerly for the gargoyle to turn and tell him, for the whole face was brimming with reflections of ideas that were engendered by what the eyes saw and the ears heard. Moreover, Quentin recognized the gargoyle. It was Twigge.

'Twigge!' he called.

The effort of speech hurt him. He panted. Pain began in him and robbed him of precious vitality. He groaned involuntarily. It was not only disappointing but vexatious as well when Twigge took no notice of him.

A peculiar thing happened. Slowly, the whole scene disappeared, and a little table with a bright lamp upon it came in its place. And the gargoyle changed its appearance and actually assumed a collar and tie and jacket. Arms appeared on it, and in its right hand it held a pen. Slowly, its head moved.

Quentin felt an impulse to laugh. How ludicrous it was that the stone head and the long neck should move, and that garments should suddenly appear on it! A sound fluttered from Quentin's lips and became a moan of pain as the agony stabbed at his lungs and throat.

Then Twigge glanced at him with a tranquil, soothing gaze. He got up from the little table and approached the bed. It was amusing to Quentin when what had so recently been a stone gargoyle delicately blew its nose with a clean handkerchief. The keen brown eyes were observing him. And the lips were smiling.

'What did you see?' Quentin contrived to say.

Twigge glanced towards the door and then back at the patient.

'That nurse would have me hung, if she heard me talking to you!' Twigge said.

'I saw you . . .' Quentin mumbled. ' . . . a gargoyle above the city.'

'Sh!' Twigge exclaimed, softly, again glancing at the door. 'She'll be in any minute now. Not another word!'

'What did you see?' Quentin asked again, ignoring the advice. 'And what are you doing with PEEPER?'

Twigge slowly rubbed his hands together and made a wry face. He laughed briefly.

'See? The same old thing: the Concrete and the Abstract. New fashions in everything: eating, drinking, dressing, and such like. New fashions in pleasure. New ideas about killing in warfare. But nothing new in the nature of man. Same old savage,' he said.

'And PEEPER?' Quentin said. 'Hasn't he found something to offset all that? You remember, we did find enchanting things, Twigge.'

Twigge wrinkled his features. 'I know, I know. But before that, there's a whole heap of badness: I mean . . . in any city—rascality . . .'

'But the spirit . . .' Quentin said.

'I was going to ask your advice about PEEPER,' Twigge said. 'I've done the best I could with him. He's popular. He's become so popular that I don't know exactly which way to send him. The fact is, he's a power in the land. I can tell you!'

He leaned forward suddenly over the patient.

'You listening, Quentin? Can you hear me?' he whispered.

There was no answer. The dark features were relaxed in sleep. Twigge stood back and sighed.

'Every time,' he murmured to himself. 'The same every time. Soon as I ask him for a bit of advice he slips off.'

He rubbed his right hand briskly against his cheek and frowned.

'I don't know . . . I don't know . . .' he mumbled; and he turned sharply to the figure in the bed.

'You'd better hurry up and take hold of PEEPER,' he said, audibly. 'Do you hear me? Because he's beyond me, and I'm afraid I'll make a mistake with him. He's stalking about the world, with his fists full of Power. I tell you, you'd better get well and take charge of him!'

He grunted softly, giggled, and turned to collect his notes from the table. A glance at his watch showed him that the nurse would return to duty any moment now. Therefore, he hurried.

When, a few minutes later, she entered the room, he had gathered his papers and put aside the pen and ink and set the table where she preferred to have it.

'Well?'

'Asleep,' he said, glancing at her robust person.

She had crossed the room and was standing with her arms folded while she leaned over and looked down at Quentin.

'I'll be off, nurse!' Twigge said.

She gave him a swift glance and a slight nod. Next moment, he was out of the room.

Quentin awoke from his brief sleep. An unfamiliar presence stood over him and firmly restrained him when he attempted to sit up. A deft hand settled the pillows beneath his head and shoulders and drew up the sheets. He was semi-conscious and could not recognize the room or the faces which, a little later, approached from the soft pools of light that were about him. He closed his eyes against the pressure which those faces made on his sight. He heard the voices whispering sibilantly. And there were other noises, loud ones, that seemed to him to have their source in something which was incongruous to the scene around him. A cup rattled in a saucer. A spoon struck a glass. The door closed softly, yet its sound came heavily towards him.

He could not relate the voices, the faces, and the noises to one another. He felt pain in his chest. His head ached. What was happening to him? Where was Twigge? He tried to speak, but only a harsh exclamation escaped thickly from his lips and brought the nurse once more to the bedside.

He remembered PEEPER. Looking up at the nurse, he tried to speak. His words reached his tongue and then retreated, making echoes across his mind and raising a turbulence which increased until it overwhelmed his senses. Again, he lapsed into a coma.

## EIGHTEEN

★

When Twigge reached his own room, he put on a tweed cap and a faded fawn raincoat into whose pockets he stuffed three bulky envelopes and a small bag of sweets. Before leaving, he threw a shovelful of coal dust on the fire and set up a wire guard in the grate. A minute or two later, he was in Piccadilly.

All day it had been blowing in gusts and raining lightly. Now, at a quarter to eight, the rain had ceased, and the wind had subsided to a soft, southerly breeze which was drying the pavements in great streaks. Far above, there were stars shining between the rents in the fleeting banks of clouds.

Twigge walked in a long, unhurried stride, keeping close to the wall and lightly banging it with his left fist. It was a habit which he had not lost from the days of his childhood. All over London, in the great streets, the walls knew the light blow of his fist and the echo of his long, slow gait.

At Piccadilly Circus, Twigge stopped for the first time. He looked about him and addressed a stranger.

'Trafalgar Square, mister. Which way?'

The man was small and sharp-featured, with a hoarse voice and a ready manner. He eyed Twigge closely, blinked, and then jerked his thumb.

'Trafalgar Square? There y'are! First on your right, go straight on. Can't miss it!'

'Thanks,' Twigge said. 'Just wanted to make sure . . .'

The other was grinning. He made a little gesture.

'Same old Twigge! Make sure!'

Then both of them laughed hoarsely. Twigge drew him aside.

'How's the world using you, Billy?'

'Can't complain. Seen Victor?'

'Yesterday.'

Billy seemed surprised. 'Oh! Yesterday, did you?'

Twigge nodded. 'Anything funny in that?'

'So damn funny, I feel like crying. I do straight,' Billy said, raising his thick eyebrows. He nudged Twigge.

'Which way you goin'?'

'Haymarket.'

Billy accompanied him a short part of the way.

'I'll tell you, seeing we're friends . . .'

It was soon told: the little bit of gossip for which Billy knew that Twigge would be grateful. Some tiny particle of news which, compared to the thunder of larger items of news, was almost negligible, but which was important to Twigge.

'I thought you might like to hear,' Billy said, waiting with his hungry gaze upon Twigge and folding his quick fingers over the florin which Twigge furtively passed to him.

Nothing more was said. They parted like two little shadows that had met, paused, and travelled together for a few minutes. Twigge reached Trafalgar Square and halted outside the National Gallery. He took his bag of sweets from his pocket and put two toffees into his mouth before continuing his journey into the Strand where once more he stopped a passerby.

'Fleet Street, mister? Am I on the right road?'

He looked up into the puffy, sullen face of a man of middle-age who was dressed like any London member of the great class of unemployables. The sour, shifty character was inscribed in the little red-rimmed eyes, the greasy skin, the dirty collar, the discoloured, diseased teeth, the thick shoulders. Yet one adjective described the whole of him Twigge uttered it softly.

' "Sleepy"!'

The man smiled. The little eyes almost disappeared under the tiny rolls of flesh.

'Lost your way?' he said.

Then he came closer. 'Could you . . . could you give us a sub?'

Twigge gave it without demur. Without a word. Another florin. And walked on; and having dropped his three bulky envelopes in the letter-box of a shabby door behind which the confidential bureau that rendered such good service to clergymen and public officials had its premises, he continued his way and stopped yet another pedestrian and asked his way to Holborn.

It was one of Twigge's ways of amusing himself. To ask acquaintances and strangers for a direction. As if he didn't know his way everywhere north of the river. As if he didn't! The buildings, the streets and squares and avenues, and the lanes and courts, all of them, as they surely knew his small being. There was a good deal of the street urchin about Twigge, both in character and appearance. The cap on his head was a tweed garment, really a garment, it was so large. Quite two sizes too big for him and, in that respect, like his suit and the raincoat which he wore. Soon, it flopped over his right ear. He raised it and settled it in such a way that his grey hair furled out from under its right side and its peak. There it remained. And more than before, he looked like an urchin, an old urchin of the stones and the streets and the life of the City.

He entered Cannon Street and turned to the right into King William Street and entered Lower Thames Street. His destination was a little café between that street and Eastcheap.

When he entered that place, there were only three persons there. One was the waiter in a white overall who stood behind the counter at an urn which was cheerfully steaming. He had an evening newspaper spread before him. His elbows were leaning on the counter while he read.

The other men were customers seated at the little tables placed at intervals against the wall opposite the counter. Black-topped tables, red-topped ones, green and yellow ones, all spaced on the new linoleum. One of the customers was a taxi driver, a very stout man of about fifty clad in an overcoat and several layers of waistcoats and pullovers and two scarves above which his little head rose like an egg. A little red egg with two blue little eyes. His hair was very short. He had enormous ears, and a large nose. His whole countenance had a battered but friendly and frank expression as he sat there with a cup of tea before him and two sandwiches gripped in his big right hand. Too friendly and confiding, and too frank. He was the sort of man who could not keep a secret. A glance at his open face related that much.

The third man was hidden behind a newspaper. Small and dressed in a shabby blue overcoat and a grey cap, he had recently finished a meal and was half-turned from the table on which one elbow rested. His elegant little feet in pointed brown shoes projected into the floor-way between counter and chairs. Twigge stepped to one side to avoid them.

And at once, down came the newspaper, like a balloon suddenly deflated and sinking. A little damp face with protuberant eyes and parted lips and a scrappy nose lifted to follow Twigge as he walked to a table and sat down. The face was void of expression. It was just a nose, eyes, lips, rather round. Nothing moved upon it. Nothing was reflected in it until Twigge sat down and faced it and gave it a quick glance. Then the eyes blinked, and the whole thing came to life and assumed an expression of momentary, acute concentration that might have expressed anything from cruelty to intense fear.

'Cup o' tea, Georgie! If you please!' Twigge said, crisply, without turning to the counter.

Georgie slowly straightened himself. He was a slim, trim man, in the early twenties, dark, with a sallow skin and eyes like two dark pebbles. He reached for a cup from a pile nearby. Reached for a saucer from another pile. Spoon from a box of spoons. All his movements had deftness and a supercilious languor.

'One tea, with sugar,' he said.

'That's the ticket. With sugar,' Twigge rejoined.

'Anything to eat?'

'Two nice sandwiches.'

'Two sandwiches,' Georgie said. 'They're all nice.'

They were under glass covers. Cheese, sardine, spring lettuce and tomatoes, sausage spread. Georgie slapped two on a plate, and lifted a flap of the counter to come out and put them with the cup of tea on Twigge's table.

'There we are! Tenpence.'

While Twigge got out the coins, Georgie glanced at the little customer who had quickly risen and gone to the door. He nodded good night to him. The door swung to. At once, the taxi driver became talkative.

'How are you, Hector?'

Twigge gave the coins to Georgie. 'Nothing to complain about, Fred!' he said, without turning.

He shot out his arms to free his hands of his overhanging sleeves, and lifted the cup in one hand and a sandwich in the other.

Fred said: 'Let's see. Mus' be . . . mus' be . . . oh, months since I last seen you.'

'October the eleventh, last,' Twigge said, with a mouthful of sandwich and after a sip of tea.

'Yes, mus' be,' Fred said.

'How's young . . . what's his name?' Twigge asked.

Fred and Georgie exchanged glances. Georgie said that young what's his name was ambitious. He stood nearby, leaning against the counter, with one arm folded across his chest and the other hand holding a pointed match-stick with which he picked his teeth.

'Oh, dear!' Twigge exclaimed.

'Has left "Flannel Foot" and joined the "Admiral," ' Georgie said in a low tone.

'I knew that,' Twigge said.

Fred guffawed at Georgie's surprise.

'Not much misses you, Hector!'

'And what about the "Admiral"?' Twigge said.

Georgie frowned. 'Not so loud! Not so loud! Not a word! Don't ask me!'

'Like that, eh?' Twigge said, while Georgie returned to his newspaper behind the counter.

'Ambitious, too?' Twigge went on. 'On the up and up . . .'

'The 'igher the fewer,' Fred said.

Georgie flicked away the pointed match-stick.

'I don't know anything, and I don't want to talk about it,' he said.

Fred got up heavily and sat down at Twigge's table.

'They don't like you, Twigge, old son,' he muttered.

'Don't they?' Twigge said, eating and drinking without pausing.

'They hate the sight of you,' Georgie said.

Twigge smiled, 'I never interfere . . .'

'I know, I know,' Fred said, with some impatience, 'but you get round and you see things and know things.'

'And they know it,' Georgie remarked, reading his paper.

Twigge was indignant. He looked like a jack-in-the-box as he put down his cup and lowered the bitten sandwich and said:

'I mind my own business! Always have!'

Fred touched him with a stubby forefinger.

'What is your business?'

Georgie looked up. 'Tell us,' he said.

Twigge looked from one to the other.

'Minding my own business,' he declared, flatly.

'Okay.' Georgie said.

Fred said: 'I'm on'y warning you, old son . . .'

'All my life,' Twigge said, 'minding my own business. Can't do more . . .'

Very quickly Georgie pushed the newspaper aside and lifted the counter flap and came to him.

'Can't you . . . blast it! Can't you get some sense? We're trying to tell you! Keep right out of the "Admiral's" way for a long, long time. and don't speak to his fellows and don't ask silly questions and pretend you're so . . . so . . .'

'Innocent,' Fred murmured.

'Anything else?' Twigge said.

He drained his cup and said: 'I'll take another cup.'

Georgie shook his head. 'No, you won't! One cup's enough for you One at a time.'

'But I'm thirsty,' Twigge said, looking up at that hard young face.

Fred leaned his bulk across the little table and tapped Twigge on the arm.

'Can't you see the red light when it shows up?'

He heaved himself from the chair. 'And that's the gen, if you wan to know. That's all there is to it.'

'The gen of what?' Twigge said.

Georgie closed his eyes. Fred flung out a hand.

'Ah, let the silly bugger . . .'

He waddled towards the door where he halted with his hand on th little catch.

'I'll offer up a prayer for you!' he said.

'I'd be very grateful,' Twigge said. 'Very grateful.'

The door opened, and Fred went out. The gust of wind which ha blown in subsided, and Twigge said to Georgie:

'Now I'll take another cup.'

Georgie lifted the empty cup and said: 'What's the plan?'

'Thirst,' Twigge said.

'Thirst for adventure?'

'No. I had fish for tea.'

Georgie said in a whisper: 'PEEPER!'

'Who's he?' Twigge said, and without waiting for an answer he wer on: 'And that reminds me, Georgie. What about Kempton Park, ne: Wednesday?'

At the counter, Georgie filled the cup from the urn and put it on Twigge's table and said:

'What d'you mean?'

'I mean a winner, Georgie. That's what I want: a winner for Kempton Park, next Wednesday.'

Georgie regarded him with his sombre stare for several minutes, and then said:

'They know all about you. All of them. "Flannel Foot," Cocky, and the "Admiral" and the rest.'

'Fancy that!' Twigge exclaimed. 'I wonder why they take the trouble!'

'Me and Fred have been trying to tell you ever since you came in!'

Twigge still did not appear to be impressed or disturbed. He sipped his tea.

'Two cups . . .' Georgie said. 'That's bad. Most people with sense just keep to one. One thing at a time.'

'Like you, for instance,' Twigge remarked, looking up at him.

Georgie took from beneath his overall a packet of Gold Flake cigarettes. He put one of them on the table beside Twigge's cup and lit another with a spill which he put against the jets of the urn.

'Your trouble is that you walk around as if you was some old daddy who knows nothing. When all the time you're . . .'

The rest of the remark was conveyed by a gesture.

'Trying to look as innocent as a babe unborn! But you're not,' he went on. 'Oh, no!'

'Oh!' Twigge breathed.

Georgie was twenty-five. His father owned this café, as well as six more in various parts of London. In addition to the cafés and restaurants he owned oyster bars, snack counters, fish-and-chip saloons in the East End, and several public houses about the East India Docks. A very rich man. A big man in the trade; and yet physically small and amiable and so encompassed by his affairs and his wealth that he led a very simple life, as though he were a prisoner who could not or would not venture beyond the territory in which he had always lived.

By comparison, his only son Georgie was a much bigger man. Georgie always thought so, for he was not afraid to venture beyond the territory in which he had always lived, although he was much encompassed in a comforting sort of way by his father's great wealth. Indeed, he existed on the consciousness of that wealth, and imagined that he slept, walked, ate, on a plane of existence which was much higher than that of all his friends. And he wanted to go still higher,

quickly. A clever man, in many ways. An estimable character in certai
things, recently demobilized after army service in several theatres o
war and once more resuming its threads of life in the Capital in whic
it had been born and reared. But inclined to be somewhat domineering
and with a habit of extracting information, which he called 'getting th
gen,' and another of disparaging his father's habits and methods an
projects, as well as those of pretty nearly everybody else with whom
he was in contact. A schemer, a twister, and a rascal. And ambitious
And yet interesting and attractive.

'I like you, Twigge,' he confided. 'That's why I warned you. Get me?
Twigge said that he got him and thanks. Georgie said:

'You want this winner?' in a whisper.

Twigge drained the second cup of tea and wiped some crumbs fror
his raincoat.

'I wouldn't mind a bit of a flutter, Georgie,' he said.

'Well, have one,' Georgie said.

Twigge nodded. 'Why not?'

'Is it a deal?' Georgie whispered. 'Something for something?'

Twigge pondered it and then looked up at him.

'Me? I've got nothing to offer you, sonny!'

Georgie clipped his cigarette and stuck the remains of it behind his lef
ear. He looked down at Twigge rather sleepily and whispered one word

'PEEPER!'

Twigge did not seem to understand what he was trying to say. H
looked around him, slowly, and without any particular interest aske
Georgie who PEEPER was when he was home.

Georgie folded his arms and leaned a thigh against the table.

'You can trust me, Twigge,' he whispered.

'That's nice to know,' Twigge said.

Georgie yawned. 'They all know who's running PEEPER,' he said
'Cocky, and the others . . . they all know. I'm telling you that t
warn you.'

'Thanks,' Twigge said.

He looked up at Georgie and grinned: 'What about the winner?'

'It's up to you,' Georgie said. 'Something for something.'

'Suits me,' Twigge said. 'Suits me.'

'What do I get?' Georgie asked him.

Twigge laughed merrily. 'Dividends,' he said, 'when they're due.'

'Could mean anything,' Georgie said, sauntering back to the counter
'Couldn't it?'

'That's it,' Twigge said. 'Something, and on the other hand nothing. Just depends . . .'

'But,' said Georgie, leaning on the counter and looking keenly at him, 'the more you invest, the more you collect.'

'Well,' Twigge said, reflectively and cautiously, 'there's that to it. That's one way of looking at it.'

'And if you invest all you've got, it shows you have faith. Doesn't it?' Georgie said. 'It shows you believe you're on to a good thing.'

'I wouldn't deny it,' Twigge said.

'Take me, for instance. Now if I was to say to you that I was willing to stand in with you from now on . . .'

He paused. Into his sombre face a smile crept. But Twigge did not seem to notice it until Georgie said: 'See? How does that strike you?'

Twigge pouted his lips. 'I'm a poor man, Georgie,' he said.

'Do you know what they're saying about you?' Georgie told him. 'Cocky, and the "Admiral," and the others. Do you?'

Twigge chuckled. 'I can guess!'

'They're saying that you're tops all over the City. You've got 'em where you want 'em. Right in the palm of your hand. And they're scared of you. I know that . . .'

'Me?' Twigge said, rising slowly. 'I'm just a quiet fellow. I don't bother anybody . . .'

'Come here!' Georgie said; and when Twigge was at the counter, he added: 'I'll tell you something. They've all got together. Amalgamated. All of them . . .'

'Except the worst one o' the lot,' Twigge said.

'Corny, you mean?'

Twigge said yes he meant Corny.

'There's nothing I can tell you,' Georgie said. 'You have all the gen. You know all there is to know.'

He smiled with admiration. 'I wish I was with you?' he said.

'Dear, dear!' Twigge said. 'So you're tired of being with the "Admiral"?'

'Browned off. Especially since the amalgamation. No future in it. Cocky and his crowd swamped us,' Georgie whispered.

'I suppose so,' Twigge commented. 'What are you going to do about it?'

Georgie frowned. 'I'd like to . . . rub 'em all out. Just like that. In one swipe!'

He made a swift gesture with his right hand.

D

'And then what?' Twigge said.

Georgie raised his eyebrows and pursed his lips and shrugged his shoulders.

'Don't know. Might turn over a new leaf . . .'

'Not a bad idea!' Twigge exclaimed. 'Not at all bad!'

Georgie nodded. 'It would give me a lot o' satisfaction to rub 'em all out in one go, Twigge,' he said earnestly. 'I'm so browned off. I am. I'm fed up with the whole shoot. I am, straight. I want to get out. Same time, I'd like to . . .'

Twigge laughed. 'You're ambitious, Georgie! You're like what's his name who was here just now!'

'If you knew,' Georgie said. 'The game they're on to now! That's another reason why I want to step out of it.'

Twigge buttoned his voluminous raincoat. The southerly wind burst against the café door and rattled the little catch.

'Must be off,' Twigge said.

Georgie put his cigarette stub between his lips and lit it with a spill. 'I never gave you that winner,' he said.

Twigge said nothing. Georgie leaned forward and whispered.

'One of the Ticker string. "Lord Punch" . . .'

Twigge was laughing derisively. 'An outsider. A rank outsider . . .'

'Remember it,' Georgie repeated. ' "Lord Punch." A cert.'

'All right,' Twigge said. 'I will. I'll take a chance.'

He glanced at the big clock above the tins of soups and sardines and spaghetti stacked on the shelf behind Georgie.

'Time to go, sonny,' he said. 'The "Admiral" doesn't like late visitors.'

He knew that Georgie was startled, for into that bland, sallow face a faint suffusion of blood swept, and the mouth opened slightly, although no words came until Twigge glanced at him.

'You wouldn't be such a fool!' Georgie exclaimed.

Twigge went to the door and lifted the catch.

'Just a chat with him,' he said.

'Twigge!' Georgie called. 'Hi! Twigge!'

The odd little figure at the door turned and halted. Georgie came hastening from behind the counter.

'I'm with you,' he said, earnestly. 'With you, all the way! One big swipe at them. At the whole crowd.'

'We'll see,' Twigge said. 'We'll see what can be done. In the mean time . . .'

He put his fingers to his lips. Georgie did the same. Then they both nodded simultaneously. Twigge opened the door. A boisterous gust of wind leapt into the narrow café and overturned a show card for somebody's cigarettes. Georgie saw the door close behind Twigge, then he folded his arms and drew in his lower lip and remained like that for some time.

He was still there when the door opened and four young people came in. Four cheerful people—two men and two women—from a theatre. They wanted soup, and spaghetti on toast.

Georgie took the order and called it down the serving hatch.

# NINETEEN

*

Coming out into the windy night, Twigge could smell the River's odour on the long, rising gusts of wind which buffeted his small form. That hard, fresh odour always made him wince. He was not cold, yet he shuddered. He did not like the river. It brought to the City an atmosphere which Twigge felt was incongruous. Its brimming level with the reflection of lights pricking the surface, and the dark ripples made by the wind or the passage of river craft, suggested the sea and the traffic of steamers, and maritime matters that seemed to Twigge to encroach upon the City's life. Merely to think of the oceans, and to smell on the wind that sharp, lusty odour of the river water gave Twigge a feeling of insecurity, as though at any moment the river would rise and hurl its waters into the streets upon a single gust of the vigorous wind. He drew his raincoat closer about his neck, and turning his back to the wind he entered Eastcheap and passed, by Mincing Lane, into Fenchurch Street.

It was the core of his world. These streets and those commercial houses. They were not mere names to him, or impersonal things. They were familiar to him since his childhood. They were landmarks, and as such they delineated his vision which, in all the years of his life, had never known space or emptiness but which had been circumscribed by buildings that had marked what was near and what was distant. Always buildings. He was a city man, and he belonged to its buildings and streets, its habits and its traditions. But if he belonged to it, it had engendered in him a curious, abstract sense of possession over it. And that idea had gradually developed until it could not be dislodged by reason or fact. Only the great River in winding motion spoiled the belief, and perhaps it was for this reason that Twigge seldom ventured near the Thames, and had never yet crossed it, even by the Underground, and had no contact with persons who lived on the south side of the River and had no interest at all in events there. The north bank was his, all the way from Canning Town to Hammersmith, for it seemed to him that everything of importance was there. The King in his Palace; the Prime Minister in Downing Street; the Lords in their House, and the Commons in theirs; and the Abbey, the Ministries, and the great seats of Commerce. And the theatres and restaurants, as well as the famous personalities, and his own contemporaries in their millions. All north of the River.

It might have been a weakness in Twigge's wisdom for him to assume that south of the River was a different city, a strange locality. But Twigge, being human, had many weaknesses, some of which gave an individuality to him, while others that were so personal to himself and so concealed that they left no indication of themselves in his behaviour, had moulded his entire character. To innumerable people, he was nothing more than an eccentric, a natural ; while to others he was the embodiment of exquisite virtues such as gentleness, selflessness, generosity and charity. But there were others—persons of the plane of life which is termed the 'underworld,' but which is actually very much above ground—who knew him as a remorseless, purposeful being. They feared him more because of his knowledge of themselves and his terrible war against all of them. A war it was.

For the truth was that Twigge was possessed of a belief which might have seemed fantastic to the famous personalities of commerce, Church, State, and aristocracy who assessed their wealth in terms of land, stock, reputation, influence, authority and power. They believed in their wealth for what it represented: its utility, its value in money, or its power and authority. Twigge believed in his wealth merely because it had beauty. He loved it. All of it, the whole of London north of the Thames. For that was his treasure, which he believed was his.

For years, his sense of possession had increased in him. He was jealous of the personalities who arose and had their day and passed from the scene. He resented some of their actions. He was the benign monarch of a territory into which millions of strangers poured, and from which the same millions receded like a tide that had flowed there during crisis. Hunted, haunted creatures remained from that tide, like its flotsam and jetsam, and were hidden by lonely women until the pursuit found them or rooted them out.

Lately, new figures had entered his territory. Already a great traffic was in progress amongst these men and women. Food was their commodity. Rationed food. The Law did not terrify them. But Twigge did, for he had the cunning ability to play one mob off against another, not openly but merely by exciting the appetites which had driven them to their purposes. Greed was his weapon against them. The very greed which was in them. And the suspicion of one another which was in all of them.

But it was not enough to overcome them. Twigge needed a greater weapon; and in this connection he dreamed of a little newspaper with a modest circulation but a formidable tone. How trenchant it would be! How powerful! It was nothing more than a dream. Until PEEPER's advent.

If PEEPER was Quentin's creation, he was just as much Twigge's. Into the thesis there had gone all of Twigge's philosophy. Consequently, PEEPER represented much of him, although what was unformulated and quaint and inadmissible had been tactfully expunged from PEEPER. Nevertheless, Twigge felt some pride in him and a sense of creation over him. And he had no scruples about using PEEPER for ends which he believed were justifiably good.

At the same time, he was cautious. Twigge was much too shrewd and much too wise to let his fancies take flight. He was still Twigge: small, outlandish in his large garments and his big cap; modest, and affable as he plodded through Moorgate into the City Road and northwards until he reached the Borough of Islington.

Somewhere in the region off the Liverpool Road, he stopped at a little house and rang the bell. No answer. And again, after pressing the switch and waiting, no answer.

He walked off. By now, he was feeling very tired. He boarded a westbound 'bus from which he alighted at an Underground station. He went to Paddington.

Coming up, he turned south. Somewhere off the Bayswater Road, he stopped at a large mansion. The rooms facing the street were lit, and curtains were drawn across the big windows. Twigge ascended the flight of steps and rang the bell.

# TWENTY

This time, he had not to wait long before the door was opened. He was pleased, for the wind was still rising and the spiteful currents whipped around him in the big porch and chilled his thin body.

A man of about forty-two, of medium height and dressed in an elegant, double-breasted suit, and holding in his right hand a long cigarette-holder with a lighted cigarette, opened the door and raised his head to discern the curious figure in the porch.

It was the 'Admiral.' Twigge stepped at once into the hall, whereupon his host signed away the maid who came in answer to the ring on the door which the 'Admiral' himself had attended, and began to exclaim with a great show of pleasant humour which Twigge ignored.

'How nice!' And he went on, drawling the words in his unctuous manner. 'How good to see you, Twigge! Come in!'

He looked at Twigge, as he looked at other people whom he wished to please, with an earnest, concentrated air of attention that was full of plausible little gestures, smiles, and twists and turns of his handsome head, and inflections of his resonant voice. Altogether a flatterer, and an ingratiating rogue, handsome and mannered but unscrupulous.

'Are you going to stay a little while, Twigge? It should be so nice, because we were just going to have supper. Shall you join us? Give me your hat and coat.'

Twigge made no answer to these remarks. He took off his big hat and coat, and at the same time he glanced at the half-open door of a small room behind the large front room. Many people were gathered there; and Twigge could hear the rumble of brisk conversation and the pleasant tinkle of crockery and glasses.

'I want a chat with you, Willie,' he said, addressing the 'Admiral' by his Christian name.

Willie appeared surprised and hurt by Twigge's refusal of supper.

'Not going to join us?' he exclaimed, raising his eyebrows.

Twigge shook his head. 'A little talk,' he said.

'Very well!' Willie exclaimed, inflecting his voice and opening the door of a room opposite the supper room.

It was a big house, furnished in fine taste and very warm and comfortable. When Willie switched on the light in the room, he stood aside for Twigge to enter. In one swift glance Twigge took in the room: the carpet; the cream-coloured walls; the pale green curtains and the mahogany furniture.

'Do sit down, Twigge! Now! Can I get you something to drink? Whisky, sherry, gin, port, a little white wine?'

Twigge said: 'I've just come from Islington.'

Willie appeared extremely distressed. 'My dear good chap! Oh, I say! Why ever didn't you give me a tinkle on the 'phone, and I would have sent the Daimler for you? After all, we are friends, I hope.'

Twigge took an armchair before the electric fire which Willie turned on for him.

'I'll take a cup of tea, if you please,' he said.

He stretched out his legs and accepted a cigarette from a silver box which the 'Admiral' offered him.

'Sure you won't take . . .' Willie began. 'Whisky, gin . . .'

'Tea, please. With sugar,' Twigge said.

'Very well,' Willie said. 'Excuse me, won't you?'

When he was gone, Twigge looked about him. The room had a feminine character from the soft colours of the carpet and curtains and walls, and the delicacy of the mahogany furniture. There were some choice little water colours on the walls above the settee and the little desk which was opened and on which Twigge saw the monogrammed blotter, the engagement diary, and a couple of envelopes.

Twigge knew that it was the study used by Willie's aunt. He had met her once, when he had come to this house to make Willie's formal acquaintance, about six months previously. She was a stringy, highly-strung woman of fifty, ornate, restless, and seated in the shade of a discreet lamp which cast its radiance on a company of about twenty foreign gentlemen who sat stiffly on the edges of hard little chairs and stirred cups of tea and spoke in guttural English, very politely, addressing questions to a commercial gentleman from London's East End who had lately returned from the Balkans. About them hovered an Italian woman dressed in black who replenished their teacups and offered them little cakes which they either nibbled or else stuffed whole into their mouths. All of them wore grey suits and big boots around which the silent Italian woman threaded her way skilfully, despite her bulk. Willie's aunt lounged and listened to the questions which her guests put to the young commercial gentleman. Questions about whether this bridge and that building were still standing. And was the so-and-so hotel and the so-and-so palace . . . were they still there? Yes, they were. General grunts of satisfaction from the company. And the so-and-so Convent . . . and the Church . . . the very beautiful one near the Hotel of . . .

'Red Army Headquarters . . .'

Something like a growl sprang from the sedate gentlemen on the hard little chairs. Square faces flashed upon square faces.

Willie's aunt had drawled: 'It's progress, and we must bow to it and trust that, in time, the more experienced parties will regain their prestige and bring some sort of education or discipline to these younger people who have voted away their rights for the sake of . . .'

More growls from the company interrupted the rest of the remark. Cake crumbs dropped from mouths. Tea slopped into saucers.

Twigge smiled at the recollection of that scene and felt tempted to go across and peep into the room to see if the same gentlemen were seated on the same chairs around Willie's aunt and growling about the present state of their homelands. But just then Willie returned with a silver tray loaded with sandwiches, cakes, biscuits with anchovies upon them, and a silver teapot and two cups.

He set down the tray on a small coffee table and poured tea for his visitor and offered him food. He took a cup himself and selected a sandwich which he ate standing with his back to the fireplace.

'Tea to your taste?' he asked.

Twigge said, thank you yes.

Willie said: 'Something on your mind, my dear chap?'

'Sit down,' Twigge said, 'and I'll tell you.'

'Another sandwich?' Willie asked, offering the plate to him.

Twigge took three and placed them on his plate and stretched out his legs while Willie sat down opposite him.

Willie was very elegant and trim, with his slender waist and broad shoulders and sleek ankles. But he was not an admiral. The title applied to his rolling gait. Actually, he had no legitimate occupation. He had returned recently from Vienna where he had been busily occupied for six months supplying cigarettes and British currency to various impoverished Austrians in return for such articles as diamond rings of great value, cameras, wristwatches, necklaces, and valuable old paintings, until his superiors had discovered something of his habits and had notified him of his dismissal from their employment.

Twigge pondered all this, for it was known to him: and he was still thinking of it when Willie spoke.

'I do hope we aren't going to become bad friends. It would be such a pity, Twigge.'

Twigge was busily masticating the sandwiches and did not trouble to answer the remark.

'I hear that you have found your feet in a rather clever little venture, Twigge,' Willie continued. 'Am I right?'

Twigge swallowed the last of his sandwiches and emptied his cup.

'Now you listen to me, Willie,' he said, flatly, as though he were suddenly tired of Willie's character and manner.

'Another cup of tea, my dear chap?' Willie said; and when Twigge shook his head, he went on, suavely: 'You were saying . . .'

Beneath his ingratiating, measured manner and speech, there was a faint sourness and fractiousness which Twigge well understood. And it was to that aspect of Willie which, after all, was the truth of him, that he addressed himself.

'I take a serious objection to the way you're behaving,' he said.

Willie seemed nonplussed. He drew back his head and looked aggrieved and surprised.

'You don't think, my dear chap . . . you don't think that you are being just a trifle . . . dictatorial?'

'Drop it, drop it!' Twigge said.

In his drawling voice, Willie said: 'I don't want to get angry. We're friends. But I resent . . . I'm afraid I resent interference, my dear chap!'

He shifted irritably in his chair. Looking at him, Twigge saw the ugliness in him. It was there, in his expression which could not conceal the greed, vanity, and wilfulness of his nature.

'Wouldn't help you,' he said.

Willie got up. 'I'm sorry, Twigge. I don't tolerate any interference with my affairs.'

Twigge got up. Very gently but firmly, he pushed Willie back into the armchair.

'I'm twice your age, Willie! You listen to me. And don't interrupt.'

Willie sank back into the chair and stared up at him with a look of grievance that swelled and pulsated in the flabby features like a thing of separate, sentient existence resident in the nose, the cheeks and the lips and eyes.

'You can diddle about with your Black Market,' Twigge said. 'I don't care. If people like to pay for what they want, that's not my concern. But this other business . . .' and he jerked his head in the direction of the room on the opposite side of the hall. 'That's ambitious. I won't stand any of that nonsense.'

'You . . . you won't!' Willie exclaimed.

'I don't like the way you're climbing, Willie. Out of the Black Market into . . . I don't know what!'

'Is that your business?' Willie exclaimed.

Twigge seemed to reflect on the question. He warmed his hands at the electric fire and eventually said yes, it was his business.

'Why? I don't see . . .'

Willie had risen again. He was taller than Twigge who had to look up at him.

Twigge laughed quickly. 'You don't see anybody, except yourself . . .'

'But by what right, what . . . purpose . . . what . . .'

Willie spluttered. He was petulant, aggrieved, truculent, and abusive.

'A little nuisance like you, Twigge! Oh, no! I'm not going to stand for that! It just isn't your business!'

Twigge turned upon him a patient, amused look.

'Who's then? Who's is it?'

Willie frowned. All he could say was that it was not Twigge's.

'Go on,' Twigge said.

'It's nobody's concern . . .'

'Must be somebody's,' Twigge said.

Then he looked sharply at Willie.

'Since nobody seems to mind, I do,' he said. 'I don't like you, Willie. I don't like you at all. I've waited a bit to see if somebody would stop you . . .'

'And so you have decided . . .'

Willie laughed. 'You're so funny, Twigge! You are, really. You stand there . . .'

'I'm going to pull you up, sharp!' Twigge said.

Willie made a smooth gesture with his hand. 'Fine, my dear chap! Pull me up, if you care to try.'

Twigge walked towards the door, with Willie following him and saying: 'It should be interesting. Quite a tussle!'

In the hall, Willie helped Twigge into his hat and coat.

'There,' he said. 'So now you're going? And you're . . . what is it? . . . you're going to pull me up?'

'Good night,' Twigge said.

Willie accompanied him to the door. 'You won't stay and join the company? You wouldn't like me to bring the Daimler for you? You won't think again, my dear chap, and stay and have a glass of wine?'

He went down the steps with Twigge and a short distance along the pavement.

'Flossie will be very upset. She's quite fond of you, Twigge. She'll be very upset that you haven't stayed and shaken hands with her. After all, you have no quarrel with her, have you?'

Twigge halted. 'I know all about you, Willie. You've had your own nasty way . . .'

'Oh, don't be silly, my dear fellow!' Willie exclaimed, taking Twigge's arm and walking on slowly with him and murmuring to him. 'We're friends, friends, really we are! I like you. So does Flossie. We both think you're a tremendous fellow! But this . . . all this is so silly between friends! Whoever heard . . . Whoever heard of anybody interfering . . .'

'That's right!' Twigge said, and he chuckled so heartily that Willie thought he had at last persuaded him of the folly of his behaviour. But suddenly, and with astonishing vigour, Twigge shook off Willie's grip.

'That's right,' he said. 'Whoever heard of anybody interfering with you? Whoever did?'

He went on, leaving Willie behind.

'I say! Twigge! Twigge!'

Twigge could hear him calling softly, until the high wind obliterated the sound. When he glanced back, Willie had returned to the house.

The last 'bus had travelled the route, and the last Underground train had made its journey. A few taxis went past, but they were engaged and did not stop in answer to Twigge's summons. He walked. He was tired and vexed.

It was past one of the morning when he reached home and went noiselessly upstairs to the studio where the light still showed. John was there.

Twigge sat down and sighed as he stretched out his legs. He asked after the patient. Joining his hands across his chest, he glanced around him and saw drawings of PEEPER scattered on the table and floor. He laughed softly.

'You've got enough there to last you . . .'

'If I had an idea,' Bessing said, yawning. 'I've been waiting for you. Belfwig says he wants something very light.'

'Can't you think of something?' Twigge said.

'Can't you?' Bessing retorted.

For quite a minute, Twigge was silent. He appeared to be in a dilemma. His lips were pursed and his brows were contracted.

'Give them a Punch and Judy show,' he said. 'Call it Lord Punch and his Lady.'

'Good enough,' Bessing said.

'They'll love it!' Twigge remarked.

# TWENTY-ONE

★

Twigge had never deliberately made an enemy, and he hesitated to do so now. He let a day or two elapse before he reached a decision. During that time, he reflected seriously on many things.

His chief problem was one which had exercised far wiser minds than his; and he could have sought for and accepted the conclusions reached by many philosophers who had examined this problem. Instead, he chose to seek his own conclusions by asking himself what degree of free will had expression in, for example, an individual such as Willie.

Twigge did not hate people for their faults. On the contrary, he loved them because it seemed to him that all their actions were the result of some enormous, mysterious process to which they were submitted and which gave results in terms of their characters and temperaments that had been fashioned by forces beyond their control. Therefore, in opposing Willie, Twigge realized that he was not condemning him for his actions as much as for the factors which compelled him to do certain things. What were those factors, those compulsions?

Willie was less an individual than a symptom of certain evils which characterized modern life. He had to be considered in relation to his environment as well as to such matters as the history of his civilization, and the development and influence of the philosophy of his time.

Twigge was amused by this. If Willie were told that he was a particle, an atom of some sort, whose degree of free will was almost negligible compared to the immeasurable, incalculable forces that ordained his

108

physical and mental existence, he would scoff at the idea. But it was true: Willie belonged as much to nature and all its phenomena as he did to the contemporary scene. And if he was a symptom of certain evils, all that he did could be explained by reference to the current philosophy which, in itself, was an attempt to understand the natural and moral forces that ordained his existence.

In order to reach some sort of understanding of Willie, Twigge was obliged to examine as best he could and without reference to writings, the current philosophy. In this respect, he believed that something very interesting and, at the same time, very startling was happening. What was it?

He was convinced that the influence of ancient philosophies was waning, and that it had been on the wane ever since the migrations from Europe to the New World when a new and very materialistic philosophy had arisen out there in the West.

From time to time, ripples of that philosophy reached the Old World which trundled on its way and lived an altogether different kind of life to that which was fashioning itself in the New World. Then a strange thing happened. The Old World, due to incredible errors in its ideas as well as to fractures in its philosophy and statesmanship, was split by two wars; and back to Europe came the descendants of the old emigrants, millions of them, millions of men who represented a new, materialistic philosophy which itself was suddenly undergoing a process of change.

The resultant intermingling of two philosophies created curious results that were far too elusive to pursue and analyse. But one thing was certain. Christianity, which had failed twice within twenty-five years to avert major wars, had lost its influence. The world no longer belonged to the Church, but to Science which, to the ordinary being, appeared detached and irresponsible and answerable to no morality

The ripples which travelled back to the West from the temporary fusion of two philosophies could be described. Twigge gave names to them.

The first was Fear. Another was Greed. Whatever they were, they had their source in a current feeling of insecurity and movement towards a kind of brink. And both states of mind and the kind of morality, or lack of it, which they produced, were readily seized upon by such persons as advertisers, politicians, speculators, Government ministers, generals, and the host of men who desired power. They encouraged the idea of Fear. Fear of being without certain goods and thereby not enjoying life to the full. Fear of nations not being strong enough to resist enemies. Fear of the wrong party coming to power. Fear, indeed, of everything in the present and the future. And out of Fear came Greed. Secure yourself behind Money and possessions! Get on top! Look after yourself! Assert your sovereign independent rights!

Twigge believed that something like a universal panic was in full swing. Willie was symptomatic of it. He represented millions who, like himself, were not really evil but only afraid. And the only good thing in that condition was this: that if Fear had driven them to do certain things, another sort of Fear could compel them to do other kinds of things.

There was something, Twigge believed, to be said after all for the awful visions of eternal damnation which the early Church had drawn for its congregation. He laughed. He was going to frighten Willie by presenting him with a warning of what lengths he would go to in his struggle with him.

Meanwhile, having given Bessing something for a forthcoming PEEPER cartoon, Twigge visited Georgie and told him what he had done.

'You'd better know,' he said, 'because there's likely to be trouble.'

Georgie nodded. 'I should say so!'

He appeared very perturbed.

'An outsider like "Lord Punch" forecast by PEEPER. That means thousands of pounds will go on him. Will worry the bookmakers. Will make Willie and his racing pals suspicious.'

'A sure winner, you told me,' Twigge reminded him.

'Only because Willie and his crowd will see to that.'

'Shall I wipe it all out?' Twigge said. 'I will if you want me to. I'll rub out that cartoon . . .'

'No,' Georgie said, decisively. 'No. Let it go on. Let's knock Willie hard. So hard that he won't get up.'

'His crowd might guess where the news came from,' Twigge warned him.

'They might,' Georgie said. 'Let them! I can take care of myself. And Fred can look after himself.'

'Then you agree?'

'Let PEEPER hit him!'

PEEPER. Twigge thought about him as he returned home. The popularity of that creature was increasing hourly, and no longer belonged to the bounds of enthusiasm. It had travelled into the realm of the mysterious, like a hot wind sweeping across the entire world, for there was news of him from India, China, Japan, as well as from Australasia, and the entire American Continent. And the effect of the news on Twigge was to raise in him a sharp presentiment of something which was too terrible to be described as dangerous.

The only word which Twigge found apt to define it was cataclysm.

## TWENTY-TWO

★

The extraordinary, hysterical affection for PEEPER, as well as the sane enthusiasm for him, were factors which all in Summariser House in Fleet Street found too large to assess in terms of net daily sales. The more cautious senior executives and journalists were not only impressed but were experiencing a solemn sense of responsibility at being confronted with such a remarkable phenomenon. Not so, Belfwig, who had much that was reckless in his temperament, much that disregarded consequences and pursued its secret ambition and indulged its delight in personal achievement. For to him this was Success! The appalling interest in PEEPER proved his acumen and his sense for originality! He took that success for himself. It was too large to share with anybody. Moreover, he was not yet finished with PEEPER. Lord Ecks had had his day with him, running him hard into the blaring and publicity of his new Cause which, as with all his former enthusiasms, had petered out like a clockwork toy whose springs had broken. That tilt at the Income Tax system! Belfwig guffawed with derision whenever he remembered it, for the whole stunt had been swallowed up by PEEPER's personality, leaving Ecks baffled and jealous. But now it was Belfwig's turn. He wanted to give PEEPER his chance and make him greater than emperors, kings, famous statesmen.

He disregarded the solemn advice of his sub-editors, his financial experts, the advisers and journalists, who trod knee deep in sacks of letters from all over the world; nor would he heed his harassed junior staff who handled the floods of telegrams and cables. He derided the resolutions passed by august City Boards condemning the manner in which this new feature of journalism interfered with public and private

111

life. And he applauded the enthusiastic retorts made by other Boards and Guilds who extolled PEEPER and daily established fresh branches of PEEPER Clubs. He ignored adverse criticism against which he could offer thousands of congratulatory letters and almost as many telegrams, as well as the world-wide admiration for PEEPER. In fact, it seemed to Belfwig that a world which was burdened with crises, wars, and the inconveniences resulting from the stupid mistakes of politicians and governments deserved its affection for PEEPER to whom it turned for relief.

It was at this juncture that Ecks paid him an unexpected visit. Had he come with the remaining members of the Board who controlled not only the 'Daily Summariser' but the forty-three publications which Summariser House published weekly, Belfwig would have been happier to see him, for alone Ecks was inclined to exercise dictatorial powers.

He entered rapidly. The door slammed behind him. He halted at the fireplace and drew breath. Then he emitted a single word.

'PEEPER!'

Belfwig was prepared for him. He had hundreds of reports from foreign correspondents in the world's capitals. They implored more news of PEEPER. They called him the biggest thing in history. Their telegrams ran to thousands of words. They wanted observers sent out to see for themselves, for words could not describe the effect which PEEPER had created.

'You can congratulate yourself!' Belfwig said, handing him a selection of copy.

Ecks had risen and removed his hat, gloves and coat. He sniffed and ran a forefinger under his big nose.

'I've had enough of it!' he bellowed. 'I'm weary of it!'

He extended his big hands. 'It's gone far enough!'

Turning his back on Belfwig, he flung himself into an armchair and sighed as he shot out his legs.

'What do you want me to do?' Belfwig said, smoothly.

Ecks growled. Nothing could be done without the consent of the Board.

'Finish him. Close him down . . .'

'On what grounds?'

Ecks scratched his neck and frowned.

'He'll destroy us if we don't put an end to him soon!'

Belfwig sank back in his chair and regarded him calmly.

112

'I'm afraid I don't follow you,' he said, suavely.

'Of course you do! You know everything about him! He's more than a cartoon! Can't have that! Realize what it means?'

The big body was slewed in the chair to confront Belfwig.

'Bigger than any personality in this mortal world!'

Belfwig smiled. 'You made him so,' he remarked. 'First the campaign of publicity, which you definitely sponsored. Then the Crusade against the method of Income Tax levy. Your plans. Your idea . . .'

'I know, I know!'

Ecks was silent. When at last he spoke again, his voice was that of an old man. Slow and tremulous.

'It's horrible, Belfwig! A terrible thing. My Crusades and Causes have always been innocent. This is abominable. Never thought it would swerve up into this.'

He got up and came over to Belfwig who saw then that he was really afraid. His resource and impetuosity were evaporated from his thunderous frame, and his little blue eyes under the shaggy brows were the visible things of an inner terror.

'Don't understand it, Belfwig. Frightens me. Keeps me awake at night. It's madness, and we're geared to it! Not as if PEEPER were a film star. Could understand the fuss if he were. Nice clean enthusiasm. But . . . a series of cartoons! And these PEEPER Clubs. Awful! Never happened in the world before, has it? Can't make it out. Can you?'

'Certainly!' Belfwig replied.

'Explain,' Ecks sighed.

'A sick world wants relief. And it is a sick world, Ecks. And it longs for release from stress. PEEPER gives it. PEEPER is universal. I flatly refuse to countenance his destruction!'

Ecks stared at him and grunted, and blinked his little blue eyes.

'Don't deprive the world of its Man!' Belfwig said. 'We in Summariser House have this responsibility. Are you going to shirk it?'

Ecks put on his coat and hat and drew on his gloves.

'Fellow is bound to become a political instrument,' he complained. 'Then what? Then we'll have trouble!'

'Leave it to me, Ecks,' Belfwig said. 'Unless, of course, the Board . . .'

Ecks shook his head. 'Be the last to interfere in editorial matters. But I do caution you . . .'

Belfwig accompanied him to the door. 'Have you been approached by the parties?' he said quietly.

'They wouldn't presume to go that far!' Ecks asserted. 'They know me. Democratic, independent . . .'

He and Belfwig laughed heartily. Ecks shook his hand.

'Come and dine with us to-morrow evening,' he grunted as he left.

Belfwig returned to his desk. The door opened and he thought for a moment that Ecks had returned. Instead, it was the Sports' Editor holding in his hands a rough proof of the next day's PEEPER cartoon.

'You know what this is?' he said to Belfwig.

Harry. Bluff, florid, and renowned in sporting circles all over the country. A famous sporting journalist who spoke like a bookmaker and who looked like one. Perhaps, years ago, he had been one. Belfwig did not know. He only knew that he liked Harry who was a very great sports' journalist and a good all-round sportsman, but who, at this moment, was truculent and angry as he slapped down the proof and stood with his hands resting heavily on the desk.

'What's on your mind, Harry?' Belfwig said.

The big eyes goggled. The lips pouted.

'On my conscience, if this goes into print!'

Belfwig had already passed it. The PEEPER cartoon which harmlessly depicted a little crowd around a Punch and Judy show. Lord Punch!

'What objection . . .' Belfwig began.

'An outsider,' Harry said, interrupting him, 'a poor outsider. Lord Punch!' he said, drawing away scornfully. 'Haven't I given my selection for to-morrow's race?'

'This has nothing to do with your page!' Belfwig said.

'Lord Punch!'

'A Punch and Judy show . . .'

'No!' Harry said, shaking his head. 'Nothing but a cheap trick to get a bit more popularity! That's what that is! Like the rest of his stunts. Cheap, and nasty . . .'

'You think so?'

Belfwig was smiling at him. Harry said: 'I know it! I know PEEPER by now. All those nasty stunts. And this . . . this bit of work . . .'

He pointed to the proof.

'Another sensation! Just another shot to get the gallery. And . . .' he added, angrily, 'and it's right across my province.'

Belfwig said: 'So you think this is a racing forecast?'

'And a pretty poor one. And a dangerous one,' Harry asserted.

Belfwig did not appear to be impressed. He sat back in his chair and smiled while he glanced again at the proof. Harry put a forefinger on it.

'It hasn't a chance in ten million,' he said, 'unless some dirty work helps it. That's why I don't like it. If it loses, you'll disappoint every backer who is fool enough to stake on it. If it gets a place. you'll have told the world that you knew some nasty business was afoot. That's my opinion.'

'If, as you imagine, there might be some underhand move to enable this horse to win, aren't we warning the authorities?' Belfwig said.

Harry stared at him in amazement.

'Any decent newspaper wouldn't involve itself in rubbish like this,' he declared. And he went on: 'Touch a stunt like this, and your hands won't be clean for years. And one more point. If that cartoon goes through, you'll risk my reputation. I won't be able to put foot on any racecourse without meeting trouble.'

Belfwig laughed. 'Harry! Do you think that I'd take things that far, if I thought for one moment that this cartoon was a poor stunt? Do you?'

'You'll walk clean into scandal and heaven's own fuss!'

'But the thing is harmless and innocent!' Belfwig said.

Harry was silent. He stood there for a few seconds longer, staring at Belfwig. Then he shrugged his shoulders.

'Very well, sir.'

When he was gone, Belfwig asked for a messenger to be sent at once to Mr. Bessing's home with a request that Bessing should come as soon as possible to the office. Belfwig was worried. He understood the violent gangs, the dangerous elements, the tricky waters of horse-racing. Harry was correct in what he had said, and Belfwig did not wish to oppose him or endanger his reputation. But there was something else which Harry had remarked and which Belfwig believed to be true. Lord Punch. For some reason, Belfwig accepted Harry's opinion. Perhaps he merely wanted to believe that 'Lord Punch' might first of all incline readers and others to stake on it. Perhaps he felt that there was a forecast in the cartoon. Perhaps he hoped that 'Lord Punch' would be amongst the first three at the winning-post. It was an opportunity against which caution went down like so much straw before wind.

Nevertheless, he sent for Bessing. He had to be sure that he was not going to walk into trouble of any sort. Also, he wished to convince Harry that he had first of all satisfied himself that Bessing had no ulterior motive in presenting that cartoon for publication.

When Bessing appeared about an hour later, Belfwig tossed across to him the rough proof.

'I wanted to see you about that, Bessing.'

John glanced at it. 'You've already passed this. You wanted something light. . . .'

'Did you know that "Lord Punch" is the name of a racehorse?' Belfwig said.

Bessing shook his head. 'Never heard of it.'

'Quite certain? Even in a conversation you might have overheard. Something like that . . .'

'Absolutely certain! You asked for a kind of pause in PEEPER, and said you'd like something light. I thought of a Punch and Judy show. There it is, with PEEPER looking on.'

'Thank you,' Belfwig said. 'I'm sure that you understand just how important it is for us not to become involved in scandal.'

'Scandal!'

Belfwig smiled. 'The title of your cartoon is "Lord Punch," which happens, as I have said, to be the name of a rather mediocre racehorse.'

'Did you think that I would have put forward such a . . . such a device?'

Belfwig interrupted him.

'Certainly not. I merely wished to . . .'

'To make quite sure?'

Belfwig smiled. 'At the risk of offending your susceptibilities,' he said, with a touch of irony.

'All you have to do, if you're still dubious, is to delete the first word. "Lord." Simple enough,' Bessing said.

'I'll think about it,' Belfwig said. 'Meanwhile, I should be glad if you would make no mention of this conversation. . . .

He checked himself at that point and was surprised to detect what at first, he suspected were signs of discomfiture and duplicity in Bessings's features. He felt nervous. He wanted nothing more than that the cartoon should appear in its present form. He did not want a confession of any kind from Bessing.

'I won't detain you any longer, Bessing. Thanks . . .'

He was relieved when the door closed behind Jayby. He was pleased, at first, then worried. He passed the proof and then regretted having done so. An error of judgment? Up there, on the dizzy, precarious heights to which PEEPER's success and his own zeal had carried him, in that rarefied atmosphere, had he been foolhardy, had he ignored

116

discretion and suddenly become nothing more than a blundering fool who was blind to obvious danger? Or had he accepted a risk with the same courage which had characterized the whole of his career in journalism?

He had his answer on the following morning when, after a tedious, anxious night, he knew that he had made his first grave mistake. He could not ignore it. Coming up to the City, he heard about him the buzz and excitement which told him that thousands, literally tens of thousands, were backing 'Lord Punch' because PEEPER had fancied him. He dared not conjecture how much money was staked. Fortunes, probably. The shillings and half-crowns, the gamblers' pounds, the fivers of the regular punters. But there was something more than money on that outsider.

There was his reputation, and PEEPER's, and Harry's. All were stupidly imperilled. Oh, the public might be satisfied, and PEEPER might gain in repute, if 'Lord Punch' gained first place! But with that success, down would go his own and Harry's and the newspaper's, for he realized it now: some sordid plan of gangs to defeat fair-play and win the race for 'Lord Punch.' And some exposure of them by another mob through PEEPER's cartoon.

And there was Harry—red and exasperated—waiting for him and exclaiming:

'I was right! It's gang warfare! Either way, we're sunk! A messy business like this!'

Belfwig said: 'I explained to you, and I had Bessing's word for it, that the cartoon has no relation at all to that race or any runner in it.'

'Tell that to the thousands who believe otherwise!' Harry shouted. 'Tell it to the bookmakers and stewards! Come down to my office and hear the fellows on the telephone asking me what the devil I'm playing at. What am I to say?'

'What I have told you!' Belfwig said, controlling his frayed temper and his nervousness.

'A bedtime story like that, sir! You don't believe it yourself. Nor do I. Nobody does. That course will be stiff with C.I.D. men, and if the race doesn't end in catastrophe . . .'

'At least,' Belfwig said, 'we can claim that we warned every-body . . .'

Harry glared at him in stupefaction. Then he exploded.

'This damned PEEPER . . . right to your head! You must be out of your mind! How many years have I been with you? A quarter of a century! And you go behind me to do this!'

'What are the latest odds?' Belfwig asked, calmly.

'Odds?' yelled Harry. 'Odds! The odds are that there is going to be the biggest turf scandal in years, with this newspaper in the thick of it, and my reputation gone for good. They'll have a punch packed for me at any future sporting event I attend!'

Belfwig got up and went out. He heard Harry shouting at him until the door closed. After that, he hurried from the building and walked . . anywhere. To get away from Harry and the telephones and the anxiety on the faces of the other sub-editors, and the atmosphere of extreme tension which hung in the air of his room. He drank cups of tea in snack bars. He had soup and two sandwiches and a cup of coffee in a crumby, cramped café, and a brandy in a sour bar, and hurried back to his office in the afternoon.

It was there, awaiting him: a murmur of excitement mingled with apprehension. It impacted with his body in which his heart thudded like a bell clanging in a fragile structure of mere paper. He thought of the hundreds of thousands who had backed 'Lord Punch' and won. They were lucky. So was PEEPER. But Success, this time, was a double-edged affair, cutting both ways.

Was it a misfortune? Had he gone too far with PEEPER? Harry was there to tell him. A pale Harry, this time. A shocked and despairing Harry.

'It isn't journalism! This blasted nine days' wonder! PEEPER. It doesn't make sense to me: a game like this.'

He got up disconsolately from the armchair.

'You'll get the letters of congratulation all right. They're the lucky ones . . . the people who staked on "Lord Punch." That'll be one side of the coin. The reverse side won't be so pleasant.'

'What have we to reproach ourselves with?' Belfwig exclaimed. 'It was pure coincidence . . .'

Harry walked slowly to the door. 'It's not the end of it,' he said. 'Don't imagine you're shot of it all. You'll see: to-night or to-morrow soon, it'll blow up. Then . . .'

Belfwig tried to concentrate his thoughts on his work. Alone in his room, he resumed his contact with affairs which he had neglected ever since he had reached his office in the late forenoon. He glanced swiftly at reports, notes, memorandum, proofs, telegrams. His head ached and throbbed. He rang for his secretary.

'You any aspirins?'

She smiled faintly and turned to go. 'I'll bring some.'

He sat back in his chair and closed his eyes. The dizzy heights! He panted and felt afraid. Up there, beside PEEPER, he felt frightened. Opening his eyes, he saw nothing but the familiar features of his room. But he knew that a presence was with him in that room. PEEPER.

It had a strange reality of its own. It was there, in its own form, intangible but real in some way which he sensed but could not describe in words. A Thing which had compelled him to commit a folly and endanger his own reputation and that of Harry. A large and potent presence, greater (as Ecks had said) than the newspaper which published him. It was a fact. It was an Idea firmly established in millions of minds. •

He got up so abruptly from his chair that he upset a vase of flowers on his desk. Some papers were swamped, and the blooms themselves lay scattered over the desk in the pool of water. He scarcely noticed what had happened. He rushed to the door.

There he checked himself. Reason, commonsense, dignity, made their appeal to him against that swift, overwhelming notion that his room was haunted. He opened the door and stood there and heard the building's noises and the sounds of the staff in the rooms and corridors. He glanced slowly over his shoulder and saw the spilled water gleaming on his desk, and the flowers lying with the overturned vase.

He was still there when his secretary returned with some aspirins and a cup of tea.

## TWENTY THREE

*

Riddle had gone into Soho that morning to commence an audit which had always afforded him a good deal of pleasure but which, on this particular morning, offered the same bleak prospect as did the rest of his work and his personal affairs.

He was unhappy; and in that sullen state of mind everything lost its lustre for him. He had left his parents' home with the determination to begin a new life for himself. He proposed to make more friends. In his flat, which he had been fortunate in renting from a friend who had recently gone abroad, he planned to occupy his leisure not only with all the pursuits which he had had no chance to extend at home, but with the gay company of other men of his own age and profession. His unhappiness sprang from disappointment when he discovered that despite all his attempts to forget Lenora, everything relating to her in his own life had followed him to this new home. She remained in his memory where her image was impressed too deeply for him to erase it. And in the silence of his flat, her subtle character in all its charm seemed defined to him by the quietude around him which took his impressions of her and gave them growth. She seemed then to await him there at the end of the day, and to exist somehow amidst the company of his friends when they visited him and filled the place with chatter and laughter. There was no real escape for him from her. He was forced to admit to himself that he was nothing more than a man in love. As such, his problems took precedence in his mind over everything else.

He had written to her. He had sent flowers to her. Also, he had enquired about Quentin. Only a brief note had come from her in reply. She was surprised that he had not called.

'Why have you stopped coming to see us?' she wrote.

Why, indeed? His idea of Lenora during those weeks was of a woman lost to him behind an intervening sensation. PEEPER. PEEPER was in the air. Riddle could not remember any event or sensation comparable to the magnitude of this present one which, instead of expiring after its peak of excitement, increased so that it went beyond the bounds of human experience into regions of hysteria where it sent its ripples across normal human life.

There were PEEPER Clubs throughout Europe and America. All the Clubs were affiliated with a central association. Against them, a prominent Archbishop had spoken severely, with the result that a petition signed by several thousands of people had been presented to the Home Secretary begging that personage to control the activities of the Clubs and prevent them from disrupting the nation's life. Several Members of Parliament who were actively associated with the PEEPER Clubs had addressed large meetings in their constituencies where processions of PEEPER Club members forming after the meetings had been attacked by hooligans. In the ensuing brawls, two men had lost their lives and some hundreds of major casualties had been taken to hospital. In other cities, mass demonstrations by PEEPER Club members had concluded in resolutions whereby the members pledged themselves to withhold all payment of Income Tax until a Select Committee, appointed

120

by the Government, had examined the entire System and suggested a reform. These were minor incidents compared to larger ones that were reported daily from other localities.

Throughout England, a rumour which asserted that PEEPER was a living personage had gained considerable emphasis, more particularly when it was declared as well that PEEPER was at present touring the Midlands. The fact that no denial of this ridiculous statement had been printed by the 'Daily Summariser' was accepted as a confirmation of the news. In consequence, PEEPER Clubs were inundated with invitations to PEEPER to appear at public and private functions. A Midland University had gone so far as to offer PEEPER an honorary degree. Directly resulting from these invitations, came reports of bogus PEEPERS appearing at City Halls, Clubs, Societies, where they lunched and dined as the guest of honour and received gifts and generous tokens of admiration. PEEPER, it appeared, had been the guest at private houses on no less than seventeen simultaneous occasions which were followed by seventeen robberies and seventeen sudden disappearances of the guest. Yet these distressing frauds, as well as the appearance at various Courts of Law of a dozen bogus PEEPERS who were convicted and fined and, in some cases, sent to prison, did not shatter the credulity of the public. Harmless private persons who walked through crowded streets and who in the least resembled that famous figure of the 'Daily Summariser' cartoon were enthusiastically mobbed, treated to incredible displays of admiration, and finally rescued only by the determined efforts of hundreds of police.

Several famous radio personalities, as well as four prominent publicists declared in statements to the Press that, in their opinion, PEEPER was a living personage. Only one famous personality of the present time offered an explanation of the sensation.

He remarked that if some hundreds of millions of people believed that PEEPER was real, then the miracle was accomplished and PEEPER existed. Because none of those millions could see, hear, and touch PEEPER, it could not be asserted that he was not in the flesh. How many of us had seen Hitler, or known somebody who had seen him? Very few of us. How many of us had seen PEEPER? According to reports, very few had seen the living man, although millions had seen a representation of him. He would be the last to deny that PEEPER was as real to those who gazed daily on the drawings of him as he was to those who had seen him in the flesh. . . . And so on.

At once, several Bishops together with some Dignitaries of other

Churches, had taken grave exception to this remarkable statement and wished for the author of it to be prosecuted under an old law laid against Heretics. It happened that on the morning on which the curious explanation of PEEPER had been printed, news of an accident on an American railway appeared in a nearby column. An express train carrying some three hundred members of an American PEEPER Guild on a visit to another city in which they proposed to meet their brethren of yet another PEEPER Guild, had come into collision with another express. All the Guild members had been killed or seriously injured. The Dignitaries of the Churches drew particular attention to this shocking tragedy, and begged Guild and Club members everywhere to let their thoughts dwell upon it.

Riddle heard much of all these items of news and the subsequent controversy which grew around them. They not only depressed him but worried him. He could not ignore them. Was it from his unhappy heart with its uneasiness that there seemed to him to come something which was reflected in the most ordinary of his contacts with other people; or was there a mysterious spirit persisting everywhere and subtly colouring all human affairs so that irritability and stress were liable to leap from expression so readily, so sharply? Was the whole human race moving in one direction, suddenly, with this fantastic figure of PEEPER as a kind of symbol of itself?

The very odour of excitement was in the air. To taste it on one's lip was to feel at once that strange intoxication which carried the sanest minds into extraordinary regions whither he himself, along with the majority of his friends, might have gone but for his preoccupation with his personal problems. PEEPER to him was a Thing, a cloudy fact that involved his friend, Lenora. He resisted it with all the forces of his mind and spirit, although daily the Thing increased in significance and extended its hold upon Lenora in his imagination.

He saw her as someone completely lost to him and yet nearby and within reach. She was behind a curtain of fame and wealth, in another world from which PEEPER had come.

Riddle was glad that he had with him as assistant a young, loquacious articled pupil whose cheerful company took the edge off his depressed spirits and afforded him an opportunity to think of other matters than his own gnawing anxieties.

Tifleigh was his name. He was seventeen. The world for him was represented by several makes of motor cars, some film stars, some racehorses and almost all pretty women of his own age. But he listened attentively to Riddle who explained some features of this audit to him when the two of them were seated in that little front room above the café in Soho. And Tifleigh was amazed by the wealth and success of this client who owned other cafés, and many supper bars, snack bars, oyster bars and public houses in various parts of London. He liked Georgie, Senior, at a glance, for that stout little Maltese with his olive skin and dark hair and handsome eyes and florid style had an innocent, friendly manner. And when Georgie, Senior, departed and his son, the young Georgie, appeared, Tifleigh felt as though the wealth of the old man was visibly denoted by his handsome son who shook hands with him and displayed some interest in him.

'New on the job?' he asked, feet apart, back to the fireplace, hands in trousers' pockets of exquisite new suit.

Tifleigh said that he was articled to the senior partner, whereupon Georgie rather pompously explained to him what a splendid profession he had entered and what a lot he could learn if he conducted himself properly. Georgie, lately a young sergeant, and still almost full of some puffy self-importance from his brief authority, enjoyed this chance to articulate very slyly his own remarkable position as the son and heir of a very wealthy man.

'As I said before, you're in a fair way to being on the road to success if you keep your eyes open, your tongue still and your shoes polished and a civil tongue in your head. Mr. Riddle will bear me out in that.'

Mr. Riddle did nothing of the sort. Instead of bearing Georgie out, he asked him a question relevant to the Stock Sheets of which he was expected to know something, but of which he knew nothing although he pretended to know everything. After a word or two, Georgie realized that Riddle expected him to deliver the Stock Sheets for the audit. He turned to go. In order to leave behind him some impressive recollection of himself, he again addressed Tifleigh and asked him if he ever fancied the starters.

Tifleigh named several but omitted "Lord Punch." Georgie smiled thinly and looked down at his brown shoes and walked slowly to the door.

'Speaking for myself . . . if ever I thought about placing a bet . . . which I don't . . . I might . . . might favour "Lord Punch," ' he said.

Tifleigh and Riddle exchanged glances. Tifleigh smiled.

Later that morning, Georgie came again and idled in the room and was pompous and inquisitive.

'How have we made out this year, Mr. Riddle?'

Mr. Riddle said that he had not yet prepared his Trial Balance and therefore could not say. Georgie asked other questions. How have we done with the supper bars, and how did we work out with the snack counters? He gave the impression of a forward, calculating spirit covered with a garment of impudent vanity through which there gleamed an unhealthy nature. But he was cheerful and generous as he offered coffee, cigarettes, cigars, and appeared with them just after an excellent lunch had been served to his visitors. When he departed Tifleigh smiled again at Riddle.

'What does he do?'

'Runs the little café near the River, near . . .'

'And what else?'

Before Riddle had time to reply, Tifleigh unfolded his copy of the 'Daily Summariser.'

'See what PEEPER said this morning? And young Georgie said the same. "Lord Punch"!'

'Come on!' Riddle said, crisply. 'Get your nose into that ledger!'

'But they both said . . .'

A glance from Riddle quenched him. A little later, the tedium of the afternoon was relieved for Tifleigh by the arrival of old Georgie who, asking no questions and making no boastful remarks, sat quietly and with an air of comfort and dignity, in the armchair, saying that it was a nice day but that life was difficult. He appeared to find a fascination in Riddle's absorbed presence at the table near the window; and for a long time he sat there, resting after the luncheon activity. At four, he left them and went down to order tea for them which was served by his prettiest waitress. He followed her up and remained to drink a cup of tea with his auditors.

The door was ajar, and from below there came the sounds of the café. An Italian waiter was softly singing. The girls were chattering in the kitchen to the accompaniment of rattling cutlery and a slamming door. A telephone rang. Old Georgie bent his head over his cup, so that Riddle saw the crisp hair flecked with grey.

And Riddle was pondering the hair and the stout neck and old Georgie's character when the head suddenly lifted and revealed the complacent face transformed and stiff with horror as the shuddering contralto scream began from below and drove itself to a piercing yell. It ended suddenly. Somebody was moaning.

The old man—and he had never seemed so paternal, so gentle and wise, and so lovable to Riddle—leaned forward and put his cup on the table. His fat, white hand trembled slightly. His breath suspired in a tremulous sigh as he rose.

'My Maria . . . my Maria . . .' he whispered, poignantly and tenderly. And he was already padding out of the room and down the stairs when she shrieked for him.

'Giorgio! Giorgio!'

An extremity of grief was in those two words. Riddle sensed it. A door slammed. The voices from the kitchen rose to a shrill jabber, and a voice called frantically up the winding stairs:

'Signor . . . mister!'

A chorus of horror joined below. Some crockery fell to a stone floor, and incoherent shouts sounded. And suddenly . . . prayers . . . intoned and then broken off . . . and sobs.

Riddle got up and went to the head of the stairs. Tifleigh followed him.

'What is it, Mr. Riddle?'

'Don't know. You go back. I think I'd better go down.'

Riddle went slowly down and joined a shuddering little group of kitchen hands, boys, waiters, and two customers standing in the passage outside the office. He asked no questions. His whole presence was a solemn expression of interrogation which, presently, the Head Waiter answered.

'Is young Giorgio . . . is shot dead in a taxi. Our young Giorgio . . . and the driver too . . . shot . . . two men fired . . .'

'Killed?' Riddle blurted, softly. 'What for? Where?'

Carried from his usual discreet reserve, the Head Waiter told him, hotly, with gesticulations, while the swarm of employees nearby jabbered and prayed, wept and trembled.

'Was with the gang . . . was mixed up . . . some fellows perhaps, some fellows from the gang . . . always trouble always . . .'

Much more might have been elicited from him had not the door opened and old Giorgio appeared. Behind him in the room, Riddle caught a glimpse of Maria sprawled face downwards on the solid little settee beneath the lamp standard and before the dark-papered old walls with their faded scrolls and roses and the numerous prints and photographs. A heavy, lax body in black, with her hair fallen loose from its high coiffure to her emerald shawl, and the rings flashing on one twitching hand, and a great expanse of white thigh where her skirt was dragged awry. All lax and motionless.

'Please . . .' old Giorgio was panting, his jaw trembling, 'please, somebody, bring a doctor, quick!'

He turned and padded back into the room. The door closed after him. The Head Waiter had gone to the telephone. Riddle turned away and went upstairs.

Tifleigh was standing at the head of the stairs waiting for him.

'Was it really? Was it young Georgie, was it?'

'Shot . . . and the taxi-driver as well,' Riddle said.

'Where? Have the police . . .'

Riddle looked up at the pale face and shook his head.

'Hand me those papers. Pack up,' Riddle said.

They put away their papers in the brief-cases and went down with the keys to the Head Waiter.

'Tell him,' Riddle said, nodding towards the closed door. 'You won' forget, will you? Say we're very sorry to hear it.'

He could hear Maria moaning and old Georgie murmuring to her. The sounds were still in his ears when he came out into Soho which was full of the sound of traffic and passing pedestrians. Life was so extensive, so indifferent to the personal tragedy which, as he saw a moment later, was nothing but a small column in a newspaper, or a cry on the lips of the old woman perched on her box and selling newspapers.

'LATEST KEMPTON WINNERS!'

It had no relation to what had happened in some quiet side-street earlier that afternoon, or to Maria and old Giorgio, until Tifleigh with a copy of the newspaper wide open in his hands nudged him.

'It says . . . "Lord Punch" . . . it says! First!'

Then it had some sombre, horrid affinity with those other events and to PEEPER as well; and, horribly, to Lenora.

'It says . . .' Tifleigh was still saying, was still trying to tell him.

'Put it away,' he said. 'And don't talk about it!'

With Tifleigh beside him he walked rapidly through a Soho which was possessed by tragic news and by a new, weird light that was not quite the soft sunlight slanting wherever it could into those streets. It belonged to the peculiar note which he imagined he heard in the air and which might have been the buzz of excitement about PEEPER'S correct forecast, or young Georgie's and the taximan's death from bullets, or something else.

He remembered Lenora, for always at the end of his day's work his thoughts swiftly reverted to her. He recalled his last visit to her: an

126

he kiss, and the life which he had tasted on her lips . . . the life of her spirit, and her world in its mystery which was now heightened and more distant than before.

Nevertheless, as he dismissed Tifleigh and was left alone to wait for his 'bus, he heard again the chatter about PEEPER. It did not trouble him as much as before. It was everywhere. It was no longer a Topic, a Thing to be discussed. It belonged to the air which all breathed. It was an Idea in all minds.

And suddenly, he felt happier. There was no longer a gulf between Lenora and himself. She belonged to the world which had taken PEEPER to itself and which believed in him. He could visit her at any time. He could believe that there was no longer a mystery.

Soon there would be nothing but PEEPER dominant everywhere.

*Part Two*

# ON THE BRINK

★

# ONE

★

The Bessings made no rules for their acquaintances, demanded nothing, expected nothing. Those who wished might come often, or infrequently, and find at last a friendship which had passively awaited them.

There were numerous acquaintances consisting of young and old artists and their friends, some writers, some young poets of both sexes, and the usual crowd who passed from scene to scene in mass migration. Of friends and acquaintances there were three only who had found in the Bessing trinity a flavour of enchantment. Riddle was one of them. Matthew, and his wife Kitty, were the others.

The Bessings had always accepted people on their own valuation of themselves when, like Riddle, Kitty, and Matthew, they approached and sought friendship. It was not from charity, or faith, or condescension. It was from love.

To see Matthew, to listen to him and try to understand him, might have exasperated formal minds and less tolerant spirits. The Bessings enjoyed him. They were unassailable, and they relished the spectacle of assaults upon their senses, their intellects, their tolerance and credulity. Matthew might believe them to be supreme egoists, indifferent at some point in themselves to all other persons, lodged in some quaint estimation of themselves, and unperturbed by criticism; yet he loved them for the grace of their tolerance of his egoism which, unlike theirs, had never truly discovered apt expression or found some acknowledgment of its gifts.

He was gifted. He knew it. Others knew it. His brilliance was exciting, although it did not compose his character or temperament in satisfaction. He sought for so much. And the measure of his success was not in himself, but, as he tacitly admitted, in his material condition. The fact was revealed in his life; and he really did not believe that he had achieved anything at all remarkable. This belief was revealed to others who accepted it from him and consequently never conceded that he was anything but a failure.

He had written three witty but sullen novels, as well as two plays that were as clever as the novels, and as sombre and sardonic. His poems had been published in a slender volume. His film criticisms

131

appeared weekly and were formidably incisive. His weekly dramatic criticism in the form of two critiques was flavoured with a salty scorn. But as a literary critic he was witty and boisterous, bringing off his epigrams with a shout which rolled through literary circles and came back to him in a giggle from his own lips. He could afford to do that because he had no faith in the novel. It was finished, he declared, used up, dead; by which he probably meant that after his third novel he himself, having no more ideas as a novelist, was finished, used up, and almost dead. The pity was that he had never conceived a comedy. It would have relieved a tragic world, and himself.

He was forty-one, and had been charmed by his own cleverness since his schooldays when he had been a quick, rather sardonic boy at the top of an obscure prep. school. The one really brilliant pupil in that absurd little society. The fact had moulded his mind. Thereafter, the world for him was like a vast prep. school wherein he selected a tiny corner which he could dominate.

Small, tubby, sulky-faced, shy, with a ready smile which was always charming because it represented him more truly than did his morose expression, he knew that his work failed because it conveyed only one aspect of him. It had been easy for him to be cruel, spiteful and devastatingly witty at the expense of others. But that was not what he wanted to do. He longed to be gracious, generous, encouraging, for he really was kind and generous and gracious. He wanted a chance to show everybody the truth of himself.

Only recently had he discovered that what he lacked was an apt subject which would release his authentic self. He had considered the novel, drama, poetry, the film, even painting. Nothing in them engaged him for longer than a year, after which he was returned to himself. He became restless and impatient. He was forty-one, and unfulfilled; and it was intolerable to think that he was not to have his chance. He blamed his failure upon the chaos and transient nature of modern life, only to become bitterly scornful of the novelists and playwrights and film directors who were inspired by that very condition of life. After that, he sulked and was almost in tears when the people whose work he had attacked did not respond to the fits of generosity and kindliness that always followed his harsh outbursts.

Kitty, who was thirty-three and quiet and self-effacing, was a mere adjunct to the edifice of his personality. At a glance she appeared complacent and happy. It was impossible to discover whether she lacked personality or deliberately refused to make herself apparent

Many people felt that she was a strong character, resourceful and confident; but she never confirmed this impression. Loyalty was, perhaps, her greatest virtue. Or, with her complacency and detachment, was she all the time rendering a comparison between her husband and herself and thus presenting him to the world for what he was?

At the Bessings' home, Matthew was happy. He was vivacious. He gave the impression that he understood that trinity and approved it. He admired Quentin and deferred to his ideas. He loved Lenora, and appreciated John's talents. Compared to him, Kitty was silent and devoid of ideas.

Suddenly, she emerged from that habit of silence and complacency and declared herself in an action which was so emphatic that Matthew scarcely recognized her. Standing at the door of his study, and holding in her hands a copy of his first long article on the PEEPER phenomenon, she waited until he looked up from his work.

'I don't like this,' she said, positively.

It was the first time she had disapproved of his work in any form or subject. Always, before, she had given a brief praise which he had accepted as though it were a caress.

He was startled. She looked so grave, so determined, that he hardly knew her in this mood. She appeared to have stepped back from his life. He felt suddenly quite alone with himself and everything of his egoism which her silence and complacency had encouraged for so long in him. The coolness with which he met her remark was more from a sudden fright than from patience.

'Why not?' he said.

The article was the first of a series proposed to him by an editor and intended to examine critically the whole PEEPER topic.

Kitty quoted a sentence and, looking up at him as she approached his desk, she added:

'You say that the enthusiasm for PEEPER is hysterical.'

'Well, isn't it?' he exclaimed. 'Haven't we seen that ourselves? Don't we know that the whole thing is nonsense?'

She put down the paper on his desk.

'What are you attempting to do in this series?' she said.

He was angry with her, but he controlled himself.

'To debunk the whole thing!' he said. 'To lay it wide open and expose it all . . . all of it . . . the entire ridiculous . . .'

'Why?'

'Because the thing conflicts with commonsense!' he said. 'Because it's a menace to . . . to any number of excellent, necessary features of life!'

'Are you sure?' she said.

'If I weren't, I wouldn't have accepted the commission!'

She looked at the article. 'You've been so . . . spiteful! Why couldn't you have attempted to explain PEEPER?'

For a moment, his anger took him. 'Because I'm opposed to him! This generation is full of little PEEPERs! The popular enthusiasms are lavished on too many effete characters! We require new standards. I want to destroy PEEPER!' Then he paused. He laughed.

'What else could I do?' he asked. 'Did you imagine I was going to applaud him? Think of him! What we need is sanity, restraint. Not this irresponsible . . .'

'You are confusing PEEPER with the people who love him,' she said. 'You are jealous of him. There is good sense in him, and a purpose. That's why he is loved so much.'

He guffawed. 'Good sense? Love? As if the mob cares about good sense! As if they are able to discriminate!'

She interrupted him. 'Do you know who originated PEEPER?'

He answered sharply: 'A cartoonist . . . some wretched man . . . one of your mediocre minds with an eye to popularity. That's what goes nowadays. Some fifth-rate intellect . . .'

She said quietly: 'It was John Bessing. See for yourself.' And opening a copy of the 'Daily Summariser' she showed him a cartoon.

'Jayby,' she said. 'John Bessing.'

His gaze swung up to hers with its question. He had no need to state it. She said:

'I met Lenora and asked her.'

He sat back in his chair. 'Well, I didn't know . . .'

'And another thing,' Kitty said. 'Quentin is seriously ill with pneumonia.'

She turned and left him. He looked at the article and at the first chapters of a new book which he was writing. And it was as though she had ripped the pages and thrown them aside. His series of articles was in the form of an attack. Oh, he had found at last an apt subject. He was the enemy of the commonplace excitements! The day after PEEPER's first appearance, when he had sensed that PEEPER had come to stay, he had hurried home and planned the chapters of a book. That work would carry him to the sort of position which he had always desired. The sensation which was current and which was rapidly

134

ncreasing awaited its critic. He was that critic. He was prepared for he task. Every feature of his character and intellect was suited to it; and he had a belief in himself which he had never experienced pre-viously. He was the only critic of PEEPER; the first to raise his voice against the madness of the applause and the gathering momentum of a chaos which nothing could check. Somebody had to say something. The whole wild business had to be examined and explained. Cause and effect must be studied dispassionately. It was essential that a sound critic should stand aloof from the contemporary scene with its hurri-canes of trite nonsense that caught and held the public fancy to the exclusion of what was good.

That was what he had planned for himself. He had not told Kitty. His intention had been to show her the completed manuscript of that book. He was going to labour at it and complete a rough draft within a couple of months.

But not now. The whole plan was ruined. He dared not aim his criticism at a friend's work. Nor could he deny his admiration for the Bessing trinity by decrying what John was doing, or by destroying John's opportunity. Despite the idea of him as a remorseless, vindictive mind, which his acquaintances had, he was loyal to his friends.

He should have been told. . . . Kitty need not have waited until this moment. But had she waited? Wasn't it true that she herself had only recently discovered who Jayby was?

But Kitty . . . How strange had been that moment when the strength of her character had suddenly declared itself. That instant when he had felt himself to be quite alone still hurt him and frightened him. Was he alone? Hadn't he always been alone? Despite his marriage to her, and the way in which she appeared to allow him to decide and appoint everything of their lives, wasn't she actually detached, living her own life?

And love? The two of them had long ago expressed it all. All that there had been to express. And, similarly, they had said everything that there was to say. They understood each other, he supposed. But he realized that he did not understand Kitty, until this present moment when her character was clear in all its strength. He knew nothing of her. Her thoughts, her ideas, her hopes, were all concealed from him. Who was she, this woman who certainly understood him, and who, in the past, had seemed to him to be unimaginative, placid, dilatory?

He appreciated her nature now that she had brought him this far. She had encouraged him in his egoism, and brought him to this juncture and turned back to pursue her own course, leaving him cheated of his

135

task which was the only one that ever had or ever could engage the whole of him.

That was Kitty whom he had always imagined to be mild and pliant and dependent upon him. He pondered her, not denying to himself that the sense of being alone, although terrifying him at first, was oddly pleasant, for no longer need he accept the little burdens of responsibility which were hers as well as his. He relished a slight feeling of freedom which disappeared when he asked himself what Kitty intended to do now. For obviously this was final, this cleavage. Her manner declared that much to him.

Suspicion, from its absurd seed, rapidly increased in him. For Kitty to come to him and give him that news of John Bessing's venture. . . His thoughts flared. He remembered incidents which had occurred during visits to the Bessings. He had smiled at them, been a little flattered by them, and even amused himself by taxing Kitty about her interest in John Bessing.

That had been one way of accepting a fact. He could not feel so lightly about it now. It was all so much larger now. Previously, it had been flattering to him that another man should admire his wife who was pretty and gentle and so many other things. What transpired now was that Kitty was in love with that man.

That was disturbing and humiliating, particularly after her remarks that had shoved him to a brink and there left him. But he was determined not to behave rashly or foolishly. He wanted to consider every relevant feature before deciding his next step. All at once he laughed loudly. He got up and hurried to find Kitty in the flat, for he had remembered Riddle.


# TWO

★

To consider Riddle was to appreciate at once how compact was the Bessing trinity and how hopeless was the position of Riddle who loved Lenora and who obviously wished to entice her from the trinity. And to study Riddle in that predicament was to realize Kitty's position which was probably akin to that of Riddle.

At first, Matthew was amused. Now he could sit back and await developments! Now there was no need for him to decide what he must do. He returned to his desk with the resolve not to say another word to Kitty about his articles on the subject of PEEPER and certainly not to broach the subject of John Bessing and herself.

He felt a slight disquiet. He didn't want Kitty to suffer as Riddle did. That was certain. Yet what could he do? Nothing had been said to him. He was not expected to understand that his wife was in love with Bessing. As yet, she had stated only the fact that PEEPER was John Bessing's creation, and another that Quentin was ill.

His disquiet increased. He wanted to act wisely not only with regard to Kitty and John but also about his series of articles concerning PEEPER. His resolve not to act disloyally to his friends by criticising PEEPER, dwindled slightly when he considered Bessing in relation to Kitty.

He could not decide what to do. There were too many conflicting arguments claiming his thoughts, and too many opposing loyalties causing him to waver. He did not wish to resign his work on PEEPER, yet he hesitated to hurt the Bessings. At the same time, he was resolved not to let John cause Kitty the kind of suffering which Riddle seemed to endure.

Matthew at that moment was sadly involved in hypothetical problems which a less egotistical mind would have disregarded or never admitted to consideration. But they were rooted in him, because his character and temperament were the especial soil on which they flourished. And suddenly, he was determined to settle them with Kitty.

He knew that this was a clumsy resolve and that he might only make a fool of himself. Therefore, he hesitated again. He was afraid of the result, really very much afraid of discovering that all these ridiculous suspicions and ideas had a basis in truth, and that after a few hot words with Kitty he would be much worse off than at present.

He could hear her moving somewhere in the flat. A door was opened, and her footsteps sounded in the hall. Then the kitchen door was closed softly. He heard the mumble of the one o'clock news.

That was typical of Kitty. To close doors behind her until she was shut away from him in this flat in a little interior of her own. As though she liked being enclosed, separate! Even in the height of summer, when London lay under a stiff pall of heat, she carefully closed all the doors—one after another—until she was at that distance. He knew why it was. He could interpret it accurately now!

It was to put barriers between herself and him, and to create of the short distance which lay between them in this flat a region with obstacles which would exclude him from her company. That, and her silence . . .

E*

137

She enjoyed silence. He had known that for years and had often been exasperated by her habit of lapsing into hours of taciturnity from which she granted him only an occasional mumble. He knew why that was. The two of them had discussed everything to a conclusion in the depths of their personalities. Almost everything which interested them was long ago pursued to an ultimate bedrock where Kitty suddenly turned and retreated into silence. She rejected his ideas that were forward and keen. That was her mode of life. To retreat into herself and seldom to venture out.

What did she intend by it? To isolate him, so that he might destroy himself in the illimitable depths of his egoism? He was an egoist. He admitted it. He was proud of the way in which he had developed. Fundamentally, most persons were egoists, but only the honest spirits and the most courageous were not afraid of being what they were. He was not afraid. But she . . .

She shut herself away from him, behind doors and relished a little world of her own which she would not share with him. Why? He wanted to find that answer. What especial fault in him . . . What impassable condition of his character . . .

He got up from his desk again. And once more he wavered. If he were to go to her now and discuss all this with her, would that be weakness? Would it afford her an opportunity to push him a little nearer to the brink of his egoism? Better to remain here! Better to close his mind to suspicion, fear, doubts, all of which had so many paths that it was impossible to choose the right one. That was the trouble. To find the correct way. Better, therefore, to cast the problems from his mind, for everything occurred in the mind, and merely by remaining silent and by not disclosing one's thoughts, the gravest problems could be resolved, the most acute disagreements erased.

Better to keep silent and not to bring it all into the reality of their life. He sat down again, feeling exhausted, and with a pulse as rapid as that of physical exertion.

He turned again to the sheet of paper before him, and lifting his pen he resumed his work. There was so much to say about PEEPER, and so much to interpret. He wrote swiftly, for his style had always been flexible and responsive to his thoughts. And for the first time he had a subject worthy of his prose.

It was only when Kitty tapped on the door and called him to lunch that his predicament recurred to him. All that work, to remain unpublished if he wished to remain loyal to his friends, the Bessings!

138

# THREE

★

He was so accustomed to sitting down to meals in silence with Kitty that it gave him no embarrassment to enter the room and take his place at the table and meet her absorbed, detached air. Usually, he read his letters, or read newspapers throughout the meal, or listened to the radio. To-day, he unfolded the *Manchester Guardian*.

When he had made notes for his book about PEEPER, he had anticipated the development of that feature into certain predictable channels of popular sensationalism, and had planned his work to embrace the possibility of PEEPER's popularity extending to other continents. He had gone further than that, and had examined PEEPER from horizons which, as yet, were either indifferent to that creature or impervious to current sensations. His vision had been comprehensive and logical, for he supposed that PEEPER was bound by some fundamentally logical condition of the human mind which applauded him. His end, he had not attempted to prophesy. But he imagined that it would be similar to that of other favourites of human enthusiasm. Throughout the book, he had decided to examine PEEPER as a Topic relative to human beings.

A first glance at the sober columns of the *Manchester Guardian* convinced him that PEEPER could not be related to anything but the most elemental aspects of human nature; and it was with a shock that he realized how much in error he had been to examine this phenomenon on any other plane but that of the crude, the primeval, and of all the curious impulses that still lingered from a distant past in the human spirit

Some remarkable items of news were reported, and editorial comment inferred that PEEPER might prove to be a curse as well as a blessing, and went on to suggest that popularity seemed to have become a gift within the power of so many people that it should be given with less generosity, just in case it might be required for a greater personage than PEEPER. Which raised at once some controversy.

Something more than controversy had occurred already. In certain territories of South Africa, the black population had embraced PEEPER with idolatrous enthusiasm. So had the negro population of the Southern States of America, thus placing the other devotees of PEEPER—

139

particularly those who were members of the various PEEPER Guilds—in a difficult position. In South Africa, the offices of newspapers publishing PEEPER cartoons had been wrecked by bands of white youths. But the reaction of the negro population in America's Southern States to PEEPER had, so far, only caused a vast ripple of laughter to travel across the entire United States which eagerly awaited the next move of the discomfited PEEPER Guild members. Except in one small township where the entire population had gone into a neighbouring desert where, led by a fervent young minister of religion, it had feasted, danced, sung hymns, and awaited the miraculous advent of PEEPER from a sacred rock. Far from quenching the ardour of these folks, PEEPER's failure to materialize had only excited it still more. The young minister warned his flock that it had evidently been judged to be unworthy; whereupon a frenzy of religious zeal had followed, with a campaign of repentance and penance in full swing.

Matthew could explain such manifestations by attributing them to spiritual boredom with a life which was devoid of movement or interest beyond a restricted area. In the next moment, his explanation was forcefully derided by a report from the English Midlands which remarked that a crowd estimated to be ten thousand strong had gathered at the principal railway station in a large city and had there awaited the arrival of PEEPER. In spite of repeated assurances from the station loud speaker which declared that there was no truth in the rumoured journey of PEEPER, the crowd had remained, had swelled, and had eventually stormed the platform and invaded the London express where it proceeded to rip open the upholstery in the compartments and tear down the doors of communication coaches. Reinforcements of police dispelled this throng which gathered again at a distance and waited throughout the following night. Elsewhere in England, similar gatherings occurred. At a large engineering works in another city, the entire personnel had downed tools and swarmed into a neighbouring park where PEEPER was reported to be asleep on a bench in the sunlight.

On the previous evening, a speaker in a public hall in Sheffield had been dragged from the platform and chased from the building by hundreds of irate women who had taken offence at his disapproval of PEEPER; whereas in Liverpool, a meeting held by several visiting clergymen and some Members of Parliament from other parts of England, to protest against PEEPER, had passed off quite peaceably, probably because nobody except its promoters had attended it.

In another city, an amazing stoppage of work had occurred when an individual purporting to be PEEPER had driven through the main thoroughfare in an open carriage drawn by a white mare. Staffs of shops, offices, hotels had left their work. Tramcars and 'buses were deserted. Employees at the gas and electricity works had swept out with the rest, on the hurricane of excitement which had blown through that little city. A newspaper correspondent, writing of the affair, remarked that a scene of festival of such joyous, spontaneous humour had followed, rendering all former occasions of public celebration trivial and lifeless by comparison. One felt, he said, that an oppressive burden which could not be described but which had always weighed heavily upon the mind, was suddenly and miraculously lifted, and that the spirit was released to enjoy for the first time the mere fact of life itself. People laughed for no other reason than that the sun was brilliant, the air temperate, the earth and its growths suddenly new and beautiful to the sight. Others declared that PEEPER would unite the peoples of the world and end for ever the stupid, arbitrary rule of men who had only forced nations into wars with one another. This statement had been repeated to the multitude by other voices. An enormous burst of applause greeted it. The same correspondent remarked that an authentic new spirit was alive amongst the throng. Whether it was a belief in the advent of somebody who would change the whole conception of human existence, or whether it was just a sudden impulse to reject the heavy burdens of modern life: taxation; the stress resulting from the stupid bitter disputes between conflicting international groups; the strikes everywhere; the false crises and alarmist nonsense daily puffed out by newspapers: it was difficult to tell, but the barriers were swept away and people of all classes united in gaiety. That night, almost the entire population of the city trekked to the neighbouring hills to light bon-fires, sing, dance, watch the winking bonfires on distant hills, and to begin from that point a great chain of signal fires that stretched to the far north and the extreme south. At the same time, groups of enthusiasts who had carried materials to the hills erected durable shrines, while people danced around them in the light of the bonfires' flames and the softer light of many stars in a clear firmament. People had discovered a new consciousness in themselves.

The same correspondent concluded his report by asserting that it was like the inception of a new era, a new civilization which vigorously rejected the old with its mistakes, its crimes, its evils and follies. It was not just a night's excitement. Upon resuming work next morning, a spirit of determination to continue in that new consciousness was current everywhere in that city. Committees were formed. Meetings were arranged. Only Authority was perturbed and apprehensive of the outcome.

Matthew read it swiftly, all of it, and looked up at Kitty. Nothing of his personal problems remained in his mind.

'This . . . !' he exclaimed, pointing to the newspaper.

His extraordinary expression startled her.

'About the city which went on a festival for PEEPER!' he exclaimed.

She shook her head.

'Listen . . .'

He read it to her, swiftly, and then laughed across the table while she sat there feeling curiously cold in herself.

'Do you realize what that is?' he was saying. 'Do you? That's not hysterical! That's not your commonplace enthusiasm! Nothing like that. It's a pagan instinct! Atavism . . . that's what it is. A terrific mood of . . .'

Kitty said: 'There was something on the one o'clock news. Something . . .'

'What was it? What did they say?'

'I didn't pay much attention,' she said. 'Something about a Bishop protesting . . .'

'Against what?'

Invariably slow in response, she was tardy in her answer. She took up her knife and fork.

'Don't let your lunch get cold,' she murmured.

He laughed. 'Good heavens, lunch! Don't you realize, Kitty? Don't you understand what's happening . . .'

She smiled at his excitement. He liked that. He loved her pretty face with its brown eyes suddenly smiling at him as though she were amused by his eagerness.

'Go on! It's so silly,' she said. 'All the fuss. Besides, you shouldn't be the one to add to it. I thought . . .'

A ripple of gentle malice hovered on her lips and then disappeared and gave place to an expression of anxiety.

'Did you?' he exclaimed, sardonically, and then checked himself and added quietly:

'I was wrong about PEEPER, Kitty. I admit it.'

His ideas had undergone a complete transformation. Now he believed in PEEPER. He realized what he was. He saw Quentin in him at last, and caught something of Quentin's mysticism. He was for him, as millions of devotees were for him.

'Don't you realize what it is, Kitty?' he said.

She slapped down her knife and fork and clasped her hands.

'It's . . . silly . . .' she gasped. 'That's all . . . silly!'

'It's inevitable,' he said, calmly.

Her retort to that alarmed him. She was so vehement and tense and angry. She half rose as she spoke.

'What is inevitable? What d'you mean?'

He knew that she was frightened, but he went on, trying to present it all to her with reason and calm.

'If millions of people suffer intense mental and physical strain for as long as they have done in this century, this is bound to be the result. That's what I mean. It's inevitable. There is a limit to human mental resistance, just as there is a limit to physical resistance, although no politician or statesman seems to think so. For ten years, this world has endured stress and horror. It still is. It's still a war of nerves, all over the world. Every politician knows it. But few of them realize that unless people are given a respite, and hope, the human mass mind is liable to go sick, just as any individual mind can suffer a breakdown from too heavy a stress. That's not nonsense. And this . . . this news . . . this is either the breakdown in full swing, or else the only retort which millions can make to the rulers who use them as slaves in the game of Power. That's my opinion. We're on the very edge . . .'

Kitty stumbled back from the table.

'No!'

He knew that she was terrified, but he had to go on.

'What else is it then? I tell you . . .'

She was standing in an attitude of extreme nervousness, some distance from the table.

'But . . . if it continues?' she exclaimed, tremulously.

Her terror touched him. From an idea in his mind, the truth became something in the air, in the events which he had just read aloud. He got up and stood at the window. Below, in the street, two women in slacks ran by. It was a tiny finishing touch in reality to his idea of a world in a ferment of excitement over the one thing which represented release. PEEPER. He saw for an instant the flushed, eager faces of those women and heard their chatter as it echoed up to him from a street which was usually full of pedestrian and vehicular traffic but which was now empty and silent.

'. . . said he was coming at two . . . so I said well I'm not going to miss that!'

He faced Kitty, saying: 'Who could stop it? It's in full swing . . .'

He flopped into an armchair.

'Think of it!' he said, quietly and slowly, while Kitty walked to the window and looked down. 'Two ghastly wars that spread over the whole world. Two! Within a quarter of a century! What do they think . . . the rulers, the whole gang of them . . . to do that? To take people that far . . . the peoples of the world, the millions who had no enmity towards one another! To make mistakes that resulted in that! People cannot endure any longer. They have had enough. They want peace and happiness. And to get it, Kitty, to get it they'll go to any lengths. They will. You'll see. They'll take anything that offers a chance. They've taken PEEPER!'

'Listen!' Kitty said, standing quite still in an attitude of concentration. 'What's that?'

Both were silent.

'Cheering . . . from somewhere . . .' she murmured.

The sound of it came faintly on the current of the south wind.

'A big crowd . . .'

Matthew went to the window and opened it wide. At once, the sound poured into the room. A car sped past in the street. Some children ran noisily along the pavement while the cheering sounded again, hoarsely, lustily, almost frenzied. He closed the window.

'Blast them!' he shouted. 'With their shifting party politics, and their rotten ideologies, and their cunning! To pile all that on us, and then talk about uniting the nations! Damn them, why don't they hide in shame and let the people talk to one another and find peace and happiness?'

He sat down and covered his face with his hands for an instant and then groped in his pockets for cigarettes and a lighter.

Looking at Kitty, he smiled thinly.

'I always said it was rotten,' he told her. 'A bad apple which would have to be cut down and thrown away. They clung to it, because they were afraid. They clung to tradition . . . that absurd old club along the Thames! That old box of pomp and words! As if . . .'

'Well, tell them,' Kitty said. 'It isn't too late, is it?'

He pointed to the window. 'Hark at that! A world that is slipping its cables and going right back to paganism to find what it must have. It wants Peace! It's got to find it somehow, and quickly!'

144

'Well, say so . . . tell them!' Kitty said. 'Write it. But write it quickly!'

'Words on paper,' he said, softly. 'As if that would help now. Why,' he said, laughing, 'even prayers wouldn't be of avail now. Nothing could cure those stupid men, all over the world. The people know that. They know it now, and they've renounced them. This is it, Kitty: the end of the rotten apple. Only one person and one thing can do any good now.'

She said uneasily: 'Who? Can't you do something . . . write something . . .'

He got up and took her by the arm and walked with her to the door.

'Quentin Bessing is the only person . . . Quentin or John . . . the only people who can help now. And PEEPER is the only thing.'

He opened the door and, releasing her arm, gently impelled her into the hall.

'Go and talk to them,' he said. 'Ask them . . .'

He went back to his study and sat down and tried to compose his mind for work. A few seconds later, he heard the flat door close and Kitty's footsteps pass down the stairs and out into the street. Then their faint sound ceased.

He looked at his notes and the few chapters which he had written and wondered what he could write.


# FOUR

★

Kitty travelled by 'bus and was faintly conscious of being hungry, although she was far more conscious of the fact that the habits of years were broken by that meal left untouched on the lunch table. But all that was immediately forgotten when she heard a passenger laugh loudly and show the conductor a copy of yesterday's 'Daily Summariser.'

'See? He gave it! Good 'nough for me. I never 'esitated. Picked up a clear 'undred and thirty quid! Just like that.'

The conductor gave him a glance and left him. Coming inside to collect fares, he laughed crisply.

'Some people think they're lucky. I don't call it luck.'

He took several fares.

'I call it a nightmare,' he went on, addressing the passengers, but looking out at the ruddy, robust man on the platform who cackled back at him and put his head into the 'bus.

'A nightmare! Then give me another, Charlie! I can take it!'

'You'd swallow poison for fivepence!' the conductor retorted. 'You would. You'd lap it up!'

An elderly gentleman looked up at the conductor over thick spectacles.

'Are you referring to PEEPER?' he said, loudly.

A lean woman in fashionable clothes spun round and looked at him.

'I've had enough of PEEPER to last me a lifetime,' she exclaimed, rising and making her way to the platform. 'I can't stand any more. I've had PEEPER day and night . . . my four sons . . .'

'Wait till the 'bus stops!' the conductor shouted.

She had jumped rashly. As the 'bus sped on, they saw her lying in the gutter.

'I told 'er!' the conductor exclaimed. 'Some people . . .'

The elderly gentleman tapped his arm. 'PEEPER, did you say? Did I hear you . . .'

The ruddy, robust passenger standing on the platform said:

'I tried, Jack . . . tried to stop her. She wouldn't 'ave it.'

The conductor leaned towards the elderly gentleman and pointed towards the platform.

'That's right. PEEPER. See that chap out there? Won over a hundred quid through PEEPER . . .'

'Really?' And the big head with its big hat swung round. 'Really? But I was going to ask you, conductor: have you ever studied "Revelations"?'

'Whose revelations? I like biography . . .'

'I am speaking about the Revelations of Saint John, the Divine . . .'

'Oh, that! Can't say that I have, mister.'

'Then you should. Everything is foretold there. You will find the whole thing . . .'

'That a fact?' the conductor said, hurrying out and winking to the passenger on the platform and then going upstairs.

'Oh, yes . . .'

'Nonsense!' somebody exclaimed. The other passengers smiled.

'No! I assure you . . . no! Let me just quote . . .'

The 'bus stopped and the conductor came rattling downstairs.

'Your stop, mister! If you want to get off here!'

The old man got up. 'I was just about to . . . to say . . .'

'Come on, sir! If you're getting off. This 'bus runs to a time-table!'

'Thank you, conductor. I only wanted to tell you . . . find it all revealed . . .'

'Mind the step, sir! You're not the first. If I've 'ad one, I've 'ad fifty. The seven angels, the Great Seals, the . . .'

He signalled the 'bus to proceed and then laughed shortly.

'Please don't blaspheme!'

He turned sharply to meet the tight little voice and the compact little face which confronted him with its anger and its fierce little courage.

'You never 'eard me blaspheme, ma'am! Not one word! Thing I never do!'

'I distinctly heard you scoff at . . .'

He turned to go upstairs. 'Pardon me, you never! If you was me and 'ad to stand 'ere and listen to what I've 'ad to listen to all day! A nightmare . . .'

The timid little woman, flushed, surprised at herself, spoke to Kitty who sat beside her.

'It's the only thing left to us. I don't like to hear . . .'

The small, gloved hands folded themselves on the handbag and she went on nervously:

'It's all so terrible. We ought to have faith, and hope.'

The 'bus turned into Knightsbridge.

'What is terrible?' Kitty said.

The plain, diminutive face, which looked as if it had been squeezed and compressed into a final shape by a lifetime of crises, presented its terror frankly.

'Haven't you seen the papers to-day?'

'I don't believe all I read in newspapers,' Kitty said.

'Oh, but it was on the one o'clock news! I heard it . . .'

It was the countenance of gullibility and panic itself. Her little blue eyes reflected nothing but their submission to every rumour and piece of rubbish blared out in headlines or breathed from a loudspeaker.

'I'm going up to St. Paul's. A lady in the next street to ours told us. She said that the Primate . . . or someone . . . was going to hold a service at three . . .'

'Evensong, that's all,' Kitty said.

'But it said on the one o'clock . . .'

'It said nothing of the sort!' Kitty asserted. 'I listened.'

'Oh, but this lady said it did! She wouldn't tell a lie! She said it's a special service for Divine aid and intercession.'

'What for? Intercession for what?'

'For what's happening. Haven't you heard? It was on the wireless . . .'

'A silly lot of nonsense,' Kitty said. 'A few people . . .'

'And the papers said, too. About PEEPER . . . about terrible things . . . about whole cities under . . . it said under a strange spell. The papers wouldn't say it if it wasn't true.'

Kitty laughed. 'It's rubbish! The newspapers print muck like that just to work you and thousands like you into a fever. They love to horrify you. They lie and distort incessantly. All except three or four. The rest . . .'

'This lady in the street next to ours wouldn't tell a lie! She said we must all go. It was our duty to the nation. And look! Look there!'

Ahead, at Hyde Park Corner, a solid mass of cars, 'buses, lorries, cycles, carts, filled the scene, with drivers moving through, gesticulating, shouting, laughing, resigned to it, cursing it, standing on running-boards, clambering on roofs of vehicles to peer ahead into the distance of Piccadilly where the tide was as black and as jammed as at the Corner.

A stout, nervous man sitting opposite Kitty sang out to the conductor.

'Back out! Tell your mate to. Go by another route. I want to get to St. Paul's!'

'So do I,' said the little woman.

'Doesn't look as though . . .' he exclaimed.

The conductor laughed briefly. 'Look behind you! Back out, you say!'

The roadway behind was full of oncoming traffic which slid tightly into place all across the road and remained there. And from it, as well as from ahead, there came one mad chorus of horns and klaxons and bells in a disharmony which was suddenly silent. Then the air of that spring day seemed to open at once to some unfamiliar quality of light which poured into it across the sunlight with a gentle, insidious motion that was new to the senses and which was remarked by the soft, southerly breeze that swept across that great black mass and the anxious faces. The trees echoed it all with their new foliage.

Kitty blinked. Was there some peculiar quality in the air, the sun-light, the blue sky above the grey stones of walls, houses, arches, and the sombre memorial? Was there this newness and freshness which the eye could not relate to any previous experience? Was there a light from some mysterious source?

Struggling with a sickness of panic, she turned to the woman beside her.

'It has nothing to do with . . . with silly headlines! It's a traffic jam, that's all!'

'Oh, no! They're all trying to get to St. Paul's!'

The conductor laughed, coming back from a parley with other conductors and their drivers.

'Take more than prayers to untie this tangle! Talk about a night-mare!'

'Listen!' Kitty said, emphatically, touching the woman's arm. 'Listen to me, please! Don't believe what you read in newspapers! Don't even talk about the rubbish. If you and all your neighbours stop talking about this thing, nothing more will happen. If you go on talking about it, it will go on happening and it will become worse. It all comes to this: if we believe . . .'

She groped for apt words with which to explain to that shallow mind and that vapid face what was happening.

'Don't let them herd you! Have a mind of your own! Think for yourself. And don't listen to what ladies in other streets tell you.'

'I'm not afraid!' the other asserted, perkily. 'I believe in the Faith.'

The other passengers had crowded the platform to besiege the imperturbable conductor.

'Don't ask me!' he said. 'You'd get there quicker if you was to walk.'

Only the stout, nervous passenger remained inside with Kitty and the little woman. He was slewed round in the seat, with his thick lower lip sagging, and his protuberant eyes looking like things that found no solace in the scene of frenzied commotion about the 'bus.

'I don't mind tellin' you, this scares me!'

His whine was like a cord stretched to breaking point.

'You ought to be ashamed,' Kitty said.

'Yes,' said her neighbour on the seat, 'you ought to find consolation in prayer instead of . . .'

The conductor came in and sat down, swinging his legs and removing his hat to wipe his perspiring forehead.

'Phew! This beats everything!'

'Do you think, conductor . . .'

He looked at the little face.

'Don't get no time to!'

'I was wondering how long . . . do you think . . . before we go on.'

'Might be five minutes. Might be an hour. Look at it! Where d'you want to get to?'

'St. Paul's.'

'If you walked, you might get there before this 'bus does.'

She pondered the reply, saying: 'It begins at three.'

'The service?'

'Yes'; and she went on, yes the service of Intercession. She wanted to be there in time. The lady in the next street had said. The papers said. The wireless said. He laughed.

'D'you ever sleep? Time you've done gobblin' up the news, and got your head out o' the loudspeaker and stopped listenin' to that lady! And this lot's the same.'

He indicated the traffic block.

'Listen to any sort o' tripe! Panic . . . look at 'em!'

He got up suddenly and joined a crowd of his mates. Kitty rose.

'It's a hoax,' she said. 'A silly . . .'

'Aren't you going to wait and come up to the service?'

'No!' Kitty said, vehemently. 'No! I believe in commonsense. Not this . . . not all this hysteria! God is Commonsense, and Patience and Calm. And all that is in you, if you want it. Not the rubbish you read and listen to all day long. The ability to think: that is God. Go home and tear up the nonsense you read and stop spreading rumours.'

She left the 'bus. But she too was afraid now. The great pulse of panic in the mass mind beat through her own heart as she edged through the traffic to the pavement and followed the crowd moving past the Corner and into Piccadilly. She saw what had happened.

Exodus had met influx at this point. Panic of two sorts had collided and intermingled, and would writhe there until Authority disentangled it, soothed it, and exorcised its fear.

Turning into Half Moon Street, she rang softly on the bell of Bessing House. A pale, dishevelled and almost shamefaced John Bessing admitted her.

'Kitty! How did you get here?'

His manner puzzled her. He had an extraordinary air of excitement and elation which he concealed so carelessly that it showed clearly. He knew it and smiled mischievously.

'I walked from the Corner,' she said. 'You know what's happening, don't you?'

He grinned like a boy caught in some mischief. But his extreme pallor indicated plainly what he was thinking.

'Well, I'm not responsible . . .' he blurted. Then he stopped. He was no longer smiling. His features were stiff with a kind of exasperation. He looked exhausted.

He said sullenly, slouching away across the room:

'If they enjoy that sort of thing, I can't stop them. It's not my fault if they let themselves be jerked into panic!'

Kitty indicated the patient's room. 'Quentin?' she said.

John sighed. 'He's had a relapse. There's very little hope.'

He offered Kitty a chair and sat down opposite her.

'John, is there anything . . . anything at all I could do?'

He shook his head. 'Nothing, Kitty, thanks. It's just a question of waiting.'

The house was hushed. The Street was hushed. The traffic jammed along Piccadilly was hushed as well. The whole of that part of the City was under a pall of silence which was deeper than that of night and which rendered the vivid spring afternoon mysterious and somehow threatening.

'Are you afraid, Kitty?' Bessing said, glancing at her.

'If it continues . . .'

She searched his features to find there the calm and grace of expression which had always evoked her admiration. He was transformed. Behind his tired eyes there was a harsh shadow eloquent only of some stubborn, almost sour aspect of mood which was inimical to his character and which seemed to her to be the source from which had come the panic, the chaos, the rumours.

'I want you to do something for me,' she said.

He would not have refused her anything had she asked for it a month ago. Now, he shook his head without even waiting to learn what she wanted of him.

'I know what you're going to ask me,' he said.

'Please!' she said.

He retorted irritably: 'I can't, Kitty! I never began this business . . . all this panic! I had nothing to do with it. If two or three newspapers try to fan things up to a gale, am I to blame? Let them end it!'

'You could make a statement,' she insisted.

'As if that would do any good!'

'It would,' she said. 'People would listen to you. The people in other cities. You know what's happening out there, don't you? Out in the provinces, and abroad . . .'

He covered his frowning face with his hands and sighed. When he removed his hands, she saw again the crumpled features in their stiff stress.

'I didn't originate PEEPER,' he said. 'You must have guessed that: you and Matthew. Quentin created him. He is Quentin. He was created to express his ideas. That's how he began. You can guess what happened when Quentin became ill.'

He leaned forward. 'Do you know what all this . . . this excitement everywhere is? It's an Idea which has escaped from its source in Quentin's mind! There it is, out in the world, loose. It's out of control. It's a Thing which anybody can have but which nobody can control. I can't guide it. I daren't even tell the truth.'

'You could, if you wished,' Kitty said.

He flared at her: 'How? How?'

He was distraught. She could scarcely recognize him. Or was it she who had changed? Was her heart cold, her senses numbed; and was her spirit presented with a reality which she could not understand? He was in a new guise. She, too, was transformed. The life of yesterday and last year, and all the years which had shaped John and herself, was dead with all its influences, ideas, and purposes. There was nothing in place of it except panic, fear, uncertainty, and the shrill enthusiasm for PEEPER.

'You could end PEEPER,' she said. 'Now! To-day. If you wanted to!'

'I can't,' he retorted, vehemently. 'I daren't. He belongs to Quentin. If I stop now, some kind of PEEPER will remain in the world. But if I return him to Quentin . . .'

'And if Quentin doesn't recover?' she asked, flatly.

'Then I can finish it all,' he said.

'And if Quentin recovers, will he be able to do anything? Will he recognize his PEEPER? Won't everything have gone too far for him to save it? Can't you do something to stop what's happening? You say something fresh every day. Why not make an appeal to good sense?'

He was slow to answer. Looking around her, Kitty saw the drawings littering the floor, the tables, and the broken stumps of charcoal lying amidst pencils, brushes, and palettes.

'Whatever harmless thing I say,' John told her, 'only carries them on. All they want is PEEPER. I don't understand it. The way they took to him, loved him. A figure in a cartoon! And the strange things that have happened. And the money . . .'

He laughed softly. 'I didn't tell you about that, did I? A few weeks ago, I hadn't a penny. To-day . . . thousands of pounds. I really don't know how much I do earn. It pours in. Day by day, some new offer from India, China, Australia, America, with lavish terms. Did you know that to millions of negroes and Indians, he's some kind of god. PEEPER! But the money . . . that's not what I wanted. I wanted to paint. Quentin wanted to relate the adventures of a Man, a soul, in this civilization. Someone from past centuries. An Idea . . .'

'Which has gone off its course,' Kitty said.

'The only good thing is that we've been able to buy a cottage in Hampshire, and a car. That's what I wanted. Somewhere to take Quentin, when he's convalescent. The rest . . . Riddle manages it all for me. You know Riddle, Lenora's friend?'

Kitty smiled. 'The accountant . . .'

'He and Lenora manage it all. I turned the whole financial side over to them.'

He stopped all at once. He looked like a prisoner.

'It's fantastic,' he murmured. 'Unreal . . .'

'If you had been in that traffic jam just now, you wouldn't say that it was unreal. You should recognize it all for what it is.'

'It's a phase.' he said.

'A cataclysm!'

'Are you still afraid of it?' he said.

'Yes, I am,' Kitty said. 'It's something . . . all this panic and the clamour for PEEPER: that's new in the history of the world. There have been little flashes of the same kind, but never anything as universal as this, or as savage. I can't relate it to anything else. I just feel that we're rushing madly through space towards . . .'

To her surprise, he laughed. In was brutal laughter, coarse and unkind. For an instant, she supposed that the madness had caught him. His derision was awful. It ended as suddenly as it had begun, but only when she knew that her sanity could not have borne it an instant longer.

'I'm sorry, Kitty! I'm so sorry . . .'

'Is there anything to laugh at?'

He was penitent but still amused.

'Yes, there is, really! There is!'

She stood up to go. 'I can't understand that, John! To me, it's dreadful. It's devilish.'

'Why?'

He was so nonchalant. She looked down angrily at him.

'You're not serious? Are you?' she exclaimed.

She was humiliated. The conviction that he had always derided her occurred to her. These Bessings, in their trinity! Their detachment, against which she had fought in order to extract from him a word which would confirm his love for her. His devotion to his brother and sister! His entire indifference to her own passion for him. . . . But that was in a past which was the other side of a brink. A past which had been orderly, despite its wars and crises. Oh, he had undoubtedly realized that she had loved him! He had never dissuaded her, although he had been amused, as he was amused now.

'You are making fun of me!' she said. 'You have always done that.'

It shocked him. She could see that. He got up and stood before her at a loss for words, with his hands slightly extended towards her, as though he wanted her to take them but could not believe that she would.

'That's not true, Kitty,' he said. 'Not at you . . . never anything but . . .'

She felt that it would be better for her to take that much and believe in it, instead of waiting for the completion of a sentence which might rob her of that fancy.

'At what, then?'

He tried to explain. 'I was laughing because you thought it terrible that people should scramble at the first chance out of this miserable civilization, this ghastly scene. That isn't a cataclysm! That's the best thing that could happen to them: to renounce it all and to make a new civilization, not out of the rotten bits of the old, but out of new ideas. The past has served them badly. They have had to slaughter one another in millions, because their leaders made mistakes and quarrelled. They have been led anywhere but in the right direction. The Church failed them because it put itself beside the rulers and governments instead of with the people. The Scientists failed them because they, too, lined up with governments. What was waiting for the People in that old civilization? Nothing but the old game of Power to be played out between rival governments. And the chance of being blown into fragments along with a hundred thousand other people in the flash of an atom bomb! No wonder they wanted an end of that! If they have united under PEEPER, I am not going to call it a cataclysm. It's the best thing. I am afraid, just as you are, because I don't know what will happen, but I am willing to trust the people, Kitty. I believe in the ordinary people—those who believe in PEEPER because through him they can find a universal peace and unity. The others—that crowd out there jammed in their own panic—they're the real savages, liable to rush down the slope at the least word. I saw them! Pouring up to pray to God, although most of them have denied Him all their lives. Or rushing out from London, with their jewels and their cash, and their flats and houses safely locked, in case there is whatever they fear there will be. A riot, a civil war, a collapse of the markets. They are the ones who make trouble.

'I saw Matthew's first article in his paper. Belfwig, my Editor, showed it to me. Go back to him, Kitty, and tell him not to waste time examining PEEPER, or prophesying what PEEPER will do. Tell him to write about the people who are afraid of PEEPER. What is happening is only disastrous to the men who have misused the power which the people gave them. The men who made terrible errors because they thought only in terms of party politics, and class, and wealth. The rotten little governments composed of opportunists. They are the mad ones, the enemies of Man! PEEPER is a threat to them. He's an Idea which I can't control, and he menaces them as much as he promises hope to the millions who love him.'

She could not recognize the man who said this to her. This was not the John Bessing she knew and loved. But it did not seem to her to matter who he was. Love was something of the past, when she had had nothing to hope for or to live for, and when she wanted a purpose. She, too, was transformed now. She had an abundant hope in a new civilization.

She told him as the two of them went down the stairs:

'If I believed in prayer . . . if I could believe in the power of prayer . . . I would pray for Quentin.'

'Because you are still afraid of PEEPER?'

She shook her head. 'No. Because I want Quentin to continue what he began.'

'And Matthew?' he said. 'Will he be convinced? What will you tell him?'

'What you have told me.'

'Don't go,' he said. 'Stay here and wait for Lenora. I'll 'phone to Matthew and ask him to come over.'

She refused the invitation, saying that she wanted to return home. Afterwards, she said, she and Matthew would come over and spend the evening with them.

Instead of returning through Piccadilly, she made a wide detour, going through South Audley Street and down to Hyde Park Corner through Park Lane. It was impossible to get through, for the immense traffic block extended far westward and into the Park and almost the whole length of the Lane, with the entire mass of vehicles hopelessly jammed there and unable to move in any direction. And the streets that ran like tributaries from it all, they too were as bad. Over the whole curious scene, a soft wind blew. Birds alighted on the bonnets and roofs of the cars. The evening sunlight was reflected on metalwork and windows in that abandoned mass which remained there like a dreadful evidence of panic which had locked and writhed there until it had exhausted itself. Children played there, in and out, over and under, thrilled by the scene and its sensation. A paradise for them.

She worked her way across and walked homewards along the thronged pavements. She was no longer afraid. Nor was the crowd whose voice rose in a single note of gaiety. She was impatient to reach home, that was all. There was so much to tell Matthew. There had never before been so much to relate, so much to discuss.

It was past seven when she reached the house and went in. He was waiting for her. She knew from the tone of his voice when he called down the stairs to her that he had been anxiously awaiting her return.

'Kitty!'

She wanted to hasten to him. She checked herself. She let him repeat that cry because in it there was all that she wished to hear. He came pelting down so that she knew the suspense he had felt and the relief which he found in her return. She met him half-way up the stairs, running up to him and, in the dim light of the stairs, seeing his heavy expression transformed into happiness which sprang quickly and lightly into his face. She knew that she was looking at the authentic Matthew and not the vexed, frustrated man of the past.

'I heard,' he panted, 'I heard about the traffic block. They interrupted the radio programme to caution people. Said that a rumour about a special service at St. Paul's was false. That people should not . . . you know . . . a whole set of directions. Said Piccadilly and Knightsbridge were completely blocked and Park Lane and Oxford Street. I was worried, Kitty, terribly worried about you . . .'

She removed her hat and dropped her handbag and gloves.

'I was frightened, at first,' she said. 'Frightened of people . . . of what they might do. In that panic. Now I'm not afraid any more. I saw John.'

She turned to Matthew.

'Did you send off that second article?'

He shook his head. 'I worked most of the afternoon on my book.'

'A book?'

'On the subject of PEEPER. A critical examination of the phenomenon.'

He took her into his study and showed her his notes and the pages which he had already typed. She looked up from them.

'Before I went out,' she said, 'you said something which John repeated. About people being at a limit of mental endurance and liable to . . . a breakdown . . . unless they are given a respite, or hope, or a better life.'

He smiled. 'They needn't necessarily suffer a breakdown. But they might do something which astonishes governments.'

'That was John's theory too. He says that PEEPER is a release for people. A kind of safety-valve.'

'I know,' he said. 'I believe that. But I'm . . . Kitty, I'm afraid of him . . .'

'You aren't,' she said. 'You are afraid of the people who fear his influence. They are the souls possessed by devils. They run in panic . . .'

'They have . . .'

'Nothing!' she said. 'PEEPER is stronger than they are.'

He sat down and was silent for several minutes. Looking gravely at her, he said:

'Or have we, too, lost our reason? Have we?'

She laughed. She forgot that she was hungry and thirsty and tired. She had so much to tell him. The whole world was new, shaking itself free of the dead grip of mountainous old systems that had bruised it and burdened it for centuries. Everywhere, it was moving off to new horizons. PEEPER was supplanting the morbid statesmen with their crazy notions, and the politicians with their cunning stunts of party conflicts, and the generals and marshals, the abstruse economists, and the scientists, all of whom had enticed the world into savage enmities. PEEPER was different. He was the Man sought by the simple hearts everywhere in their longing for happiness, peace, unity, security. There had been others before him: statesmen even, and actors and actresses of stage and screen, and singers, and dancers. But PEEPER was different. He belonged to the whole world. Being only a figure in a cartoon, there was no fear of his dying, retiring, becoming disagreeable or outmoded. He was there, on the page, day after day, and he did not disappoint. He was amusing.

He was the Ordinary Man, not a tyrant with a cunning brand of nationalism. He was for the whole world. A universal Man.

*Part Three*

# THE IDEA

★

# ONE

★

The celebrations in Paris to commemorate the founding of the Fourth Republic were planned on a lavish scale. France Resurgent intended to offer her people an occasion which would find its place in the pages of the nation's history, and which would be engraved in the happy memories of her subjects, and recalled vividly and with pleasure by the thousands of official and unofficial guests. Once again, France stood amidst the great concourse of nations: liberal, free, artistic, fashionable. And anxious to hold a party.

Commencing with a solemn service at the Cathedral of Notre Dame when the President of the Republic, the Marshals, and the Ministers of Government would make a vow of dedication, France would rejoice for a whole week. There were to be Pageants in the great Places, receptions and dinners at the various Ministries, balls, ballets, operas, drama.

France, ever hospitable, had provided comfort and luxury, had summoned its cleverest managers and chefs to the Capital where thousands of experienced purveyors, caterers, servants, clerks, valets, cashiers and interpreters were busy. Famous hostesses had made their personal plans in accordance with the express wishes of the Minister concerned. The proprietors and licensees of the famous theatres had received their directives and had submitted their plans for approval to the same Minister. Hotels and mansions by the score had been requisitioned and were in process of renovation. Generous contracts had been given to reputable firms to illuminate the Capital. All of it! Not only the bridges, and the banks of the Seine, but the boulevards, the avenues and parks, the squares, the monuments and finest buildings. Floodlights; miles of coloured lights; beams and globes; festoons of lights amidst the trees. Paris was to be a jewel of lights whose brilliance would fill the darkness. The adults would gasp at that splendour; the children of France would remember it throughout their lives.

From all parts of France, there had come the best musicians, famous orchestras, great virtuosi, renowned poets and writers. France had beckoned from sunny retirement her mellowed genius. Ballet, opera, comedy and tragedy, concerto and symphony, all were planned. And, being not unmindful of the diversity of human taste, France had summoned its masters and mistresses of revue and vaudeville.

The political parties had prepared their own rival plans. For the especial delight of the Soviet party and their friends, the French Communists and their allies intended to present a classic example of Western decadence, 'An Ideal Husband'—in the original text. M.R.P. and its friends proposed to retort with 'Le Malade Imaginaire,' while the Socialists who had decided to relinquish party rivalry at such a time had chosen to present 'Much Ado About Nothing.' The Right Wing group, detaching itself from such shameful conflicts, was satisfied with its plans for a performance of 'The Devil's Disciple.'

France had been busy long before the publication of official plans. Throughout Paris, the rattle and thunder of hammers echoed from the requisitioned hotels and mansions where armies of workmen sedulously argued the future of France and now and again drove in a few nails, dropped planks, and marched off to the neighbouring bistros. But in numerous offices where the involved machinery of this affair was being set in motion, the real tasks were lifting their horrible heads. Particularly in the Deuxième Bureau, which had never worked as hard.

Suddenly, when thousands of official guests had already arrived, a crisis arose. A postponement of the whole business was announced from Paris.

What had happened?

The first official guests to arrive had been the Soviet Representatives, together with the Polish, Roumanian, and Yugoslav parties, as well as the delegation from the newly-established Republic of Plebs. Paris had placed nine hotels, all of which were adjacent to one another, at the disposal of these guests. It was insufficient. Five more hotels had to be rapidly emptied of certain trappings and given over to the guests from Plebs who, to the consternation of all Paris, had brought with them their own cooks, managers, waiters, clerks, cashiers, porters, secretaries, typists, messengers, interpreters, as well as their own large company of actors and actresses, dancers and musicians, and no less than six travelling cinema units with thirty classics of Plebs' films. The entourage was completed by a portable printing press, capable of printing thirty thousand copies daily of *Plebs Comet*, for which a staff of editors, journalists and special correspondents had travelled with the party. It would be a pity not to mention at this point that the printing press had with it a radio reception and transmission outfit, to which were attached a competent staff of operators, and some private censors.

Paris, tactful and discreet as ever, merely raised its eyebrows and ventured to ask for a Press Conference to attend this amazing mob which had pushed and scrambled its way with hobnailed boots from the railway station to the sumptuous hotels. The request was politely refused. Then the doors of the hotels were shut noisily, bolted from the inside, and almost immediately sentried by stocky little guards in the uniform of the Plebs Republic. Not long afterwards, the Republic's flag was unfurled from the standard on the principal hotel. A Comet, in the faintest of pinks, enclosed by broken chains of blue, on a white background.

When Paris announced the postponement of its Celebrations for a period of one week, the delegation from Plebs applied to its Government at home behind the mountains of Transplebia for permission to remain on holiday for that extended period. It was granted immediately, whereupon the entire crowd sallied from its hotels and spent one whole day studying Paris, being particularly interested in its public utility services, its industries, and its public health services. Punctually at midnight, it returned to its hotels. An hour later, every window was alight. The party from Plebs was hard at work printing its newspaper and preparing its report on its study of the public utility services of the French capital which, it subsequently appeared, were much inferior to those of the Plebs capital.

A curious thing occurred early next morning. Watchers at a little distance from the principal hotel saw the main door open and a diminutive man step out into the soft sunlight. The guards stopped him and examined his papers and then signed to him to proceed on his errand.

He hurried away at a great pace, with head down and senses obviously quite indifferent to the charms of that district of Paris. The newspaper correspondents who followed him saw him stop at a newspaper kiosk. He purchased several English newspapers, back numbers. He hurried away to another kiosk and purchased other back numbers, as well as some current ones. And so on, for the next three hours, after which he hired a taxi into which he dumped his purchases and then got in himself and was taken back to the hotel where the guards passed him in. Again the main doors were closed.

PEEPER! Enquiries at the kiosks elicited the information that the gentleman from Plebs had asked for PEEPER papers! Paris smiled. The little gentlemen from Plebs were human, after all! In spite of the sentries posted at their hotels, and the printing press, cinema units, radio transmitters, the citizens of the fabulous, new Republic

163

whose glories already astonished the decadent west, laughed merrily at PEEPER! And Paris, although gravely concerned with secret problems, smiled.

In Transplebia, PEEPER was as popular as he was in the rest of Europe, America, the Far East. The two men who presided over the lives of Transplebia's millions of subjects drew some derisive comment upon PEEPER in their national newspaper by remarking upon the wild enthusiasm in the capitalist West for a new kind of toy which represented a tall, starved Englishman trying to smile. An example of this toy was on view in the Museum of Capitalist Decay, in Transplebia's capital, where it was seen by thousands who watched an official work it by squeezing together the two sticks that held the string on which the figure was suspended. Transplebia laughed because PEEPER was what the Government press described as 'a typical example of Feudalism—starved and ill—lingering in the decadent West and elsewhere.' And it demanded more of him to laugh at. It was given great doses of PEEPER. Its District Councils distributed tens of thousands of PEEPER toys that were said to be replicas of those with which the British Members of Parliament amused themselves during long debates. Block Committees, Efficiency Brigades in Transplebian factories, House Parties, clamoured for PEEPER toys. The national newspaper reported that whole cities in England and America had been deserted by the populace in order that PEEPER might be extolled in idolatrous meetings on nearby hills. Chaos and unrest reigned in London and New York, where PEEPER was more popular than the white-haired, ancient Colport or Senator La Guardia.

Transplebia could not be satiated. It wanted more and more of PEEPER. Until, all at once, a curious silence fell upon that extensive country behind the lofty mountains. News leaked out a day later. The two rulers of Transplebia's two hundred million souls had discovered that the laughter over PEEPER was not the right kind of laughter. All PEEPER toys had been withdrawn, and anybody found in possession of one was liable to suffer the death penalty. All newspapers bearing PEEPER cartoons were taken from circulation and forbidden to be read. All drawings of PEEPER were transformed overnight by an army of artists skilled in depicting the sullen frown of both of Transplebia's rulers. The impenetrable curtains of censorship were lowered upon all incoming news dispatches, as well as upon outgoing press telegrams. But one redoubtable American correspondent of the internationally famous magazine, *Dime*, contrived to export a sixty-thousand-word article which described the state of Transplebia due to the advent of PEEPER. He could have said it all in six words. The people of Transplebia wanted PEEPER.

The Foreign Minister of Transplebia, and his enormous suite, reached Paris one day before the curtain of censorship was lowered. Paris apologized for having to ask for a postponement of one week, but was certain that the guests would find means of amusing themselves while certain important matters were smoothed out. The Foreign Minister of Transplebia, who had spent eight years of exile in Paris, said that he was sure that he and his staff could spend that week profitably and happily.

The matters to be 'smoothed out' related to the increasing collapse of local government in England due to the rising popularity of PEEPER. A glance at English national life would have revealed little to the casual observer, for on the surface the same old currents streamed, and the same observer would have looked in vain for a reference to PEEPER in *The Times*. But had he been admitted to the meetings of City Councils, County Councils, and the Cabinet, the whole alarming scene would have disclosed itself to him.

No Government could have handled this crisis, for the methods of most governments are conventional and are based upon experience. Such a crisis had not previously arisen and could not be approached by government upon the lines laid down by former occasions. Moreover, in spite of rumours of treason, revolution, and civil war, the people were not in any mood of violence. In hundreds of thousands, day by day, they were merely widening the gulf between themselves and governments everywhere. It was not difficult, for most governments had maintained themselves behind a ditch of formidable dimensions and had come across it only at the end of a term of office. Also, the very speed of international communication enabled people everywhere to acquaint their fellow mortals in other parts of the world of their interest and love for PEEPER. And that alone was all that was needed to unify millions under one Thing. The fact could not be ignored. Man had turned his back on the trivialities in his own countries and was at last united in a common interest that had no relation to governments, wars, crises, mountains, rivers, seas, or other national boundaries. No government, no matter how adroit, could expect to overtake Man on such a flight. In England, hundreds of clever orators, sent out by the Government to lecture the people on the folly of PEEPER, all failed lamentably in their attempts to raise scorn for that amiable feature.

People laughed. Their retort was that there was less harm in following PEEPER than there had been in following certain Governments of the past into follies that had resulted in national distress and crisis.

By a common consent, essential services were maintained. Nobody required to be told that it was necessary to work, to earn money, to run trains and trams and 'buses, and to keep going the gas, water, and electricity supplies. What people flatly refused to do was to heed the old cries of nationalism which opposed world unity, or the old ideas which had resulted in distress, or the old systems that were now out-worn. Instead, national life was slowly being related to universal life. It began, one might say, overnight, and surprised governments. It horrified millions who could not take this plunge into sober sense. It sent into panic whole sections of communities. Prayers were of no avail against the rising tide of the new era.

People were laughing. Across the world a weird joy was travelling. Meanwhile, in London, at the heart of the PEEPER affair, all manner of events occurred. Out of obscurity had come old politicians. Colport, in particular, skilled in the formation of coalitions, his venerable presence soothing to his contemporaries and menacing to his enemies. After a stormy debate, a Coalition Government had wobbled into being. What to do, and say?

Not until the second day of its existence did it realize that the people had withdrawn their mandate from Authority which had betrayed them for century after century by involving them in narrow nationalisms, petty international rancour, wars, and personal quarrels between statesmen whose vanity was always inaccurately described by historians as 'personality.' Authority could no longer awe the nation. It had suffered the loss of its power. And as well as from outside, there came from inside, too, an apathy, an indifference, and a loss of faith in the old ponderous systems of government. All over the land, civil servants resigned, or went on long periods of leave. The involved machinery of government rapidly collapsed from inertia. And the same condition prevailed in local government circles. Hundreds of tedious official Boards that had never accomplished anything except new rules and regulations, no longer sat.

Addressing a packed House of Commons, Colport said bluntly:

'The cataclysm is unique in the history of human life on this planet. We must recognize it for what it is: a revolt of the human Will which can be contained within the bounds of wisdom only by the most prodigious efforts of all of us in this House. Let us look to ourselves and admit first of all that the People have outstripped us in vision and have attained the first stage of universal brotherhood. From long ages of tribulation, mankind has boldly set its foot upon the promised land towards which we, in our humble way, have led it. If, in its initial joy, it appears to run from guidance, we must be patient and hopeful. Like wise shepherds, we must again herd the flock and fold it safely by going ahead of it, by going to right and left of it, by gently impelling it from behind, and by leaving open the one channel into which it can proceed.

'Let us not be terrified by the miraculous concept of life which the people have achieved in their millions! When, many years ago, I myself was accorded remarkable popularity, I felt then that I was but a symbol of what that universal Will sought and terribly demanded. I am an old man who has seen much of the manifestations of that Will. In my years of semi-retirement, I have frequently realized that Mankind desires an end of Party Politics, and wishes for nothing more than universal unity and brotherhood, beyond the insularity of nationalism, creed, and the vision of its rulers. I say to you now that the time is ripe for that brotherhood! I urge this House to resign at last all the conflicting ideas of Class, of Party enmity, of small things that have not only divided us, but have tended to divide our own people and the people of other nations. How is that transformation of ourselves to be achieved? Well might all of you demand an answer from me!

'The hope and expectation—nay, the demand of Mankind!—is for Universal Unity. I proclaim it here to-day, in no spirit of fear, but with the most profound prayer that we move forward ourselves and offer Mankind a direction by inviting to London the governments of the civilized world so that we may unite with them under one banner, one glorious Idea, one purpose and one hope!

'This is our moment! This is our last chance, and our first glorious opportunity! This is the tide which the universal Will, as expressed by the peoples of the world, has awaited since the sombre dawn of history! As I travelled from my orchards and vineyards to this ancient House, there entered my compartment an old woman, white-haired as I am. We looked at each other. Her recognition of me moved my heart, and I asked myself if I knew her and her people as shrewdly as she knew me. I was no stranger to her, yet in my soul I was troubled that, despite my many years of leadership, I still knew so little of her. Let us take example from that one old woman! Never again must we remain aloof from the People by burying ourselves in our conclaves. We have this day learned our lesson. I say to this House! My Sons! Be mindful of your tasks and duties! Guard well the precious mandate which the People gave you, and which they have taken away, but which it is within your power to recover!'

No sooner had Colport resumed his seat and enfolded himself in his dark blue mantle, than uproar occurred. Some Communist members objected to his statements. The Socialists smiled. The Conservative members cheered and jeered. The Speaker called for order, but the outburst of disorder continued until the Speaker rose and left the Chamber.

The speech was mentioned only in *The Times* and the *Manchester Guardian*. The remainder of the daily Press gave headlines and most of their space to news from the world concerning the increasing demonstrations of enthusiasm for PEEPER. Meanwhile, after a resumption of the debate in the Commons, the new Coalition Government sent immediate instructions to its Ambassadors and Consuls throughout the world, requesting them to invite Presidents, Foreign Ministers, Prime Ministers, Dictators, and other rulers to a Conference in London. Its next step was to inform the French Government that in view of the crisis in world affairs it could not, for the time being, commit itself to any participation in the approaching Celebrations in Paris.

A fortune had been expended on the preparations for the Celebrations. Other fortunes would be expended on the Week itself. Public expectation in France was at a tremendous pitch of excitement and could not be cheated. Nor could national wealth be squandered in delays.

But France, too, was in the grip of PEEPER fever. The genius of France, resident for an instant of time in the mind of the President, suggested politely to Britain that the Celebrations should proceed on the date arranged, but on an even more lavish scale than had been planned, and at greater length, thus offering the world a diversion from PEEPER which might result in that phenomenon expiring within a day or two. In a confidential paragraph, the genius of France added that unless a completely satisfactory reply was forthcoming within twelve hours, the Celebrations must continue without the presence of the British party, and that the Republic could not be expected to delay its official business, or to take heed of the disruption of affairs due to a stupid enthusiasm on the part of sections of English life for a figure in a newspaper cartoon.

Within five hours a reply was presented. It begged for a postponement of the Celebrations for a period of one week. France gracefully acceded to the request.

These volatile English!

But what to do now with the guests who were already in the French capital? The little gentlemen from Transplebia? The guests from Poland, the Soviet Union, and Roumania, were enchanted with France, and had departed for a week to the south-west, and to Nice. But the party from Transplebia politely refused such trips, although France offered private trains and private hotels. The guests bowed, smiled, and shaking their heads firmly declined the offers. Whereupon, France's famous hostesses were asked to issue invitations to them. Dinners, balls, receptions. With the same result. But in return, the party from Transplebia offered to send on a week's tour through France not only its travelling cinema units with the classical Plebs films, but its dramatic companies, and its opera and ballet companies as well. France, ever tactful, could not accept the compliment, saying that the population was preoccupied with the forthcoming celebrations. The gentlemen from the Republic of Transplebia smiled, and returned to their hotels to work.

Always work! In those lofty hotels, the lights shone all night; the printing presses clanked and whirred and thundered; the radio transmitters chattered their codes; the messengers hurried in their hobnailed boots about the corridors. In the early morning, thirty thousand free copies of *Plebs Comet* were piled into vans and rushed off to be distributed to the citizens of Paris who, on opening the pages, discovered that France was 'a prey to Black Markets and the devastating PEEPER sickness which has laid low so much of England and other continents.' They learned, too, that in Transplebia the harvest would exceed that of last year by seven million bushels of wheat, four million tons of maize, twelve million bushels of potatoes. The steel output of Transplebia had increased eight hundred per cent within one year. Eleven new cities for the aged had been built. Eight new cities of Rest and Culture had been erected for sick workers of the Republic. Photographs were reproduced. The Republic's army of twenty-seven million men was now on spring manœuvres in the plains and mountains of Transplebia, led by Grand Soldier Karavit who, seven years previously, had been a corporal in the infantry. Photo on page nine.

The wit of France was overwhelmed. Paris gracefully bowed its acceptance of this twelve-page daily relating to the glories of Transplebia. The Government smiled. But the Deuxième Bureau perspired, and at last revolted.

Its experienced, patient and faithful staff had recently discovered that the Foreign Minister of Transplebia was in the habit of nightly escaping from his hotel with two of his party and joining old friends of his exiled days in one of the most disreputable cafés of Paris. In itself, that did not tax the resources of the Bureau. What the Bureau complained of was something far more serious. Its spokesman visited the Minister of a Government department and angrily exhibited the latest PEEPER cartoon.

He pointed to a figure drawn in the cartoon.

'Why was this person not listed to us as dangerous, sir?'

The Minister gravely examined this copy of the 'Daily Summariser.' At home, in the heart of his family, he was an ardent PEEPER fan, and carefully preserved all the cartoons in an album into which his enthusiastic daughters daily pasted them. But at the Ministry he knew not PEEPER.

'Alors!' he rejoined, shrugging his shoulders.

PEEPER was depicted on his way to embark at Newhaven. He carried a small suitcase. Ahead of him in the crowd, was a sullen, tight-faced young man in a raincoat and a cap.

'WHAT'S-HIS-NAME goes too,' said the caption, below which that morose man had a square to himself. The next two squares showed PEEPER on board the cross-channel steamer, with 'What's-his-name' amidst the crowd and concealed from PEEPER who seemed to be anxiously looking for him.

'I DAREN'T LOSE SIGHT OF HIM!' PEEPER said.

Again the Personage of the Ministry said 'Alors!' and shrugged his shoulders.

The official from the Deuxième Bureau stabbed his forefinger at 'What's-his-name.'

'An anarchist!' he said, sharply.

The Personage said no, at least twelve times, and shook his head emphatically. He rose. He smiled. He said that although he respected the pertinacity of the Bureau, he must pronounce that the figures in the cartoon were not relative to facts. He indicated the cartoon with a graceful motion of his right hand.

'This is fiction,' he said. 'Obviously, this man PEEPER has an enemy—"What's-his-name"—or perhaps the man is his valet.' He adjusted his spectacles and looked closer at the cartoon. 'Yes! I should say, an enemy . . .'

'An anarchist!' the man from the Bureau repeated.

'But . . . no! No, no, no! You persist in mistaking what is fiction for fact! Consider! If this . . . what is his name? . . . if he were alive, real, a person, would not Scotland Yard have listed him in their Memorandum? But no! He is in the category of PEEPER! A fiction!'

The official from the Bureau said most emphatically that 'What's-his-name' was a criminal, an anarchist, in London. Of that, all the members of the Bureau were convinced.

'Alors!' shouted the infuriated Minister. 'Alors!' Then he flopped into his chair and moaned, saying:

'And has the entire Deuxième Bureau become one shrine for the adoration of PEEPER?'

His eyes flashed. 'Have all of you lost your senses, as the rest of the world appears to have done? PEEPER!'

He sighed loudly. 'My god! PEEPER! What next?'

The persistent official from the Bureau said:

'The cartoon is a warning, sir! We do not propose to disregard it.'

The Minister turned pale. 'Then . . .'

The other sighed tremulously. 'A grave situation has arisen. Because he was not listed, no watch was kept. Therefore, he has entered France.'

'A fiction . . .' murmured the Minister.

The spokesman from the Bureau shook his head and raised his hands.

'Remember,' he said, 'the prophecy . . . the forecast not long ago. "Lord Punch." I myself . . . and you also, sir, I have no doubt . . . I accepted that forecast and am the richer by ten thousand francs. Those who scoffed at the forecast are the poorer . . .'

'Certainly!' agreed the Minister, whose wife was the richer by eighty thousand francs. 'But it is not relevant . . .'

'Sir, the Bureau dares not take the risk of ignoring so obvious a warning.'

The Minister swayed in his chair and flung out his hands in exaspera-tion.

'Very well! And if we ask for information from Scotland Yard, basing our query on . . . on this! On a piece of PEEPER!'

He exploded. 'Is that what we have come to? That the Government of this country must tremble at a cartoon!'

The servant of the Bureau was adamant.

'I beg you, sir; I plead with you to request immediate information. Even now, it may be too late! Nevertheless, in the name of safety, honour, the reputation of the Bureau, the comfort and peace of mind of all France at this time . . .'

171

The Minister sighed. 'Very well! I shall see that the information is requested.' And with another sigh, he added:

'This PEEPER! This . . .'

He could not find the apt word by which to describe PEEPER. Nor could the personage from the Bureau who, having achieved what he had come to do, departed after expressing his humble thanks, leaving the Minister faced with yet another manifestation of the power and influence and foresight of PEEPER.


## TWO

★

In the fine house not far from Paddington Station, Willie had breakfasted in bed and was shaving in the bathroom when he heard Aunt Flossie calling to him. The bath water was running, and he had already shaved his left cheek and was working round to the stiff patch of stubble under his chin when her shrill, imperative squawk swept up the stairs.

Almost immediately, a door slammed. He heard footsteps thumping somewhere below. Voices joined in a sudden, high-pitched gabble. He cursed. The mob of Flossie's patriots. And then Flossie's nasty, shrill voice yelling at him.

He wondered what had happened. Flossie gave to the most trivial matters the same heated exclamations which the most important affairs evoked from her. She could never discriminate. Her first impulse was to yell for him, which was flattering in one way but annoying and alarming as well. Moreover, by her tone, she proclaimed that he was living in her house, at her expense, and that it was her fortune that financed him. He could not forget it. His own fortune was settled upon something else. His own house was blitzed. He had taken control of her fortune and her home—all for her own good—yet she would not cease inflicting her imperious manner in this way. Screaming at the merest trifle! As though he were a lackey!

Fortunately, his nerves were strong. He continued shaving.

'Willie!' she screeched. 'Quickly, Willie!'

He swore. He turned the key in the bathroom door so that when she came panting upstairs, the door was locked against her. She thumped into his bedroom, and out again, and about the landing. Like gabbling geese the patriots followed her, weaving a pattern of dismay and terror throughout the house. Doors slammed. Somebody tried to make a trunk call. A loud argument began below.

Willie sighed. He finished shaving and slipped off his dressing-gown and got into the bath. The water was very hot. He sank into it with a sense of extreme comfort and contentment.

Flossie beat with her hands upon the panels of the door.

'Willie! Please come out at once! Please! There's important news!'

He was prone in a liquid paradise, his mind drowsy, his senses at peace. Flossie's voice, in its various inflections, drove him from that peace and brought him to consider what the news might be. Good? Hardly! Bad? Very bad?

Flossie seldom had good news to impart. Her temperament was the kind that relished its importance when it gave bad news. Removing himself from the bath and sitting down on the cork chair to towel himself, he tried to examine all the factors that might have changed overnight and resulted in bad news.

He remembered Flossie's patriots and the extremely dangerous projects which they had persuaded Flossie to enter and which he himself had accepted. It was money, of course. And it all seemed simple enough. Flossie's part in the affair was to provide a place where the patriots might meet whenever they wished. His task had been to find . . . he flinched from the word, although it was the only one . . . an assassin.

He unlocked the door and strode to his bedroom. She came panting from her room and almost collided with him. Her face was deeply cut by lines of anxiety and impatience.

'Didn't you hear me?'

He tried to close the door against her.

'I must dress first . . .'

He unslipped the cords of his dressing-gown. Flossie caught his arm and shook him.

'That awful creature . . . that Twigge!'

She thrust a copy of the 'Daily Summariser' into his face and stormed at him in a torrent of words while he stood there and saw What's-his-name' accurately depicted in the squares of the cartoon. He sank into a chair and continued to stare at the drawing. Above him, around him, Flossie panted and reviled him.

'You blundering fool! To let Twigge do that! After you had taken such drastic measures against that Georgie man and Fred! To let Twigge thwart us like this! I told you . . . I said . . . if I said it once I said it fifty times . . . that Twigge must be taken care of unless you wanted this . . . this to happen! But no! You wanted your way. You said he wouldn't dare, wouldn't try. Well! Well, now you can see for yourself! Our man is in France, and then this appears! Look at it! What chance has he against the French police in their . . . their Surety or whatever they call it? That poor boy . . . surrounded by them! You realize what that means, don't you? You must know that he'll never stand against them. He'll confess! He'll tell them everything. And then . . .'

'Be quiet, Flossie!' he mumbled. 'For heaven's sake . . .'

She was a stream which could not be checked.

'And all of them . . . downstairs . . . what do you think I am to do with them? They want to know. They want their money back. They say . . .'

'Send them away, Flossie. Just for a little while . . .'

She seemed aghast. 'Where to?'

He hadn't thought. He supposed that they might decide their own destination.

'For a week or two until . . .'

'Until when? Where to?'

He did not know. He had never calculated for a possibility of failure. He had spent so much money, bribing people, buying a forged passport, arranging for 'What's-his-name' to travel to France, coaching him in his job. And all that activity was in addition to his own affairs which extended like roots into the City's life and ran clean against Twigge.

He was afraid of Twigge, especially since he had acquired a kind of control over PEEPER whose artist seemed quite willing to enter the game with him. But although Twigge terrified him, and in spite of the fact that the two of them were rivals, he had never expected that Twigge would dare to oppose him after the stern warning which he had given him by dealing with Georgie and Fred. And yet Twigge had not been silenced. And there was this awful disclosure.

He got up and languidly dropped the newspaper on the chair. He stood at the window, looking out on a spring day which was delight-fully attractive to the senses. It was one of those days when London looked clean and vivid, and when the clouds in the blue sky above it were white, and the air clear, and the colours of everything suddenly and mysteriously enchanting. It was especially vivid this morning, and he could not help remarking on it.

'It's a beautiful morning, Flossie! I can't remember . . . even in Vienna it was never . . . really, it was never as bright as this!'

He thought that she was going to push him through the window. She came at him with such speed and fury.

'You chattering potterer! You . . .'

Then she stopped. 'What are we to do?' she wailed.

He took another glance at the enchanting morning.

'All right,' he said, decisively. He saw Flossie stare apprehensively at him. He made a curt gesture.

'Close this house for a week,' he said, his eyes reluctantly withdrawing their gaze from the window. 'Send everybody away. Go away yourself. Go to Harrogate.'

'When?'

It was a harsh sound which he answered impatiently.

'Now! This morning! As soon as you can!'

She threw back her head and laughed in a way which made him feel suddenly very cold.

'You're out of touch with things!' she exclaimed. 'The trains are packed. Go to any main line station and see for yourself. Go round the corner to Paddington and see the queues. A mile long, day and night. Waiting to get out of London at any price!'

'Take the car, then! Travel by road!' he shouted.

'Take the car, he says! Travel by road!' She thrust her head forward. 'And where, if you please, are we to get the petrol? Tell me that.'

He sat on the edge of his bed.

'From Harold, or Louis, or Ernie!' he exclaimed. 'From a dozen sources.'

She seemed to enjoy presenting one by one these little defeats to him. She laughed.

'There isn't a pint to be got in all London! Try for yourself! I have. It's all gone! I've asked all your men. They are sold out! There isn't a drop to be got anywhere. The new Government has put an embargo or something on supplies. People are offering a hundred pounds a gallon!'

His flabby face sagged in sullen rage. 'Ernie should have plenty! I have fifty gallons stored with him.'

'Ernie's store is empty. And Ernie is half-way to Wales by now, I should think.'

'Then Harold . . .'

'As if he'd save some for you, when he can sell it at a hundred pounds a gallon!'

He got up and fingered his smooth chin. 'There should be some . . . somewhere!'

'Just for you!' she taunted him. 'Just so that . . .'

He said coarsely and loudly: 'Well, walk then! Walk! And tell the rest of them to do the same. Or go and queue at the station.'

And just as coarsely, in a tone which matched his, she answered him: 'Is that all you can suggest?'

He laughed. 'That, or stay here. But I advise you to send the patriots away. Get rid of them . . .'

Her laughter interrupted him. Hard and mocking, it hurt him.

'The way you allude to them!' And like a machine wound up to repeat the trite old phrases, she went on:   'They are the last bulwark against . . .'

He finished the sentence for her. 'The wicked Bolshies!'

It was like a match to a keg of gunpowder. She exploded violently: 'Yes! Don't you dare laugh at them! Hitler was right! A pity he didn't get his way and teach a lesson to . . . to . . .' She screamed the rest at him. ' . . . these wicked Socialists!'

He had heard it all before, from her: the whole sick, frenzied idea, like a malady which would not end but which had its germ in her.

'Shut up!' he said, 'Oh, shut up!'

He went to his wardrobe and chose a suit. From his chest of drawers he selected a shirt and tie to match.

'And you tell me to send them away,' Flossie was saying. 'As if they'll go! Would you? Suppose you had handed over something like twenty thousand . . .'

'Which I have disbursed fairly,' he said.

'Even so. Would you be prepared to go away at a word? When somebody whom you trusted had blundered? Would you?'

He spread the suit on the bed. 'Let them stay then. I don't care. I was thinking of their safety.'

'All I can say is, you had better think again, Willie!'

He went into his dressing-room and stood at the window there. Such an enchanting morning. Really, something new and dazzling in the very air. Flossie had followed him into the room.

'It's funny, Flossie,' he said, slowly. 'No matter what men and women do, or what happens to them, the birds go on singing and the sun still shines and the beautiful blue sky is . . .'

Flossie collapsed in tears. 'I wish you'd stop talking drivel and tell me what I'm to do,' she said, sobbing into her handkerchief.

He had suddenly noticed that the street below was quite empty of traffic except for people riding cycles. And the pedestrians who moved in the street went without hurry, as though London were on holiday.

Ever since he had returned to London after that adventure in Vienna, he had been so intensely occupied with his affairs that he felt a keen pleasure at this moment when he realized that at last he could relax. Everything was slowly coming to a halt. Even the extensive Black Markets which he controlled. Literally coming to an end, simply because the hundreds of persons employed by him to do this or that, to run, to fetch, to contrive in their way a tiny part of the involved machinery of it all, were gone, or could not be found, or said no when he requested them to act for him. Crime itself was ended, along with all manner of other things. He was not worried, or unhappy. Instead, he was glad.

One final opportunity did, however, bob up and occur to him and tantalize his greediness.

'Just think, Flossie!' he exclaimed. 'If I had only concentrated on petrol! If only I had known. Even a couple of hundred gallons. Just think. Twenty thousand pounds! And I could easily have got it, I could really. Double that amount; treble that amount!'

Then he came out of that little dream which a shrewd Coalition Government had forestalled. For the Government had a firm hand not only upon all food but upon petrol and transport as well. With that experienced old patriarch in charge, that fabulous old pilot who, like an embodiment of national destiny, had accepted premiership, and would steer the Government safely through this period, the hands and eyes of Government were everywhere. Its hands held food, petrol, all transport, and the Banks, so firmly that there was no public anxiety about any of those things. Hundreds of PEEPER Restaurants had been established by the Government, with the help of the PEEPER Clubs, so that one might eat twenty times a day of excellent, wholesome food for no more than a shilling a time, as indeed some had attempted to do. The old order might be tottering into ruin, but a spirit of sobriety and joy, unity and hope, was increasing. There was the usual panic mob, rushing to escape from its own fears. But for those who remained, here was that solid, indefatigable little Premier, with his blue cloak and his venerable white hair, smiling upon the millions of PEEPER adherents, even when the Government itself had no more lease of life than the next hour. Colport was out of party politics. Next to PEEPER, he held popularity, as of old. He had Power as well, although he had not yet declared it by any action. He had the reins of Government, and he might have driven somewhere if there had been the People between the shafts. But there was nothing but the reins. Willie knew it because he had heard it. Colport dared do nothing except feed the people, guard the money and petrol and transport and shipping, and pretend to admire PEEPER. PEEPER was greater than any Premier on the planet. And like a wary bull, Colport watched him.

'If only,' Willie murmured, 'if only Colport would destroy PEEPER!'

'And to think of that poor little wretch in Paris!' Flossie moaned. Willie came slowly towards her and gently patted her shoulder. He had a special reason for this attempt to placate her.

'Oh, he can take very good care of himself, Flossie!' he said, buoyantly. 'He's very experienced. Why, he was born in what you could term the lap of anarchy. Out there, in Danzig. From his youth up . . .'

'But if he does anything now! Even if he succeeds . . .'

'He will,' Willie whispered, soothingly. 'Of course he will.'

Her sodden, horrified face was lifted to him.

'But if he does, it will only put PEEPER higher than ever! Everybody will say that PEEPER has prophesied again!' she exclaimed.

Willie's flabby face was a void at that moment. He was not thinking of PEEPER but of Twigge. How powerful Twigge was! Not only in London, and the rest of England, but throughout the world. For Twigge held PEEPER firmly. Willie had discovered that. One Bessing brother was dying, and the other was effete. Twigge was the mind behind PEEPER. He had Power in abundance, and yet all he did with it was to slap his enemies across the knuckles and offer their plans like prizes to the Government! Weird, mysterious little Twigge! And if . . .

But Willie could not trace all the patterns which had their source in that word. He was surprised to find Flossie patting his head.

'Willie, dear! Willie! What are we to do?'

'Go down and wait for me,' he said, gently. 'I must dress. Run along and tell the others . . . get them together . . . and I'll be down directly.'

He did not expect her to take it reasonably. It was a surprise to him when she meekly blinked away the last of her tears and gave him a watery smile. Yes, she was saying, yes, well after all the best thing would be to get them together and try to induce them to disperse for a few days until . . .

'Quite right, Auntie!'

He closed the door behind her and noiselessly locked it. He dressed in a hurry, and sorted out his papers in a hurry, burning some of them in the empty grate. He had a considerable amount of money, in notes, which he pocketed. Ten minutes later, he unlocked the door and tiptoed out to the landing.

Flossie and the patriots were in the room behind the big one which faced the street. He could hear them jabbering away while Flossie tried to say:

'. . . but just for a day or two until . . .'

He knew that they would talk noisily for hours. He went quickly and silently down the stairs and out through the door near the kitchen. Nobody heard him or saw him. He was running away, with some thousands of notes, and a wallet of securities.

He laughed softly. To run away, to decamp, was a new experience for him which he enjoyed.


## THREE

★

He laughed louder . . . he had to stand there and laugh at himself . . . when, a few minutes later, he unlocked the door of the shed in which he garaged his car and found nothing there except a 'bus ticket. His Daimler, with seven gallons of petrol in its tank, was stolen. And the six tins of petrol were missing.

He laughed because the situation was ironical; but he felt suddenly weak and shocked. He sat down on an empty box, knowing that it was foolish of him to admit failure merely because his car had been stolen. Failure was a condition of the mind which he refused to suffer. There were other ways of escape, surely.

He sniggered softly. He had always done things like this. Kept a door open behind him so that he could quickly retreat. Kept his car ready, with plenty of petrol in the tank. Kept a reserve of petrol, and a large reserve of ready money. But all at once, he knew that the ways of escape were closed. He could not travel, except by walking. Destinations of safety no longer existed. There was nowhere to go. Safety, as he wanted it, was no longer a condition to be sought and found.

That amused him; but not until he walked off, southwards, did he realize why he found it amusing and even exciting.

He was laughing from relief. The London which he had known from childhood was undergoing a transformation. It was no longer a scene of boiling activity and tense speed. It was calm, even complacent. For the first time in his life, he enjoyed its sunlight and freshness. Looking about him, he noticed first of all the absence of all but two or three 'buses, some Post Office vans, a couple of Army lorries packed with meat, and one Police car. But the cyclists! There were hundreds of them. He thought that a Cyclists' Club was holding a parade, until he saw that the cyclists were dignified City men, with brief-cases strapped to their machines or dangling from the handlebars. They wobbled along beside young clerks and typists who were obviously more accustomed to this means of locomotion. Nobody hurried. The pedestrians who filled the pavements strolled as though they had nowhere particular to go. And the sounds of pattering feet and cycle bells was so altogether new to Willie that it seemed to him to remark some especial quality which his senses discovered in the enchanting scene.

He felt that happiness was in the air for everyone to experience. Looking about him, he saw nothing but smiling faces and heard only the sounds of thousands of footsteps and ringing bells and laughter everywhere. He knew that the great Exchanges were closed because markets had collapsed or had been taken over by the Government. By Government orders, all the Banks were closed. All hotels had been shut by another Order, to prevent people from flocking into them. Transport had been commandeered. All food markets were under Government control. Luxury was dead. Class—that peculiar remnant of Feudalism—was dying in the PEEPER Restaurants where, perforce, everybody—literally everybody—ate because food could not be purchased for consumption at home. A few shops which sold luxury goods were still open, but sales were negligible.

It was collapse. It was financial ruin for thousands; yet in the air there was that joyous note which Willie not only heard but which he felt rising in himself. He felt free, miraculously free of innumerable cares as well as of a kind of weight which he had borne for years along with other people. Collapse was real; so was ruin. Yet it all did not seem to matter, because in its place there was promise of something new. A new civilization.

Willie had not a profound mind, yet he could appreciate that that new civilization was imminent. He stood still and looked about him. He felt a peculiar fear begin in him at the thought of what the future held for the world. The familiar systems were gone. A whole way of life was ended. He felt as though he were nude. He wanted the comforting touch of garments of current ideas, current laws and orders and systems on his life.

He walked on again, and presently stopped at one of the many Government Bulletin Boards on which news posters were pasted every hour by hundreds of men and women who, a week ago, had been civil servants in offices that were now obsolete. A little crowd was around the Board. Willie worked his way to the front.

COALITION GOVERNMENT REQUIRES IMMEDIATELY UNEMPLOYED PERSONS TO ACT AS MANAGERS, CLERKS, WAITERS IN PEEPER RESTAURANTS. APPLY NOW TO NEAREST EMPLOYMENT EXCHANGE FOR LIST OF VACANCIES. GOOD PROSPECTS. JOBS FOR ALL

COLPORT'S PLANS FOR FEDERATED STATES OF WORLD ACCEPTED IN OUTLINE BY FORTY-NINE GOVERNMENTS. DELEGATES ARRIVING HOURLY. SCENES OF REJOICING THROUGHOUT INDIA, AMERICA, AND AFRICA. SESSION OF UNO ENDS IN REMARKABLE DEMONSTRATIONS OF CONFIDENCE. TRANSPLEBIAN DELEGATE ABSTAINS

THEIR MAJESTIES WELCOMED BY RECORD CROWD IN EAST END
PEEPER CLUB MEMBERSHIP REACHES FORTY MILLION MARK IN ENGLAND
CELEBRATIONS IN PARIS POSTPONED FOR ONE WEEK

Willie walked on. Entering Hyde Park, he went into Kensington Gardens and sat down. Twenty years had elapsed since his last visit; but he remembered distinctly how the hollow roar of London's traffic had boomed on the air and obliterated the sound of the summer breeze which had boisterously agitated the foliage of trees and bushes. Never had he imagined that a day would come when, as now, he could sit here and actually hear that soft spring breeze coming from afar and stirring the fresh leaves and passing into the distance of a London whose iron roads no longer emitted their thunder. How calm was that air, this scene! And how exquisite was its effect upon him! Gone was the compulsion of that tense, stiff pace, that goading scramble. In its place there was something which was attuned to the unhurried progress of nature in its seasons.

Around him, on other seats, sat City men, and typists and clerks. The sound of their laughter and conversation had an exciting note, as though the enforced idleness was not from chaos or collapse but from a universal inclination for an altogether new conception of human existence.

He turned to a smartly dressed man of about fifty who sat at the opposite end of the seat.

'It's so funny,' he said, laughing. 'All you fellows coming up to Town as usual, just to walk about and sit around and chat! Why don't you stay at home and have a real holiday? Cut the lawn and just potter about the house, or have a round of golf?'

The stranger smiled and shook his head.

'No, you wouldn't get the proper feeling of holiday, at home. It'd be just like Saturday or Sunday or a Bank Holiday. Whereas, coming up to Town and just walking in the Gardens, you really do get the full flavour of things. Wonderful! A real treat!'

He got up and sat down next to Willie and went on:

'I've never enjoyed life so much! Just sitting about in the sunlight and the silence and doing bugger all! Just listening to the birds!'

'Yes, but my goodness aren't you worried about the collapse of . . . well, of trade and all that?' Willie said.

The other lifted his hat and settled it again on his head.

'Awfully, at first. Nearly put me off my rocker. I thought it was the end of the world. I mean, no trade. I'm in leather and fancy goods. Commission agent, no income. But then the chaps who usually travel to Town with me every morning told me to join their PEEPER Club, so I did. Not so bad then. Job right away, with lots of other chaps like myself. I start work to-morrow in a PEEPER Restaurant. Clerk in charge of supplies. Three-fifteen a week. My wife and I worked it out, and we'll just about be able to manage without breaking into our savings. The President of our PEEPER Club at Surbiton explained the new order to us only last night. Nice chap. Used to be a big shot at Lloyd's. Said we were all moving forward. A sort of tide in life. I must say, I think none of us really regret the change. Not since we're all in it. Really, when you think of the old life, it was pretty awful. You never really knew . . . you didn't, did you? . . . just what was going to happen. War, or some sort of business that worried you a bit more. All the time. Never a rest. Something sick and patchy about it all. We all wanted something new. Except the ones who were well dug in. I must say I like this new way of things. Suits all of us. In our PEEPER Club, we've got all sorts, and no politics. Thank God that's all over! That awful game, squabble, squabble, squabble, all the time! As if you could get anywhere with that sort of caper! Not that I'm for Fascism or any Dictatorship stunt. Far from it. But a middle way, with all parties taking a share. After all, there's not much to choose between a Dictatorship and a Party Government in power for five years, is there? Best thing is to have a Coalition. We were only saying last night, at our PEEPER Club: thank God all that party politics tripe is finished for good and we can begin to live instead of having to die for some fathead's mistakes! Wonderful! To come into the daylight at last.'

'Yes!' Willie said. 'It is wonderful.'

He got up and walked away. He supposed that he, too, could take a job and rub shoulders with stockbrokers, merchants, and their former employees, at three pounds fifteen a week. But he trembled at the thought of a new currency, and the loss of his fine fortune, and the metric system coming into being overnight just as the experts always wanted it to. You never knew, with Colport holding the reins.

Still, three pounds fifteen a week. Not so bad, when the price of breakfast, or any other meal at PEEPER Restaurants, was not more than a shilling or one and threepence. Rents could not increase, for the Government had slammed down on them with a swift, flat hand. And there was little else upon which one could spend money. The theatres and cinemas were temporarily closed. But the Pools and the Saturday matches still continued. Life was on one economic level.

Coming from the Gardens and turning left, he walked towards Knightsbridge. All along there he saw the derelict cars and lorries, midst which the nightly petrol thieves had reaped a harvest and left that mass without a hope of locomotion. The doors swung loose in the breeze, and the children swarmed noisily in and out, over and under, their voices lifting into the vivid sunlight. All along Piccadilly, that black, motionless tide remained. It filled every yard of ground at Hyde Park Corner, and flowed along Park Lane: a sea of dead things, motionless, with sunlight flashing in reflection from it. The wind played over it, and the ear awaited an impatient chorus of klaxons. But all was hushed in that hopeless entanglement.

On the lowest step of a tall house along Piccadilly, Willie saw an elderly gentleman seated with his grey head bowed in his hands. He was sobbing. A liveried servant standing on the top step answered the enquiring glances of sympathetic pedestrians with a shrug and a grimace.

'I can't do anything with him! He keeps on saying it's the end of the world. He won't come in.'

The crowd smiled and passed on. Willie went with it. He turned into Bond Street and went through to Oxford Street and along to Tottenham Court Road. It was the same all the way: the crowds on a kind of holiday, filling the pavements and roadways, their voices rising in wonder, gaiety and freshness into the air which was free for the first time of the seething roar of traffic. Here and there, little knots of people danced in the roadway, having come up from the East to look at the West. And the West watched it, having dined or lunched at PEEPER Restaurants beside people who were agreeably astonished to find that such hotels as Claridge's, the Savoy, and the Berkeley had been converted into PEEPER Restaurants which were open to all, literally to all.

Willie was stunned by the thought: 'Not for to-day. Not just a holiday, and back to work to-morrow! Not a sort of V-day or something like that. But for good! A new era!'

He stood with his back to a shop window and pondered it all. Was it actuality? Could the enormous routine of life suddenly transform itself? Could these people break away, and begin a new life? Was this sort of thing happening throughout the world? *The Times* had said so yesterday. For once, it had a headline across an entire page.

## UNIVERSAL REJOICING AT THE PROSPECT OF AN ERA OF WORLD UNITY

Willie walked on. He had lunch in a PEEPER Restaurant with a cheerful swarm of people of all types and classes, paying a shilling for which he was given soup, mutton and potatoes with spring cabbage and what was described as 'Colport Pud.' For threepence he had a cup of excellent coffee. Passing out, he was able to purchase a small packet of 'Player's' at the counter. Ambling eastwards, he had to admit that within a day or two his digestion could accustom itself to that kind of fare. It was not bad at all. And it was plentiful.

By four, he was in Leadenhall Street. He heard a shout. The crowd turning and hurrying towards three speeding newsboys, carried him with it. Newspapers! They were almost a novelty.

He darted through and ahead and bought a copy and then edged out with it and stood in the porch of a tobacconist's shop to read.

## ASSASSINATION OF PLEBS FOREIGN MINISTER
## TWO COMPANIONS GRAVELY WOUNDED
## ASSASSIN SHOT DEAD
## GRAVE CRISIS DEVELOPS IN EUROPE

There were columns of news. His gaze sped down them. In his imagination, he saw the whole scene. The disreputable little café, with its loafers and pimps and prostitutes, and the party of five or six old friends making merry in a corner. Then the entry of 'What's-his-name,' and the sudden outburst of firing. Shrieks and shouts; overturned tables and chairs. And the body slumped across the table and then falling to the floor. The two wounded men. Then the arrival of the police.

The newspaper mentioned 'an angry mob.' Willie shuddered. The newspaper reported that the assassin was shot dead while trying to escape through a rear door, and that an examination of his wallet revealed that he was a stateless person carrying a forged passport in the name of Smith. His real name was understood to be Vatsitzgnom.

Willie folded the newspaper and shoved it into his raincoat pocket. Then he set out to walk home. He had a long way to go, and since there was no public transport operating, he was obliged to walk. It was after eight o'clock when he reached Flossie's house and, after glancing cautiously around him, hurried up the steps and into the porch.

He let himself in carefully. True to his cunning instincts, he left the door ajar behind him so that he could retreat if . . . well, if the police were awaiting him in the empty rooms from which, it appeared, Flossie and her patriots had departed. He made a tour of most of the rooms and satisfied himself that the house was deserted. Then he went to his bedroom.

He did not turn on the light. He locked the door and crossed to the bed. Without removing his clothes, he threw himself down. He slept at once. He fell into a deep sleep, forgetting everything: Flossie and the patriots; Vatsitzgnom; the crisis; Twigge and PEEPER; the police; and the house door which was still ajar.

# FOUR

★

It was broad daylight when he awoke from that long, dreamless sleep. Finding himself fully clothed, and seeing the clear flood of daylight about him, he could not at first recall what had happened. A party? He struggled with memories of outrageous parties in Vienna. Was this Vienna? Was this the old Palace, or that ornate Hotel, or little Lisa's flat, or . . . But no! His head was clear. His tongue was healthy. He was sober; and in his mind there remained an impression of some exciting event of world importance, and a recollection of something else, not quite clear as yet.

He sat up on one elbow and drew a deep breath. When he expelled it, he remembered yesterday. At once, he got off the bed and went to the window.

It was a tall, old-fashioned window which opened on a balcony. Willie could see a strip of the roadway, but since the balcony hid the pavement immediately before the house he saw nothing at all of what was happening outside the house. In the road, there were cyclists passing; and along the pavements the people were strolling. He was reminded again of yesterday and its peculiar air.

He could not adjust his sleepy mind to the idea of a transformed world. His heart pounded in nervousness. Had he been dreaming? Was that recollection of a long walk nothing but the memory of a dream? Surely! The august City of London did not slip so easily into such abrupt changes! But as he yawned and dug his fists into his eyes, he saw again the cyclists, and the pavements thronged with lounging hundreds. So it was true!

He drew back from the window as though he were struck. He was not going to believe, even if he saw down there what he had seen yesterday! No, sir! He was going to remove his clothes and take a nice hot bath; and after that he was going to ring for his breakfast . . . and . . .

He removed his jacket and suddenly remembered Vatsitzgnom, and Flossie's patriots, and Twigge and PEEPER, and the news which he had read in a shop doorway last night. Horrible news! Of little Vatsitzgnom . . . pulped by blows and buffets and . . . and the police!

186

He felt sick, really very sick at the thought of what might have transpired during the night. But still . . . that was yesterday. That was all over and done with. To-day? Why, to-day belonged to the new order which was rolling across the whole world and carrying mankind on its high crest! It was hardly likely that Authority would bother itself with the affairs of the little assassin whose body was lying in a Paris morgue along with the body of the Foreign Minister of Plebs.

Willie's nerves were always particularly good. They had resilience and could suffer shocks. In this present trouble, the fact that he had not to take care of Flossie or her patriots left him free to concern himself with his own safety. His sleep had refreshed him. He wanted only a hot bath, a shave, and his breakfast in order to confront this new day with perfect equanimity.

From early manhood, and throughout the war, Willie had never gone without breakfast in bed. First his mother, then Flossie or one of the servants, then a former servant of an aristocratic Austrian family, had brought his breakfast to his bedroom. To-day, the habit of a life-time was broken. He was fully dressed, not yet bathed or shaved, and not yet breakfasted. A day so strangely begun could hardly continue satisfactorily.

He opened the door and crossed the landing. In the bathroom, he turned on the hot tap and waited. It ran cold. He sat down on the chair and swore again. He might have known that Flossie and her patriots had taken all the hot water. Flossie always ran a full bath, and her disgusting patriots were never done rushing to the bathroom to spend hours washing their feet. Willie sighed. All manner of anxieties rose and fretted him then. The silence of the house seemed to him to be full of them. They were like things left on the air by Flossie's irritable presence. The whole house was tense with them.

Grimacing unhappily, he went down to see about his breakfast. When he was half-way down the stairs, he had an uncanny feeling that he was not alone in the house. He halted. The faint but unmistakable odour of cigarette smoke was in the air. He saw that the house door was slightly opened.

It depressed him. With mingled anger and anxiety he hurried down, never for an instant supposing that it was a stranger. In imagination, he saw Flossie and some of the patriots sitting, just sitting in the study, and waiting for him to think for them. Anger swept through him and drove him through the hall. He flung open the door and strode into the room. Three men stood there. Strangers.

He was within a yard of them when he stopped. The three pairs o
eyes seemed to him to hold him at a distance. He stood there, numbe
by surprise.

All three men had an authoritative air. They were dressed alike
Their attitudes were alike. One of them spoke, naming him and askin
him if he was that person.

They were detective officers. He knew that. As usual, when he wa
taken by surprise, his lower lip sagged. He looked what he was:
determined crook who wanted to speak. He had that sudden, inordinat
desire to talk; and the men thought that it was only a nervous reaction
But this time, he did not wish to explain away a felony, or wheedle
superior into supposing that he had committed a mere error. This time
he had no excuses. Instead, he wished to ask about . . . well, about th
world. But the words would not come to his tongue. He was dumb.

He was cautioned and then arrested. But he could do nothing excep
stand there, listening, and feeling despair, regret and frustration. H
was afraid, too, for the spokesman charged him with the murder o
Fred and Georgie, and with illegal dealings, and with another and mor
terrible crime.

He had not expected that the Law had such a perfect knowledge o
his activities, especially at such a time as this when order was rapidl
changing. To be arrested gave him an acute sense of disappointmen
He wanted to ask the officers, for surely they would be able to tell hir
if there was this end and beginning.

They gave him no opportunity. One of them accompanied hir
upstairs and waited in the room while he changed. Willie was told t
hurry himself. And the silent presence of that stranger in the bedroor
exerted a horrid pressure on his mind and prevented him from gatherin
his thoughts into cohesion. But at last, he managed to speak.

'I should rather like to know what has become of my aunt who live
here,' he said.

'You mean . . .' the man began.

He had a frank, open face, except when he seemed to be suspiciou
of Willie who moved to the wardrobe and chest of drawers.

'She was here yesterday,' Willie said, sitting down on the bed an
folding his arms. 'When I returned home last night, there was no sig
of her. She hasn't come back. I'm very worried . . .'

'Dress yourself,' the man said, pointing to the fresh suit whic
Willie had set out. 'No need to worry. She's quite safe.'

'Where?' Willie said.

'In custody.'

'What?'

Willie asked several questions in rapid succession. None of them as answered by the detective officer who merely said: 'Hurry.'

The other men entered the room.

'Not ready yet?'

'He's dressing, sir.'

He asked the senior: 'My aunt . . . I was asking . . .'

'He's worried about his aunt,' the one in charge of him explained.

All three smiled faintly. Willie drew on his trousers.

'You'll see her soon,' the senior said.

Willie put on his jacket and filled its pockets with the things from his crumpled suit.

'How are things . . .' he began. Then he stopped. He had an overwhelming curiosity about events in the world and in England, but he could not find the apt words. He made a wide gesture.

' . . . everywhere?' he stammered.

Before he could realize what had happened, the junior officer slipped a handcuff on his wrist. Willie gaped, and raised his arm. The officer's arm lifted with his own. Willie was handcuffed to him. But he went on:

'I mean . . .' he gulped back a sickness of humiliation and surprise. I mean, the universal . . .'

All four of them were going downstairs.

'The universal what?' the senior officer asked politely.

They reached the hall and went to the door and down the steps leading to the pavement. Five small children stared at them and nudged one another. Two passing adults stopped and watched as Willie and his officer got into the back of the car. The second detective took his place on Willie's left side. The senior sat next to the constable who was driving.

'The universal era . . . the prospect . . .' Willie stammered, still struggling to maintain his thin courage against an overwhelming sense of shame.

The three officers all looked at him.

' . . . of world unity,' he said.

The three men laughed loudly and cheerfully.

'World unity!' one of them exclaimed.

It was nothing but a fabulous joke to them. The car was speeding towards its destination, taking Willie to Justice.

'Surely . . .' he ventured to remark.

The men guffawed heartily. Willie was some sort of joke to them and their laughter was a sufficient answer to his question.

The man next to him on his left said: 'You shouldn't believe all you read.'

'But this!' Willie exclaimed, angrily, pointing to the streets in which cyclists wobbled along. 'All this . . . this . . .'

'Oh, that!' said the senior officer. 'They'll wake up soon.'

'So,' Willie rejoined, 'it's all nothing but . . . but a . . .'

'A bubble,' the officer murmured.

'But the Government . . . the Coalition . . .' Willie went on.

The officer was quite chatty. He leaned an arm along the back of the seat and turned round.

'The Coalition Government knows all the answers,' he said. 'Nobody need worry. Everything will settle down nicely, and one morning everybody will wake up.'

'To what?' Willie said.

They all laughed.

'They'll just wake up,' the senior officer said.

The old, familiar things resumed in Willie, with a dull pulse which hurt him. Once again, he experienced the old impulses and appetites and feuds. And quite suddenly, the image of Twigge glimmered in his mind. He knew then that he had lost a final conflict with that adroit being.

'I wish . . .' he exclaimed, loudly and roundly, with his old truculence. But he said no more. The image of Twigge grew to horrible proportions in his mind; and for the first time he recognized in that shabby, lean little figure something that had encircled all his affairs and defeated him.


# FIVE

★

That afternoon, Belfwig had before him on his desk a file of press telegrams and reports relating to the shocking affair in Paris. Also on his desk was a copy of yesterday's PEEPER cartoon, as well as to-day's. And in the room, he had a visitor.

The latter was an official from Scotland Yard. He was a young man of quiet, direct manner; and watching him Belfwig envied him his mild air and his personality which was without show or fuss and which had a charming strength that was in contrast to his own ornate personality.

'Our theory is that your artist, Jayby—John Bessing—is an extremely well-informed man in such matters,' the official said, pointing to the file and the cartoons.

Belfwig shook his head.

'Have you ever seen him? Spoken to him?'

The visitor said no.

'I thought not,' Belfwig said. He looked at the window. 'He's what I might term an ingenuous sort of chap . . .'

The young official laughed.

'Must be, to rip the lid off a gang like that, on two successive days, and show us two of the most dangerous numbers on our files!'

'I don't accept that idea,' Belfwig said, blandly, giving him a glance and then examining his fingertips.

'We do,' the other said, quietly. 'The connection is just too accurate to be a mere guess or coincidence or anything else. "What's-his-name" is Vatsitzgnom, and Willie is Willie, alias the "Admiral." '

'You must remember,' Belfwig said, 'that PEEPER has this rather remarkable gift of prophecy . . .'

There he smiled. So did the young man from Scotland Yard who said: 'I've explained what happened to Fred and Georgie, haven't I? No need for either of us to try to explain anything more, is there?'

Belfwig examined his fingertips again.

'Whatever you wish,' he said.

'May I see what you intend to publish to-morrow?' the visitor said.

Belfwig passed him the proof cartoon.

'Is that an order, or a request?' he said.

The other grinned. 'Just curiosity,' he said. 'We wouldn't dare to touch PEEPER!'

'I should think not,' Belfwig exclaimed, laughing. 'Not when he serves you so well. According to your ideas . . .'

'But we are watching him pretty closely, Mr. Belfwig,' the visitor said.

Belfwig explained the cartoon:

'I advised Bessing to refrain from what might be provocative or controversial.' And indicating the cartoon with a gesture of his hand, he added: 'It's a comment on events at home.'

PEEPER was shown surveying one of the many traffic blocks that remained at the great intersections of London's roads.

191

The young man from Scotland Yard returned the proof to Belfwig and then pointed to to-day's number.

'And how do you describe this?' he asked.

In the forefront of a disappointed crowd of travellers who were unable to find accommodation on a cross-channel steamer stood Willie.

## BUT WILLIE DIDN'T GO

Yesterday, Belfwig had supposed that it was nothing more than an amusing comment on the scramble to visit Paris for the Celebrations. Willie was typical of thousands. He looked nothing more than the average Englishman; and it was a shock to Belfwig to learn from this young official that Willie was not only a crook but an extremely dangerous one whose activities had resulted in that horrible affair in Paris.

'The curious thing about that cartoon is that we haven't had a single letter or telegram from our readers,' Belfwig said. 'That puzzles me. So far . . . not a word about it. Thousands of letters, yet not one reference to . . .'

'It's early yet,' the visitor said.

'By this time of the day,' Belfwig said, 'we have thousands.'

'Perhaps you've shocked your readers,' the official suggested. 'Perhaps they suspect this newspaper of playing all sorts of games with PEEPER. For instance: setting one gang against another; or informing against criminals; or pretending to forecast race winners, when all the time it had certain knowledge that a race was going to be . . .'

Belfwig slapped the desk with his hand.

'Rubbish! If you think . . .'

'I don't, sir! But your readers might. It's possible that you've strained their credulity.'

Belfwig dismissed the idea with an abrupt gesture. He knew the public. Its credulity could never be overtaxed, nor its great, gaping mind satiated. It had an astonishing belief in the printed word. Which was one of the reasons why he himself had always respected that mind and felt a grave sense of responsibility towards it. And in spite of its astounding gullibility, it awed him. It had such latent power.

'That's nonsense,' he declared. 'Our readers have faith in us. And I must tell you again, most emphatically, that we have printed PEEPER for what he is: a lovable personality, above politics, above suspicion. You are incorrect when you say that he expresses these . . . these . .

The visitor smiled and said without anger and with a considerable degree of patience:

'I've told you, sir. PEEPER has given us quite a lot of useful information. We were only sorry that he didn't give it in time for us to get hold of Vatsitzgnom.'

Belfwig laughed. 'Rubbish! The cartoon said "What's-his-name."' It just happens . . .'

'Too much has happened!'

'Very well!' Belfwig said. 'Tell me what you want me to do. Give me orders, advice . . . whatever you have come to give me. I'm quite ready to . . .'

'That's kind of you, Mr. Belfwig. All I came to tell you was that you should have a serious talk with Bessing.'

'Why?'

Belfwig did not wait for an answer. Instead, he leaned forward and grabbed a file of letters and opened it. He smiled sardonically as he glanced at his visitor.

'Listen to this,' he said. He read one of the letters:

*Dear Sir. You think Jayby does* PEEPER *don't you? Well, you are crackers if you think that because he doesn't. Jayby does the drawing but a man called Twigge puts up the ideas. He is the real brains behind* PEEPER *and you ought to know it.* A FRIEND

'We get quite a lot of letters like that. Every day, some ridiculous correspondent, always anonymous, writes to tell us something like that. That Jayby is not Jayby but Colport, or somebody else. See for yourself. Read some of them. They're choice. There's one there which says that Jayby is Hitler! Another says that he is a new sort of Fifth Columnist, sent by Russia to destroy us! If I paid attention to them for an instant, where do you think my sanity would be? I'd lose it!'

The visitor closed the file and pushed it back to Belfwig.

'The one which names Twigge,' he said, putting on his hat. 'I'd certainly pay attention to that.'

Belfwig rose and accompanied him to the door.

'And who is Twigge?' he said, jocosely. 'Another crook? On your files?'

'Look out for him, Mr. Belfwig!'

'An international . . .'

The young man said: 'Ask Bessing.'

When he had gone, Belfwig closed the door and walked slowly back to his desk. He felt perturbed and apprehensive. Outside, in the Street, a sound like a distant wind in the tree tops of an immense forest wa audible in the silence which persisted throughout London. Belfw knew what it was. Standing at the window, he saw the mob pour in the street like a black wave which flowed towards him and stared up him with its thousands of eyes and yelled its hoarse fury at him. H felt that rage like a palpable thing that drove him back at the insta when the burly Commissionaire burst into the room.

'Sir! Communists, sir! I've 'phoned for the police! Barricaded a the windows downstairs, sir! Better get away from your window, sir

The crash of breaking glass sounded from a lower corridor. A missi struck Belfwig's window. A second struck another and split the bi pane wide open. A bottle crashed into the room and thudded agains the wall.

Belfwig ran into the corridor with the Commissionaire.

'Everybody quite safe, below? What about the rear doors? And th roof?'

'I gave orders, sir . . .'

Belfwig sped down and met an aghast knot of typists and clerks Some compositors ran in from the machines. He could hear the mo battering at the main doors and crashing the windows.

'Lock those doors!' he said, taking charge. 'Get the staff out Barricade the doors. Get the women out through the rear doors, a once!'

He strode swiftly to another corridor.

'Get the fire extinguishers ready! Tell Johnson I want him. And Sergeant! Sergeant, get some of the men to hold the doors!'

Upstairs, the editorial staff was coming from the rooms and crowding into the passages, calling, running down to him, meeting the clerica staff from the ground floor. He went amongst them, cool and active and inspiring, giving orders. Once, he paused at a window on the firs floor and looked down. The crowd below moved like a sea in com motion. He had seen many crowds in the course of his life as a young daring reporter and as a foreign correspondent. Mobs in Paris and Berlin; rebels in Dublin. And throngs in what had been St. Petersburg. He was familiar with the note of anger, frenzy, recklessness and brutality which rose from them. But this yelling swarm!

It horrified him and fascinated him. The arms upraised, gesticulating. Those shaking fists. The bare heads. The eyes in the thousands of little shapes that were angry faces. And the mouths that were wide open to emit that awful volume of rage.

It was the sound of a threat. It was a seething wave that grew, swept up to him, burst, and began again in the next instant. It was the spirit of Revolt, and it reminded him of the pages of history that were torn and spattered by the bloody tramplings and slashes of mobs. He thought of the insensate violence which had no conscience, no mercy.

A sudden sharper note from that multitude startled him. He saw the whole crowd swing its gaze to the right. Following it, Belfwig saw mounted police riding at the mass.

Derision spurted into the yell and became a higher note of anger when the big batons were used. The pressure from the right was momentarily answered by a lurching movement of the mob. Belfwig saw it. It was exciting and yet terrible to observe and to hear. He stood with his face touching the window.

Somebody pushed him roughly aside with a muttered apology, and, to Belfwig's horror, flung up the window and mounted a Press camera on the sill.

'Once in a lifetime, sir!'

As though it were a Cup Final! That apparatus, with the film spooling through it! While like a gale of wind, the yells from below swept into the room. A bottle rose from the mob. The photographer ducked. Belfwig dodged to one side. The missile struck the sill and shot off into the room and thudded against an old oil painting of a former editor. The staff photographer laughed hysterically.

The mob was tightening its pressure against the mounted force which was striking right and left with a heavy, almost rhythmical motion of batons on heads, shoulders, upraised arms. A horse reared, and its rider slid heavily off and disappeared beneath a scrambling mass of rioters who recoiled at once when the riderless horse pressed forward and two mounted officers rode at that boiling group. At that edge, where Authority met Disorder, the forces were so compact that only a kind of shove and thrust was possible from the rioters who were as much confined and hurt by their own supporters pushing from the left as by the whirling batons. Belfwig could see that. It had become a fight between a kind of solid force and those mounted police whose trained horses knew where to thrust forward and whose batons walloped and thwacked at the least sign of a weak point. Belfwig himself, as well as the little knot of sub-editors around him, could feel the fury and menace in that conflict. He heard the tone of the shouting gradually change as the huge crowd, like a single thing, slowly yielded to pressure. And suddenly broke.

'Like a spring!' he exclaimed. 'It always happens! I've seen that happen dozens of times!'

The agile staff photographer was aiming his camera at the breaking-points. Other employees crowded into the room and clustered at the windows.

In the street, a scream of panic travelled over the mob from its right edge. The left thinned out suddenly, and the whole mass swayed back. At once, foot police poured in. At the extreme left, the mob was scattering. In its centre, it was breaking open, like a cracking surface of ice. Its right fringe was crumpled beneath the batons and the darting foot police.

Figures sank beneath the horses, under the batons, or scattered to doorways. The foot police grabbed at them, grappled, slithered about, marched off with single, tattered rioters. The gaps widened, and the running figures became more numerous but assembled again to fight it out with single mounted police. The horses rode in through the main mob which fell back swiftly, leaving behind the appalling aftermath of all riots: the prone bodies like heaps of rag in little pools of blood; the stragglers; the litter of hats, coats, boots and shoes, sticks and bottles, and paper, so much paper that Belfwig could not understand where it had come from.

He heard the gruff shouts of the police. Orders were given. The dishevelled captives were being led off to vans. A few of the rioters still resisted in little clusters against which the batons banged and thrust. Voices yelled. But the uproar was subsiding, and the hoarse chorus of the mob had faded into the distance into which the remnants of the multitude had fled.

Leaning out of the window, Belfwig saw the last rioters being rounded up and dragged off. A horse delicately avoided the prone bodies which remained in the roadway and which were so still and like so many bundles of rag flung there. Symbols of dead violence!

'In the can!' the staff photographer said, still directing his camera at the scenes below.

Turning, Belfwig met the grave faces of his sub-editors. The photographer brought in his camera. Somebody closed the window, shutting out the beat of horses' hooves and the explosive shouts from the road-way. The immediate hush in the room seemed to Belfwig to have its source in the features of his editors. They awaited his comments. In their eyes he read a single question. What report was to be printed? What news?

Before he could speak, the door opened and Lord Ecks entered the room. The door slammed behind him. He smiled through the cuts and bruises and smears of dust on his face. A long streak of blood trickled down his right cheek. He was without a hat. His hair was more untidy than ever. His collar and tie were hanging loose over his jacket which was ripped at the back from the seam to the top. He flung down his raincoat and seated himself on the arm of a chair.

'Gentlemen!' he exclaimed, panting. 'For your information . . . they were not Communists!'

A mumble of astonishment came from the others. Ecks went on: 'The first organized opposition to PEEPER! Nasty! If you like, you can call it the first mutter of civil war. Or revolution. Don't like it! Would get to my knees at this moment, and pray. If I could bend my legs. Pray that the spark has been extinguished.'

He dabbed his face with his handkerchief. Limping to the side-table, he poured water from the carafe into the glass and drank it.

'Mustn't intrude on your responsibilities, gentlemen,' he continued. 'Thought I'd come here and take your advice.'

He turned to Belfwig. 'Major crisis, Belfwig. Whatever you and your staff decide, I'm content to follow.'

Belfwig motioned with his hands to the chairs and addressed his staff. 'Sit down, please.'

They sat on the chairs, on the arms of the chairs, and on the edge of the table, and heard him give them the news from Paris as the official from Scotland Yard had related it to him. Vatsitzgnom, and Willie. And Willie's connection with Fred and Georgie. And somebody called Twigge. . . .

'A Park orator,' Harry said, flatly. 'I've known that little nuisance since I was a nipper. Biggest little know-all outside of . . .'

They were all laughing. They all knew Twigge. All except Ecks and Belfwig.

'A character. Writes sermons for the bureau along the street . . .'

'But a personality. And a philosopher . . .'

' . . . my foot!' Harry growled. 'A little nuisance . . .'

Belfwig put up a hand. 'That's beside the point. What we have to decide is this. Do we continue PEEPER? I put that to you as a major point. You understand that PEEPER has become much more than we ever imagined for him. You might wish to put forward your own views. PEEPER is extended across the whole life of this newspaper, and I don't wish to withdraw him without first of all giving you an opportunity . . .

Somebody said in consternation: 'You're not proposing to kill him off?'

And all of them, in unison, and then singly, said no, couldn't do that, impossible.

'It's gone too far to stop,' somebody said. 'It's not only a national institution. It's world-wide. . . .'

Harry shook his head. 'If I had my way . . . after that "Lord Punch" affair . . .'

They refused to be persuaded by him. They laughed at him.

'What is it to be?' Belfwig said.

They told him. To continue. Whereupon he professed to be pleased and grateful. But had they said no, he would have replied in the same words. That riot in the street had frightened him and aroused his conscience and given him a feeling of guilt. PEEPER had gone far enough. The whole, fantastic business must be ended. Ambition had had its moment. Courage had taken him far out, beyond the regions of reality, into this . . . this horror. Now it must finish.

That was what he longed to do before PEEPER took him deeper into danger. He wanted a release from PEEPER and the crisis and madness. He was appalled, for he was not going to be so easily released. He had to go on, deeper and deeper, to an ultimate cataclysm beyond the worst horror. And he dared not run away. He had too much self-respect to turn tail and cancel PEEPER at this first whiff of danger.

So he stood his ground and made his brief speech and then left his staff. He went back to his own room with Ecks beside him. There, he flopped into his chair and was silent, until his own guilty, fearful gaze met that of Ecks. Then Ecks spoke.

'Have to, I suppose. Can't cut and run just because . . .'

He pointed towards the street.

'It's the grinding feeling of responsibility which hurts me,' Belfwig said. As though his collar stud hurt him. And he went on, angrily:

'I can't understand why the blasted Government doesn't do something, say something to us, show us its hand!'

Ecks guffawed. His swollen, gashed face had a devilish look.

'Think they would? Think they'd let us know what they had in mind? Not likely!'

'At least they could give us a chance to help!'

'We are helping!' Ecks said. 'If we weren't, they'd soon let us know. Off with our heads! Whoosh!'

198

'Then why don't they say so? Why don't they do us the honour of inviting us to a conference and letting us put forward some constructive views?' Belfwig said.

'Because we're doing nicely thank you for them, without any conference!' Ecks chuckled. Then he said seriously:

'You have no political intelligence, my dear Belfwig. None at all. Can't you see what the Coalition is doing?'

Belfwig snorted. 'Of course, I can! Keeping the world quiet with our doses of PEEPER!'

'Right!' roared Ecks. 'While they push on beyond the people and erect the stockade into which the whole world . . . the entire world . . . will stampede like wild elephants being rounded up!'

He guffawed again as best he could with his swollen face.

'Fascism! A United States of Europe . . . of the whole world! That's the game! That's the bloated dream bred from the itch for Power! A Federated States of the World, with about six men bossing it!'

Belfwig sank into his chair, huddled and fearful. He was pale.

'Afraid?' Ecks said.

'I never imagined . . . I never thought for one moment that . . .'

'Should have done, my boy,' Ecks said. 'I did. Saw it from the outset. Follow it yourself. Colport. Coalition. Government slyly links up with PEEPER Clubs by getting Club members to fill up the new forms, wash and scrub, fetch and carry. What for? National unity? Not a bit! National hoodwinking, until the plans for Universal Government are worked out and safely passed clean over the heads of the people. Tell you . . . politicians are always a jump ahead of the people. Thrive on crisis. Makes 'em active. They make crises. Love 'em. Gives 'em a sense of importance. But that riot down below was the first resistance. The Government anticipated it and stamped it out quickly.'

'I don't understand why the crowd came at us,' Belfwig said.

'Easy!' Ecks explained. 'Because it knows we are just the pawns of the Coalition. It expected us to tell the people the truth. We didn't. We haven't. So along they came to kill us.'

'And we go on?' Belfwig said.

'Until the Government wants us out of the way. Then we'll know what's what!'

Ecks got up and stood beside him.

'Now listen! This fellow Bessing. Fetch him here. We'll talk to him.'

'What do you propose to say to him?'

'I'll tell you. But before that, let me say this. I'm not going to let

199

this newspaper become a yes-thing in any big political stunt! Not even for the chance of historical fame! I keep my hands clean!'

Belfwig laughed derisively. 'After PEEPER has become the biggest pawn in any game yet!'

'He won't be a pawn any longer, Belfwig!'

'It's too late. If we move against the Government now . . .'

'Bah!' Ecks shouted. 'He'll become the champion of . . .'

Belfwig groaned. 'The public hates champions! It can't tolerate champions of liberty or justice . . .'

'That mob in the street,' Ecks said. 'It saw the way things are going! Now! PEEPER must warn the People of the new dictators . . .'

Belfwig shook his head. 'Read the latest telegrams. From all the continents. The Governments have joined hands with the PEEPER Clubs. Government delegates fly to London. Universal Unity accepted in outline by sixty-one nations. . . .'

He looked up at the battered face of Lord Ecks.

'Freedom is dead! All the birds . . . elephants you called them . . . are in the cage already. And those who tried to escape are down there, in the roadway, dead. And that's where you and I will be, if we raise a word against the idea of World Unity.'

Ecks was silent and quite still. At last, he sighed.

'I never thought PEEPER would make us his slaves!'

Belfwig laughed tersely. 'All of us,' he said, 'caught in the greatest deadlock in history. All of us, governments and the governed, the slaves of PEEPER!'

'Governments?' Ecks said.

'There isn't a government anywhere which dares to touch PEEPER. And . . .'

'In that case, we can make PEEPER speak out!'

'And there isn't a living soul that dares to make PEEPER speak out! If we act, the Government will crack down on us. If the Government stirs against PEEPER, the People will crack down on them. Deadlock!'

'Then there's no hope?' Ecks asked.

'A little,' Belfwig said. 'Just a little. If we leave Bessing alone.'

'Oh, but the fellow . . . I mean, he's hand-in-glove with some little fellow in the Park! One of those fellows on a tub!'

'He's done pretty well so far,' Belfwig said. 'And it's my firm belief that he's inspired. Having got us into this blasted dream, he'll . . . he's the only one who can get us out!'

'I never heard,' Ecks mumbled, 'never heard of a strip-cartoonist coming to such influence!'

Belfwig laughed. 'Haven't you? Why, only a year or two ago, Europe was nearly bossed by a little artisan, a fantastic little screamer to whom every diplomat in Europe bowed graciously at one time or another. I tell you the real potential leaders of the world are the little people: the stage and screen actors, the popular dance band chaps, the crooners and dancers. They have the real hearts of the people. All the time.'

'Pity they don't do better with them,' Ecks said.

'There's a tiny possibility that PEEPER might,' Belfwig said.

Ecks grinned. 'All right. Leave it like that. Let's see what this artist and that fellow Twigge can do. Must go and eat now. Lend me a shilling, will you?'

# SIX

★

It was time, Twigge thought, to return PEEPER to the course which Quentin had determined for him and from which he had been enticed so wilfully. It had been easy to persuade PEEPER to fulfil certain personal tasks, for the distracted artist was ready to accept any idea which offered to maintain PEEPER'S popularity and influence. But Bessing was no longer content to follow Twigge's advice. He was suspicious of Twigge's ideas, although his own were too thin to sustain PEEPER.

Twigge was proud of his success with that famous character. If PEEPER had failed to persuade the police on both sides of the English Channel that Vatsitzgnom was dangerous, and if that assassin had succeeded in spite of all Twigge's efforts to draw attention to him, Twigge could not be blamed. He had been daring enough. He had informed against Willie while the danger from that quarter was very real. Nevertheless, some hours had elapsed before Willie's arrest. They had been uneasy ones for Twigge. Now they were ended. Vatsitzgnom was dead. Willie, Flossie, and those bony gentlemen who sat on the edges of chairs and stirred tiny cups of tea, were arrested. Twigge rejoiced. His kingdom was his once more. But he was afraid of the enormous power which PEEPER held.

PEEPER had come to life, had spun the world on a new axis and set the people of the world upon a new path. The wily governments, clinging to the shreds of power, pretended to applaud him; but Twigge knew that they feared him, dared not touch him, and were awaiting an opportunity to destroy him. The face of life wore a new expression which was one of jubilation. Behind it, there was disorder, confusion, and increasing crisis. The new era could not lift its enormous feet and take even the first perilous step forward, although the will of the people desired that movement. Instead, it was retarded by subtle governments that knew how to thwart it while pretending to encourage it.

In its exhaustive reports, *The Times* mentioned only the so-called terrible disorders in Transplebia where PEEPER was being ruthlessly snatched from the people and exterminated by all manner of decrees. These reports gave the impression of a country which was alone in its ability to retain the old order. Side by side with them, there was news of a much more serious character. Throughout the world, the people might imagine that a rosy dawn was opening on human existence; but already the first dark cloud was moving across that dawn.

It came from the Rosy East. The Government of the Republic of Transplebia had sent a stern Note to the Coalition Government in London, accusing it of deliberately neglecting to control the activities of a certain Displaced Person who had been harboured in England and finally allowed to cross to France and assassinate the Foreign Minister of Transplebia and attempt the assassination of important members of other States. The Note demanded enormous sums in compensation, apologies, the punishment of officials, and the handing over to the Government of Transplebia of certain criminals who were under arrest in London and who were known to be associated with Vatsitzgnom. A time limit of twelve hours was given for a satisfactory reply. But the whole world knew that excitement in Transplebia was at such a boiling-point that General Mobilization had already taken place. Several Embassies had been raided by armed bands. Members of the staff of an English firm with a branch in the Plebs capital and selling a new brand of floor polish had been murdered by the same bands. And already, the army and air force of Transplebia was on the march and on the wing, although the destination of both forces was difficult to determine since the whole of Transplebia, as everyone knows, is surrounded by the territory of the Soviet Union.

Two months ago, such behaviour would have alarmed the civilized world. Crowds would have gathered in Downing Street and other vantage points to study the faces of Cabinet Ministers. The newspapers would have puffed up every item of news into enormous significance. Big Ben would have boomed out its bogey notes in millions of homes where a hush of expectation of news, and more news, and still more news no matter how trivial and disturbing, was current. The entire world would have demanded news, even if it related merely to the particular suit or tie or hat worn or gesture made by a statesman on his way to a meeting. And that demand for news, as well as the inflaming of public opinion by every ridiculous little item, would have compelled Government to some course of action upon which the virtues of Time and Tact and Wisdom had had no chance to operate. War would have resulted.

To-day, solid behind PEEPER, the nation was unimpressed by the Note. It did not care what Colport said in reply. Colport, in fact, had said nothing. No Cabinet meeting was boosted in the newspapers. Big Ben did not boom bogey notes into homes. Nobody ran hysterically to Downing Street. Transplebia's General Mobilization created no more interest than a strike of dance hostesses in Blackpool's ballrooms.

But Colport had not yet spoken. Twigge was worried, for a card—a trump card—had been presented by Transplebia to that astute old politician and statesman. It was a trump card for possible use against PEEPER. Twigge appreciated that. Therefore, it was time to bring PEEPER back to the course which Quentin had determined for him in his thesis.

How? By what subtle device, and in what sort of episode which John would illustrate?

Twigge examined the pile of notebooks in which he had written in shorthand Quentin's comprehensive ideas of Man. Twigge understood that philosophy, having taken his share in determining its expression in the various chapters. He subscribed to its mysticism. Yet he could not find the especial path which PEEPER must take in order to return to the great avenue along which Quentin intended to travel.

He had done impudent things with PEEPER. And imprudent things. Like a traveller finding convivial company in some obscure little inn, PEEPER had loitered, had taken sides in sharp disputes, had laughed and found popularity. What Quentin would say when Twigge confessed to him, Twigge knew well enough. He was prepared for a reprimand. Against it, he wanted to be able to say that he had contrived not only to make PEEPER a figure of immeasurable importance and power but had returned him to his proper course. Therefore, he searched the notebooks for a suggestion, for the genii was rapidly becoming the

Master and Twigge required a subtle idea by which to bring him under discipline.

Days, weeks, months, perhaps, would elapse before Quentin could discuss PEEPER with him. Upstairs, Quentin remained at an extreme edge of life, in a coma which, when he came from it, left him too weak to speak. Once, Twigge had been allowed to visit him during one brief period of consciousness; but the patient had not spoken. His dark eyes were dim. He smiled at Twigge's eager expression, as though he recognized what evoked it and was mocking him. Twigge waited hopefully; but the vague consciousness which Quentin attained at that moment was so unsubstantial and so defined by the dwindled forces of his life, that it seemed to be no more than a strip of ice in a river already thawing. How frail was his existence on that foundation he himself seemed to realize, for he appeared unwilling to expend energy in an effort of conversation or movement. Even his smile had been so light that it was scarcely discernible. It visited his gaunt features like a tremor upon a bowl of water shaken by passing traffic. It was a tiny gleam of recognition to which Twigge had responded with a broad grin and a slight motion of his hand, which appeared to satisfy Quentin who gave no other sign but remained quite motionless with his eyes reflective of the distance of thought into which his mind was withdrawn.

Twigge returned to his own room and sat there in a dilemma of fear and doubt and guilt. PEEPER, for him, was a master who wandered freely throughout the world while his creator lay unconscious on a sick bed. Presently, Twigge left his room.

He entered the passage and glanced upwards before ascending the stairs. He knew that there were nurses in attendance all the time. One at night; the other during the day. Their duties were heavy, for the extraordinary events which had transformed human existence necessitated such tasks as the purchase of food for Quentin from special Centres, and the preparation of that food, as well as special journeys to Fuel Centres where permit orders for supplies of fuel for invalids were granted, and visits to Nye's surgery for drugs and medicines. Lenora took her share of these tasks with John. Twigge, too, assisted. And the two capable nurses, being forced by Orders to bring their own food, while the rest of the household was allowed to eat only at PEEPER Restaurants, prepared Quentin's meals and took their share of the household chores. Twigge knew it. He knew, too, that there were occasions when the nurse on duty was absent from the sickroom for as long as fifteen or twenty minutes.

He hoped that she would be absent from the room now. He reached the landing and stood there. Almost immediately, he heard her in Quentin's room. Twigge sighed. He strolled to the big studio.

'I was wondering,' he said to John who was working there, 'I was wondering if I could nip in and take a look at the invalid.'

John gave him a glance and continued his drawing.

'No visitors. No talking,' he said, curtly.

Twigge tapped his shoulder. 'Just nip in there yourself, and tell her ladyship that the kettle's boiling or the milk is hot. Out she'll come. And in I go!'

John yawned. 'What for?'

Twigge grimaced. 'He asks what for?'

'Do you want to confess the mess you've got the world in?' John said.

'Is it in a mess?' Twigge said. 'Did I get it into that state? Think again!'

John was silent.

'I must have a word or two with Quentin,' Twigge said. 'I want his advice. The sooner, the better.'

'It's too late,' John said, throwing down the stub of charcoal, and leaning back in his chair.

'You think so?' Twigge asked, gravely.

'He wouldn't recognize the world now,' John said. 'He wouldn't believe what he heard or saw. He'd want time: weeks, months.'

'I suppose so,' Twigge said, sitting down opposite John.

He sighed loudly again. 'I was never a humorist,' he said. 'But I wish I were one now. Right now. To raise a bit of a laugh. To get the world giggling. That'd show the governments that we still hold the crowd!'

Bessing frowned at him. Angry and puzzled, he said:

'Governments! What's all this? Governments . . . holding the crowd?'

He got up from his chair and stood with his hands on his hips. Twigge crossed his feet and joined his hands. He smiled faintly while Bessing went on:

'What do you want to do now? What's the next little trick? You've had your way with PEEPER. Aren't you satisfied? What more do you want? Governments! Holding crowds!'

'Now! Now!' Twigge said, softly, holding up a hand for silence. 'I'm not denying . . .'

'But now you want to wriggle your way into something else! Another little bit of mischief!'

John's exhausted, nettled spirit shot out its rage at that small, patient figure in the chair.

'You've put Willie and his friends away! You forecast a winner. You as good as betrayed Fred and Georgie. Do you care? Not you!'

Twigge shook his head. 'I told Georgie,' he said. 'I had his permission . . .'

'What you wanted was a sense of Power,' Bessing said. 'Well, you've got it. Nobody in this world ever had as much. PEEPER is yours, and he'll do what you say, Twigge. I can guarantee that to you. He isn't mine. He never was.'

Bessing leaned over Twigge and said slowly and incisively:

'He's all yours! Yours, and Quentin's. Keep him. Take a bit more Power. Meddle with things that concern governments, if you wish. I won't mind! But there's one thing I won't let you do, and that's to go in there and worry Quentin. The rest . . . what you do with PEEPER . . .'

John shrugged his shoulders and turned about.

'Don't you care?' Twigge whispered. 'Things are in a shocking mess!'

Bessing laughed. 'Care!'

'As an artist,' Twigge said. 'Haven't you ideas?'

'Ideas,' John said, 'but no ambition.'

Twigge twiddled his thumbs and grimaced.

'What am I to do with him?' he said.

'Are you afraid?' Bessing said.

Twigge got up and rubbed his hands briskly together.

'Not a bit of it!' he exclaimed. 'What is there to be afraid of? I admit there are a few difficulties. Nothing much. Why should I be afraid, when the people are still fond of PEEPER, and when they have in their hands all the Power they need.'

'The people and their governments are one and the same thing,' Bessing said. 'Read it! Federated States of the World. It's on the way. What's the sense in talking about the people having Power in their hands when . . .'

Twigge interrupted him sharply.

'Federated States of the World! A fine bit of rubbish! That's what that is! Cruel rubbish. The biggest enslavement of man by a handful of crafty statesmen since the world began! We'll soon stop that caper. Make a note of that! Put it down for PEEPER. THE OLD ROAD. PEEPER watching the delegates to the World Conference of statesmen. WORLD UNITY, AT A PRICE.'

'Do you want that to go down?' Bessing said. 'Is that what I'm to do with PEEPER?'

'Why not?' Twigge said.

Bessing said: 'I don't care one way or the other. But if you begin to meddle with high politics, they'll come at you, those delegates.'

'At PEEPER?' Twigge said. 'That's what you mean, don't you?'

He laughed. He rubbed his hands together briskly.

'They wouldn't dare,' he said. 'He's too big for anybody to touch. Not even Colport . . .'

Bessing took up the charcoal and slowly seated himself before the board. Twigge watched him, noticing the strained features in their pallor and heaviness. All Bessing's old placidity seemed to Twigge to have degenerated to this. This boredom and unconcern.

'I don't care . . .' John said.

'Come on! Come on!' Twigge retorted. He appeared lively and happy. 'There's hope yet! PEEPER is on the crest of the wave . . .'

'PEEPER,' said John, as he clipped a fresh sheet of paper to the board, 'was Quentin's creation. He'll go with him.'

Twigge had no answer to make to that statement. He watched the charcoal making outlines on the paper, and at last he turned silently and went out.

# SEVEN

*

He loitered outside Quentin's room and, in desperation, crept to the door and stood there, listening. He could hear the nurse in the room. He grimaced and stepped back.

Instead of returning to his own room, he ascended the stairs which led to the second floor. He passed Lenora's room and continued to the narrow flight which spiralled upwards to the attics and the roof. They were bare, and their dusty boards creaked beneath his weight.

He groped his way through the darkness and the inactive, dry air. Up there, the odours of the house remained in a thick staleness and hollowness through which his footsteps trod furtively as he entered the long attic. The door handle was stiff and rusty, and the door itself yielded only after he had pushed heavily against it. In the darkness, he could make out very little at first; but as he stood there, his eyes became accustomed to the murk. He saw the old canvases standing on the floor against the wall. The dim light which came through the roof-window revealed broken, discarded furniture upon which a few rusty palette knives had been tossed. The lumber of paraphernalia from the studio downstairs had been set here. Twigge groped his way through it towards a short ladder above whose head was a trap-door.

He tested the ladder with his hands, and having found it secure, he began his ascent. When his head almost touched the woodwork, he stopped, lifted his right hand, and shoved.

The weather and grime of many seasons had almost cemented the door which yielded only after considerable exertions by Twigge who worked his way up until his back was against the wood. He gave a great heave of his shoulders. The rusty hinges creaked. One of them snapped. The door lifted grudgingly, sending down on him a shower of dust and dirt and cobwebs. He went on, pushing over the flap and feeling at once a gush of sweet air rush past him into the attic. He stepped out on the leads and saw around him in the darkness of night the squat shapes of chimneys and their masonry. A wall about three feet high surrounded the roof.

Twigge had come up here twice previously. Once, on a summer night, with Quentin; and again, last winter, after a heavy fall of snow, when the scene had extended on all sides under moonlight which had made eerie shadows and which the snow reflected in glistening delicacy from innumerable, frozen surfaces. On both occasions, he had heard the incessant mumble of traffic rising from near and far and making a monotonous thunder. That sound was expired at last; and the scene was all the more mysterious and awesome because of it.

Looking about him, he saw the rooftops and chimneys of all sizes and shapes standing like motionless yet sentient things in an extensive forest of stunted growths. A few lights showed in near and distant attics, or in some lofty window. The darkness of night possessed the entire scene; but when his sight was accustomed to that immense ocean of darkness, he discerned distant horizons where the skyline with its irregular buildings met the city's extent. Twigge knew that those horizons were no more than a mile or so distant, yet because his senses were unused to the freedom or scope of space, he relished this scene whose features belonged to the city but which showed no road, no route which the eye must follow. But principally, it entranced him because of its silence which seemed to him to denote the end of an Age, and the forces which were latent in the organism of mortal life and which were defining themselves at this time. What those forces were, now that they were imminent in expression, Twigge did not care to remark. Nor did he care to decide which one of them would predominate. They were numerous, and he was aware of them. That was all. Eras of life had brought mankind to this moment in Time. Time alone could create the new era and, from the mysterious forces in the organism, formulate Man in it.

With his hands gripping the rough brickwork, Twigge looked about him. Everywhere, the silence reigned, like a substance which carried him and held him poised on a crest while he stared about him at a scene which, for centuries, had been clamorous with the activities of men and women. But now that the clamour had ceased, the silence which had been pent for so long was released. It awed Twigge who, glancing upwards and seeing the stars in their constellations, knew that that silence was the essence of their existence, and that the planet Earth was a part of that universe to which the faintest prick of starlight in the sky contributed light and a presence.

Suddenly, the southern horizon was scratched by the ascent of a rocket. The streak of light burst at its zenith. Coloured fragments unfolded and disappeared. Fireworks. Some local festivity in that quarter. Again, the light streaked upwards, burst, and spread its fragments fanwise. Soundless in the darkness.

Far below, the city's population existed. And farther away, over the land; and, beyond the intervening oceans, in other lands, other continents, were millions upon millions of other beings. All . . . all of them the devotees of PEEPER; and all of them stepping forth from an old civilization, and beginning a migration of thought, of faith and hope which would create a new civilization.

He knew at that moment that PEEPER had not achieved that remarkable change. PEEPER was but the key (as he had told Bessing) which had unlocked the door and released Man from a long confinement in outworn systems. And it was Man himself who, suddenly united in a mood of weariness and impatience with his rulers, had stepped boldly forth of his own volition, recklessly perhaps, to pursue his own idea of Freedom and to escape at last his awful fear of himself. Fear of the horrors which he had endured from savagery right through to this last year. Horror upon horror, despite the vaunted Progress of Civilization, the achievements of Science, and two thousand years of Christianity. That was the nature of this cataclysm. Man had at last seen his reflection: that savage, merciless thing, not truly Christian but still a pagan, still bloody and fierce. And it had appalled him. He turned from it. He had renounced it.

His existence now was in some strange desert wherein he had escaped forms of government that were so old and outworn that they could not attune themselves to what was new even in the old civilization. Instead, they prided themselves on their obsolete, fantastically old traditions and habits and fatuous pomp! But Man no longer obeyed the old governments, or the old ideas of trade or nationalism. Their reins barely touched him. He had overthrown governments almost everywhere. He had set up Provisional Governments which were afraid of him. He was free of his rulers for the first time in history. Except in the Soviet Union and the Republic of Transplebia which, Twigge supposed, looked with some misgivings upon the new order. But it was an uneasy freedom. Man himself could not go back, for his own instincts prevented him. Inquisitive, venturesome, he belonged to Time, Space, the Eternal, and his gods. He had to go forward. Whither?

Power was what he sought. Over himself, over his Earth and its environment which was the Universe. He hesitated. He consented to live in makeshift fashion for the sake of peace and security. He even accepted the commands of the Provisional Governments which, being composed mainly of members of the old Governments, had hastened into conclave while Man lingered a little way ahead in that desert. And already a new and terrible Power was being fashioned to drive Man back to Law and Order.

So thought Twigge, the King of London, the eccentric, the Human Encyclopædia, the glib-tongued soap-box orator. He had a suspicion regarding the form which that Power would take. Fascism had blared a brief note that still lingered in the memory of many statesmen who might think of trying a little sweeter music on the same instrument. That worried Twigge. But an instant later he was reassured, for he knew that by nature Man was stronger than any Dictator. His one weakness was in his belief that he was superior to the earth, to the other manifestations of life, and that he was the especial thing upon which sunlight fell.

Whereas, as Twigge knew, Man was of the earth itself. For centuries, he had ceased to identify himself with natural forces and had associated himself with a curious conception of his own immortality. Now, after long and painful experience during which he had discovered that his priests always allied themselves with his rulers, he was back to earth. But he was happy. He had suddenly broken the systems that had

210

imprisoned him. And in PEEPER he was united. Only Power threatened him. The Power in himself, and the insidious Power fashioned by governments to drive him.

Power, Twigge thought, as he stood there, was nothing but the echo from the sky of the shout of ambition. It was a ridiculous delusion which, time and again, had destroyed those who sought it. Yet it remained to fascinate the mind and cheat the spirit.

Twigge smiled slowly as he turned and made his way back to the attic. When he reached the landing outside Quentin's room, he halted. The door was ajar.

He hesitated for no longer than a few seconds before tiptoeing to the door and pushing it open and peering into the room. The nurse was absent.

He closed the door and locked it behind him. Then he crossed to the bed.

# EIGHT

*

Quentin was asleep. Only his head showed amidst the pillows and the white sheets that were drawn up to his chin. His dark hair had grown very long and lay untidily across his head and about his ears. A thick stubble of beard on his cheeks rendered his face almost unrecognizable to Twigge who stood looking down at that gaunt countenance.

The natural relaxation of the features in sleep, and the mist of dark beard on the face, concealed the hollowness of the cheeks and the strain of the long illness. A kind of peace and contentment hovered in the expression. It was of the spirit.

'Quentin!' he said, softly.

It was as though he were calling that spirit from a great distance into which it had retreated. The features moved only in the act of respiration.

Twigge repeated the summons, a little louder, whereupon the patient opened his eyes, stirred slightly, and stared up at him without recognition. He was about to close his eyes again when Twigge leaned closer to him and rested a hand on the clothes over his shoulder and repeated his name.

Into the eyes there travelled a ripple of vitality which was so fleeting and faint that Twigge knew he must grasp it swiftly and yet so delicately that nothing of its precious substance would be injured. He leaned down even closer and rested both hands on the shoulders.

'Twigge!' Quentin whispered.

'Easy . . . easy now!' Twigge whispered. 'I just popped in to tell you . . .'

'PEEPER?' Quentin said.

'That's it!' Twigge said.

'Tell me . . .'

Twigge sat down on the edge of the bed and told him quickly. The whole story, ending in the pronouncement of a universal revolution of ideas, a relinquishment of old traditions, and an exodus from the tiresome systems and the old forms of government. He related it all with a shamefaced, anxious air, his tone being modest and penitent.

'It's the best I could do . . .' he concluded.

Quentin shook his head slowly.

'I don't understand . . .'

'I've just told you,' Twigge said. 'That's the picture . . .'

'Is there a war, or a revolution, or . . .'

'Just what I've told you. That's how it is,' Twigge whispered.

Quentin's expression suddenly changed to one of resurgent vitality. He struggled to sit up. Twigge, momentarily startled, sat there watching him, and then gently restrained him.

'Sh! Easy . . . easy . . . If she comes back and finds you . . .'

'Why didn't you tell me before?' Quentin gasped. 'Why didn't you let me know?'

Twigge sniggered. 'So you're not mad with me for . . . for . . .'

Quentin's long, thin hand clutched him. He sank back on the pillows saying weakly but excitedly:

'Tell me! I want to know everything! What's happening? Show me some PEEPERS! Haven't you brought any newspapers?'

'Sh! Listen . . .'

'Tell me . . .' Quentin demanded. 'What are they doing?'

'Things are calm,' Twigge said. 'Very, very calm. The people are like lambs, except for one riot. But the politicians, all over the world, putting the bridle slyly on the creature.'

'And what does PEEPER say?' Quentin said.

Twigge wrinkled his forehead and pursed his lips.

'The best he can . . .'

'What?'

Twigge fumbled and stammered with his words.

'I must confess . . . I played about with him . . . on some local business . . .'

'Well, get hold of him again!'

Quentin gasped with the effort of speech. Twigge said:

'I want your help in that.'

'I must . . . see for myself,' Quentin said, softly, breathing the words and trying to raise himself on his arms.

Twigge restrained him. 'I'll tell you, I'll tell you,' he whispered fearfully. 'It's come to this: A struggle for Power.'

Quentin relaxed. He sighed. 'I guessed it,' he said. 'I knew it would result like that. I felt . . . from the outset . . . that if PEEPER achieved anything, he would upset the governments, and . . . and . . . make that conflict.'

'It's this way,' Twigge went on. 'The People have come out. They're ahead, but they daren't go too far. Can't see the way. But the conference of governments . . . they're at work all the time. And I'm afraid it's going to be a terrible business.'

'Power . . .' Quentin mumbled, closing his eyes.

Twigge touched him to prevent him from falling asleep.

'That's what they're aiming to take . . . the conference of Provisional Governments, and our Coalition.'

'What did we say it was? Power . . .' Quentin mumbled.

Twigge said: 'I said it was a shout into the sky. You laughed and said that I must define it in terms. We could never quite agree on that point. I said it was abstract. You defined it as a virtue which had been debased . . .'

Quentin regarded him with eyes into which the old vitality had returned. He smiled.

'They always forget,' he said, clearly and vigorously. 'They always forget that they are of the earth. Animals. They believe they are almost divine. But they are of the elements . . .'

He sat up. For an instant, Twigge only gaped at him, surprised by his sudden access of strength. Then he gently pushed him back, at the same time glancing apprehensively towards the door and whispering:

'No! Stop this! If she heard us . . .'

The long, thin hand suddenly gripped Twigge by the arm.

'Help me up! Get my clothes, Twigge!'

'Back to bed!' Twigge exclaimed in a whisper. 'Back to bed before she comes banging at that door!'

He saw the bones of the arm and shoulders jutting from the flesh that had shrunk around them. It was the body of a dying man; but the feverish heat that flowed from the hand into his own body, and the strength with which that hand held him, was of life. And in the earnest face the same vitality filled the features and gave impetus to words.

Twigge tried to release himself. Gently but firmly, he tugged at the hand which clenched his arm. He drew back a step.

'Help me to dress!' Quentin said. 'I want to go out, Twigge, and see for myself! Come with me! Show me! I want to hear them!'

He drew Twigge closer to him.

'Now look here! Back to bed!' Twigge exclaimed. 'Hear what I say?'

But Quentin's other arm came from under the bedclothes and clutched Twigge's jacket at the collar. The panting voice, hoarse and whispering, sounded harshly in his ears as Quentin dragged him closer. Whether it was anger, or only impatience or pleading, Twigge could not decide; but in an instant, those two hands had seized him by the neck and brought his face within a few inches of that contorted, furious countenance from which the words broke with a rising hollowness.

'You help me! Get my clothes! I want to go out and see. You take me . . .'

The emaciated body suddenly heaved itself with astonishing energy in a lurch forward. Twigge pushed him back.

'That's enough! You be quiet now! You'll . . .'

He was being shaken like a soft bundle of rags by those terrible hands that brought him nearer until he stared in fright into the face of PEEPER. He struggled to escape. He pleaded. With his own hands he pushed, grappled, trying to tear off the hands, while all the time the fury of strength in that frustrated spirit shook him, demanded his obedience.

'You'll . . . my God, you'll kill yourself!' he exclaimed.

One hand swiftly dropped from his neck and tore back the bed-clothes. The body swung round. Twigge forgot that he was struggling with a very sick man, and instantly grappled with that taut body. He threw himself to one side. He tried to step back.

'You think . . .' that hoarse voice said, ' . . . you think I'm going to die here . . . without seeing . . . while you . . . you . . .'

It was PEEPER returned to Quentin and demanding a release. Twigge felt the horror of it well up within him. He wrenched himself free and stumbled backwards. The little table against which he collided over-turned. An empty glass in a saucer fell to the floor. Glancing down, and

214

still stumbling, Twigge upset a vase of flowers on a larger table. He heard PEEPER cry aloud in a curious, smothered exclamation that was of anger, of pleading and disappointment. And turning, he saw him, hanging over the bed's edge, lax and helpless.

Twigge was afraid to move. He stood there, trembling and fearful, unwilling to go within reach of that violent body, appalled by the disorder in the room and the awful effort which Quentin had made. But all at once, he stepped forward. He put his hands under Quentin's arms and lifted him back into bed.

'You stay there!' he said, angrily.

PEEPER panted. A smile began on the dark face and spread maliciously over the features while Twigge swiftly settled the sheets and blankets and pillows.

'Don't speak!' Twigge said. 'Don't you dare! Not another word! I've heard enough . . .'

'Listen to me, Twigge!' And the voice was hollow and flat, like a sound which travelled from a great distance and was emitted at last through those tremulous lips. 'You be careful what you do with PEEPER! I'm coming to see for myself . . .'

'That's enough of that!' Twigge said.

He turned and lifted the overturned table. He put the fragments of the broken tumbler into his pocket, and set the broken vase in the grate, and the flowers in the basket.

' . . . see for myself what's happened!' the voice behind him continued. 'We'll walk about together, Twigge, and you can tell me . . . and show me . . .'

Twigge put his hands on his hips and faced him and saw again the smile, and heard the threat in the words. He took a step nearer.

'All right,' he said. 'That'll suit me fine! I'm ready when you are. Any time . . . Only I'll tell you this: you'll need all your strength. You'll want more than you've got at present. . . .'

The smile on that face which was PEEPER's remained in all its terrible vigour.

'I'll find it,' the voice said. 'I'll gather it. Then we'll go out, Twigge.'

'You'll have to get well first,' Twigge said. 'Stand on your feet. Ready for a long walk . . .'

'I'll do it! '

Twigge nodded and smiled back at him.

'Whenever you're ready,' he said. 'Suits me. Only you'd better hurry.'

He saw the smile slowly disappearing, and the eyelids trembling, and the eyes becoming misted with exhaustion. He went to the bedside, and looking down at the face over which a great volume of weakness was mounting and drifting, he said gently:

'I'll wait for you, Quentin! I'm ready, any time.'

He rested a hand on the head. The eyes closed, and the harsh, shallow respiration which sounded on the lips gradually became easier.

'Ready when you are,' Twigge whispered. 'Only you'll have to hurry. Gather your strength. Get well . . .'

He knew that Quentin was sleeping. He drew away from the bed, and after a quick glance round the room to satisfy himself that he had sufficiently tidied it, he crept towards the door. A moment later, he was on the landing.

When he was half-way down the stairs, he heard the nurse come from the kitchen and pass towards the patient's room. He stopped and glanced up. She saw him beckon to her.

She was a plump, jolly woman of about thirty, dark and attractive, brimming with splendid health. Twigge always amused her with his eccentric manners, and she could never resist pausing in her work to watch him and listen to his chatter which never failed to induce a broad smile of the frankest humour on her face.

'How is he?' he whispered.

She stopped on her way to her patient, and then crossed the landing and stood looking at Twigge who had come back so that his face was on a level with hers.

'He's holding his own,' she said.

Then she began to shake with laughter, for Twigge looked more odd than ever, with his abundant white hair tousled untidily and his collar and tie broken loose and swivelled far to one side, and a great streak of dirt running down his cheek. And an expression of the keenest confidence lifting his features and somehow expanding them so that they beamed at her with the impudence of a schoolboy's perky face. She could hardly contain the laughter which rose to her lips and which was already bubbling in her breast.

'That's the ticket!' Twigge whispered hoarsely, tapping her arm and moving closer to her. 'He's on the mend. You'll be surprised . . . you won't credit it . . . how quickly he'll recover.'

She giggled softly. So did Twigge who suddenly took her chin in the palm of his right hand and gave it a shake.

'You'll hardly believe your eyes!' he added.

Still laughing softly, she stepped back a little.

'I should hope so!' she exclaimed. 'After such a prediction.'

He winked at her and turned to descend the stairs.

'All you've got to do, nurse, is to tell him,' he said. 'Whenever he's awake, just tell him he's doing fine.'

He shot out his arms to free his wrists of the overhanging sleeves, and went on down with the quick agility of an urchin, leaving her still giggling on the landing.

Looking down at him, she saw him stop and glance back. The light caught his face, and seemed to transform it. Perhaps he had heard her giggle and resented it. Perhaps he imagined that she was mocking him. His expression was serious, and full of dignity.

'Go on,' he said. 'In you go! And tell him.'

He disappeared from sight a moment later; and she too stepped quickly back and entered Quentin's room. She was no longer laughing. Her broad, energetic face wore an absorbed expression; and presently she stood quite still, glanced over her shoulder at the door, and then at the patient. She smiled faintly as she went slowly towards the bedside and stood looking at Quentin.

# NINE

*

The entire household, including Twigge and the two nurses, as well as Matthew, Kitty, and Riddle, was gathered devotedly to succour Quentin. It had come together in that way because each day presented problems that could be solved only by the efforts of all of them.

It was easy for the able-bodied to walk to the nearest PEEPER Restaurant which might be a former Lyons Restaurant or a famous hotel. Class was extinct. Privilege was swept away. Life had a new hue, a different face, as one sat with hundreds of other persons of all ages and from all degrees of what had been class. And it was amusing and exciting to eat with them, to get a good meal for a shilling or fifteen pence, to hear the comments and to study the faces. Life was reduced to simplicity, said the women who, formerly, had catered for large families. Life was a monotonous level, and noisy, said the single man. Laughter spilled across the great crowds at the trestle tables.

But it was no laughing matter to obtain food for the aged and the patients in bed; and it was much more difficult to purchase the trivial household commodities such as matches, soap, pins, wood for fires, cotton, and bread. Despite the Coalition Government's optimistic tone, and the spirited enthusiasm of people for what seemed to be a new order, the mass of trivial details was slowly becoming a burden which retarded the belief in a universal motion towards what was new and different. Government, with an apologetic mumble had pushed ahead of the people, was everywhere, was at the old game of 'systems' with forms and thousands of temporary civil servants temporarily parked in handsome buildings requisitioned for the purpose.

To obtain food for Quentin, it was necessary to attend one of the special Food Centres set up in various parts of the Capital. Thousands of people waited patiently in long queues, often in wind and rain, and trudged homewards because all means of transport had been removed. Within a period of one month, most shops had sold their stocks of minor commodities and had closed down, thus leaving the population without an opportunity to purchase small necessities. The famous stores were empty, and their staffs had passed at once to Government employment. In all the great streets and avenues, formerly so busy and so thronged and noisy, a perpetual Sunday seemed to have descended. An air of silence and cessation prevailed, and through it the pedestrian hurried on the way to work, or to some obscure little shop still open. Convoys of 'buses and army lorries laden with food roared past. The pedestrian stopped and stared at this wonder, and watched with envy the thousands of civil servants being taken to or from work by fleets of requisitioned 'buses. No waiting. No scrambling for seats. Room for all. 'Buses for all who came under the wings which, daily, seemed to grow larger, until the average civilian began to wonder if, eventually, there would be only one employer in existence, and only one way of earning a livelihood.

The period of transition had lengthened and become an arid prospect without a single oasis. Hardships became more numerous. Or was it that the first impulsive hope and courage which had taken humanity on that journey, was now expiring? The luggage of one set of ponderous, outworn means and ends had been discarded, but another was growing hourly. It loomed higher than mountains. It increased like immense clouds in the firmament. Daily, an optimistic Coalition Government issued its Bulletins, announcing that Colport had become President of a PEEPER Club whose headquarters were in the House of Commons. Almost hourly, Colport extolled the idea of PEEPER-ism, until it might be suspected that doses of PEEPER were necessary, as drugs were to a nervous invalid. And all that had appeared in the early spring to be a novelty and but a temporary arrangement until something new could be contrived by the will of the people was now part of existence itself.

The desert was barren. Moreover, it was beginning to be obvious that the Government had gained control. Had it? Did it say so? Did anybody know?

Nobody knew. An oppressive note of irritation began anew every morning. But the mere physical effort of walking to the nearest PEEPER Club for the early morning cup of tea and breakfast, and of hoofing it to whatever work was not under Government control, and of eating with hundreds at PEEPER Restaurants, soon deprived the spirit of its sharp edge. Then one yielded with the rest, or gained a momentary optimism by contact with the civil servants who, being sheltered under the wing, had no cares and could afford to disburse much optimism. It did not seem to matter that the Government of the Republic of Transplebia had severed diplomatic relations with England, and had massed its armed forces along its frontiers, and violated certain Treaties, and already parachuted an entire division into the Libyan desert on what it called 'extra-territorial manœuvres.' Who cared, except the Coalition Government which, hourly, spoke of these 'grave moves'? Was not World Unity imminent? Or was it a dream which had vanished at the instant when the world had set out to march to it. Only PEEPER remained. The whole world still clamoured for him. But at home the individual, exhausted by a day of difficulties, was at peace.

Family life, and communal life offered wonderful personal oases, like a foundation which could not be destroyed. Neighbours discovered one another, shared, grew into communities around the local PEEPER Clubs into which companies of Government Ballet, Opera, Orchestra stars came on tour. Everything of the best for PEEPER and the PEEPER Clubs. The best entertainment, the best facilities. Join now! Don't be left out! Become a PEEPER Club member and get free milk, free soap, free matches!

But it was family life which was steadily growing into its former importance. Colport extolled it, and gained the Churches' approval for the remark, although the Churches refused to go with him when he added that 'in every home there is the invisible, kindly guest, PEEPER.' Nevertheless, moral authority became warmer to him from that day and gave its blessing to his new pension scheme for all newly-wedded couples. The family, it appeared, was receiving the closest attention from Colport.

At the home of the Bessings, the life of the family and its friends revolved very closely around their patient. A rota of duties had been formed to procure food for him, to prepare it, to obtain information about the likely sources from which small but welcome luxuries could be purchased.

Daily, John delivered to Belfwig a PEEPER cartoon which appeared on the following morning and which was welcomed as warmly as before by the millions of PEEPER fans in the British Isles, while elsewhere in the world yesterday's cartoon, or that of the day before yesterday, was excitedly awaited and finally greeted with an enthusiasm which increased as the days passed and the Idea of PEEPER became a feature of human existence.

John took Twigge's advice. Whatever Twigge suggested was acceptable and became illustrated in the four squares. Belfwig expressed satisfaction; so did the multitudes of PEEPER fans in the thousands of letters which daily reached the offices of the 'Daily Summariser' by the hundredweight, in sacks, along with presents of fruit, cigarettes, matches, sweets, wines and spirits, cigars, furniture, and numerous invitations to PEEPER to address public meetings. There came, too, many offers of marriage, and hundreds of threats of violence.

John ignored them all: invitations, praise, threats, gifts. His one purpose was to keep PEEPER active until Quentin recovered. He tried not to ponder PEEPER. He was appalled by the entire fantastic affair and regarded it as a universal fever, a sudden, inexplicable flaw or loss of equilibrium in the human consciousness. There was no other feasible explanation.

'Did he cause it all?' he frequently asked Lenora. 'What do you think? What's your explanation?'

She laughed. 'Of course not? How could he have done? What has he said that could possibly have resulted in this? Something about the Income Tax? As if . . .'

Her manner, in spite of her laughter, was nervously vehement.

'But how can it be explained?' John said. 'What began it all? Obviously, PEEPER has something to do with it! What other explanation is there?'

She turned almost fearfully to him. 'PEEPER had nothing to do with it! It's nonsense to believe that from this house, from Quentin, from you, all this . . . this . . . madness began!'

Her hands were clenched. She appeared to be answering questions stated more by her own mind than by John's words. She spoke emphatially, yet there was a quality of conviction lacking in her manner, as though from repetition the words had lost the flavour of her own convictions and had become meaningless.

'It was from the world . . . from outside this house,' she continued. There was something in the air . . . something which awaits every actor and actress and every screen personality. That's what it was. It found PEEPER and has taken him. It might just as well have turned itself upon a new crooner.'

John laughed. 'No, Len, that isn't what you think!'

'It is,' she said.

He came over and sat on the arm of her chair.

'No,' he said, pensively. 'And I'm the same. I keep trying to convince myself that PEEPER wasn't responsible for it, and that Quentin wasn't, either. I tell myself dozens of times a day that the Thing didn't come from any of us. But I can't quite make myself believe that. Nor can you. And Twigge is the same. And Riddle and Kitty and Matthew. We all think the same way and admit that PEEPER was the cause of it all. And that's why we are all of us hoping so frantically that Quentin will recover and . . .'

He got up, lit a cigarette, and added: 'Set everything straight again.'

'But I can't believe that so much . . . all over the world . . . all that, springing from PEEPER!' she said.

She appeared quite calm, but John saw the nervous fracture in her manner and the fears which were resident in her mind and which found expression in her slightest movements.

'I can't believe it,' she said. 'If I try to, it begins to destroy something in me . . . my reason . . .'

'But we have to accept it,' he said. 'There's no other explanation, is there? Don't you realize that? Don't you understand, Len, that we're all afraid. All of us: Riddle, you, Kitty and Matthew, Twigge, and myself . . .'

'I don't want to talk about it!' she exclaimed. 'Please . . .'

Both were silent. At last, she said pensively:

'If he had made the world laugh . . .'

'He might, yet,' John said.

Again, they were silent: and again Lenora spoke.

'There must be another explanation,' she said. 'The right one. I feel that there is one.'

John sat down and stretched out his legs and yawned.

'Is there?' he said. 'I give it up. I can't think of it.'

221

# TEN

★

To Riddle, the problem was simpler, and he imagined that he had practically solved it. Several aspects of it still baffled him, but the rest was quite explicable. He was a rationalist. He believed in cause and effect, a beginning and an end, a corresponding debit for every credit and an ultimate balance.

Through his contact with many trade interests, he learned of what was happening to the markets, the sources of manufacture, the distributive channels, the intermediate exchanges. He traced the hand of Government adroitly taking control at the springs and at the selling end. He did not know what to call that. Totalitarianism, or Socialism, or Communism. But since the nation appeared to be satisfied, he supposed it was Patriotism. It had to be something which deserved a fair label.

But there was something before that, something which had burst into life from people the world over and overthrown old governments and demanded new ones, and which was still not satisfied. He remembered the early reports of news relating to events in English cities. Curious, spasmodic moods of rejoicing, with PEEPER everywhere. Oh yes, that was amusing, that was very peculiar! But he could explain that. It was easy to see why that had happened. People wanted a change. That was all.

They made one. They downed tools and went on festival. It was a fever, and like some fevers it was infectious. Other nations took it. It spread throughout continents. The idea that human existence must be related only to work, to the great harness of earning money, making profits, creating huge edifices of wealth, was momentarily rejected. The idea that human existence might be for another purpose such as the pursuit of happiness and peace and security through leisure took sudden hold of people. They were tired of the old, overwhelming systems at one of which PEEPER scoffed. Off they went to dance, light bonfires, sing.

But they forgot that a day's work lost to production was like a stone cast into a pool. It sent out ripples which other industries felt. No coal for one day; a drop in steel production; a decrease in a thousand types of production. No cotton; no materials in the shops. No shops; no employment. All over the world. Factories, robbed of fuel supplies by days of idleness at the mines, closed down. Harvests rotted for lack of harvesters. All over the world, a breakdown.

World unity! Riddle laughed. Of course there was world unity! What else was there when every nation depended on its neighbours who, in turn, depended on it and on one another! What more could the cleverest statesman accomplish? What more was necessary, unless one thought in terms of bloody rivalry? To summon those bluff politicians from old and new governments and to pretend that World Unity was their object was only a handful of dust thrown into the eyes of people to blind them until the time came to reveal what the true purpose of that hasty conference was going to be.

Riddle believed that he knew what it was. Hadn't the Coalition taken control, with food, money, vast stocks of goods, railways, shipping and every other form of public transport firmly in its grasp? Hadn't it cut out the middlemen? Wasn't it steering the entire nation cunningly into a new kind of order which had no name because it was new and undreamed of and never even calculated by the most assiduous government of the past? Hadn't the Coalition brought into its employment millions; and weren't millions more pouring in daily, so that soon the nation would be its own employer? Wasn't that a fantastic drive towards a new civilization? But the conference of members of the Provisional Governments?

It was nothing more than a lecture on How to Behave at the Present Time. How to control the People. PEEPER realized it. PEEPER warned the world of it. Millions of PEEPER fans in the British Isles discussed it. Some argued yes, some no. Nobody cared very much. Why worry? Grub was plentiful, in the PEEPER Restaurants where you could eat twenty times a day, if you paid. Beer was coming along. The Pools and the League matches were not cancelled, although the season was now at an end. But there were the Dogs, and the Horses, and a hundred other amusements. And the PEEPER Clubs.

Abroad, it was different. Riddle was told of revolution and terror. Governments sought to destroy PEEPER, whereupon PEEPER in the shape of millions of revolutionaries destroyed governments and their adherents and all manner of other enemies judged fit for extermination. By comparison, the position in Britain was of paradise, although even at home new things had arisen from the remnants of the old. That swollen, privileged mass of temporary civil servants, of which Riddle himself was one. That, for instance. And others.

It rode to and from work free of charge. It had extra clothing coupons. It sat in its own PEEPER Restaurants. It had its own PEEPER Clubs, affiliated with one another under a special Guild. It was flattered by a wily Coalition which advertised in this way the vacancies still existing. Jobs for All! Why remain outside? Come in; and when all are in, Riddle thought, the doors will be closed. Colport will make a speech. The Coalition will announce that World Unity has been achieved. And PEEPER will be extinguished.

In Riddle's heart there was fear. He had never concerned himself with politics, principally because he had been in love with Lenora for several years and had been too preoccupied with that matter to think of politics. Love such as Riddle's for Lenora swallows the vision, puts politics below the level of dog racing. But he believed that he saw the truth in home affairs and world affairs at this juncture. And he was afraid because he felt that the statesmen were afraid of PEEPER. And he knew that when statesmen are afraid on their side of the gulf which they always erect between themselves and the People, horrible events ensue. He had been told of the ghastly civil wars in other countries, and of revolution and anarchy as well. Nothing of those events was reported on the Coalition Bulletin Boards. All appeared to be well, except in Transplebia where the armed forces were preparing to invade somebody. The fairest news was presented in the few remaining newspapers and was concentrated mainly on the headway in the establishment of World Unity. The Bulletin Boards reported leaps in public savings, and increases in membership of PEEPER Clubs.

When would the fever abate and sanity resume? What fresh crisis would arise when the gullible ones, the millions of stupid minds, the hysterical and impulsive spirits discovered that the bonds were upon them once more, this time so closely that never again would there be even a moment's release? Riddle asked himself that question and was afraid of the answer which his own mind gave to it.

There was something else which troubled him at the same time, although it was not as important as the current events. He could explain the collapse of industry, and the swift seizure of the chance to go in and take the whole machinery of trade under its wing, which the Coalition had cleverly effected. He could follow the course of events at home and abroad. But at home, the Coalition had said nothing against PEEPER who, quite obviously, was its enemy. And abroad, whenever governments had quashed PEEPER, terror had resulted. He knew why that was. He could explain so much, but not the inner phenomenon, not the mystery. Man had his laws, and he tried to live by them.

Morality plotted a course for him. Philosophy explained him but did not unriddle his existence, no matter how glibly it was applied to him. For at the core of his nature there was Mystery which defied examination.

He spoke of it to Matthew and Kitty with whom he spent much of his leisure during those days.

'Do you know what we are doing?' he said, referring to their devotion to Quentin, and hoping to continue from that to a more particular subject. He made the suggestion with a conclusive air, although he was really offering it for Matthew's approval of it as an idea which was reasonable.

'We're putting our faith in Quentin, because he's the only person who can clear up the mess. We're doing all we can for him because we want him to live. And that means that we acknowledge that he really had an original Idea and a purpose for that Idea, but that when he became ill the thing went wrong.'

Matthew and Kitty exchanged rapid glances. Both of them looked intently at him.

'It's true, isn't it?' he said. 'And another thing: behind all the wild enthusiasm for PEEPER . . .'

Matthew interrupted him, 'I wouldn't say . . .' he said, thoughtfully, 'I couldn't commit myself to . . .'

'You mean that you can't admit that from the mind of one man, so much could result . . . that an Idea could come . . .'

Matthew nodded. He removed his spectacles and rubbed his eyes with his right knuckles.

'No,' he said, 'I can't.'

'But it had to come from somewhere,' Matthew said. 'Where else, but from Quentin who created PEEPER? Or was it . . . was it from all men? Was PEEPER somebody or something which they wanted and waited for and suddenly found?'

Matthew exclaimed: 'A figure in a strip-cartoon?'

He shook his head, 'That's going a bit too far.'

'Then where, what . . . what caused it all?' Riddle said.

Matthew said: 'I don't know. I wish I did . . .'

Riddle laughed. 'Come on, confess it! Confess that you believe Quentin has an Idea and that if he gets well he can continue the purpose of that Idea and bring order. Say that you are as afraid as we all are that he'll die. . . .'

'You are,' Kitty said to Matthew.

'Only because . . .' Matthew tried to explain.

'Because he is PEEPER!' Riddle declared.

And suddenly Riddle no longer appeared like a man with an argument which he wished to exert over them. Instead, his round, chubby face had a wistful, pleading expression, as though he were imploring them to give him the truth.

'You do believe it, don't you?' he exclaimed. 'That he has this Idea? That he is PEEPER. Quentin, the mystic: I've heard you call him that, often. I believe it. I believe that PEEPER is his, and that when Quentin recovers he'll set things to rights. You believe it too, don't you? Anything else . . . I mean, if we thought for a moment that the Idea is from people . . . that they were the source of all this . . . that PEEPER became popular only because of his appearance, and that he has nothing to do with events . . . if we thought that . . .'

He stopped suddenly, for Matthew had sunk into a chair and covered his face with his hands.

'If I could pray,' he was saying, 'if I believed in the efficacy of prayer, and the existence of God, I'd pray.'

And removing his hands as rapidly as he had put them to his face, he continued:

'That's what we should do: pray! Pray for Quentin's recovery, and for the recovery of the entire world!'

'Then you believe . . .' Riddle said.

'I don't know what to believe,' Matthew said. 'I can't find a satisfactory explanation of it all. Did PEEPER begin it? A figure in a cartoon? Or is he just a symbol which people have accepted as something which represents unity of mood? Or is there a universal . . . insanity? And are we included in it? Is the entire world mentally sick after ages of wars and a vain search for abiding peace?'

There was silence. After a few minutes, he went on slowly and pensively:

'I've searched for a cause, an explanation. I can't find one. I examined history. I believed that I found long periods during which the race existed happily in security. But I was deceived. We have all been deceived. History has been faked up to represent Glory from Conquest, and to put before Man ideas of Duty and Freedom and Allegiance and Patriotism that served only to support the ambitions of ruthless leaders, or to correct the mistakes in the policies of others. It ignores the spirit of mankind and pays service only to Pomp and Might. It has never penetrated below the uniform of the common soldier to find the darkness and cruelty and squalor and ignorance behind Victories that were said to settle favourably so many human affairs. And there was never a

Golden Age, for Man is nothing more than a part of the natural life of the world, subject to laws of nature and essentially pagan in his spirit. The proof of that is in the remarkable scientific discoveries. What happens to them? Are they preserved from the pagan, savage spirit of Man and turned to true Progress? Never! They are rendered back to that implacable, heedless nature which uses all of them to blast and wither hundreds of thousands of human beings. Every amazing device is focussed upon destruction: of cities, of man. And do your philosophers condemn this, or your scientists suffer remorse? Never! It is accepted and explained away in terms of whatever condition it served. It is an act of despair! The universal mind realizes that it is collapsing under centuries of strain. Look at us, in this century! We are degenerate intellects. We are debased because we are worn out by incessant conflict and bitterness and suspicion. The people cling to PEEPER. Can he save them?'

Riddle and Kitty were silent. A little later, Riddle departed. He walked to Bessing House in Half Moon Street, taking with him some delicacies which, through his employment in a Coalition Government department, he had been able to obtain for Quentin. Lenora met him.

He was agreeably surprised by her mood. She appeared refreshed and full of the old vivacity.

'I needn't ask . . .' he began.

'Yes,' she said, going up with him. 'He's much, much better . . .'

'I knew it, Len, as soon as you opened the door.'

'A wonderful change for the better. He's sitting up! We're all so pleased.'

She accepted the parcel and opened it. Looking at Riddle and turning to him, she said quietly:

'You're so good . . . so good.' And taking his hands in hers, she added slowly and thoughtfully: 'I love you because you solve so many problems for me. You help so much.'

Her remark, Riddle thought, was some kind of answer to what Matthew had said. It offered a suggestion which leaders could consider, and which all the workers in the field of scientific and philosophical research might have accepted; for the so-called 'progress' which had been achieved had only increased the problems of life.

Riddle thought that it would be better if the whole purpose of human existence was declared afresh, and the efforts of all minds devoted instead to the problems which 'progress' itself had piled so heavily upon people.

# ELEVEN

★

In undertaking that extensive study of the crisis and of PEEPER, Matthew had been considerably encouraged by his editor who had released him from the series of articles, and who had opened to him sources of news which, by consent of certain subscribers, were operated under a strict, private censorship.

Through these reports, Matthew obtained an immediate, comprehensive picture of world events. Twice a day, he or Kitty visited the office and received several typed sheets which, later, Kitty analysed and indexed, so that Matthew could see at a glance the course of events in a particular country or district.

It was a sad picture, of violence in all its forms, of revolt, anarchy, civil war, and tyranny. Through it, there ran the threads of drought, famine, and disease. Rich crops in more than one country rotted for want of harvesters, while in another drought or freak storms had ruined vast fertile regions whose crops had been almost ready for the harvesters. In other countries, where an early summer occurred, and where the great plains had yielded magnificent abundance, the grain could not be distributed owing to the breakdown of systems of transport. In Capitals and the large seaport cities, riots, revolts, and chaos alternated with curious periods of calm.

Across the East, famine was on the current of the hot wind. Hapless thousands trekked from one region to another, first southwards, then westwards, until the West became a kind of legendary sanctuary towards which the gathering millions turned when they discovered nearer goals to be as empty of food as their own homes had been. But in the cities, astute speculators waddled like symbols of greed and cruelty, waiting, waiting just a day longer, two days longer, for a better price for maize, corn, rice which, when it would come at last from them to the markets, would surely enrich them a thousandfold. And in the same teeming cities, disease burst into wild epidemics which a harassed Government stemmed in one locality but could not prevent in a dozen others.

Unrest was in the air which encircled the globe. The usual repressive measures failed completely, or achieved only a temporary success which was insufficient to provide a foundation for any sensible government. Governments fell, rose, struck right and left in attempts to terrorize, and sank suddenly. Provisional governments were out of office even before the swiftest 'news-hawk' could report their election! New ones lasted a week, and were overthrown.

In Europe, astonishing features of the crisis had occurred. A Germany which had been stripped to the thinnest garments of hope and national unity was, of all the nations on the Continent, the calmest, the most peaceful, the most orderly and the most hopeful. It was her neighbours who displayed the greatest threat to peace. They armed. They marched. A sudden change of government threw them into spasms of civil war in which thousands slaughtered other thousands for policies of this or that. The Republic of Transplebia thundered its air forces over the air of other nations in warlike displays. It seized barren deserts in other parts of the world, much to the annoyance of Colport. But that was all.

In France, the Fourth Republic had been established with acclamations but without the Celebrations. Postponement of those celebrations had cost the Government its life, since when five other Governments had arisen, had fallen, had spermed other Governments. But France was thriving, as usual, on crisis. And it was from France that PEEPER resounded louder than ever.

PEEPER, in fact, was universal. Civil war could not extinguish him. He belonged to all parties, all creeds, all factions. He was beloved everywhere.

Matthew, studying the items of news, realized that. He could not understand it. Collapse was everywhere. Ruin and starvation, disease, famine, all were actual. Yet the acclamations for PEEPER continued without abatement.

It was the last thread which remained whole. It coursed vividly through the horrors of chaos, like a safety rope which all might clasp. Friends, foes, the bitterest antagonists, the tyrant and the oppressed, the anarchist and his victim, all clutched PEEPER. His devotees were whole nations.

Yet the exact nature of that enthusiasm for him still defied Matthew's pursuit. He sought it through the cities, the plains, the mountains. He pursued sudden strange reports which led him into silence, emptiness, and failure. PEEPER was elected a member of a new Provisional Government of a South American republic. His salary was to go to a special fund to promote educational facilities for the children of peasants. His vote was to be given by his 'disciple' who would be chosen by the population and who would sit on the Council. Matthew smiled. It was baffling.

In Africa, natives had deified PEEPER. But natives! Again, Matthew smiled. He had in his hand several curious and alarming reports from Wales, and from India, which related to some extraordinary rites which had been performed amidst the Welsh mountains, and not far from the city of Benares. PEEPER . . . Matthew read the reports again . . . PEEPER had been represented by exquisite statues at those rites at which pagan ceremonies had been performed in his honour. A little shrine had been erected by a band of enthusiasts gathered on a mountain and surrounded by an amused throng of Welsh people who, far from participating in the ceremonies of these visitors from England, had chattered and laughed all the time. But outside Benares, a crowd estimated at about thirty thousand had conducted a solemn ritual around a stone statue of PEEPER which, from that moment, was regarded as sacred.

The smile passed from Matthew's face as he sat with that sheet of paper in his hands. A baleful flicker of light caught his imagination when he pondered the chaotic human scene. It increased, shedding its radiance everywhere on that sombre panorama, and lighting a path for Matthew to follow. An Idea gleamed fiercely with its own remarkable light behind the dust of revolution and the murk of civil war. It appeared suddenly in all its startling reality. His soul flinched from it, yet he remained staring at it with the entire, inquisitive strength of his imagination.

In the city of Benares, there was a belief prevalent amongst a band of holy men that PEEPER was not one person but three. A trinity composed of two men and one woman, all celibates, the woman being the sister of those two brothers. The same report which mentioned this item of news told as well of the belief of this small sect in certain miraculous manifestations given by PEEPER, notably his influence upon many thousands of merchants in the City of London, and his remarkable success in destroying the former Government and opening the way for the Coalition. That sect worshipped PEEPER and attributed divinity to him.

That was the Idea, and Matthew believed that his search was successful. Man who had created his gods from awe of the glory and power of Nature and who had attributed divine omnipotence, agelessness, and omniscience to them, and had heaped upon them the responsibilities and the sins of the world, and had sacrificed them at the spring of the year and revived them a little later, had created another god. PEEPER!

230

The Idea flared through Matthew's mind. He could not grasp it immediately. He was afraid of it and of the vision of a new conception of life which that new god would encourage in the world. He dared not trust himself to believe that Man, in this century which was said to be progressive and rational, had reverted to the savage mysticism of his remote ancestors and created a new god. Oh no! This was an Age in which Man himself had the power of gods! This was the Century of Progress in which Man took unto himself the power of life and death over millions of human beings! Man had come to see with the eyes of a god, to hear with the ears of a god, to penetrate substances, to fly like a god! He was on the threshold of his own Apotheosis! He believed so much in himself that he had ceased to believe in a true God, for if he had believed in that God he would not have disobeyed Him. He had lost Faith. Yet he longed to find it. And true to his pagan, savage instincts, he had created a new god for this new age. The god's name was PEEPER! The god of millions and millions who had forgotten other gods.

Matthew went to Kitty. He stood before her, panting as though he had been running.

'Found it! At last! The Thing . . . the Idea . . .'

His expression frightened her, and she stammered uneasily, struggling with an inexplicable panic which his shout of excitement and his curious manner created in her.

'Have you?' she said.

He shouted with laughter. 'Have I? Have I? You're so matter-of-fact, Kitty! I stumble across the solution to the whole terrible business, and you stand there . . .'

She interrupted him quickly. 'What is this . . . this . . . explanation . . . solution . . .'

He took her by the hand and dragged her back to his study.

'A new god!' he exclaimed, 'Mankind has created a new god!'

She stood back from him and smiled, perhaps to placate his temper which, at that instant, was at a peak of frenzy with the Idea. That smile was full of her terror; and seeing it, and hearing her taut exclamation, he checked himself.

'No . . . how?'

He put his hands on her shoulders and wanted to force her to accept the Idea, to reflect his discovery of it, and to hear from her the encouragement which he felt he deserved. But he saw her terror in her eyes. It angered him, but he controlled himself.

'We have always had gods! Age after age . . . always with its own gods. They are inherent in our idea of existence. We must have them, above us, around us, like garments. PEEPER is the new one, born out of a desire for him!'

He waited for her approval, her comprehension of the Idea. She wrenched herself from him and stood back.

'I'm not going to believe that!' she shouted. 'I won't!'

'Well, what else? It's the only explanation . . .'

His anger rose to fury in him. But her expression had changed, and she had come over to him and was saying gently and reasonably:

'Don't believe it, Matthew!' Then she laughed gaily. 'It's so . . . really, it's ridiculous!' Suddenly, in another tone, she said: 'And it's evil. You mustn't admit it.' Her manner was becoming positive and solemn. 'I don't want you to write about it! I won't let you! You are not to do it! You hear?'

Astonishment melted his anger. Curiosity compelled him to question her.

'Why not? It's the only explanation! Think of it. What else is there. Study all the popular enthusiasms and see the instinctive desire to create gods of mortals in all of them! And that's what is happening to PEEPER. Whatever he was at first, he is a god now!'

To his consternation, she conceded that point.

'I don't deny it. But I don't want you to mention it. I want you to keep that out of your book.'

'If I do, what will they say of my book in the future? If I omit the explanation . . .'

'What does it matter what they say?'

'It's important . . .'

'But it's monstrous!' she said.

She put her hands over her ears. 'Aren't we sane? Haven't we advanced? Aren't we free of . . .'

'We are pagan, savage, all that! But we are miraculous, too! We discover nothing! We create everything, dreaming of what shall come next, and then bringing it all into the light of fact. That's Man. God-like, the eternal creator of gods! Part of the Will, and therefore endowed with its Power.'

Kitty heard him, but had nothing more to say. His Idea in its enormity swept over her, swamping her senses and transforming her own ideas, heaping them like dead leaves, and rendering all the familiar objects in the scene around her in the room curiously new to her sight.

232

She looked quickly around, seeing in the soft sunlight which poured into the room a terrifying new quality, and detecting in the shape of vases and the colours and subjects of the oil paintings something . . . an expression or quality which belonged to an older life than that of the body or the mind. She rushed to the window, to verify . . . what? That the world was as ever. That in the street there were people, walking people, talking and laughing people. Yes, they were there! But different . . . strange now that she believed . . . But did she believe?

She felt herself to be like something of the air, something which did not belong to notions of civilization and its routine, but to ageless conditions. She was afraid, and yet suddenly enchanted. This ecstasy! Was this the experience which belief in PEEPER had rendered to the millions?

She heard Matthew running quickly downstairs. She supposed he was going to the Bessings. But he was right. She had an impulse to follow him and overtake him and tell him that he had discovered the truth. But first of all, she wished to relish this new experience and this new belief which he had communicated to her.

She walked slowly from room to room, touching the vases, the bowls, the little pieces of sculpture, the chairs. She saw them with a clarity as of a new sense of sight. She recognized their relation to profound things, their submission to an Idea, and their belief which their creators expressed in this simplicity. How fresh they appeared, how exciting, as though they were released at last from a confinement which her own senses had imposed on them. And even the commonest articles of utility seemed to her to have acquired light and daintiness from the effulgence of June sunlight which filled the air.

Turning away at last, she paused. The hush that was upon everything! Her sense of touch and sight had experienced so much that was new and thrilling. And her heightened sense of hearing, seeking the ordinary sounds, discovered only silence. A deep, mysterious hush that had descended upon the house, the road outside, the city. And perhaps the world.

She could hear a few summer flies buzzing lazily in the air and against the window-panes. They were the sound of summer: languid, soft, contented. The summer air which, with its heat and sharpness, possessed the streets, the buildings, defining everything in a clarity which her sight had discovered. But the extraordinary hush: that was not of that summer air. It was of the stealthiness of the earth's immense vigour which held all life in its pulse and breathed its stillness and tranquillity upon everything. She listened to it as she might have done to music in a new rhythm or phrasing. It took her upon its current and increased her consciousness of what was new.

It was suddenly ended by the sound of running feet on the pavements in the street. And at once she was returned to the old consciousness, and its old ideas.

She looked around her in fear. Upon everything there remained that freshness and brilliance as of something new. It was still there, but she herself was no longer a part of it. The sound in the street had carried her back. And with a rising terror she was asking herself what was actually happening to the visible world, and to herself, and to Matthew, as well as to human society in its communities and in its trade, its beliefs, its aspirations.

She was dazed. She had tasted for an instant something altogether new which had enchanted her. But the recollection of it stupefied her. She closed her eyes. She put her hands over her ears. Her mind sought a point upon which it could trust itself: a point of stability from which sanity could renew itself.

She was at a dizzy height of consciousness from which she wished to descend to the levels of familiar things. She had seen and experienced a momentary phenomenon. But there were other and more normal features . . . little, everyday things that held the mind within limits. She longed to return to those limits. She opened her eyes and cautiously withdrew her hands from her ears.

Upon everything there remained that newness and freshness. The subtle transformation was complete; and from the hushed air there came that hollow, thunderous sound that was like the pulse of earth itself and which was repeated by the sounds of running feet in the street below.

She tried to reason with herself. Glancing around her and noticing again the peculiar access of colour in the paintings, and the strange definition of shape in the vases and bowls, and the hard clarity of detail in the designs of the carpet, the curtains, the tapestry of the screen, she told herself that the transformation was not in the things themselves but in her mind that had yielded to an Idea and whose faculties were more acute.

She could not convince herself of that. She ran from the flat and into the one above. The tenants had left, weeks ago, on the first wave of panic. She paused, realizing that the place was empty. Fear seized her. She could feel it, hear its approach.

Fear of what? She asked herself, aloud: 'What is it?'

At the windows, the flies still buzzed. Below, in the street, the feet thudded. The ponderous pulsations were still audible. Oh . . . it was nothing . . . nothing extraordinary! It was thunder, perhaps, in the distance. A summer storm from which people hurried. Or a procession, headed by drummers, towards which people hastened. But that explanation did not serve. It did not dispel her terror which remained because she knew that what she heard was not thunder, not drums, but something from the earth itself. The tread of thousands of feet. Or the reverberations from the earth of the shouts of a multitude.

She turned abruptly and sped back to the flat. She ran into the rooms, looking swiftly around her for something . . . some small thing, anything, which was not touched by the peculiar light and which would return her to the familiar things. She halted once. What was she doing? What foolish panic was this? What madness?

She was driven by fear from the little hall and down the flight of stairs into the lower hall. She ran into the porch. The street was deserted. The stiff, vivid sunlight possessed the scene. And over the hot roadway the heat hung, rendering the air tremulous. She had seen that before: the shuddering haze. But it terrified her now, and for an instant she imagined that the earth itself was vibrating and emitting that thunder, and that people had fled. . . .

She stumbled hastily back and closed the house door and stood there panting, fearful, astonished at herself and yet unable to calm her terrified mind. She took a step towards the stairs. Upstairs? That hush, and the subtle transformation of all things, and that immense pulse which claimed her senses and against which she was all the time struggling. Upstairs . . . the atmosphere, the ripples of an Idea which Matthew had discovered and which remained like an extraordinary substance!

She hammered with her fists on the door of the first flat. A surveyor and his wife lived there. She and Matthew spoke to them on the stairs, were affable to them, supposed them to be a couple of unemotional, easygoing and conventional people. Had never gone beyond the cheerful greeting. But to think of them now . . . their rational manner . . . their solid temperaments . . . was comforting. And to realize an instant later that they, too, had fled from the city on the first panic exodus was distressing. Had they foreseen? Had their heavy instincts warned them? She turned from the door. Again, she opened the house door and rushed into the porch and looked to right and left along the street.

And recoiled after seeing that hot, shuddering haze and the emptiness into which the hard sunlight poured.

She stood in the hall, in the silence, and spoke aloud.

'It's the heat . . . that's all . . .'

She remembered the last three days of abnormal heat and perfect weather.

'Summer . . .'

The words came back to her in a sibilant echo. Eerie and monstrous, they were. She gasped. Her heart thumped in her breast. She called loudly:

'Matthew!'

He was out. He had hurried away, somewhere. She was alone. Nobody else was in the house. The street, too, was deserted. And out of the silence, the echo of that single word poured towards her from a hideous, glaring world that was like a keen eye watching her.

'Matthew! Matthew!'

She sped again to the house door and opened it wide, starting back when the heat poured in past her like an inquisitive, jealous force taking possession of the house. She heard her own shout echo about the building, and was momentarily appalled by its frenzy. She made an effort to compose her fearful thoughts. But the knowledge that she was alone in the house, alone in the locality, with that pressure of heat and silence and the living light of an Idea, grew in her mind, taking hold of her and sweeping across her consciousness. She stumbled towards the stairs. When she reeled and fell, with the pulsating thunder breaking at last from the hush and overwhelming her senses, a minute fragment of intuition remained to her.

She knew that she had fainted but that she was not utterly overcome. In the curious darkness and tumult of unconsciousness there remained that particle. It was of herself. It glittered as she considered it. She had a feeling of being a part of it, and yet being able to detach herself from it to verify it. And looking at it with a desperate stare, she saw in it the entirety of life as she had known it, experienced it, believed in it.

It was indestructible, aflame with eternal life. In her coma, she discovered it in the same way in which a patient excavator, centuries hence, might find in the rubble of a buried building fragmentary evidence of a lost civilization. A fragment of glass in which, miraculously, an Age was reflected.

# TWELVE

★

When Matthew reached the house in Half Moon Street, John came hurrying down to admit him. He was jerking his arms into his jacket. His tie hung loosely in his collar.

'I'm glad you've come, Matthew!' he said, rapidly. 'I was in a quandary. Nurse is off duty for a couple of hours. Len is out in the Park for a stroll. Belfwig says he wants to see me very urgently.'

He settled his tie. 'Can you . . . would you mind?'

'Of course!'

'Only for an hour, at most.'

'How is he?' Matthew said.

John laughed. 'He's a miracle! Go in and see him. He's dressed and sitting up. Nye let him walk to the end of the road and back, yesterday!'

John knocked on the door and pushed it open.

'A visitor!'

Quentin was fully dressed and sitting out of bed in his long chair. Matthew halted a few paces inside the room, for it was certainly Quentin who turned to him and smiled, but it was PEEPER as well. The quick, keen smile; the brilliant eyes, the flicker of irony in the expression; and the long, sensitive hand extended to him.

'Quentin! To find you up!'

Quentin looked past his visitor to the door.

'Do you mind, old boy . . . closing it?'

When Matthew turned again to him, Quentin had risen. He was in an attentive attitude.

'I'm awfully glad . . .' Matthew began.

Quentin made a slight motion with his hand. The house door slammed. At once, he turned to his visitor, smiled, pointed to a chair.

'Now! We have the place to ourselves.'

He came slowly to Matthew and stood before him.

'I want you to do something for me, Matt.'

His voice had a disturbing flatness and hollowness; and the smile on his face was stiff, like a mask clapped over his features and concealing their authentic expression.

'I want you to help me . . . take me out . . . give me your arm,' he said. 'I want to walk. I must see . . .'

Matthew shook his head.

'I daren't do that! Sit down, and let's talk.'

The taut smile remained on that dark face, and the words that followed next had a tone of authority.

'Do what I ask you, Matt! Give me your arm . . .'

Matthew got to his feet and stood away from him.

'Don't be idiotic, Quentin! I couldn't do that. If I did, I'd never forgive myself . . .'

The smile suddenly broke, snapped. Anger flowed into the features, ripped across the expression, wrenched it. Words came in a shout of disappointment and frustration.

'I've been shut up in this room . . . for weeks! In that bed!'

He moved towards his chair and sat down with his hands on his thighs. Lifting his head and looking at Matthew, he said:

'I know what's happening, Matt. I've heard about it. And I got John to bring me newspapers. There they are, in that corner. But I want to get out and hear and see for myself.'

'There isn't much to see,' Matthew said. He laughed briefly. 'And there is certainly not much to hear. The traffic has gone.'

Quentin lay back on the cushions.

'Not that,' he said. 'That I can take for granted. What I want to see and hear is of the spirit. I want to experience it. I can't do that while I'm imprisoned in this room.'

'You needn't hurry,' Matthew said. 'You have time . . .'

Quentin folded his arms on his chest and looked up at the ceiling.

'I haven't,' he said. 'At any moment . . .'

'Don't talk like that,' Matthew said. 'You are recovering! Look at you! In a week . . .'

Quentin again interrupted him. 'I'm referring to events,' he said.

Matthew laughed loudly. 'There is one event—if you could call it that—and I should think it will have become much more interesting at the end of a week or two. . . .'

'Another revolution somewhere?'

The big, sombre eyes turned their gaze to Matthew. They had an expression of despair which the rest of the face augmented until the whole countenance expressed a sense of failure.

Matthew shook his head. 'Something else . . .'

Quentin turned his head. His features expressed the sourness of disappointment.

'I know,' he said. 'Revolution . . . chucking over governments and

238

shoving up others. What a tribe! Letting the harvests rot. Squabbling over the same old things.'

He grimaced and stirred angrily. 'If they have a new spirit . . . which I doubt . . . why haven't they ventured? I'm tired of reading about revolt and civil war. I've searched those newspapers for something else. I want to go out and convince myself of something, Matt. I must. I want to find something which I was sure they would have done. . . .'

'You needn't go out,' Matthew said. 'They have done it. They have reached it at last!'

He saw Quentin turn and stare up at him. He shouted the words at that image of PEEPER.

'A god! A new god! They've made a god of PEEPER! In India . . . millions . . . and across the world . . .'

Quentin got up and stood facing him.

'I knew it! That's what I knew they would do! I was waiting . . . I searched the newspapers . . .'

'Oh, no word of it there!' Matthew exclaimed. 'They censored it. They are censoring it all. It frightens them.'

Quentin interrupted him. His face gleamed.

'I knew they would. No more revolution or civil war or war of any sort. It's the one remedy which they have always found! Somebody to idolize. No longer a leader, a general, or a politician. Somebody who cannot tyrannize them!'

He laughed gaily. He walked to and fro, no longer an invalid, his step so firm and his body so erect that Matthew forgot that a week ago this man had been dying.

Quentin stopped at the little table near the bed and took up the carafe. It was almost empty.

'Would you mind, Matt? A glass of water . . .'

Matthew said: 'But, you know, Quentin, there's . . . it's a perilous moment. This moment in Time . . . these few days. Be prepared for     '

'I know,' Quentin said, handing him the carafe. 'The final struggle between the People and their governments. Oh, I know! The ultimate battle for Power.'

He sat down on his long chair and said quietly:

'A glass of water, old man . . .'

Matthew went out. He threw out the stale water which remained in the carafe, and carefully washed the vessel and refilled it. He did the same with the tumbler, and returned to the bedroom.

Quentin was not there. Matthew set the carafe on the table and waited. Suddenly, he grabbed his hat from the chair and ran to the door. He sped across the landing and down the stairs. Hastening from the house, he looked quickly along the street and was in time to see that tall, lean figure turn the corner into Piccadilly. A minute later, he overtook him.

'You fool! Wait! Come back!'

Quentin laughed gaily. He seized Matthew by the arm and walked on with him.

'A little way,' he pleaded.

Matthew tried again to stop him, tugging at his thin arm.

'Listen, Quentin! Please! Don't be a fool . . .'

Several persons in the throngs on the pavement and roadway heard him, and stopped when Quentin stopped, and stood watching the pair. Quentin was laughing.

'Don't be an old woman, Matt! I wouldn't miss this . . .'

He stood gaping about him at a changed Piccadilly. It was empty of traffic except for a few Army trucks that hooted impatiently at the crowds strolling in the roadway and making one stream that filled the entire space between the buildings. In the leafy Green Park, thousands idled: and somewhere in the blue, hazy distance a band was playing. The nervous, frantic haste of London had subsided to this! This idleness and ease! This idyllic mood and pace on a summer afternoon!

Quentin's laughter was loud above the patter of footsteps and the chattering voices.

'But what do they do? Isn't there work?'

'Plenty,' Matthew said. 'Jobs for everybody, in the Government service. Three pounds ten per week, rising by annual increments of seven and twopence to a maximum of five pounds thirteen.'

Quentin guffawed. 'Almost Utopian!' And like a complete stranger to the scene, he stared around, seeing the faces with their expressions of release.

'They look happy enough,' he said. 'But what are they all doing? Why aren't they at work, or rushing home?'

'A thirty hour week,' Matthew explained. 'And a shift system. This must be the three o'clock lot . . .'

'No 'buses?'

'Only for Government employees. And free to them . . .'

Quentin's explosive laughter sounded loudly again.

'And do these,' he said, lowering his voice, 'do these believe in their new god?'

'Not yet,' Matthew said.

'Why not?'

Matthew appeared suddenly nervous. He drew Quentin slowly on, away from the inquisitive stares of little groups that had stopped and gathered nearby.

'Perhaps they will when . . .'

He pointed to Quentin's reflection in a shop window, and added: 'When they recognize him! When they see him!'

Quentin smiled lugubriously.

'Do they know what they've done with PEEPER, do you think, Matt? Do you think they realize that they have made a god of him?'

'Good Lord, no! But the Church does, and the State.'

'Is there a schism yet?' Quentin said, 'or are Church and State still one and indivisible?'

'Colport has settled it,' Matthew told him.

Quentin halted. 'What!'

'The Church . . . all the Churches have approved his policy regarding the family. Everything for the family . . .'

Quentin walked slowly on, shaking his head.

'They have always been ahead of the People, everywhere,' he said. And after a pause, he added: 'Twigge was right. It has come to the final struggle. The battle for Power. The Rulers versus the People.'

He glanced back at the little knot of idlers following at his heels. A word rose quickly.

'PEEPER!'

Matthew drew him on. 'I don't like it, Quentin. Let's turn back. Come on!'

'As far as the Circus,' Quentin said.

The little knot increased to a small crowd. People came scampering across from the opposite side of the road to follow the tall figure which was visible from that distance and which was remarked as well by the noisy swarm at his heels. Pedestrians walking ahead of Quentin and Matthew stopped, stared, and joined the crowd. At the Circus, Matthew hoped to be able to elude them. He had a vague plan of escape. To go down and, in the maze of the Underground, to dodge them.

It was impossible. They swarmed around Quentin and himself at the moment when he stopped. The way down was blocked by them. He walked on. At Leicester Square, the shout which had arisen repeatedly behind him burst into his face from two hawkers, and was echoed by a couple of idlers against a wall. Within an instant it became a roar from

I

all sides, with the word rising from faces suddenly contorted with a frenzy which sent its shock at Matthew with the force of a blow. It dazed him. The swelling crowd pressed forward to see, to touch, to shout the word at the tall, motionless figure that stared back at it with a curiously bland gaze. It encircled the two of them. In another moment it might have hemmed them in without leaving them a single chance of escape, for it was swelling like an ocean. The roadways with their dense masses seemed to pour thousands towards that spot. The stiff summer sunlight streaming upon the scene seemed to Matthew's nervous sight to focus upon Quentin and himself. Panic touched him in a sudden, cold instant. He looked swiftly around.

Standing at the kerb was an Army truck. He thrust Quentin towards it, into the cab. The yelling mob parted to let them through, cheered while he walked round and got in, waved while he fearfully started. But its cry swung up to a note of disappointment when the vehicle gathered speed, and swelled into anger when Matthew drove into a side street. It tore after him, clambering aboard, swinging to the step when he halted at traffic lights, overtaking him in a panting rush, hands tearing at his hands on the wheel and the gear handle, faces thrusting at him. He jabbed his fist at them. He accelerated in those narrow streets. He ignored traffic lights and sped on. Swerving, he crashed into a hawker's barrow and saw it spin round, mount the pavement and collapse, its fruit rolling off. Voices yelled. A wild face burst through the canvas flap and emitted a name.

'PEEPER!'

He jerked back his fist at it, and heard the next word come in a squashed mumble. And felt a hand claw at his shoulder. He drove swiftly on and drew up suddenly and got down. The solitary, yelling passenger in the truck was beckoning to the oncoming crowd.

'Get off this truck!'

The man suddenly gaped at Matthew and lowered his arms. He smiled sheepishly.

'But you got PEEPER in front! It's PEEPER!'

'Off!'

He climbed down, grinning. Matthew ran back to the cab. A police car slid in closely against the truck. Matthew hesitated. It would take minutes to explain to the young sergeant who was alighting that Quentin was a convalescent, and that that vociferous mob was pursuing him. And it was impossible to expect the sergeant to understand why traffic rules had been broken, lights ignored, a collision disregarded.

Minutes would elapse before an explanation could be given and accepted. And within that time the mob would overtake, swarm over . . .

The severe young face was uplifted.

'Hold it! Hold it! I'll see your licence, please!'

Ahead, the road was clear. Matthew drove on only to escape the pursuing crowd. He tried to signify that much to the officer who made a sudden grab towards him and then stood back. Matthew accelerated. He chose the narrower streets. Within five minutes, he was in the Strand.

He had to go slow there because of the packed roadway. Drawing in to the kerb, he was prepared to halt and await the oncoming police car. He believed that he had a reasonable explanation which that young officer would accept.

Standing on the kerb were the inevitable loungers, hot faces submitted to the afternoon's hard heat, little eyes half-closed against the strong light. But sleepy expressions swiftly changing, eyes opening wide and staring at Quentin. And voices rising, as before. And for every man or woman who recognized in Quentin the likeness to PEEPER and who assembled about the truck, there were ten, twenty, hundreds who moved forward, stood there to discover what was happening, who it was, why there was shouting, and who recognized at once that lean, dark presence.

The shouting began, the clamouring, the excited pointing and pushing and closing in. Matthew drove on, trying to move faster, sounding the horn against the packed roadway. In the mirror, he saw the police car reflected. It was less than fifty yards distant, but the crowd had closed in, checking the car's progress, letting the vehicle through as slowly as it allowed Matthew to proceed,

He reached Fleet Street. To make headway there was almost impossible, for a multitude was flowing there, packing itself outside the newspaper offices and standing about the Government Bulletin Boards, waiting. He stopped for an instant. And again the eyes saw Quentin, recognized PEEPER in him.

'Try the "Daily Summariser"!' Quentin said. 'They might be delighted to see us!'

Matthew sounded the horn repeatedly. He let the truck creep slowly on against a dense throng which parted grudgingly and which closed in again immediately afterwards. A sound like a prolonged yawn of satisfaction rose when the eyes found Quentin. It travelled around the vehicle and rolled into the distance and echoed back, while the crowd pressed forward, swayed, came up again, swirling about and clambering over the bonnet, clinging to the sides, climbing aboard, chanting its chorus.

To stop and explain to the sergeant was impossible. To attempt to turn was impossible. To devise a plan of escape from this heaving crowd which glued itself to the truck and made the vehicle the core of an explosion which held its sound at a shrill peak and which gathered to itself hundreds, thousands from near and far, was likewise impossible. Matthew attempted to drive faster. He felt the truck jolt. Somebody screamed. A face contorted. Matthew was aware of a body slipping down amidst the feet and of hands grabbing that body and dragging it aside. And of shrill voices shouting into the cab a swift sentence of abuse which was smothered by cheering as the thousands recognized their Peeper.

It became a fantastic procession of triumph, with the single word being repeated with a horrible monotony. An ocean of faces spread around the truck and sent its yell at the pale, dazed figure beside Matthew, who searched for an opening, a thinning, a weak point through which he might dart into a side street and from thence back, westwards, swiftly. The crowd prevented him. It hemmed him in, until he made a wide gesture and jerked the truck into a spurt of speed. The throng parted slightly. He saw it open in a cleft through which he sped.

Dimly, he saw where he was. Ludgate Hill. He went faster, streaking into what had been Paternoster Row. He had room at last in which to speed the truck and decide his course. He stopped. His plan was to leave the truck and take Quentin into shelter and there wait until the pursuit had fizzled out.

He had no chance. The mob was coming up. It followed him into Cheapside and Poultry. He thought for an instant of entering Threadneedle Street. There was a teeming crowd there, filling the roadway. He turned into King William Street. And it was there, in the dense heart of another crowd which was pouring in and boiling around, that the sergeant of police made his leap, swaying beside the truck and suddenly jumping from the running-board of the car to the truck, swinging open the door, crushing him from the wheel and shouting at him.

The crowd emitted a great exclamation of derision. Its laughter cracked across the hot air. What that multitude was pouring citywards or, Matthew did not know. He heard its derisive taunts as the sergeant furiously shoved him aside, and had a momentary impression of its myriad faces in the sunlight.

'You mad dog! Didn't you see me? Didn't I stop you?'

The flushed face was no more than an inch from Matthew's when Quentin collapsed. The Sergeant's cap had fallen off. His crisp, fair hair clung in a wet streak across his forehead.

'A nice, wild run! You'll answer for that . . .'

The voice came from over Matthew's shoulder and was suddenly obliterated by the word which exploded from the crowd, and which travelled to that spot from another crowd running in.

'PEEPER!'

Matthew thrust back with his elbows and shouted over his shoulder. His hands were under Quentin's arms.

'Can't you see? I had to get away from them! Clear a way for us, or come round and help me get him out!'

'If you'd said when I first stopped you . . .'

The Sergeant swung off and pushed his way round. His driver joined him. There was no need to explain. The density of that crowd increased swiftly, cutting off all possible hope of getting Quentin across the road, to the nearest pavement, and into the only building where a staff was in occupation. A bank.

Matthew got down after the Sergeant had lifted Quentin bodily out. He pushed towards them. There was a chance . . . the crowd was like water which flowed back after an impact . . . the two waves had not yet merged, were straining, did not quite know where PEEPER was, were looking, were halting. The Sergeant and constable had Quentin between them. A way was cleared for them. And closed swiftly, because the crowd saw.

It saw PEEPER staring at it. It saw a movement at that place. And it heaved itself in a sudden, massive thrust forward, closing upon Matthew as he lurched towards Quentin. He went down. Individually, those near him tried to step clear of him, tried to hold away from his prone body, but were carried forward in a rush. Over him. Their feet upon him. And a surging wave of packed humanity flowing over him, over something which feet touched, mounted, went past like a thunderous, pummelling Thing which could not check itself but which was urged in swift, swaying motion, first to the right, then back, then checked, then forward again.

Matthew knew what might happen to him beneath the surface of that mass. He scrambled up. The flowing weight sent him down again. It was like so much water, a rushing wave, heaving around him, riding over him and burying him in its scuffling, trampling feet above which the single word boomed, muffled, incessantly.

'PEEPER!'

He heard it while he struggled to rise, and until the last moment. It was the sound of a breathing multitude that had come together at news of a Cabinet meeting which had been in progress all day. It wanted more news. It filled the streets. But a rumour had blown it together. It was frantic to see, to hear, to touch PEEPER. It roared for him, angrily, the sound beating thinly upon Matthew as the ponderous, merciless wave tore brutishly at him, rolled his helpless body, broke him beneath its massive weight and trampled into extinction the last particle of the Idea.

Quentin looked back, seeking him. He appealed to the two men who brought him through the edge of the crowd.

'My friend . . . back there!'

The Sergeant had hold of Quentin. Sergeant rushed him at last to the doorway, while constable wrenched from his path a gesticulating ruffian with upraised fists. Sergeant and constable almost hurled Quentin through the doorway which seemed to open grudgingly as an elderly Commissionaire stepped out.

'Can't hold 'em . . . if you don't hurry!'

And before the door closed on the lax, lean figure which the police officers thrust in, a deft, ludicrous little being in an oversize suit darted in, panting, pushing as though he were in flight from pursuers. But who were pursuers in the fringe of that crowd as it flowed in a shouting rush to the doorway through which PEEPER had vanished, and who were the pursued, was impossible to decide. The old Commissionaire put up his hand, whereupon the adroit little man, elderly himself, and as white-haired beneath his big cap as the Commissionaire, swept it aside.

'Twigge!' the old employee exclaimed.

Twigge was in. The door closed on the yelling crowd. The Sergeant and constable faced round.

'The other one?' the constable shouted.

The Sergeant shook his head and looked anxiously at the swaying thing that filled the entire street.

'In that lot!'

Even to get back to their car was impossible.

# THIRTEEN

★

For Twigge, in those days of early summer, London was especially beautiful. It was disclosed to his sight at last. His kingdom. No longer cut and bisected and filled with noise by the incessant streams of traffic, it had a grace and repose which delighted his senses. For the first time, he saw its distances, its sweep of crescent, its pride of avenue, its composition in squares, and its abandoned sprawl. Its grandeur of perspective excited his admiration. And over it all was the comparative silence, while far above that was the peace of the sky and the smile of the sunlight.

Twigge was happy. He felt supreme when he walked by day and by night through the streets of the city. If, around and about in the world, there was trouble amounting to a terrifying chaos, Quentin who was PEEPER would solve it. Twigge had no doubt of that, for the patient was improving. His recovery astonished not only all in the household, but Nye too. Nye could not understand it. He used the phrase frequently, shook his head, was loth to allow the patient to sit up even for an hour or two. But in the end he gave his assent to the proposal that Quentin should take a few steps around the room, sit up, and later spend a couple of hours in the studio.

Twigge knew that the couple of hours had included a walk down the stairs and into Twigge's apartments where the patient had learned more within ten minutes than the nurse had permitted him to read within days from the newspapers. Quentin was hardly back in his own room before the nurse returned from her hour or two of leisure.

The recollection of that visit filled Twigge with confidence. He cared no longer about affairs in the vast world. He was concerned with his own kingdom which he loved with an inordinate passion that was as sublime as it was ridiculous. He had vanquished his enemies. In the process, he had made others. He knew it. He expected them to make a sortie against him. Meanwhile, there was PEEPER, daily as popular as ever. And that other PEEPER, the living being, soon to return and guide the shadow into a better path. Twigge was contented. For the time being, his rule was absolute.

But in making enemies for himself, he had made them for others too.

For Jayby, and down a long list which included Belfwig, and Harry who was suspect amongst the sporting confraternities of all shades ever since PEEPER had forecast 'Lord Punch.' Twigge knew it. He heard the chatter. He was told it. And if he wanted confirmation of it all he could find it whenever he wandered in and out of the narrow streets and the back streets and byeways, and met there the malice in the stare of nondescript characters: deserters, crooks, little scavengers of little opportunities, who composed the thick sludge of a great city. There was awe as well as threat in their glances. In his present mood, Twigge was flattered by it.

Vanity had withdrawn him from his pitch in the Park where, previously, the gusts of laughter that came at him had evoked his best rhetoric and his keenest wit. Now he scorned them. His philosophy had found expression in a full-blown medium. He need no longer stand to be gawked at, smirked at, or potted at by anybody.

But he had still to earn a livelihood. There was a fortune of money pouring into the family purse upstairs; and he had been given a share of it, a salary almost. He would not use it. He had lived from the age of thirteen by what he had earned through his own resources. He did not care to break the habit now.

On this June afternoon, his errand citywards was to deliver four sermons to the Bureau which distributed them privately to country clergymen. Twigge had never yet failed the Bureau. Other sources of supply might arise and flash brilliantly through those quiet premises; but Twigge had never had a rival.

The fact was that his heart was in his sermons. Twigge was a believer, in spite of his philosophy which could readily mould itself into mysticism. He believed in many particles from many Faiths, decrying no man's creed, nobody's god, but seeing in all of them the yearning towards a pure Faith and a True God. Tolerance gave him Charity, and from Charity he wrote very well, remarking upon the Will, the Godhead.

With the four sermons in his jacket pocket, he left for Fleet Street, walking in the sunlight. Except for the throngs filling the entire route, London had a Sunday aspect. He could even hear a bell tolling, and a band playing in the Green Park. The air was clear, curiously clear, but hot. He felt it. A drowsiness of contentment settled upon him.

He left his sermons at the Bureau and ambled slowly on. The crowds worried him. He knew why they were there. The news from Transplebia had taken a graver turn, and the Coalition Cabinet was sitting on it.

Had been sitting since ten this morning. Was it to discuss the latest ultimatum? But who cared? Not this idling multitude in the heat! Not these loungers and chattering pedestrians who appeared to be waiting? Waiting for what?

Twigge did not know. Even when he stopped and listened to the chatter, he could not discover why the thousands were there. That was irksome to his spirit which surmized that something was afoot, some personality awaited and expected.

Royalty? Twigge enjoyed the passage of Royalty through the streets. But in all the talk there was no mention of any function. He walked slowly on. Through Long Acre. Across Drury Lane and into Kingsway, where he turned right and strolled towards Aldwych. There the crowds were denser, and so many people brushed against him and buffeted his slight figure that it simply did not attract his notice when, on either side of him, against his arms, he felt a simultaneous pressure. Two men. Neither of them looked at him. Nor did he glance at them. They were two fellows in the crowd of which he was a particle. But in the Strand, as all three turned into it, they were joined by two more. One a step ahead; the other so closely behind that his shoes scraped Twigge's heels. Twigge halted.

In one glance, he recognized the quartet. What were they . . . oh, yes, there was Charlie, and the other was Hossy! Fringate was there, and Koggs. Names. Twigge laughed. Charlie and Hossy were burly men of about forty-four, with florid faces gleaming with perspiration. The others were unhealthy fellows, untidy, in greasy suits; both of them being nothing but refuse on the tide of humanity in this city. Nondescript, with nothing to remark them except their shabbiness which was somehow like an expression of their characters, they had a furtive air from little eyes that were almost hidden by the puckers of flesh drawn up to screen them from the sunlight. All four wore soft hats with the brims brought down to shield their eyes. All four had little of personality or individuality to distinguish them from others who were their counterparts in the society in dirty bars, cheap lodging-houses, cafés. But together they created a menace which they expressed truculently.

It did not impress Twigge who suddenly laughed into their stiff, greasy faces.

'The four sawnies! Well, I never!'

'Quick march!' Charlie growled.

And it was a quick march. For all of them. They had Twigge between them and were hurrying him off through a dense crowd, pushing him, laughing hoarsely at what they all supposed was a great prize. The afternoon heat was stiff in the air, like a yellow flame. It brought the perspiration streaming down those greasy faces. Until, all at once, by unanimous impulse, the four of them stopped.

Two stunted fellows with the same kind of expression as the rest were instantly beside them. Damp little faces creased to focus the sight of weak eyes upon the burly bodies, upon Twigge. Little heads jerking with the words, like the heads of birds.

'You got 'im! You picked 'im up!'

'No need to notify . . .' Charlie growled.

'Twigge! In the bag! Prop'ly in the bag!'

Charlie and the other three silenced them.

'All right! All right!'

And the five of them, with Charlie giving them a frown of anger, began to argue their destination, their voices joined in a rapid tangle upon which Charlie threw his order.

'We're going to Corny's! Now then . . .'

They protested. Three against two, with Charlie still outside the argument.

'What's the sense in that? Cocky told us . . .'

'We got orders from Corny . . .'

'Nobody ain't giving no orders! Cocky and Corny teamed up when Willie . . .'

Charlie put his hands out and pushed, his head to one side, his glance skywards, the tip of his tongue protruding slightly from the right corner of his lips.

'Get crackin'! Get started!'

They moved. The five of them, with Twigge between them and Charlie, who made the sixth. A bunch of seven men.

'Well, I on'y said . . . I was on'y saying Corny and Cocky . . .'

Then the heat seemed to Twigge to silence them as they panted along. In the crowd, it was not easy for them to make headway in such a formation. They were constantly obliged to separate, to open out, to dodge about and proceed in single file, But two of them had hold of him, firmly, their grip hot on him. They were a tawdry lot, a frayed handful, blinking in the sunlight to which they were obviously unaccustomed, with their furtive glances telling of the murky depths to which they belonged. It was their momentary unity in what Twigge knew was a plot that gave them a curious air of purpose. Singly, they had nothing but their deceit, cunning, and knowledge of crime. But in this party they created something that was truculent, impudent, and resolved, merely by their proximity to one another. Twigge was amused. It had a smell, like the odour from their dirty clothes that made a single, steamy taint upon the air. He was not afraid of them, for he could match and outclass all their cunning. But he was curious about their plan which, as they all plodded on, came slowly to his knowledge from their words and the direction which the group was taking.

Corny's, they were saying. The other side of the Bridge. Twigge did not like it. He knew Corny who was ugly and sly. The ugliness was not Corny's fault. But the slyness, the soft voice, the hypocrisy, the rapacity of that soul, the disease of that spirit . . . Twigge was revolted. He had never crossed to the south bank of the River, never ventured there to oppose Corny. But frequently, when Corny's slow fingers had travelled northwards to meddle with affairs there, Twigge had slashed at them. And this, he supposed, this . . . kidnapping . . . this was Corny's revenge. Or was it something larger than revenge, seeing that Cocky had joined hands in it?

Corny was one who preyed upon fools. He worked dodges. He bossed a school of tricksters who daily wandered northwards and westwards to wait patiently along the counters where, like spiders, they spun out webs of words for the gullible flies. But Cocky was bigger. A hunter of big game.

Twigge knew him. Twigge was pondering him when the party suddenly stopped and turned back to Ludgate Circus. It hurried from there to Ludgate Hill and into Cannon Street. What had made his kidnappers turn and streak off in that fashion? Twigge could not discover. They were afraid, and excited. Their pace, and their fragmentary conversation disclosed that much to him.

By the time they reached the corner of Queen Street where Twigge supposed that they would turn to the right and cross the River by Southwark Bridge, it was plain that some opposition from rivals had upset their plan. He was amused. All six men were under orders which bade them do certain things. Opposition had prevented success in the execution of those orders, and as a consequence the whole party was in a dilemma. Twigge listened to it. It could not think properly. Left to its own devices, it had no initiative. It was weak and inept and divided.

Twigge wondered what had opposed it. Another gang? The Law? He had time to consider it in Queen Street where the men halted. All of them were out of breath and perspiring. Twigge, too, was glad of a respite. He drew breath and glanced quickly around and wondered what the pedestrian throng was doing in that street. Its presence there was suddenly more important to him than his predicament. He sensed in that waiting swarm something of intense, excited curiosity. About what?

They were there in hundreds and thousands: clerks, accountants, cashiers, assistants, typists, directors, together with a sprinkling of persons from the outer boroughs. The routine of years drew them daily to the city, although many of them now worked near their own homes in the localized Government offices. Yet all of them, at some time during the day, wandered back here, to meet in the buildings, to hear the news which, hitherto, had always had its source in this district.

The throng suddenly stirred. A sound swept over it and drew it into motion and greater sound. Twigge shuddered apprehensively, for that sound had a terrible element of expectation. It gathered the multitude into a solid thing and impelled it towards Eastcheap.

Twigge's captors did not move. They appeared to be waiting for somebody.

'He said he might . . . about this time . . . might be able to make it,' Charlie said.

'No sense in waiting! If we wait . . .'

They all said it to Charlie. What was the sense? Why wait? He weakened beneath their persistent argument. Twigge could see him waver, look anxiously around. It was so funny that Twigge chuckled.

'Can't you make up your mind, Charlie?' he said.

The taunt added its weight to the pricking arguments, and Charlie swung round as if he had been goaded.

'All right, all right then! Only don't blame me if . . .'

He pushed them before him, and the party set off again, going with the crowd which had swelled from the addition of hundreds from Aldersgate, Cheapside and Moorgate.

' . . . don't blame me if we've missed him!' Charlie shouted.

At the corner of King William Street, they turned to the right and halted again. Twigge realized that they wished to cross to the opposite side and join associates. The six of them began to wave and whistle and exclaim excitedly amongst themselves. To cross the densely crowded roadway was impossible. To attract the attention of their friends on the opposite side seemed just as difficult. Again, they all spoke at once. You go! No, you. Somebody go! Too late. They're gone. You'd never get through. And so on, until Charlie swore thickly at them.

'A lot of . . . as if one of you . . . instead of bobbin' up an' down like . . . like tarts at the races . . . as if . . .'

He shoved them off again along King William Street on the pavement above which groups of clerks and typists leaned out from windows. And little knots of people were hurrying towards Cannon Street, some of them trying to run, all of them chattering incoherently, the sounds being obliterated by the sounds from other directions. The dizzy heat pressed over all; and in the shimmering haze the dust from the scuffling feet rose like a mist kicked up from the stones that had gathered a thick film of dirt during a fortnight's drought.

And already through that pungent air Twigge could detect the pervading odour of the River. Something in him flinched from it, and a vague despair began in him. To cross the River! To be taken forcibly from his territory! His captors were putting on speed. Their grip on his arms was tighter and hotter. Twigge frequently stumbled as he was dragged, shoved, and raced through the street, southwards to within sight of the expanse of hazy sky above the River. He was prepared to resist. And resistance, he thought, might bring help to him from the passing crowd. He need not have worried, for a scattered crowd that cohered as it came towards him was pouring northwards from the south side of London Bridge. A tumult of excitement was in it and rising into the air and preceding its swift flight. It came on like a wave against which Charlie's party could not move, dared not try to move. Charlie stopped. They all stopped. They all broke apart, started to retreat, yelled to one another, and were smothered and separated and carried farther apart by the onrushing crowd that swept past and filled the air with its thunder and its word.

'PEEPER!'

Twigge was carried with the wave. If Charlie had not held him, he would have fallen. He was grateful to Charlie for that much; and he presumed that Charlie was grateful to him when, suddenly tripping, he was pulled up by Twigge. The rest had vanished, carried out of sight by the rush.

Charlie turned a damp, fearful glance to Twigge.

'Where is he?' he yelled.

Twigge did not understand. He shook his head. Charlie dragged him into a shop doorway.

'PEEPER! You little runt!'

Twigge struck at his belly with a sharp elbow.

'As if I know!'

253

The big, perspiring face gaped at him, its lower lip sagging as it breathed through its mouth.

'Corny said . . .'

The rest was smothered by the volume of sound from the crowd which must have collided with a flowing wave of humanity coming along Gracechurch Street and pressing forward. All around Twigge, the mass was halted for an instant. Then it flowed back and was pent in by oncoming thousands from the Bridge. And he could hear the word rising like a chant:

'PEEPER!'

Charlie wrenched him round and screamed into his face.

'I'm askin' you . . . where is he?'

The entire scene was becoming dense. Somebody stumbled towards Charlie and shouted. One of the gang. A stranger, well-dressed, agile. He saw Twigge and grabbed at him.

'No!' Charlie yelled. 'He doesn't know . . .'

There was some commotion near the opposite pavement where an Army truck had halted. A police car had swerved in. Twigge saw a sergeant scrambling into the cab of the truck and shoving the driver aside. Momentarily, that little incident was closed for Twigge by the swirl of persons before him. But he heard the note of the multitude leap into shrill exclamation. He wondered what had incited those thousands to shove, to flow in and yell. He was hemmed in there, jammed against the wall by a solid press which moved in a compact mass. How many fainted or went down, he could not tell. So many. At the fringe, the crowd passed them out, made little lanes that were quickly closed by the sudden pressure that travelled over the multitude. Twigge was carried by that motion, and then swept back again to his original position opposite the truck and the police car. Charlie still gripped him by one arm, and the agile stranger had hold of him by the other arm. Twigge could not understand what they intended. The dense crowd was yelling for PEEPER, and dimly from the distances the echo came back from the throngs there. In that swaying commotion, Twigge thought only of keeping his feet, of not going down, of not being crushed. The same immediate difficulties kept Charlie and the stranger silent. Until the stranger recognized an associate. Somebody very much like himself who had worked through but could only flounder with the scuffling edge of the crowd. The stranger stretched out his hand. An instant later his companion was beside him. And it was then that Twigge saw Quentin.

A momentary glimpse of him as the sergeant and the constable got him safely to the pavement and across it. Perhaps Twigge's expression betrayed not only what he had seen but what he was thinking. Charlie and the others saw him. They followed his gaze. And they saw. They let go of Twigge.

He saw them push and punch their way towards that doorway. He knew then that they had wanted him only as a pointer to their prey. They were smashing forward, and the angry fringe was closing behind them. To work through was impossible, for the temper of that section was high after the blows.

Twigge gained the wall. It was easier to dart forward there, with the wall so solid at his side. He saw light gleam on steel, and the hand coming up to aim the weapon whose dark metal gleamed balefully and seemed to him to become at that instant the very note of the multitude. He made one last effort. He smashed the upraised arm and saw the hand open and the weapon drop out of sight. A woman screamed. The stranger spun round to seize Twigge. The crowd thereabouts pushed him aside to pass into the building a fainting girl. Twigge saw a gap.

He pitched himself into it. A yard ahead, they were shoving Quentin into the bank. The elderly Commissionaire holding that door passed him in and swiftly pushed the door to exclude the pouring edge of the crowd. He saw Twigge. He recognized him, shouted something at him, helped him with one hand, kept open the door a little.

Twigge darted in. He heard the door slam behind him and the boiling roar of thousands of voices fade to a muffled sound. He flopped to the stone floor and took off his big cap and dabbed at his streaming head and face. Set in a long line were the injured and the unconscious. Beside them knelt the staff and the few who had found safety. And apart, against the opposite wall, was Quentin at whom the staff kept staring and around whom three or four elderly clerks stood, with the old Commissionaire expostulating to one of them and occasionally pointing to the windows on the ground floor where a dark line of figures stood with inquisitive faces pressed against the panes to peer in.

Twigge got up. He was stiff and bruised and dizzy. He went over and nudged the Commissionaire.

'Leave him to me, Bertie . . .'

'Oh, Twigge! Here . . . this man . . .'

The Commissionaire explained to one of the older clerks who Twigge was, what he was doing there.

'Yes, well . . .' that grave official said, looking towards the windows where the excited faces were pressed. 'I think you had better get your friend here . . . get him away somehow. Those persons seem to think that he is . . . that he bears some resemblance to PEEPER. They're not far wrong, I must say.'

Twigge spoke to Bertie.

'Somewhere through the back? Could we get out?'

'Take them,' the old clerk said, 'through Mr. Heggins' room. And into the yard.'

The Commissionaire was helping Twigge to get Quentin to his feet.

'And don't forget to lock the doors after you come back, sergeant. We simply can't have anybody rushing in. I don't know what the Directors would say . . . I mean, all these people. The place is becoming like a . . . worse than the raids . . . all these people being brought in!'

At the door of Mr. Heggins' room, Quentin spoke to Twigge.

'Matthew . . . find Matthew . . . he was with me, Twigge.'

Bertie opened the door. 'If you mean the man who was with you and the sergeant and that constable . . .'

'Where is he?' Quentin said.

'Don't ask me,' Bertie said, leading them through to the yard. 'I've seen Cup Final crowds, and Rugger Internationals. This crowd . . . And if you ask me, he's still where he dropped. A crowd . . .' He shook his head. 'Got no conscience. Is just a Thing with a voice and a will. Hark at that!'

The voice of the will thundered its terrible chant into the hot afternoon and the stark sunlight.

'We want PEEPER! Bring out PEEPER!'

The yard was very tidy. Its pavement was recently flushed with water. There was a large cycle shed used by the staff. It stood against the high wall to the left. Beyond was a gate into a private alley which led to St. Swithin's Lane.

'You could hide yourselves in the cycle shed,' Bertie said. 'I'll get the key for you, if you like. But if I was you, Twigge, I'd cut on while the going's good. I would. You can't trust crowds. Awful things. No conscience. And this one . . . this one means murder.'

Twigge bit his nether lip and looked round the long yard. Quentin said:

'I'd like to sit down.'

Bertie stared hard at him and then turned to Twigge.

'They'll lynch you,' he said. 'They mean murder.'

Twigge swung his perky face up at him.

'I don't see why! I can't understand why.'

Bertie impelled them towards the gate to the left.

'Then you haven't heard the news. All over the City. They want PEEPER . . .'

'What for?' Twigge said, at the gate with Quentin.

Bertie took the padlock in his fist and inserted the key.

'Who knows what a crowd really wants? To pat somebody on the back and yell in his ears! Think of that, Twigge! Would kill anybody. And besides . . .'

He unlocked the padlock and swung open the high, wooden gate. Quentin stepped into the little alley and leaned against the wall while Bertie beckoned Twigge back into the yard.

'Who is he?' he said to Twigge. 'Looks to me like . . .'

'Like PEEPER?' Twigge asked.

'The image of him!' Bertie said. 'Take my tip. Slip in somewhere and hide until they're gone. Hark at it!'

The air was thunderous with it. The sound poured over the high buildings and fell heavily into the yards and back premises.

'WE WANT PEEPER!'

'It's sheer murder!' Bertie whispered.

He took a last glance at Quentin and shook his head.

'I'll have to lock this door, Twigge.'

Twigge stepped out into the alley. 'If you must, Bertie, that's all there is to it. So long!'

But it was not a question of hurrying away safely. It was one of finding a place in which to hide. Already, Twigge could hear the crowd pouring round. And by craning his neck he could see faces at some rear windows. He pulled Quentin down. Taking off his cap, he exchanged it for Quentin's soft hat.

'Put on that cap,' he said. 'Pull it down over your eyes.'

'If I do, I won't see . . .'

'Doesn't matter,' Twigge said. 'There's nothing to see.'

His optimism was expiring. And he was exhausted and in pain from his bruises. Also, he could hear a vociferous crowd yelling up to the faces at the windows and demanding PEEPER. To have escaped one mob and its horrid nucleus, only to walk into another! He looked about him. Lifting the latch of the first gate along the alley, he opened that loose, wooden board and looked into the yard. Bins, a couple of cycles, an old tea chest full of waste paper, and a coal shed.

'Here!'

257

He drew Quentin in and showed him the shed. He closed the broken gate and slid over a bolt.

'As quickly as you can, Quentin!'

He got him into the shed, amidst the small coals and the old sacks and the cobwebs, and then flopped down himself and lay at full length. And groaned with his numerous aches and stiffnesses, hearing the horrid clamour of the crowd. He drew a deep breath and expelled it. Weariness took hold of him.

'I can't make it out,' he said. 'I don't know why . . . or what. And that nasty customer with a revolver . . .'

He saw that Quentin was sitting fairly comfortably with his back against the side of the shed, and his legs outstretched. He closed his eyes.

' . . . a wink or two . . .' he mumbled; and in a moment he was snoring.

Quentin rose slowly. He went into the yard and drew the bolt and opened the gate. The alley was not very long. Fifty yards, at most. He went along with one hand resting against the wall, guiding himself. At the end, he reached the door leading into the Lane.

The bolts were stiff and he had to work at them for several minutes before they slid back. Outside, the crowd was thick. He could hear its mighty voice calling for him; and although it frightened him, he felt enticed by it to open the door and go out and discover what that multitude wanted, what it had to say, what it wished to ask him, what it demanded when it thundered. It had taken Matthew. Would it take him, too, and destroy him?

He hesitated. He was afraid of it, but he was not afraid of its individuals. He longed to speak to them, ask them questions, hear what they had to say. But to do that he would have to open the door and move out into the mass, and by some means silence it.

He remembered how, when he had glanced back to find what had become of Matthew, he had seen thousands of faces turned to him. They glistened in the afternoon's stiff light which revealed them like things with a curious similarity to one another. Thousands of white blobs, with eyes, nose, mouth. And all the faces emitted words. A millions words which, in their unison, made only one word: PEEPER. But that was not what the faces wanted to say, for each face actually uttered a different word. That was the impression he had at the instant before the heavy door shut out the faces and the enormous sound.

Now he thought again of those thousands of little white blobs that were actually the single words of a magnificent narrative which awaited a gale, a cataclysm that would release them one after another in their proper order, so that all might hear, or all might see, at a glance at the ocean of uplifted faces. And he drew open the door and stepped slowly out.

The screams from the crowd struck his ears like blows. And the seething press of faces that swung round to him destroyed some subtle thread of consciousness. But he remembered the words that awaited some mysterious event which would give them proper sequence, and he smiled when he heard the thunderous voice call its one word.

'PEEPER!'

The word destroyed some essential sense of hearing in him, so that from that moment he heard nothing but a single note, a boiling roar, futile and yet magnificent, which ascended into the afternoon's haze and which struck the high walls and poured down them, and never ceased. It had hope and desire and a resurgent courage. He stepped out blindly into it, and felt as though its sound were lifting him.

Hands seized him, shouldered him aloft, and carried him thus, while the cheers came only faintly to his deaf ears, and the faces that uplifted to him swam for him in a misty wonder of one exquisite sea whose soft waters reflected all the glory of sunlight.

The faces had merged together. Not so, the words. In a subtle sequence he heard them with an inner hearing. The first words of a universal Faith springing from the soft ocean and ascending and carrying him upon their sound.

When his champions who had shouldered him realized that he had fainted, they gently lowered him and cleared a space about him. The roadway thereabouts was shaded. The little circle around him grew hushed, for he was dead.

The hush travelled from that little cluster far outwards beyond the ragged edges of the enormous crowd, on across the City from whose streets the thousands had hurried at a rumour that PEEPER was in Piccadilly, was in Leicester Square, was going towards Fleet Street, was in Threadneedle Street: the real PEEPER. It went with the speed of sound. It was the cessation of the sound of a multitude which wanted PEEPER, which had chosen him instead of Colport, which had found him at last, and lost him.

The hush descended on the entire city. It was everywhere. It travelled through streets that had resounded all afternoon with the distant thunder of that multitude. It invaded the Park which, like the streets,

259

had gradually emptied of their strolling public and become full of the weird pulsations of sound from the City's heart. It was an end of something.

Lenora hardly knew what it foreboded. Walking in the Green Park, sitting in the sunlight and noticing a gradual excitement pass over the public, and then seeing the quick departure of hundreds towards the East, she had presently heard that roar coming from afar. And, at last, had heard it subside.

She got up. The weird silence which had fallen upon everything was like a substance through which she hurried homewards. It was heavy about her as she crossed Piccadilly and entered Half Moon Street. It was in the house when she entered through the doorway. The door stood wide open, as though that massive silence had burst the lock. It was all about her on the stairs. And in Quentin's empty room, as well as on the landing outside, it persisted as though it were aimed at this house, these rooms. And it was in Kitty's presence as she stood in the studio confronting Lenora.

For an instant, both women were silent. Words sprang to Lenora's lips, and to Kitty's. But when they were uttered they were only a murmur which the vast hush received and quickly consumed. And after that there was no necessity for speech, for the heavy silence related the magnitude of an event that touched both women.

They sat down and waited.


# FOURTEEN

★

Belfwig and Bessing heard that hush after the frenzied shouting. They glanced at each other.

'It could mean anything,' Belfwig murmured. 'We must wait.'

He had explained to Bessing earlier in the afternoon:

'Colport wishes to resign. We have that information from Lord Ecks. Colport's contention is that he has done his best to bring the countries of the world through this crisis which he blames on PEEPER. He says that he can do no more until he has a Vote from the People. PEEPER or the Coalition. The Cabinet has been in session all day. Colport is adamant. If the Cabinet will not agree to this Vote or Plebiscite, he'll resign.'

Belfwig had pointed to the window below which thousands were hastening eastwards.

'And that,' he said, gravely, 'is the People, giving him its answer.'

They could hear the cheering and the single word lifting into the drowsy air:

'PEEPER!'

'But there's something which the People have not been told,' Belfwig. had continued. 'This morning . . . a final Ultimatum from Transplebia. In effect, it says: "Get rid of PEEPER, if you wish to settle the differences between us." Colport has never had such a strong card in his fist. He's playing it now.'

The afternoon passed tediously and ominously. Until that hush began. John walked to the window. Belfwig examined some current reports and proofs and signed several letters. Suddenly, the door burst open and Ecks entered. Dishevelled as usual, he strode to the desk.

'It's finished, Belfwig! In St. Swithin's Lane, at the moment of his triumph! Fell dead! I saw the body . . .'

He stopped suddenly when he saw Bessing who turned and came towards the desk.

'I beg your pardon! I . . .'

'Who fell dead?'

Ecks and Belfwig glanced at each other.

'I want you to tell me!' John said.

Ecks said: 'He was PEEPER, wasn't he? Your brother . . .'

Harry entered the room at that moment and stood a little way inside. He saw Bessing lean across the broad desk and take a sheet of note-paper from Belfwig's blotter. From his pocket John took a charcoal pencil and drew three squares on the sheet of paper. The first and second squares were left empty, but in the third he wrote:

'WE REGRET TO ANNOUNCE THE PASSING OF PEEPER'

In four heavy strokes, he encompassed the whole with a band of mourning.

'Publish it, to-morrow,' he said.

He took his hat and went out and never returned. He went home where Lenora and Kitty were waiting with the nurse; but he could tell them very little. It was not until Twigge returned that they heard what had happened to Quentin and Matthew; and it was only when Riddle arrived that they learned more details, for Riddle, practical as ever, had done all that was necessary for them: he had been to the police; he had arranged with the hospital authorities all that there was to arrange; he had been told what must be done about inquests. And more, he had brought copies of three evening newspapers, and an extra edition of the 'Daily Summariser' which had been rushed out.

The six of them unfolded the newspapers and looked in vain for a reference to PEEPER. There were only headlines:

### WORLD UNITY ASSURED
### ERA OF PEACE AND PLENTY OPENS
### COLPORT FOR TRANSPLEBIA

Column after column of it, page after page. And on a back page, a small paragraph:

### JOY RIDE ENDS IN FATAL ACCIDENT

> Shortly after three this afternoon, a man described as a free-lance journalist, together with a companion said to bear some resemblance to a popular figure in a cartoon, drove away a military vehicle from its parking place, and after a reckless journey through congested streets came into collision with a police car. Both men died almost immediately from their injuries.

Of PEEPER, there was nothing except a small paragraph on the back page of the 'Daily Summariser' reporting that the cartoonist, Jayby, had resigned from the staff, thus bringing to an end the amusing PEEPER series that had been so popular with the newspaper's readers.

### LOOK OUT FOR THE NEW SERIES IN TO-MORROW'S EDITION!
### THE ADVENTURES OF VIRGINIA!

The rest of the newspaper was devoted to Colport. The Great Peacemaker! The Architect of Universal UNITY! Life story on Page Three. Village Schoolmaster who rose to be the greatest Statesman of All Time.

'That's all,' Twigge said, softly. 'That's the fall of the curtain. Farewell to PEEPER!'

The nurse had left them. Twigge sat down. PEEPER . . . he was thinking . . . PEEPER would subside in the minds of men all over the world. He would die, as he had died in reality. That shocked Twigge, and he glanced suddenly about him, as though his eyes were seeking the amiable, enchanting presence of Quentin and could not believe that that being was gone.

It was less a universal tragedy than a personal one. Twigge felt it in himself. Nothing mattered, except that he had lost a friend. But in his lifetime, he had lost many friends. He could remember them still and live with something of them still in his heart. It was the same now.

And looking at the others in the room, he knew that grief would soon end. That was the natural ability of the heart: to recover; to realize what was good and noble in a friend who had departed. But he knew that the passing of PEEPER had released those four people. They were no longer bound by themselves. The trinity, too, was ended.

He got up and returned to his own room. He sat down and thought of Lenora, John, Riddle and Kitty. They were released to find themselves. For it was a natural quality to seek new friendships, to go on, never to halt, never to lose hope. Life was the journey which all were making through Time.